The Rapture of Michael Pryor

The
RAPTURE
of MICHAEL PRYOR

a novel

by

Kent Richter

RESOURCE *Publications* · Eugene, Oregon

THE RAPTURE OF MICHAEL PRYOR
A Novel

Resource Publications
An Imprint of Wipf and Stock Publishers
199 W. 8th Ave., Suite 3
Eugene, OR 97401

www.wipfandstock.com

PAPERBACK ISBN: 978-1-6667-3313-6
HARDCOVER ISBN: 978-1-6667-2748-7
EBOOK ISBN: 978-1-6667-2749-4

VERSION NUMBER 041122

For the Unenlightened

CONTENTS

BOOK ONE

Where the Body Is . . .

1

MICHAEL PRYOR

Michael Pryor awoke slowly, rolling over easily between the soft sheets and reaching gently for the form beside him. She was warm, as she always was, and he nuzzled her blonde hair, drank the smell of it. He would have thought of sex, but he was already growing more aware and awake and he knew how deeply Desra slept. That was why she needed an alarm; Michael never needed one, had never used one in thirty years of life. He felt a curious pride.

Michael slid away from Desra's sleeping form and lay on his back, his eyes finally open to the soft morning light. "Time," he whispered into the air, and instantly digits appeared on the ceiling overhead: 6:48, still twelve minutes before Desra's alarm would go off. He decided simply to lie still, and, as he often did, he considered the day ahead. Busy, of course, especially with the press conference in the afternoon, not to mention Desra's meeting about her designs for the Japanese condominium complex. For a few minutes, her day filled his mind more than his own, as he considered how important her professional achievements were to her sense of fulfillment, and he allowed himself to want for her what she wanted for herself. She was, after all, a good woman, perhaps the best companion he had ever had. She had guts and drive, put up with none of the nonsense of professional manipulation, and sought to do great things on her own strength. She was, he realized, a lot like him, and he liked that. He, too, was disdainful of nonsense and the pitiful self-indulgences of modern professionals, and he imagined himself at today's press conference being incisively obnoxious. He smiled crookedly.

Desra moaned and rolled onto her back. Her alarm must have been going off, though, of course, Michael could not hear it. She had gotten the alarm implant while she was in college, and she insisted that, far from being

a techno-copout, as so many implants were these days, this was a recognition of her biological inclination to sleep late and, at the same time, an act of
self-discipline. Seven o'clock every day, no matter what the day, work or vacation. For there was always something important to do, something to learn
or consider, news to watch, maybe even something to read. She was, after all,
still one of those people who read. It was another reason Michael liked her.

Her alarm must have been beating at her cortex pretty hard by now,
for she winced and rolled her head, finally moaning, "Okay, okay," as if that
would make it stop. But she had to be erect, she knew, and erect for five
minutes continuously, or it would start again. The chip could, moreover,
adjust itself to a dozen different frequencies and made automatic alterations
whenever one stimulus began to lose its rousing effect. It was physically
bonded to sensory neurons in the parietal lobe near the pain centers and felt
sometimes as if her teeth were vibrating, at other times as if her nose itched.
The one that made it feel as though her back were tensed up was genuinely
unpleasant; the others were just sufficiently annoying to be useful.

Beside her, Michael folded his hands behind his head and watched the
events of her awakening. He had seen them before, but it was often entertaining, since her facial expressions were occasionally comical and, even gri-
macing against the implant's stimulus, Desra was beautiful. Her hair strayed
across a softly tanned face and across her thin shoulders to the straps of her
pseudo-silk gown. Beneath that gown, he knew, the curves of her body were
soft and delicious, something she offered him as a gift, but something she
maintained for herself. Her regimen of diet and exercise was as controlled as
her work schedule, but was, according to her very vocal insistence, a point
of pride for herself alone, a psychological empowerment independent of
the force of beauty in the social and business worlds. The independence of
a woman's psyche, she told him often, like the independence of the woman's
body, was sacrosanct.

Finally, Desra sat up, and with a few sighs, resigned herself to being
awake. She stretched a little, her thin, smooth arms, making a skyward *V* in
the dim light, and then reached down to pat Michael's leg through the ther-
mal sheet. Eyes barely open, she looked back to him and smiled. He beamed
back at her, his eyes wide, his torn smile announcing his own wakefulness
in contrast to her own condition. "Smart ass," she said.

Desra struggled up and managed to leave the bedroom, calling up
the lights in the bathroom and stating in centigrade her preferred shower
temperature. She ordered horizontal spray and a sonic rinse of her hair, so
it wouldn't need drying. There was a good hour and a half before her meeting on the Japanese condo designs, but she wanted to phone in early, just
to be prepared.

"There's lots of time, isn't there?" Michael called form the bedroom, hearing Desra's commands and recognizing their meaning. "When is the meeting?"

"Nine," she called back, speaking easily over the hiss of the misting spray. "But I intend to show enthusiasm in approach. I've seen some of the competing designs, and I want it to be clear that I have every confidence in my own. Approach is key."

"So what does the competition look like?" Michael asked.

"Highrises have no chance," Desra answered with a kind of professional-sounding assurance. "They're out aesthetically. And anybody who has done homework knows the Japanese want to fit into the hills, not stand over them."

"Nice line," Michael called.

Desra ignored his comment and told the shower to stop. "Even midrise will seem too extrusive, I think," she went on, talking more to herself than to Michael, "and that's why Brandon's design won't go, in spite of his 'fluent Japanese.'" She wagged her head and mocked a snobbish tone at the mention of her colleague's ability with Japanese. She was no fool; she knew the language capability was valuable, but there was nothing grand about Brandon's abilities. His Japanese was, after all, only a chip on the side of his brain.

"So my stairstep lowrise use of the Kowa hillside is best," she went on. "Of course, Tharese's scattered lowrises plan is very similar to my version, maybe even gentler in space usage, but by the same token less efficient. I saw, of course, that stairstep terraces don't have to be rectilinear, but can sweep and dip, adding an extra dimension to dynamics and matching again, in my view, the Japanese aesthetic. Tharese's isolated multiplexes will make more use of the trees, and I guess that's Japanese, too. She did her homework, all right. But the view-of-Ise idea was mine all along, and Kevin knows it."

Michael took the long speech silently, ignoring its pauses and accepting it as a rehearsal as much as an answer to his question. He knew she would do well in the meeting, and he admired her work for its thoughtfulness and originality, as did Kevin, her office director. Of course Kevin was, Michael believed, something of a fluff, having the political insight necessary to run a design firm with international connections, but not with any genuine concern for creativity beyond sales. Kevin recognized talent well enough, but Michael knew in this case that talent might not be enough.

Desra knew Kevin even better than Michael did, and she knew much more than Michael ever could how undependable her boss could be. So even though she could assert her own skills and knew the value of her work, there were no guarantees that her designs would be accepted. She knew her own strengths, of course, and knew well the empowerment of appropriate boldness. Indeed, she knew how to present her ideas with a delicately tuned balance of power and politeness that was designed as carefully as her architectural concepts. But nevertheless, floating somewhere in the miasma of highly trained self-esteem, she had doubts, and as she reemerged into the bedroom naked, she felt Michael's attention become visual and accepted it as evidence of another, unspoken power. She let him admire her and lingered before the closet mirror, pretending she had yet to decide what to wear. She admired herself, accepting her beauty as a mark of self-discipline as well as natural gift. Smoothly, she reached forward and touched the console, and gradually her own image became wrapped in her chosen apparel, as the lasers produced the clothed image in the mirror. Another touch to the console added a slightly deeper blue to the tint already chosen, and another touch dropped the neckline slightly. The skirt was mid-length, a mock denim but with a flow over the hips given a slightly lighter color. The dark boots were, for her, standard.

"Fine," she spoke at last, and with a final touch to the console, she moved forward with gentle patience as the mirror slid aside. The buzzing of the assembly beams was barely audible. In seconds, the door was open, and her chosen wardrobe hung there, created of beamed-in paper particles.

Michael had watched with some amusement. He was often fascinated by the vision of Desra's bare back alongside the clothed reflection in the closet mirror. He enjoyed her beauty as he enjoyed her intellectual abilities. Yet perhaps even more than both, he admired her forthrightness, her willingness to state her mind and play no games. Her slimness and beauty were the product of her own will, her own concentration and effort, as her architectural designs were the product of her own research and invention. When others took pills and got implants, Desra thought and chose.

Michael smiled at her as she slipped into her paper underclothes and paper dress. His smile was crooked; it always was. The scar that marred his left upper lip made every smile into a sneer, and that sneer had made him enemies and denied him friendship his entire life. He knew it was so, and knew it had been so since he was ten. But Desra, precisely because she was forthright, had liked his sneer. Or perhaps, Michael mused, she had taken her own ability to love his sneering smile as a form of safe rebellion. Just as Michael himself could sneer at the world whose opinions he could disregard, so Desra could let him sneer and treat the world's response with the same disdain she portrayed in her pretended self-confidence. Perhaps it occurred to neither Michael nor Desra that each loved the other only as a reflection of each one's private self-assertions. Even so, it allowed them to be themselves, and for some time it had passed as love.

Desra was dressed and disappeared back into the bathroom to brush her hair. Michael finally slipped out from the sheets and sat up on the bedside, stretching. "Wednesday," he called out to the closet, and stretched again as he waited for the machinery to produce his clothing. He was not as concerned with his appearance as was Desra; indeed, he took a peculiar satisfaction in having the same clothes for any given day of the week. Even though he was somewhat in the public eye—especially at these press conferences—he took a silent pride in rejecting the self-presentation strategies of reporters totally enslaved to video. Michael could have been a video newsperson, too, he told himself sometimes. He was handsome enough. His dark hair was thick and flowing, swirled up at the top of his high forehead by nature, and he had dark, rich eyes beneath almost-bushy eyebrows. And the catch in his lip, that scar that made his smiles crooked, could have been made an attractive quirk. Or so Michael insisted. For Michael maintained his choice to be a real reporter as a point of pride, a declaration of honesty and not merely a presentation of a face, as it was for the video talkers. Those presenters of news were actors, after all, and not really reporters. Even among the real reporters Michael knew, those who prepared the information and did the research the actors presented, there were few real writers left. But that was another of Michael's points of pride. He was a writer, not one of the talkers, and certainly not one of the actors. He intended to make that clear by the way he dressed as well as in the way he talked and wrote. And in the way he smiled. Of course the actors were richer and more famous; most of the American population would never see Michael Pryor, nor would they want to. The TV-news-watching public knew the permanently tanned face and careful coif of news-actors like Martin Mauer and D'bon Sanders. "The Six-O'clock News with Martin Mauer." Sure, everybody knew the resonant voice and the pained squint he could muster for every tough, "exclusive" newsbreak. But when there were real press conferences, when real people asked real questions, instead of having actors read lines, Michael knew—and so did they—that he was the only one who could press the speakers for explanation. He alone seemed to differentiate between a probing question and one of those carefully ambiguous insults that pass on the video news as "investigative reporting." Michael would push for reason, whether he was questioning a major political leader or God Himself.

Desra emerged from the bathroom with her hair brushed, her make-up gently applied. Then, as if she had read Michael's mind, or suddenly realized that he, too, had an important day ahead of him, she asked, "And what about your meeting with God?"

Michael finished a yawn and stretch. "Well, I'm up for it," he said with a thin-lipped nod of mock self-confidence.

Desra rolled her eyes. "I'm surprised you're up at all," she said.

Michael finally began slipping into his clothes. "Should be interesting," he called back to her. "Quite a guy, so the files say. Degrees in psychology as well as the doctorate in physics. All that beyond the official recognition as master, minister, rabbi, *et cetera, et cetera*, in something like nine different religions."

"I thought you said it was eight," Desra called back as she moved into the living room and gathered papers from the table.

"Nine," he called back. "Recent, finally-official recognition by the Catholic Council of Bishops. Of course the American Bishops practically voted him greater than the pope last year, but now, even Innocent XIV, has praised this guy as a spiritual master or a hidden saint or something. A Tibetan *tulku* being canonized a Catholic saint! Kind of like the Tooth Fairy kissing the Easter Bunny."

"Nice line," Desra called back. "You should use that."

Michael coughed sardonically. He did like the line. He could add, then, that at least the Tooth Fairy and the Easter Bunny hugging was better than watching them trying to kill each other. He could emphasize the value in seeing religious leaders getting over any sense that they're talking about anything more than their own imaginations.

Michael broke his own train of thought. "But you know," he decided to add, "this interview isn't coming from his center in Boulder. We're warned that this isn't about some new spiritual achievement."

"Where's the interview, then?" Desra asked from the other room. "The Vatican?"

Michael laughed. "Nope," he responded, "from Albuquerque."

"What's there?" Desra asked, passing from the living room to the kitchen with a briefcase in her hand.

"Sandia," Michael said. "He's got his own labs at Sandia, and the word is that the press conference is meant to be about some scientific research he does."

"Well, you'll get him," Desra said mindlessly, now with toast in her other hand. She could enjoy Michael's wit for a while, enjoyed his tangled flair for criticism. But she had her own day to attend to, and although her common air of confidence was a necessity and a carefully cultivated image she used to cloud even her own view of herself, she was beginning to feel nervous. Her day, she knew, was the center of reality, not Michael's, and so almost automatically she used mildly sincere encouragement as a way of announcing she was done listening. It was a skill she had found useful in dozens of professional meetings.

Michael heard her distance and let her go. He mentally dropped his own concerns and followed her toward the phone booth.

"Going in now?" he asked.

"I told you I wanted to be there early," she said, her nervousness becoming a little annoyance in her voice.

Michael touched her from behind. "Well," he said, "you'll get 'em."

For a second, she seemed to shoot him an angry look, as if he were dismissing her concerns. But at least for a second, she caught his sarcasm and its rightness. She nodded. "Okay," she said. "I'm sorry. Look, you let me go, and wish me luck. I'll wish you luck, too."

He nodded. They kissed gently. Desra touched the ID reader on the wood panel on the living room wall. It slid aside silently, and the booth lit up. Its aluminum foil walls shone back her near-perfect form, and for an instant, she wondered if she should have chosen a different dress—something a bit sexier?—and if she should have tried to learn a few more words in Japanese. There were tricks to this business, like the Japanese language implant, and she usually resisted them with a firm defiance. Yet for a second, she was unsure. This was a crucial day, a crucial task, with dramatic possibilities. For a second, staring into the shimmering, metallic gateway of the phone booth, she hesitated.

"Good luck, then," she heard Michael say.

She stepped into the booth. Michael's twisted smile gave her a strange confidence, maybe because it was twisted and her own was not. "Good luck," she said back to him, reaching out to close the panel. But even then she felt the need to prove something, though she wasn't sure what.

"And Michael," she called to him from the booth, "don't forget your brother's birthday tomorrow."

Desra didn't wait for Michael's response. With renewed self-assurance, she pressed the Close and Send buttons. The silver panel closed Michael from her view, and she heard the soft hum of the laser guns powering up. She looked at her watch; it was 7:37. To her right, the countdown clock projecting onto the silvered foil hit 15. Then she heard the familiar hiss of the gas that would numb her slightly to the soft sting of the first impact. She took a deep breath, then another, as the clock fell toward zero. She was relaxed, and she felt sure it was her own doing. There was a flash of light, and she disappeared.

Michael, of course, didn't see her go. The flash of the lasers as they disintegrated and mapped the body was much too fast for anything but special video to catch. The technology no longer interested Michael. When it was new, of course, it revolutionized every industry, not just transportation, and he remembered as a child being fascinated by the news. Eventually he had realized it was the *news* that fascinated him, and from then on he had wanted to become a reporter. It was nice to be wealthy and influential enough to have his own phone booth, but beyond that, he simply used it.

Daniel had a different view. From the beginning, Michael's older brother had found the technology fascinating. Kits and tools were in his hands as often as he could find them, almost as often as their parents could afford them, and Daniel had dreamed that, somehow, he would be on the front edge of the next wave of technology. Ironic, really, that he had over the next ten years trained himself into a relatively low-level job as a laser technician. The front edge of technology had just charged ahead too fast. And what really could one do with only a Bachelors degree?

Michael had been luckier. Their parents had not been able to send him to college either, at least not beyond the state-supported bachelors. But he had been a writer from the beginning—and obnoxious enough to force himself into every opportunity. Daniel had always been too nice. That was why he was married; that was why he was Christian. Nothing like marriage and religion, Michael mused, to keep a man down.

For half an hour Michael wandered the apartment. Microwaves cooked some oatmeal while he poured himself coffee. He ran the video wall through a few channels for about five minutes and sneered at everything he saw. There were dozens of programs to choose from, for indeed, any program that had more than a few episodes could, these days, have a channel of its own, or at least share a channel with another mediocre comedy with its machine-made laughter or another bloody crime drama with enough sympathy to make us concerned and enough mayhem to keep us interested. Then there were the news programs. Michael flipped through a number of those mostly to practice recognizing the difference between news and acting. His own acquaintances and colleagues appeared before him one after another with their alternations of whimsical smiles and thin-lipped grimaces, all made to fit the tenor of the news item, never longer than the magical forty-three seconds most optimal for audience attention, as determined by the most recent electronic study. Michael humphed at the entire medium as well as at his peers. He almost couldn't wait to insult them subtly at the news conference in Albuquerque.

He called again for the time, and this time it called back to him audibly: "8:16." If he phoned in before nine, he would beat the crowd and not get a busy signal at the booths in the building transportation center. His magazine office was sufficiently modernized, but the traffic into the building was always horrendous.

So Michael scratched around in the apartment, gathering his chips from the desk in the living room. A file with the chips contained hard-copy prints of news stories and photos of the man he was calling 'God.' He pulled out two pictures, one of the shaven-headed young man in red and orange robes, bowing humbly before a short line of teachers in Burma, and another of the same bald head covered with a mortar board as he graduated *cum laude* with his first degree in physics. There were other pictures, Michael knew, of this same man being ordained, graduating from other universities, and even meeting significant government figures in various nations, as he was called in here and there over the last half-dozen years as an adviser on everything from solar energy development to multi-cultural peace ideologies. And today, a new breakthrough, dealing this time with some intersection of his many loves: psychology, religion, and science. "So God shall reveal to us the truth of these matters," Michael muttered.

Michael decided he had to hurry. He had some further information to tap into at the office before he beamed to Albuquerque for the press conference. He could spend all afternoon and evening there and beam back tonight, leaving more than enough time to put some book-credit or food-credit onto Daniel's accounts, along with a list of "suggestions" chosen by computer from purchase history data. Then he'd have a free day and enough time to beam across the city for Daniel's thirty-fifth birthday party.

"Ooh, that'll be a wild one," Michael laughed to himself. "Maybe we'll play charades." Daniel and his friends were anything but exciting, Michael thought. It was almost humorous to imagine running from meeting "God" to having a party with the godly.

Michael Pryor put his hand to the fingerprint scanner that opened the phone booth and met its metallic glare with a frown. His own face frowned back, its dark eyes deep and swirling with a buried anger and sharp wit that spared no one. He followed the first of the thirty-year-old's wrinkles down from the eyes, beside the sharp nose, to the thin lips and the scar that curved up from the edge of the reflection's mouth. Over the years, because that scar had turned every smile into a sneer, Michael had learned to give up sincerity and caring, learned to match the visual sneer with good reasoning and the rejection of others with shrugging self-justification. His parents hadn't had the money to have the scar corrected, and when the psychological-medical technology industry determined that facial cosmetic surgery was no longer a luxury, but a necessity for an individual's self-esteem—and therefore deserving government coverage—his parents still resisted making him have the scar cleared. And by then Michael himself was increasingly disdainful of cosmetics: he didn't need correction any more than he needed acceptance.

He stepped into the booth and slid the silver panel closed. There came the common pause as the mildly anesthetic gas slipped softly down from the ceiling of the booth. Michael held his breath. For a few years now, he had refused to suck in the gas and instead allowed himself to feel the sting of the lasers' impact. It left him clear headed when he stepped from the booth at the office, in contrast to most people who blundered out of the phone booth shaking off the anesthetic effects. But more importantly, it proved something to Michael himself. As the clock hit zero, he let the flash hit him like something solid. It was only a millisecond of intense pain, but somehow, like the scar on his lip, it proved he was honest.

2

DANIEL PRYOR

In another part of the same city, Daniel Pryor was already at work, wrestling in the midst of his labor with his own thoughts of God. In a small utility closet, its fluorescent lights glaring like something from an old movie, he leaned with quiet efficiency into the wall opening where lasers were housed. As his brother had been thinking earlier, Daniel occasionally wondered how his interests in the breaking edge of technology had brought him to this job as a technician for the phone company. There was something softly disturbing about having had dreams, ideals even, and then to end up simply so average. It was strange to expect so much from life and to find it so mediocre. It was as if he had expected more of his God.

With trained deftness, he pulled the cover from one of the laser housings and exposed the flash source and medium tube. These would be the old argon medium tubes, he knew, and the excitation had to be kept high or they could fade. Even a slight fade on these old things could cause data loss, especially after the beam was split a couple times, and the result could cost some traveler a couple million molecules. But Daniel knew well the sequence of adjustments. Easily, he uncoupled the optic fiber at the court junction and drew aside the test thread. It plugged directly into his tester and would read back to him the photon count. Adjustments to the power source were then digitally indicated, so there could be no slip. Daniel found it easy, maybe too easy to really be challenging.

In a way, of course, Daniel didn't mind his situation. God had always been good to him. He still had a strong body, even at "almost thirty-five," and his black hair was only beginning to show scattered strands of stark white. He could walk to work from where he lived—a practically unheard-of luxury—and with both him and Helen working, there was always enough money. With some joy and a sense of satisfaction, he thought of his wife, and he smiled easily, with gentle wrinkles barely visible beside his dark eyes. She loved him, and that was miracle enough. But she was also like a spiritual power, a mind and a soul that constantly impressed him. Of course, few people saw her as he did, he knew, and to most people she was probably nothing special. That was the funny part. Daniel was handsome, dark and square-faced like his little brother, but a big man. He simply looked strong, capable in sports, good with his hands. In college he seemed to be on the road to just about any possibility, with a quick mind for technology and an erect, noble bearing that attracted more than a few women. But then he had met Helen and he had met her Jesus, and he had changed, become perhaps somewhat more like them both, though Daniel himself might never have said so. For Helen was gentle, quiet, almost innocent in her simplicity, yet also a wonder of insight veiled with humility. He had always wanted to be like her, and, denied that, he had wanted to be *with* her. And now, after twelve years, they were still together—practically a record among all their friends. Here he was, just a phone technician, and Helen working only as a legal aid. But he had learned so much from her, seen so much good, that it was partially her sheer presence in his life that kept him trusting God.

But then there was the problem with children. There was always that problem.

The laser checked out fine. That was odd. There had been indications of power fluctuation at the computer, and only automatic rerouting had prevented some danger. But of course that had tied up other lines, and there had been a traffic jam into this building yesterday. Daniel stepped back and rubbed his chin. His dark eyes bore intensely into the hollow where the lasers and splitters fanned their energy into literally a thousand bundles of glass fiber that could carry a billion digitized codes and even solid molecules over tremendous distances at the speed of light. Human beings lived by the motion of those molecules, he knew, and he took seriously the need to have it all working properly. But these old systems had their ways of covering up problems. Sometimes there were just unexpected errors, and they were often hard to find.

Daniel didn't know what the "error" was in the whole children issue either. The "plumbing," as he playfully called it, seemed to work fine. But maybe it wasn't his plumbing, maybe it was Helen's. Maybe they were making babies every month and somehow they just never took to the walls right. Of course she could be fixed, or something could be done to make the pregnancy work. There were always ways to make children happen, as well as ways to make them not happen. Lots of people take all those steps, making and unmaking babies with simple pills or doctors' help. Friends of theirs had children after years of "trying," but that was an in vitro/artificial womb project, and Daniel, for the life of him, couldn't get himself to accept it. Somehow the idea of picking a zygote from a dish and calling it "my son" felt foreign to his conscience. From the pile he could pick any boy and dump the girls, make sure there would be no birth defect, even get a reasonable guess on IQ. But somehow, he felt that this strange and wonderful event of child-making was supposed to be a little less manipulated, a little more "natural." Of course he couldn't deny the validity of these technologies, but both he and Helen had always hoped to let nature—to let God—take over this particular area of life. Life was, after all, God's specialty. And yet . . .

Normal. The laser registered on the check fiber with the standard settings, and Daniel shook his head. What was it about these argon media that caused problems? Some had been retrofitted with direct electron-beam excitation, once accelerators had been simplified, and those changes had caused some pulse fluctuations. But this was an 8415 model, and longitudinal electron beam excitation was built in. Daniel sighed. If everyone would just convert to the newer semiconductor lasers, there wouldn't be half the accidents one sees with any of the gas type. It would be nice if things just worked like they were designed to.

But that was the problem, wasn't it? God had designed life, had made it all to work through its own power, though a power given motion by divine love. Daniel had always had a kind of automatic sense of God's hand in the way things work, and especially in love and life. Of course he knew the real stories, the basic lessons of natural generation of life in simple forms, basic truths one has to know to get out of college. But Daniel couldn't be anything but a believer, a watcher of miracles. "The firmament declares the glory of God," he quoted to himself, and added, "I am fearfully and wonderfully made." He smiled. And yet the design of life wasn't quite working for him and Helen, and though solutions were many, there was just that hesitation, that sense of compromise that haunted him like a demon—or like the voice of God. Yes, medical technology could make a pregnancy work, could practically infuse life into dead gametes, creating a thousand children in a laboratory dish. But for Daniel, simply to use that science, at least in this case, was to do more than just compromise. It was to admit that God had lost, that the tough kid had taken over the old man's territory and established a new order. Daniel laughed to himself. "New order." Of course that order had been in place for centuries now, but at least until now it had not taken over Daniel.

Daniel's phone sounded and made him jump. He took it from his belt and held it up to view. With a button pressed, the tiny screen glowed soft green and a face appeared. It was Morris.

Morris had a young, round face, light-complected even in the odd green of Daniel's telephone screen. Light hair was tossed easily across his head, and he was smiling. Morris was always smiling.

"Hello, Daniel," he said, beaming. "How's your end?"

Daniel tried to smile back. Somehow he always felt like he should smile with Morris, and yet he knew he didn't quite understand what it was that Morris always found so good about life. Somehow Morris knew what he was, knew what he wanted, and, above all, knew that it was what God wanted for him. Daniel did smile back. There was something good about Morris's happiness, and Daniel could be glad that Morris felt it, even if Daniel himself did not.

Daniel pressed the send button on his cellphone, and the screen filled suddenly with his own face. "Checking the main laser still," he said into the screen. "It's one of those argon jobs, and you know how those go." He paused, felt the silence, saw himself in his own hand, somber, looking for something, until, with a start of memory, let go of the send button.

Morris's face reappeared. The smile was back. "Yep," he said, "you can count on those things to go wrong some time, and worse yet you can count on the trouble being hard to pinpoint."

"Well," Daniel took over, "so far the basic check is negative. Readings indicate normal, and the fluctuations don't seem to be in the system origin. Could be in the fibers, I suppose, but it seldom is that, and the whole system is basically impossible to check. Bomb out."

"Well, praise God in all things, Daniel," Morris responded. Daniel took the rest of Morris's advice mechanically, as he did the biblical quotation. He knew his job, knew the checks that had to follow, and knew that the whole affair would probably end with replacing the laser entirely with a newer model. But he let Morris go through the explanations and directions, since that is what Morris liked best about his job. And Daniel didn't mind letting him feel good about what he did.

"By the way," Morris was adding, "I'm looking forward to the party tomorrow night. Should be a blessing."

He was referring to Daniel's thirty-fifth birthday party, arranged by Helen for a "change of pace." They had celebrated birthday after birthday alone, she had said, and maybe it was time to have some people over. He had nodded and smiled, but he had also felt a sting, realizing the hint of resignation in her voice. They had wanted children; she still wanted children, and still he resisted the technology that could make it happen. They had wanted children, but the "blessing" never happened. They had wanted children, and yet "they had celebrated birthday after birthday alone." The party suggestion, therefore, was supposed to be a way of expanding his and Helen's

world, a way of including his friends in their home life. It was part of her gift
to him, and yet it also seemed a sign that she had given up. So she gave him
a party with friends, and Daniel accepted it, even though he very much liked
being alone with Helen. Short of being surrounded by Helen and children,
he was content simply to be with her, quietly enjoying her gentle spirit and
silent joy, a joy so unlike Morris's.

"But I'll have to leave kind of early, you know," Morris was going on,
"since God wants me to go to the praise meeting at church."

"Sure, I know that," Daniel responded automatically. "No problem." He
hesitated, then remembered to release the send button.

"Course, I know you couldn't come along tomorrow night," Morris
continued, "but you know I keep thinking you'd be blessed at these praise
meetings, you and Helen both. Right?"

There was the standard invitation. Daniel had heard it before and had
even responded before. But the "praise meeting" made him feel uncomfortable. The dancing, the repetitive singing, even the "tongues" just seemed
strange. He knew the scriptural justifications, verses Morris could recite by
heart. For that reason they seemed like ideals he was supposed to desire,
but not anything he could achieve. He knew well all the Spirit talk, and
he understood most of the theology. He had even prayed for wisdom and
"gifts," though only in the privacy of his heart and in the calmness of his own
midnight silence. And there had come nothing, not a syllable, not even a
"sense of peace." Somehow he saw in Morris that these feelings were perhaps
what God meant him to have, and yet they were not something he could
muster. They were God's gifts, yet something God withheld. Like children.

"No problem," Daniel was saying again, without thinking. He knew he
had nothing more to say about it, at least not to Morris.

But Morris spoke again. "Well, OK then. I'll see you in church
Sunday, then."

"And tomorrow night," Daniel put back. "Right?"

"Sure. And tomorrow night." There was a pause, and Daniel waited for
Morris to close out. But he could see his friend's hesitation, as if the younger
man was scratching for something else to say.

"Oh, and one more thing," he finally tossed in. "I just heard that David
Roberts is going to be in the city some time next month. Pastor Hubble will
probably be able to get us tickets." There was a pause, as Morris seemed
to be thinking.

Daniel puffed out his cheeks and rolled his eyes a little. He scratched
his head with his free hand and pressed the send button anyway. Morris
probably already knew he was not nearly so much a fan of Dr. Roberts as
Morris himself. Daniel was not so much a fan of Hubble either. "Hard to

plan," he said, "but I'll hear the details when you have them." He hoped he wasn't being too short with Morris, even though he wanted to be.

"Fine," Morris smiled. "It's one of his big Ministerings, and Hubble predicts there may be some hoity-toity types in the audience. Pretty well-respected, gifted teachers, you know."

Daniel let Morris see him nodding. "Let me know," he repeated. "Guess I'll get back to this argon job. See you tomorrow night." He made the standard disconnection, and Morris's smile faded away.

"Sheesh," Daniel said to himself, and he immediately felt a little guilty. He didn't mean to be hard on Morris or to dislike him. Morris was a genuinely nice man, a man with a strong heart for God and a commitment to Christ that Daniel himself almost, but not quite, envied. Morris was, after all, full of life, full of God in ways that seemed attractive. Yet it was also something Daniel couldn't quite follow. All the blessings, all the fullness, all the miracles of daily life—Daniel knew where they were supposed to be, and sometimes he saw them, but they seldom filled him with "praise the Lord." He wondered if it was his fault.

He bent to the laser and checked again the test fiber. The pulse read normal, and he leaned back to scratch his head. What was he missing?

What indeed. The Holy Spirit? God living in his heart? All the lines and clichés filtered back through his memory like soldiers on parade, and he watched from a distance, like an unconscriptable cripple. Their march was well known, and yes, they said something he was supposed to hear. But he couldn't respond; he wouldn't respond. All the talk, all the "word of God," was overpowering, tiring, and Daniel felt himself become angry. He didn't know what to do, and God wouldn't tell him. And he would not join the parade just because it was the only thing moving.

Daniel snapped the testing box from the fiber with such an aggressive yank he surprised himself. He paused, and then snorted a laugh. Shouldn't be angry, he knew, and he even knew that his own anger was probably a sign that overall Morris was right and he was wrong. "Guilty again, I suppose," he said to himself. And he laughed.

With accustomed motion, he slid back to his tool box and pushed the testing unit into place. He drew out a beam splitter and another testing monitor, this one with a recording system. He drew a blank chip from the compartment—noting in passing that he had only one left and would have to requisition more—and dropped it in the recording slot. Spinning, he attached the beam splitter to the test fiber, attaching the *A* exit fiber into the recorder and the *B* lead back into the phone system. It was easy work, but it would not repair the laser by itself. That was still his job.

"Guilty again, I suppose," he repeated. Daniel felt guilt like a common headache: not so terribly painful, but uncomfortable and wearying. He felt it when he thought of Helen and her loneliness for a child. He felt it when he thought of his parents' euthanizing, barely more than two years ago. He felt it when he saw Morris—it was probably a good thing Morris would leave the party early.

Daniel looked at his watch: still an hour to lunch. He could quit early today if he wanted and be home before Helen so he could get the shopping done for the party. Then tomorrow they would have everything they needed for preparation and could just look forward to visiting. Daniel looked forward to seeing the few guests, though admittedly some more than others. Morris was OK, but maybe on the negative side; Daniel's brother, Michael, was certainly on the positive side. Even that somehow seemed wrong, and Daniel winced a little. Wasn't he, as a Christian, supposed to enjoy the fellowship of Christians? Yet the unbelieving brother Michael was any day a thousand times more interesting than the ever-so-Christian Morris. And funnier, too. Of course, looking at Michael always made Daniel feel a little guilty, too. The scar on his lip was, after all, Daniel's fault.

Daniel missed Michael when they stayed apart too long. Michael's lover—what was this one's name?—would probably not come, he knew, and Daniel smiled at himself ironically, knowing she would probably stay away thinking that he and Helen didn't "approve" of her. As if they weren't long used to Michael's way of life! Michael had his own confidence, as Daniel had his guilt, and just as the guilt of the elder moved him to a two-millennia-old Christ, so the younger's confidence made that Christ unnecessary. But they were brothers, and they shared stories and humor from home and family that no one else could share. Daniel smiled. He loved Michael, and if he wished his brother were a Christian, it was because he thought Christ good. And Daniel always wished Michael good, even when they could not agree on what *good* meant.

Their mother had been the ultimate example. For as brothers who shared family and stories, they had also shared the decision to sign for their mother's euthanizing. The reasoning had been standard, the justifications agreeable to both brothers, and yet while Michael felt proud for what the advertisements called "the final act of compassion," Daniel had felt again his tiring guilt. Their mother's illness had been degenerative, and Daniel knew well that for degeneratives there was no hope. "Even cancer can be cured these days," the case workers had told the brothers, "but once the brain structure degenerates, there's nothing to do but watch the decline and see the pain." And stopping pain is what death is all about—or so the advertisement goes. So the brothers had signed the authorization, while their father sat aside and watched the inevitable. Two months later, their father had signed his own authorization and took the drip, saying, like he was supposed to, "It's for the best."

Daniel hadn't been so sure. As he grabbed his toolbox and moved out of the utility closet, he cast a last look at the panel and the troublesome laser behind it. He wasn't sure. But then that was always the problem, he was never sure. Everybody else was sure: Michael, Morris, Pastor Hubble. Not Helen; Helen was still a wonderer.

And Marta. For the first time that morning, Daniel thought of Marta and smiled. She would come to his party, and that would be good. She was something else, and he wasn't quite sure what. He smiled again, and like a flash he felt a moment's musing about whether he might have married Marta, might have made her pregnant. Then, just as quickly, he wondered at his own thought, and then wondered if, just then, in his mind, he had been unfaithful to Helen.

At that thought, Daniel Pryor threw his head back and laughed aloud in the hallway. "Oh, hell," he said to himself, "maybe it was lust, and maybe I'm guilty again." He shook his head and laughed again. Guilt's a funny thing: you feel too little and you're not quite honest; you feel too much and it becomes silly. Besides, for Daniel, he knew that even if one could never be quite sure what the right amount of guilt was, and even if he carried all the guilt in the world, there was something greater than guilt. He knew the Christian story, and he knew why he believed it. So he smiled and talked to God: "This is what we're all about, You and me," he said in his thoughts.

So Daniel headed back to the floor lobby, where the public phone booths stood. He smiled easily to a stranger coming along the halls, and in a moment of easy inward acceptance, prayed for the man's peace. In the next moment, of course, Daniel knew that the prayer was not enough, and that if phones weren't fixed anyone could be lost, their molecules simply spat into some submicroscopic plane, never to be reassembled. But there were failsafes, systems and subsystems meant to protect the phone traffic as much as technology can, and Daniel accepted his limited and fallible role in that protection. If gloom and guilt were realities he had to face, well, he knew he'd face them soon enough in any case. Were there chemical cures for his kind of gloom? Of course; and Daniel knew those drugs could help him out of guilt whether he deserved it or not. But for now, at least for one more day, the "cure" he knew and loved would have to be enough. He smiled and thanked God. Guilt is OK, he decided with a smile, if you just know what to do with it.

3

MARTA SANCHEZ

"How about that Pope, eh, Marta?"

Marta Sanchez looked up from her dictation to find two of the design engineers buddied up in front of the counter. Of course, she already knew who had spoken. It was Ben Bodine, or Ben Bovine as she liked to call him in the privacy of her own thoughts. He was leaning over the counter, staring down at her with his deep blue eyes. He had long blond hair tied back across the hairline by a thin, black strip of leather. He thought it made him look like a blond Indian, or maybe like a king. She had heard he considered himself the reincarnation of an ancient Celtic druid. This twenty-first-century rebirth, she decided, was definitely a big step down.

"Hi, Ben," she said politely, looking up. Marta herself had dark eyes, almost black in their depths, so one couldn't tell pupil from iris. Her hair was the same raven black, and it hung around her oval face like a wavy frame. Had she been standing, it would have been evident how short she was, and hence also that the moderate, round plumpness of her cheeks was a consistent trait throughout her body. That build, like her dusky skin, and her surname, expressed her Latina heritage. And it was that heritage, indirectly at least, that made her the object of Pope jokes. But she didn't feel much like talking about the Pope just now, especially with someone who barely knew what a Pope was. "And what're you engineers creating these days?" she asked.

"Oh, nothing new with us in the back rooms," he said, straightening himself up and stepping back a little from the counter. He seemed to want to sound humble while presenting himself physically in such a way that he could make it clear humility was no easy feat. Marta kept a straight face.

"But we heard the new Pope already caused a big stir at the Vatican," the other man said. Jason Washington was a bit less pompous than Ben Bodine and could be quite a nice guy outside the clique of engineers. His skin was ebony, his eyes dark circles inside brilliant whites, and his deep, resonant voice could almost be relaxing when he talked about home or jazz. But that same voice was just annoying when he got onto his kick about the ancient historical foundations of Kwanzaa. It was also annoying when it was delivering an obvious straight line.

Marta sighed resignedly. "And how was that?" she asked.

"Instead of praying to the Virgin Mary," Jason said, already laughing, "he prayed to the Virgin Maybe."

"Funny as death," Marta thought. She also pondered for a few seconds the obvious difference between *Maria virgine* and *Maria fortasse*, and realized that the joke was nonsense, since she knew that the erstwhile Cardinal Prusko liked to pray in Latin. He liked to prove he understood and honored his religion's historical roots, even though on a hundred other points it was clear he didn't.

"Don't take it too hard, Marta," Ben added as the men's laughter faded. "This new election marks the first time in two hundred years that something Innocent has come out of Los Angeles."

Marta smiled and nodded. Of all the new Pope jokes, that was the only funny one, but of course she had already heard it several times. Innocent XIV, newly elected Pope, recently Cardinal Prusko of the Los Angeles archdiocese, was a topic for many jokes these days, even—or especially, thought Marta—by people who usually hadn't a single thought about anything religious. But then a lot of the joking concerned whether or not this particular Pope was himself anything religious.

And that, for Marta Sanchez, was not funny. She was raised Catholic, of course, but had also converted to it later, as she liked to say. Her college years saw her throw off her traditional religion, embracing a kind of biblical evangelicalism that made her dive hungrily into the greater depths of her faith. That Bible-diving had sparked in her a desire to understand the original languages of her scriptures so she could read and study the old texts, and that desire over time became a love of ancient language itself. Her biblical period, as she called it, had also created in her an historical consciousness that tied her indelibly to the foundations of Christianity and awakened her to the importance of the formative years of the faith. Thus Christ, scripture, and tradition gave her her mind, and she loved them for it. But that same love soon drew her well beyond her peers, other Christian fundamentalists who couldn't imagine trying to read their own New Testament in Greek and certainly saw no use for the Latin of those almost-pagan Fathers. Marta soon found she could not understand, and was certainly not understood by, her Bible-believing friends, who loved so wisely and deeply God's Word and who had utterly abandoned the early Christian thinking that had formed most of their own well-received doctrines. So she had "graduated" from evangelicalism, as she liked to put it. Or, in another of her favorite analogies, she had decided that fundamentalism in Christianity was like socialism in political economics: it may be a necessary system to bring the peasants up to the middle class, but it stifles itself if it doesn't eventually give way to something much more free and creative.

But that had been a decade ago, and her new peers, these men before her, for instance, were anything but evangelical. Indeed, they had so little linguistic and historical sense, that it made Marta long for a Bible-banger. These men thought they were innovating when they used terms like *groovy* and believed that "All you need is love" was a line from the Sermon on the Mount. Or was it Shakespeare?

"I heard the Pope's first official act was to change from bread and wine to pizza and cappuccino." It was another joke from Ben Bodine, and Marta shook her head, trying to smile.

"You know, you guys are real godwits. No question about that," she said, nodding appreciatively. She felt a curiously guilty sense of satisfaction when both of them seemed to take the statement as a compliment.

There was a merciful hiatus, as the two visitors seemed to run out of jokes and the conversation floundered. Marta realized she could just turn back to her work and the two would probably simply wander away. But she watched them for a moment as they chuckled and reminded one another of witty lines or possible variations on them. Marta tried to enjoy their enjoyment: at least they thought they were funny. But as even the humor dimmed and finally fell into nods and nasal chuckles, she began to feel embarrassed for Ben and Jason. God bless them, they didn't really have much to say.

"So, Marta, you going to go out with me tomorrow night?" Ben asked, as if from nowhere.

Marta smiled genuinely and shook her head. It was a joke between them, and when Ben had nothing left to say, or only a passing moment for a bit of personal humor, he would ask for a date. A year or so ago, he had asked her genuinely, and she had hesitated long over the answer. "It would be like dating a rock with a penis," she had said to herself. But after a month of *no*'s, she had given in, become convicted—as the fundamentalists say—of her self-righteousness and judgmentalism, and had tried to find out who Ben Bodine really was. Besides, she could barely remember the last time she had had a date of any kind, and she had wondered if the key were just a matter of willingness. But then he had canceled at the last minute for reasons she still didn't quite understand. From then on, neither of them felt comfortable enough to talk about the matter seriously. Ben's way out of that discomfort was to pretend it had become a joke.

"You never give up, do you?" She smiled at him.

"Well, you know what they say," he answered, "eight-hundred-and-twelfth time is a charm."

For a second or two, Ben Bodine actually seemed to have charm of his own, and Marta met his blue eyes with a hint of longing. Those eyes could have been looking at her, and she would have liked that. She felt a familiar pain and laughed at it.

"Ben," she said, shaking her head, "you're too late. I've already got a date for tomorrow night, so you'll just have to stay on hold."

"What's the gig?" Jason asked her, apparently with genuine curiosity. "Some new beau you haven't told us about?"

"A friend's birthday party," she said, straightening herself as if with prudish pretension. "And his wife will be there."

"You've got friends?" Ben threw in with a laugh.

For a second, Marta was stung, and she saw in Jason's reaction that he, too, was afraid of how serious the question might be. He had some sensitivity, she knew, whereas Ben, obviously enough, did not. At the same time, Marta knew well that Ben couldn't really be malicious. So she poised on the edge of decision only the briefest instant. She knew a lot of words, could be quite eloquent in fact, and she delighted in using them. With a little time and many words, she knew, she could express her feelings or apply humor—or both. And sometimes such explanations were simply honest, and the humor was evasion. Yet evasion, too, could be justified on healthy moral grounds. Such thought, easy enough for Marta, went quickly, automatically, and left her simply with a choice, *de voluntatis arbitrio*. With practiced self-control, she chose to laugh.

"You know how it is," she shook her head and grimaced, "some people have no taste."

Marta laughed easily; it was OK. Chances are, she thought, Ben didn't even know there had been a tense moment. Jason knew, however, and with some general words of parting, he managed to draw away and to take Ben with him. Marta let them go.

They weren't bad men, she said to herself, but neither were they good men. She wasn't quite sure what she wanted from men, but with a smile of self-recognition, she knew she wanted something from them. She had no long-range interest in celibacy, she thought, and yet neither could she imagine finding much worthy companionship in a Ben Bodine or a Jason Washington. They were both brilliant men in their way, and yet they were like aliens to her concept of humanity. They were hardware designers, experts in the conceptualization and development of the miniature mechanisms Prescott Medical Technologies used in its programmable IVs and insertable medical apparatus. Software design, they contended, had become the easy part of miniaturized medical technology, and even the design of chips made to work in pumps or in human brains really required little technological innovation. But hardware was an ever-changing field, where every new materials development could radically change the miniaturization potential of programmable pumps, heart inserts, and chemical implants. Jason had said only yesterday that the development of a recently formulated quasi-fabric might make it possible finally to finish developing inaortic sub-pumps that could both re-enable weak hearts and make most aortic valve replacements unnecessary.

The run of Marta's thoughts brought her back to her work. She was dictating a report on developments in the miniaturization of dialysis machines, making them for the first time portable. It was only a matter of time, the report said, until filtering materials and pump apparatus—which was Prescott's specialty—would make it possible finally to implant the machines inside the body, thus making the first genuine transplantable artificial kidney. And with the breakthroughs made thirty years ago in immunology—thanks, ironically enough, to the AIDS epidemic of the last century—there was little danger of rejection.

Marta actually understood most of this technological lingo, though she had not pursued much in applied sciences. Everyone had said, even her religious peers, that studying classics was fine as a hobby, but she had better be practical and recognize that the only real work was to be found in technology. So she had read up on technological issues, but had found them most fascinating as historical milestones, rather than as ways of getting a job. She understood, for example, the practical aspects, even if not the molecular theory, behind high-temperature superconductors and the revolution their development had caused earlier in the century. Just when world political and economic tensions were beyond hope of peace, as the industrial powers spied on each other and bargained and fought over the last drops of oil, that technological breakthrough had changed the world, making possible for the first time the economic viability of solar and wind energies. Thus deserts and wind-swept coastlines had replaced Saudi oilfields as primary energy sources, and within a decade, the high-technology cultures dropped utterly their Middle Eastern dependence and ran massive voltages without resistance or heat loss from seashores and wastelands to cities and industries. So the technological industries of Europe, America, and the Asian rim had erupted, while the Arab nations had degenerated into barely-noticed warring states, a chaos from which they had never recovered. Meanwhile, computer efficiency went astronomical, with memory capabilities in the billions, and with laser technology, the possibility suddenly arose of literally disintegrating a solid body, encoding its microscopic structure, pushing molecules along fiber lines at the speed of light, and reintegrating them at their destination. Again, Marta did not understand the details of how it was possible, though she had the historical sense to see the immeasurable changes it brought to human life when distance became meaningless. Others could produce equations, software, and hardware to carry the weight of the world's numbers, but she alone, of all the people she knew, could gasp at the historical consequences, how it changed human economy and human consciousness itself.

Marta smiled at herself. She understood historical consciousness, she crowed mentally, and yet, here she was, an office clerk, transcriptionist, receptionist, and general information-finder for Prescott Labs, stationed at one of a dozen or more of their research facilities scattered across the nation, serving the billion-dollar, multi-national power of PMT. Of course, even this had not been something she had planned on as a career. She had learned to do research and how to order information, how to write it out coherently, and how to run it through any number of word-processing systems, only because she had wanted to write for her own purposes. She might have been a scholar had she had the patience for the nonsense of academic politics; she might have been a writer had she been interested in constructing fictionalized versions of current gossip or change-the-names revisions of tired, but ever-popular sexual romances. But instead she had just finished that utterly useless degree in Classics and gone on to be one more anonymous member of the other great area of employment, the "service" industry. So, at age twenty-nine, she wrote and corrected papers and presentations on the new medical technology developed by engineers like Ben and Jason. And while those who thought they produced something of practical value to human society might disparage the "mere" thinker and the "mechanical" writer, Marta knew everyone appreciated a clearly formed sentence when they found someone that could still construct one.

Marta looked again at the notes in her hand, the scribbled work of Elizabeth Parsons-Ostremsky. It was brilliant work, no doubt, but it was just notes. She shifted the sheet in her hands and glanced at the few following pages to construct in her own mind the flow of concepts. She shook her head. "Foreshadowing is a great tool, Elizabeth," she said aloud, "but this section is on filter design." Marta decided to save the paragraph on rehydration for the Future Analyses section. Then she said, "Record," out loud to access the computer's microphone, and she constructed Elizabeth's report verbally, while the computer mechanically translated her voice into the ones and zeros that became typed words on the monitor.

"The multiple layers of the custom-fabric filters will be kept separated by less than 5.7 picometers to allow for natural filtration and the removal of inorganic salts without sterile solution counterflow. The optimal number of layers can be determined by bench tests, but current figures suggest a range between 2300 and 2650. The great number of fabric layers and the current fabric designs do allow for significant water exchange, so that salts discharge easily. Problems of dehydration will be addressed in section six."

Marta stopped as the words glowed on her screen. "Problems of excessive peeing will be addressed in section seven," she added with a smile and laughed to herself as the words appeared on the screen. She swiped her finger across the screen to delete her last sentence. It was funny, though, she thought, and wondered genuinely if anyone had thought about that point. Insert an artificial kidney that allows "significant water exchange," and whoever has one of those things will have to drink a lot and go to the toilet every ten minutes. She laughed again. No, probably no one thought about that much, and indeed, someone with a new kidney would hardly find such a problem significant, compared to their prior situation. Still, Marta knew it was typical of her own way of thinking to find the peculiar catch. She used to talk to the engineers and researchers about their work and their thoughts, but it always seemed she asked the wrong questions. And as she sat at her computer, she recalled one of those carefully crafted and optimally timed—using the Johnson-Shimoda business efficiency model—office parties where they celebrated as a family the company's success. She remembered trying to discuss politics with those so inclined, but she found most of the conversations to be made up of complaints about how politicians wrangle and manage to change little. When she had argued that, in fact, a great deal had changed in human self-concept and the laws that reflect such ideas, the politicos hadn't been able to see her point. When they had insisted that governments continued to fail to give adequate concern for economic inequities, she had asked how a government can adopt clear principles for economic alleviation while pressing at the same time for legalizing the imposition of chemical brain adjustments and euthanization for chronic depression and failed socialization—noting in passing that these were services performed in hospitals and clinics with Prescott machines. And once again, no one had been able to see her connection. And the suggested challenge to the value of their own work, especially at a company celebration party, had not found much welcome.

Marta sighed. She did have a way of ostracizing herself, she realized, but at the same time she couldn't help believing that it was because she expected people to make sense. "Boy, was that a mistake," she thought, rolling her eyes. But by the time she had learned the startling fact that people don't want to make sense, she had created in those around her an almost tangible sense of threat. And so finally, when they discovered she was something of a "devout Catholic," it was practically a relief to all concerned. They at last could label some reason for her strangeness, even though the dozen other "not-so-devout Catholics" at this particular Prescott research facility were utterly unlike Marta. "Oh, that's right, you're Catholic," they could say, and therefore never have to respond to any argument. She had decided that was OK.

"Agh," Marta said aloud and kicked herself mentally for getting so distracted from her work. She shuffled through Elizabeth's notes again and looked up at the monitor. The clock read 3:42, and she realized she wouldn't get much more work done before it was time to go. She also realized that the conversation with Ben and Jason had apparently upset her more than she had realized. Her mind had wandered—no, sprinted—along a dozen pathways and returned where it had started. Ben Bodine had once found her attractive—a rare-enough event in itself—but she found very few men interesting. There were always men who found themselves interesting, but they just seemed to her tritely self-indulgent. Of course there were also men who had genuine ideas that they found worth believing, but Marta ached to ask them why and to see the reasons and history behind their beliefs, while so many believers had trained themselves simply to collapse back into subjectivism at the first sign of rational inquiry. Marta knew she was lonely, and she had no trouble using the word in self-analysis, but men had become in her mind a subspecies of idiot savants with a sexual surcharge, while she had become to them a kind of pudgy inquisitor, with arcane test questions dredged from some fuzzy, ancient tradition and with an annoying tendency to drop words in Latin.

And where was she then to go? "Prescott Labs is populated by the mindless heathen, and an antipope is sitting in Peter's chair," she thought, and then laughed out loud. "Well, now, there was another obscure connection," she added to herself, but in Marta's mind it spoke her life. She reached up to tap the Save key on her console, and in an instant her thoughts became stored in magnetic ones and zeros somewhere in space. She tapped the screen of the monitor, and it went blank. In the blackness, Marta saw her own reflection. With a curious pride, almost excitement, she knew she had behind those dark eyes a mind that really wanted to know and understand. With another instant, she also recognized the line of her full cheeks and the trace of the curve of her neck to the body below. So she was a woman, too, and that was good. And with such wonder, she thought of God, and so of history and tradition and so of Popes and antipopes. "*Habamus papam*," she said.

4

GOD

By four pm, Michael was in a foul mood. He had gone into the office in-tending only to do some research on "God," in order to prepare for the press conference. He had managed to get a couple hours of research done before being called in to answer for a piece he had finished earlier in the week regarding an education firm in the south suburbs. He had contended in the article that the firm's education evaluations were so substandard that their marks, which were excellent, really reflected nothing in terms of con-crete educational skills. At the same time, they had mastered so well the various psychological and behavioral sciences of self-affirmation that the children graduating from their high school were both self-confident and illiterate. The result of such a combination, he had contended, was that not only could they not read or do simple mathematics, they didn't think they needed to learn.

Michael had expected some flak from Arthur, the legal adviser, as well as the usual critiques from Melanie, the editor. But Arthur had shown more than his usual self-protective vehemence in decrying Michael's language and questioning his statistics. He had raised himself up to his massive six-foot-four stature and scratched at the chest hair he liked to let bubble out of his shirt like proof of his virility, and had taken up his imperious voice that commanded like a general while pretending to consider only the good of the magazine. So, while the legal office had no authority to cut entirely an authorized piece, Arthur could and did line-veto it into uselessness. Arthur had insisted he needed only to take some of its teeth out; Michael had in-sisted the procedure was more like castration and hinted that Arthur always was trying to remake articles in his own image. Questioning Arthur's sexual prowess was about the only way to strike back.

Then, to add irony to the rejection, Melanie had gone into one of her tirades about the evolving nature of English grammar, insisting that Michael "come out of the second millennium" and give up his tired habits of "grammatical imperialism." She usually indulged him and let the copy people split his infinitives and replace his nominative pronouns with accusative, but this time she gave him the whole sermon. She had delivered the homily before, of course, and Michael usually just let it run its course, responding with a few jokes and intentional solecisms, only then to go on his way. But this time he got angry; having just come out of Arthur's unmanning of the article, he blew up over the irony of being forced to corrupt his English on an article complaining of a corrupt educational firm. That had led to Michael relating the recent discussion with Arthur and his own long complaint about the legal costs of honesty. At that, Melanie could take on the air of commiseration and sit with him on a jury of two, judging as incompetent and unwanted the legal wrangling of the whole Legal Affairs office. And that had been lunch. Yet even with Melanie's indulgent amicability over lunch, Michael still had to rewrite the school article; that had taken him most of the afternoon, given the many breaks required for cooling off his anger.

So here it was four o'clock, only two hours until the press conference. Chances were that most of the video vermin were already there, since they had to prepare themselves for the visual feat of looking interested and positioning themselves in the right light. Many of them wouldn't have to do much research, since they had communications implants that could feed them basic dictionary information if they got stumped. And there was, with this "God" fellow, a good amount to get stumped over.

With some aggression, Michael slammed the chair back from his desk and threw himself into it. His desktop was awash with printouts, most still on the scroll-like sheets his printer spat out. He was one of the few writers who cared to print at all—of course, most "readers" didn't print either—but he had always liked to hold his own writings. Paper and ink, after all, had a feel, a weight to them, that seemed to fit with the weight of the words they contained. To Michael, that always made sense. Consequently, even in a world where video was the only thriving game and writing came out as artificial voices for almost all subscribers, Michael liked his pieces of paper; he insisted on them. When he read from a printed page, he held the words in his hands, even as he heard them in his head in his own voice and not just from a computer speaker. Melanie, in one of her clever moments, had called it his "literary atavism," and admittedly, his piles of rolled paper sometimes looked less like work done and more like trash left behind. OK, Michael thought, boxes of data chips have their benefits, take up less space, but even those could look like someone had just clipped his fingernails and tried to hide the evidence.

Michael smiled crookedly at his own humor, pushed aside his printed rolls, and pressed his right thumb to his terminal screen. Internal lasers logged him onto the system. The computer system at *The Tempo* was already three or four years out of date. Nevertheless, Michael could call up the information net with a few taps on the screen or with voice commands. He preferred contact with the screen. Within seconds he had access to encyclopedias and practically limitless files of newspaper and magazine articles from the recent past. His terminal still registered his search from the morning and so simply called up again the vast amount of information on "God."

Richard Padmaram Gesar, Tulku, was the man's real name, of course, and Michael's source said that the last word, *Tulku,* was in fact a title and not part of the name. Thus Richard Padmaram Gesar was a *tulku,* one considered a reincarnated lama of a special order, a teacher of the great esoteric truths of Tantric Buddhism accumulated over lifetimes of study. Michael knew the basic concepts of reincarnation—who didn't?—and it was no surprise to him that another spiritual master would claim to be some further development in a long line of kings and sages. But as Michael called up a file entitled "spiritual biography," written only two years earlier by some devoted follower, he found the claims of spiritual lineage were downplayed. The primary references in that article seemed to be about the discovery of Richard Gesar as a four-year-old boy living in Sacramento. His parents, devoted followers of the Nyingma sect, had from the beginning claimed auspicious signs and dreams heralding the boy's birth, and they had from the boy's second birthday asked their teacher for confirmation of the boy's lineage. But the teacher had resisted such hyper-spiritualism, as all parties agreed it was healthy to do, until a visiting lama two years later met the boy and was converted. Apparently, the boy of four "recognized" the seventy-seven-year-old visitor and called him by a pet name. From that point, standard tests had been applied, during which the boy recognized certain artifacts as significant to a long-dead but highly revered and quite mysterious monk who lived at a small monastery outside Lhassa in the late twentieth century. Even then this monk's spirituality and dedication to esoteric practices of Tantrism were well-known, and at his death he had prophesied his rebirth in "some land of the West." With the young Richard's recognition of these articles—bead strings, a prayer wheel, and frayed straps from ancient sandals—the prophesy was considered confirmed.

A beep announced that a call was coming, and Michael reached toward the screen, pausing with a finger over the conference icon. The voice was Melanie's. "Michael? You still here?" she asked.

Michael touched the screen, and Melanie's face replaced the text he was reading. "Still here," he said, with a little annoyance in his voice, "trying to catch up on the real work at hand."

"Hell," she said, "you better get off your butt and get going. The gig's at 5, ain't it?"

"Albuquerque time," Michael responded casually.

Melanie nodded exaggeratedly. She stuck her cigarette in her mouth and drew hard. "That's right," she said with the smoke. There was a pause, and Michael watched her puff again on the cigarette. Her small, gray eyes seemed even smaller through the round wire-rim glasses she carried on her nose like proof of intellect. Her hair was bleached white and stood up straight on the top of her head like albino wheat, with other layers falling evenly all along the sides and back. He had known her since she came to *The Tempo* from the *International Review* five years before, and they had instantly been friends. She had been a sex partner once, maybe twice, and he had liked her gruff, rebellious nature. But it hadn't been long before she rebelled even further. It was clear by now that she didn't care much for sexual relationships with men, and from what Michael heard, even her lesbian relationships were a bit rough. As for his own status, he had learned quickly that he sometimes was required to act like a friend but at other times had to be carefully professional. It all depended on her mood, and after this morning, Michael wasn't sure what to expect. But as the pause lingered and her eyes shifted left and right, Michael saw a conciliatory gesture coming.

"Listen," she said finally, "don't let all that shit this morning get to you. You know I'm with you on this trip and all, and don't let that asshole Arthur spook you. I've been reading up on this God guy myself, and I'm kinda hoping you'll puncture his condom a little, you know what I mean."

Michael smiled crookedly. "You can turn a phrase, Melanie," he complimented.

She laughed out another cloud of smoke. "Yeah," she said, looking side to side. "But you know what I mean. I want you out there 'cause this guy really does seem to think he's god or something, and I keep reading all this panegyric shit . . ." She dramatically dropped a chip that hit the desk somewhere slightly out of sight of the computer's camera. Michael heard it tinkle.

"Yep," Michael inserted. "I see it, too. Don't worry about me, Melanie. If you keep Arthur from reeling in my leash, I'll see what God is up to. But you know I can't go down there just to break the altars. I mean, what if he really is God?"

"Yeah." She laughed. "And I'm the Virgin Mary."

"Well, I'll interview you later," Michael said with mock seriousness, "and if you can prove it to me, I'll say you a novella, or whatever it is."

"Fine," Melanie said, looking around her and puffing again. "That's all I wanted to say. You know, I'm trying to be encouraging, like a good editor, and all that shit."

"Thanks, Mel," Michael said into the screen with serious grace. He had seen her nervous jitter and tendency toward angry brazenness for years. She seldom looked anyone in the eye anymore, and she couldn't really be nice. It'd kill her. But this was a genuine effort to encourage him. Michael recognized it as the best she could do. "Thanks," he said again.

"Yeah," Melanie said, looking away. Her hand jutted toward the screen, and her image disappeared, replaced instantly by the text Michael had been reading. He shook his head and tried to get back to his research. A glance at the upper corner of his screen showed him it was 4:23. "Damn," he breathed.

With a touch on the screen, his reading continued. "Richard Gesar," the article continued, "was directly given to the care of personal tutors, and indeed he excelled at spiritual practices from his first days." According to the article, this reincarnated holy man showed signs not only of spiritual interests, but also interest in mathematics. Indeed, his early interests in geometry were compared to Blaise Pascal's—Michael tapped up a quick reference—and "like the eminent French physicist" the young Buddha's aptitude for mathematics translated easily into success at physics. Apparently, money poured in from thousands of sources to pay for the extended education of the child, and by his fifteenth birthday, he was enrolled in an undergraduate physics program at Stanford. At the same time, he took over teaching positions at four separate Buddhist communities in the Bay Area, eventually uniting them into one community under his guidance.

Michael sat back and exhaled loudly. There was a lot here to digest. As he looked again at the clock, he realized there was not sufficient time to get it all. He made a decision. He already knew, at least by rumor, most of the success story regarding Gesar's religious life. The young man, in his early twenties, was a world-recognized Buddhist master and had established his center in Boulder, Colorado, although groups from many sects and from all over the world recognized him as teacher. Moreover, at one point, a few years later, he shocked his community by leaving the organization and joining a Catholic monastery somewhere on the East Coast, only to leave that group and study for a full year with a very old Lakota man. That pattern continued for five years, as the young master seemed to have a collector's attitude about spiritual perfection. Everywhere he went he absorbed esoteric teachings with startling facility, all the while—so said many witnesses—bowing to his instructors' superiority with a humility akin to Jesus before the Baptist.

But that was all the parts Michael knew. All that had been in the news in some form or another, especially whenever Gesar appeared at any of the many hot-spots of world violence as arbitrator or single-handed peace-keeper. His recognition as master of Brahmanical ritual and Vedantic techniques, for example, easily earned him the Mahatma designation in the Upper Bihar district a couple of years previously, while his remarkable ability to use Quranic, Hadith, and even Shariat sources had quenched the fears of even the most resistant Muslims in the same region. Eventually he had traveled, "merely as a tourist," the reports said, to Kashmir, where, somehow, his presence and "spiritual power" helped settle age-old tensions. Simply enough, the admiring crowds claimed, he had found it possible to utter prayers that the most devout Muslims and most inspired Shaivites all found moving.

With quick taps, Michael designated the Stanford and physics connections in the paragraph and watched new content appear. Here was the information he would need, for it was evident that "God's" interest in the physical sciences was the key to today's conference. The BS in physics was dated sixteen years ago and might have seemed unremarkable but for the man's relatively young age and the even more remarkable fact that he seemed to have maintained a relationship with a primary research fellow there for the next twelve years. Dr. Beslow—now deceased, a quick tap revealed—had continued to invite Gesar to the Stanford labs, even while the young man pursued his PhD at MIT and even in the midst of the young man's remarkable spiritual journeyings. Whatever research they had pursued, it had apparently been interesting enough to Gesar to compete even with his Latin chanting in Georgetown and his Hebrew davening in Jerusalem. Dr. Beslow's specialty had been optics and photon generation physics.

Michael tapped up the information on photon generation and was soon overwhelmed. He started to read the opening source but quickly gave up, as the text was generously interwoven with equations made up of Greek letters and strange H's. Shaking his head, he tapped down a level or two to find a simpler source, one more like an encyclopedia and less like a professional journal. There the text was larger and the equations more rare, and he still had some difficulty figuring out what the issue really was. Michael Pryor was more comfortable with argument and description than with the energy levels of subatomic particles.

The clock on the screen read 4:45. "Photons are discrete energy quanta without mass or charge and assumed to have one unit of spin," the source began. Michael knew only a little about quantum physics—the implications for uncertainty and indeterminacy had been popular and almost certainly misunderstood notions in his school days—and he could only employ the basic, and essentially discredited, metaphor of spinning balls to visualize particle physics. The article went on to describe ways in which photons may be emitted as light—"on high and low ends of the radiation spectrum, as well as in the form of visible light"—due to energy-level decreases as atoms pass through fields of radiomagnetic energy. Apparently, the text explained, the measurement of such emissions was the standard foundation for all applications of spectroscopy, both astronomical and geological. A tap on the atomic composition of stellar objects and another on innovations in geological prospecting were unhelpful.

Almost five o'clock. Michael shoved himself back from the computer, and put his fingers to his lips in a thoughtful pose. "What is it?" he asked himself. "What am I looking for?" He didn't know. All the talk about photon physics was fine, and he knew he could get at the information, maybe even understand it, if he had the time. But here was something more than just physics. "What is the connection with the *tulku*, anyway? I mean, if he were to invent a really great light bulb, would we all shout *alleluia* just because he's God?" Michael wondered with a sneer if the master would demonstrate how to float above the ground, as he had heard some Hindu and Buddhist mystics could do. Michael was hardly a believer; he didn't put much stock in the whole reincarnation saga in the first place, in spite of all the "evidence" people were nowadays finding through hypnosis. And what would floating have to do with light anyway?

It was five, and Michael groaned. If he didn't start soon, the lines might be busy and he might never get to Albuquerque on time. And then it struck him that he might have gone the wrong direction in his search, looking for simpler instead of more difficult writings on photon physics. Quickly, he slid forward and tapped up the directions for high-level professional journals. Under that heading, he typed in the name of Donald Beslow. Several pieces leaped up, and he scanned their titles. Several referred to specific elements and their photon generation under excitation by laser radiation, and for the most part the titles meant very little to him. But Michael wasn't looking at titles much anyway, but at the authors. Finally, one article caught his eye: "Electromagnetic Enhancement of Photon Residue from the Compton Effect," written by D. Beslow and G. Richards.

"There you are," Michael said, and he called up the paper. Again it was mostly text and equations he couldn't comprehend, but this time he forced himself to read. A high-energy photon stream, the article maintained, can be fired into any energy field, and with the concentration of the electrons in the energy field, there will be an increase of collisions and a corresponding increase in the lower-level rebound of the photons. That "photon residue," the essay declared, can be enhanced and read as electrochemical energy, in order to determine the energy level of the field in question. It seemed that this method of energy-level determination was most appropriate for measuring extremely low levels of energy, especially in ill-defined fields. None of that made a great deal of sense to Michael, and yet he felt he had found something significant. And that significance lay as much in the name G. Richards as in the content of the paper.

Finally, Michael reached forward and tapped outside the screen. He watched it fall back to the opening screen that would continue glowing at his desk until he again logged into his personal user interface. Mechanically, he pulled out a drawer and retrieved his recorder. Just as mechanically, he stepped back from his workstation and told the desk to lock up; it did.

"Photon enhancement from a low-energy field?" he thought as he walked past other workstations. "Light used to measure low energy? Light produced from low energy?"

A distant voice called out to wish him luck, but Michael barely heard it. He stepped out of the newsroom and wound his way through the white-flooded hallway to the lobby of *The Tempo*'s offices. Phone booths were there, and they too were awash with the white light of the ceiling's barely shaded fluorescent. The entire wall across from the booths was a video panel, and as he walked the last few steps, Michael watched the images shift and dance, with new scenes enlarging to cover the wall as another screen appeared in some distant corner. Michael pressed his hand against the access panel of the nearest booth and waited for the lasers to read his identity and give him travel access. There was a hiss, and the door of the booth slid aside to reveal its glaring, mirrored interior.

Light. What would God do with it this time? Color it, move it, measure it, or create it from nothing? A new energy source would indeed be worth a press conference, Michael hought, though there was nothing like the energy deficit there used to be, thanks to superconduction and solar development. And measuring or moving light? What was there that optical wires and phone company meters couldn't already do?

A thought of Daniel flashed through Michael's mind, and with a shock he wondered for an instant if he was missing his brother's party. No, that was tomorrow night. More than enough time to get this Albuquerque conference out of the way, get back, and buy him some token for the party.

Michael slid into the booth and positioned himself for the flash of laser light that would, in effect, destroy him, only to push his molecules over approximately 1500 miles of glass fiber and reassemble him in Albuquerque. He punched in the number and waited for the computers on both ends to make their connection. The only trouble with these long-distance beams was the increased chance of an accident. It only takes a small cough in some line or some relay along the way, and you find yourself beamed in with only half your liver, or perhaps beamed out into literal nothingness, where

Michael Pryor becomes a cloud of molecules floating off in the middle of a Kansas cornfield. He watched the digital clock hit its fifteen-second countdown. "Still safer than flying," he said aloud.

The clock hit ten seconds, and Michael readied himself for the anesthetic gas. He was ready to feel pain, as he was ready to doubt the claims of any new inventor or public savior, even if it's God himself. It was his job to find out what God was up to, he realized, and his job to see if in fact this was "God" doing anything. Michael had made a profession of being a skeptic. Yet there was some truth in what he had said to Melanie. If this is God, perhaps we should listen. And perhaps for a second Michael Pryor felt the stir of hope. But he quenched it quickly and held his breath as the gas hissed forth.

He steadied himself for the light. Light. What was God doing? Perhaps we shall see creation out of nothing after all, he thought. Aloud he muttered perhaps the only Latin phrase he knew: "*Fiat lux,*" he said, and the flash struck.

5

THE SCIENCE OF THE SOUL

Michael was surprisingly satisfied with his place in the array of reporters crammed into the Villard Conference Hall in Building 973 at Sandia National Laboratories on the south side of Albuquerque, New Mexico. He had been placed almost directly in the center of the group and only two rows from the front. He expected the placement behind the video reporters; they were always in front. They wanted it that way, of course, and for the most part so did those who arranged the interviews. It had been long noted in the statistics of all the major "viewer psychology profiles" that the general audience was more likely to believe true the reports presented by recognizable figures, and since the video reporters were often more well-known even than those they interviewed, it only made sense to put those recognizable and well-trusted faces in plain view. They fought among themselves, Michael always noted, for light and position in the front rows, and he easily felt himself somewhat above such trifling. Almost unconsciously, he scratched gently at the scar on his lip. He was not video-presentable, and in his usual rebellious sense he liked it that way. But it was all the more surprising that he had even the position of third-row center.

Michael smiled crookedly. He found that he commanded a strange but genuine respect from the video people, partially because they knew him to be a useful ally and partially because, as a mere writer, he was no threat. He had already shaken hands with D'bon Sanders, a black-skinned, giant man with slightly graying hair that made him seem at once powerfully virile and wisely fatherly. A resonant voice made him as commanding audibly as he was visibly, and earned him, besides his status as news superstar, a good deal of money as a popular narrator for any number of documentaries and children's shows. So for Michael it was a real treat when even the famous

D'bon seemed to step down a little from his superiority and ask Michael, a little sheepishly, for his "angle." Michael admitted he didn't have one; he wasn't sure if D'bon believed him.

But even with the respect Michael knew he deserved, it was rare to be given a seat in the direct line of on-stage cameras. It was almost as if the director of the conference was trying to fight the video system, at least a little.

There was a shuffle of footsteps and the barely audible whir of electronic machinery as an aide moved across the platform and up to the podium. She was tall and thin, with almost bony cheeks beneath short blond hair, and Michael suspected a nice shape beneath the flapping white lab jacket. She turned at the podium, and he could see the gentle hollow of her cheeks and a firm seriousness to the set of her lips. He smiled slightly with easy appreciation. He expected her to announce the speaker, although it was still a little early, and the activities of the other reporters showed they expected the same. Several, Sanders included, touched fingers to their ear implants to make sure they were receiving well and settled themselves for the act they would put forth. But instead of the announcement, the aide merely touched a finger to the flat mic on the podium. "Band three," she said aloud, even in those two words betraying a slight accent Michael couldn't immediately specify. He looked down and pressed the 3 on his recorder so it could record the short-range broadcast of the microphone. By the time he looked up, the pretty blonde was already disappearing through the side door. Michael looked to his right and shrugged at Brian Church, standard columnist for the *Denver Times*. Brian shrugged back, as if to admit the curiosity, and then looked forward again. Michael knew Brian only slightly but accepted the acquaintance with neither worry nor interest. A nice-enough guy, Michael said to himself, but writing for a daily meant to Michael that one just can't probe too deeply into any material. Dailies meant fluff.

It was a full five minutes before the side door opened again. The man who emerged unannounced seemed to bow slightly to whatever orderly had opened the door before he turned to look out at the crowd of reporters. There the man paused and smiled shyly. It was as if for a second his dark eyes scanned the entire group and knew them all. His round, almost circular face was topped by a deliberately short carpet of thick, black hair that clearly defined a high natural hair line. His skin was light and smooth, like polished bamboo, and might have classified him an ethnic Caucasian. But the broad nose and gentle, almond-shaped squint of his eyes betrayed a more East Asian background.

With a slight bow that seemed both to acknowledge the attention of the audience and to confer blessing, he moved to the podium. At first he might have been walking with his head slightly bowed, as if embarrassed by the gazes that followed him, but then, as if without any transition, he was suddenly as erect and forthright in his gait as a giant. His shoulders beneath the white lab coat seemed to fall vertically from his neck like water, and the same sense of fluidity moved throughout his body, down to the footsteps that tapped barely audibly on the wooden platform.

At the podium, he turned, and again his dark eyes scanned the assembly gently. A bare smile curled his lips and made the eyes shine. "Hello," he said softly. "Thank you all for coming. Please be seated."

It was only then that Michael realized he was standing. They had all stood, as if in rehearsed unison, as the man entered. Michael felt embarrassed and let his embarrassment become a hint of cynicism. But he did sit down, along with the rest of the audience.

"I am Richard Gesar," the man said softly, though he didn't need to. He was well known to this crowd, as many had covered his earlier accomplishments, especially his peacekeeping efforts, and all of them had seen his face at one time or another in some news medium. He was a welcome guest at dozens of palaces and government leaders' offices around the world and had been videoed at a thousand state functions with the highest officials beside him. He had also been followed by the more aggressive reporters into ashrams and seminaries, as they tried to cash in on his status as seeker of the world's wisdom. In those places, the news hunters and paparazzi were much less successful, and not a few who tried to interview this man in his religious nests not only failed to make their stories, but finally left their occupations for higher callings.

For a minute or two, the *tulku* looked across the room again and actually named some of the news-people in the room. Here and there, he actually thanked them by name for flattering stories or gently chided them for misunderstood facts. Michael looked down at his recorder to watch the voice-level indicator, just to make sure the voice was being received properly. When he heard his own name, he looked up startled and saw Gesar's deep brown eyes trained on him. As if for a full minute Michael just looked back, and when the eyes moved on, Michael felt himself relax.

At last the speaker ended his rove through the audience and seemed to straighten himself even more. With a childlike pride, he seemed to beam as he brought his hands, palms together, to his lips, as if saying a prayer, and took a long breath. And he spoke.

"I am truly pleased that you all are here," he said, with his same slight bow. "I do hope I will not disappoint you. As you can discern from our venue, the announcement I would give today is rather extraordinary. Some of you, I know," and here he spread a hand across the group, "have been kind enough to report my doings in matters political or spiritual, but here the matters are otherwise. Yet here they are no less dear to my true heart."

As the speaker paused, Michael steeled himself. He let the recorder run, but he still liked to take the notes on the pad in his left hand, as he kept his eye keen for signs of insincerity and pretense. He still felt a bit embarrassed at having stood involuntarily at the man's entrance and at having been shocked by his gaze. He would be more wary now.

"My friends," Gesar continued—and Michael felt himself sneer slightly at the appellation, almost happy to find it such a transparent pretense of familiarity. "My friends, I would like to show you some projections we have recorded as exemplary of our findings here and at other sites over the last eight months."

Suddenly the room darkened slightly, and on the platform, just barely in front of the podium, a glowing holographic projection appeared. It was a human form, naked and spread eagle, something like da Vinci's vitruvian man. It spun slowly in the air to show every side. Below the man's feet, a letter and number code glowed with the same soft pink as the body.

"This man is a friend of mine," Gesar was saying, "who volunteered for these tests back in January. You are seeing here a simple, natural projection of the body. When we overlay this projection with the results of our research, the picture changes to this."

Without transition, the projection changed from the pink glow of a naked Caucasian to a deep crimson. The entire skin area—and even the code designation—were now this solid red monochrome, but even more significant was a band of the same color that stretched out from the body along its vertical axis. Like a crimson aurora, it beamed out in streaks from the back of the head, along the spine and through the crotch, flowing undiminished up the front of the body to the head, over the crown and back to its beginning. In most places, and especially down the spine, it was a thin, vibrating band that emerged from the body only a few inches, but at a few places, the same color shone out farther, like a blood-red sail at the forehead, the back of the neck, and at the pelvis. For a few moments, the image spun on silently, with only the soft whir of machinery.

"My friends," Gesar spoke at last, "you are seeing for the first time the human soul."

In the audience of reporters, there might have been a gasp or two, or perhaps responses more like whispered questions than surprised shock. But mostly, the response was silence. Perhaps for many of them, as for Michael, Dr. Gesar's announcement seemed merely a prelude, and they all expected him to continue. But he didn't. Instead, he just smiled broadly, as if he were enjoying a joke. "OK," Michael thought, "it's the soul. So what?" Later he could only imagine that all the other reporters in the room were waiting, as he was, for some explanation. The soul? Michael didn't need to touch any information implant to register the common term and its wide range of meanings, but none of those meanings had much significance for him. Had the man announced the discovery of the unicorn, his words could not have been more foreign to Michael Pryor. Surely some explanation was forthcoming, but Dr. Richard Gesar merely waited, as if he were a school teacher waiting for his class to ask a question. So Michael asked it.

"What do you mean *soul*?" he said aloud, but the words were never heard, as many others in the room were just as quick—or just as slow in this case—as Michael. Like a flood, questions or simple requests for explanation bubbled up from all over the floor, and Michael's voice was lost like spit in the ocean. Then he realized that the flood was his competition, and he, like all those around him, raised a hand to throw questions toward the still-smiling speaker.

Gesar was like a beaming child at a party. His smile was wide and glorious, as he waved toward his clamoring audience and spoke calmly, asking for order. "Please, please," he said softly, "do forgive me my playfulness and let me explain it all in my own way. Please." As the questions continued, the man set his head back and laughed with a pristine good humor that by itself began to calm the group. That laughter was like a second mystery, and in a few moments, as the laughter continued, the imploring died away and the waving hands went still. Michael himself had gone silent right away, gathering a sense of the broad scene, starting from the curious announcement and continuing through Gesar's laughter. Michael wondered fleetingly if the whole matter were, after all, a hoax.

"Please, please let me go on with my prepared speech," the *tulku* finally continued, but his smile still raged like a storm of delight across his face. "You cannot know," he said gently, looking away toward the back of the room as if some vision lingered there, "how long I have wanted to make this announcement to the world. You cannot know how it delights me now to make it. I feel like a child who watches with joy as a beloved parent opens a present the child has made."

"Then you are serious?" a question flew unsolicited from someone in the front row.

"Serious? Oh, yes indeed, Mr. Hartley. I'm very serious."

"But the soul?" Sanders asked, putting one finger to his face in his common pose of thoughtfulness. "What does that even mean?"

"And what does it mean to see it?" Michael himself threw in the question almost automatically. "Isn't this bit like saying that we are seeing the invisible? Or the mythical?"

"Yes, yes, excellent questions," Gesar responded, reclaiming his air of seriousness. "Thank you, Mr. Sanders, Mr. Pryor. These are exactly the right questions. So please allow me to explain." Gesar seemed to gather his thoughts. He began.

"Again, I apologize for the way I've announced our discovery, and I confess that my feelings are a bit childish. But it is indeed such a delight for me to talk about this, to announce this discovery. I have simply had to contend with my own enjoyment." Gesar's voice was strong and clear, with no accent that might have suggested anything short of fluency in English. Indeed, while earlier there had been a lightness or a giggle in his voice, at last he seemed to stand back and take a slow breath, his childlike smile settling to a thin, horizontal line. His face calmed and he seemed to nod at his own composure.

"Perhaps I have been unfair already to call this," he waved at the image still spinning before him, "the soul, for as some you have suggested already, the term is problematic. As you are all undoubtedly well aware, there are religions represented among us that take the soul to mean something very different from what is meant by the same term in another religion And some take the soul to be, in fact, no 'soul' at all. Let us then call it the spirit, or the aura, if you would like a less-religious word. But the point of the discovery is that, whatever you call it, you may now see it. Yes, Mr. Pryor, see it. For if we could once know what we are looking for, perhaps we can decide what it means to see. And if we can see it, we may now study it. And if we can study it, we may now understand it, seek out its strengths and weaknesses, and, where necessary, heal it."

He paused to smile again, but with more of a simple acknowledgment than his earlier childlike delight. "But I get ahead of myself again," he said. And he took another slow breath.

"My friends, as some of you know, I have spent some time over the last years familiarizing myself with the world's spiritual traditions by meeting some fine, fine representatives of those traditions. As a consequence, I know a number of men and women who are acknowledged saints, truly people of the best spiritual quality. I have been impressed by them, impressed by their sincerity and love of humanity, love of their God or gods or Formless Truth. My friends, there are any number of wonderful saints in this world, and if I could present to you the teachers I have had and the friends I have found among them, they would be enough to reawaken in the most cynical among you a great hope and a sense of the glory of what it means to be a sentient being.

"But my story is not just of them, though any one of their biographies would almost bring flesh onto the bones in Ezekiel's valley. Nor is this story only about the things they have taught me regarding the great wonder of truth, of the absolute, of the great reality that glows and moves and lives beyond and within us all. Rather, my story is of us. It is about the fact that we know this truth, that we touch this absolute, and that we, even we, can gain a share of this reality."

Gesar was beaming again, and again he seemed to catch himself. "But I must speak today of science, as well as glory. And I mean to do that now." Another pause. Calm.

"Why shall we not believe what the overwhelming mass of humanity has known since our species began? Why shall we not believe that our spirituality is real, a fact as true as that atoms bond to form molecules and that our earth orbits our sun? Why shall we not believe that our spirituality manifests itself in reality and not just in the dreams of Freud's neurotics or Marx's bourgeoisie? I tell you today that the fruit of both our science and our spirituality is born.

"Spirit, my friends, is energy, and if it is energy, it can be measured. What Sankara called the Atman and Eckhart the birth of the Son in the soul is, in essence, light. We know it flows, or it can flow, throughout the body of every one of us, and what you see glowing red here, my friends, is that spirit."

The speaker paused and looked down at his hands, as if collecting his thoughts. There were no sounds in the room beyond the buzzing of the newscasters' machinery.

"It is well known in my tradition," Gesar said, as if beginning a discourse, "that there exists a direct connection between physical states and spiritual states. It is no accident that there arose in the East the traditions of yoga that demonstrate this connection. The orthography we display here," he ran a fluid hand up the front of his body, "is reflected in the spirit itself. It is no accident even in the western traditions that the very word *spirit* designates both the religious soul and the physical act of breathing.

"Therefore, it is possible—no, it is necessary—for us to understand the physical reality of spiritual well-being, and this, my friends, is that understanding made visible. There is, along the vertical axis of the human body, from crown, through the sternum and back up the spine, a circuit of spiritual energy, an energy the human will can control and that science can measure. The tantric traditions have known of this system for millennia and named its various centers. The centers, called *chakras*, are hubs of spiritual insight and energy, indications of life and spiritual health.

"My friends, it was only a matter of time until someone who knew both the pattern of spiritual development and the nature of photon projection could find the means for enhancing the emanations of spiritual focus and give us this." The *tulku* again lifted a hand to the still-spinning image. "Spiritual health, my friends. A saved soul."

There was something significant in that last addition, Michael knew, a subtle but important change of emphasis. But he didn't quite know . . .

Gesar went on. "Here is another case," he said, and before them all the whirling image changed. This time it was a woman, naked and spread-eagle like the last, but very different in color. For here the circle of light that moved down her spine, around and up between the breasts, was a moderate blue, almost pastel, like a too-hot summer sky. The numbers at the bottom, Michael noticed, were also blue and read A112.

"This young woman," the *tulku* was saying, "I met while visiting a friend. She came to him disconsolate, angry, tired of life and its tired ways. She confessed a weariness of spirit and allowed us to make a subject of her.

"I admit we hid from her our first studies," Gesar went on with a new solemnity, "for up to then, we had been studying the teachers, the gurus and rabbis, pastors and sages that had led me along my own path. And when we studied this woman, the readings perplexed us. Here the blue emerges at a wavelength of about 480 nanometers. We were all surprised, since previously we had seen mostly red and orange emergence, up to a maximum of around 660 nanometers.

"But now look at this." The man paused and with a slight hand motion changed the projection. The same figure, clearly distinguishable by hair and body, now took on a nearly reddish-purple hue, almost as deep as that of the earlier subject. The label read A112b.

"This is the same woman," Gesar explained, "but you see her converted. She was coming to my friend, after all, for spiritual counsel, for meditation, and for instruction. And one day, she became born again. One day, her life changed. And it changed," he paused and beamed, "into this."

Then Michael understood the point of the earlier adjective. There was more here than description, and it took him a moment to understand the possibilities. Could it be that the "saved" soul is measurably different from the unsaved soul? He had to ask, and he almost threw up a hand to press a point.

But before he could act, he saw D'Bon Sanders move his hand from the receiver in his ear and throw that hand skyward. Michael sneered. Another insightful question beamed to him by those more intelligent than he. As usual.

"Isn't this just Kirlian photography all over again?" Sanders asked with an appropriate thin-lipped, sidelong glare of doubt. "There, too, some believed we were viewing the aura," he huffed the word to give it an air of skepticism, "but in the end all they were measuring was body heat brought on by emotional changes. What do you have that, um, Dr. Kirli, did not?"

Michael was annoyed at the question, so obviously one torn out of some encyclopedia file back at the office. But Gesar seemed amused, as if both entertained by the question and sincere about seeking an answer. "I understand your concern with the comparison, Mr. Sanders," he said, "and you are right to note that the Kirlian effect measured in high frequency electric fields really designates something more like eccrine-gland activity than spiritual existence. To sound a bit like Ebeneezer Scrooge, there was more of sweat than soul in Dr. Kirlian's work."

Here the *tulku* smiled, appreciating his own joke. Michael smiled too, partly in realization that Sanders had gotten the name wrong.

"At bottom," Gesar continued, "Dr. Kirlian's research was limited by his lack of technology and, I fear, by simple ignorance of tantric traditions. The *chakras* and the power they channel and magnify are here, down the center of the self," and again Gesar drew his hands gently down his sternum, "not fluttering chaotically out every pore." He wiggled his fingers out away from him with a fluttering motion. There were a few light laughs in response. "One advantage I had over Dr. Kirlian is that I knew where to look.

"I—or rather we—also knew better ways to look," the speaker continued. "We have developed technologies that can pinpoint our essence down to the molecular level, label it, project it, and now with the help of some brilliant—I must say brilliant—scientists, we have something significantly more precise than Kirlian photography. We call it Spectrographic Aura Enhancement Imaging, or SAEI. Not a very elegant acronym, I'm afraid, but truly, finally, a way to see the soul, the aura, the spirit, the *chakra*."

"*Chakras*," came the voice of Brian Church from beside Michael, and Michael was surprised. Brian was not usually one to leap in, nor did he have an information device planted in his skull to help him ask technical questions. Yet Brian's question rose over the crowd, like a hungry seagull. "*Chakras* are a Buddhist thing, aren't they?" he asked sincerely. "Is this then a Buddhist discovery?"

"Oh, my no; I mean, yes." The *tulku* seemed suddenly genuinely perplexed, and with a hint almost of sorrow, he drew his hands palm-to-palm at his lips. Finally, he spoke. "Yes, the emphasis here is Tibetan Buddhist, though the *chakra* concept goes back much further into earlier tantric traditions, such as the Hindu tantra. But please do not misunderstand me. I am not here today a teacher of Buddhism, whether the Tibetan or Zen or hot tub varieties." He allowed himself to smile. "For the *chakras* you see illuminated are, I suggest to you, the very spirit of holy life, confined neither to Buddhism nor Christianity nor Wicca. This you see is the breath of God as much as it is a *chakra*. Oh, why would I ever say otherwise!? When you have seen the holy men and women of all traditions as I have and when you have seen the path they light up as they walk, you could never say that this," again he pointed open-handed to the revolving image, "is Buddhist. Indeed, the first man you saw was himself a Jew and knew nothing of *chakras*. This energy, therefore, is, yes, *chakra kundalini*, but it is no less the *Shekinah*, the Buddha Mind, the Son in the soul, the inspiration of Wakan Tanka, the *Tathagatagarbha*, the Holy Spirit." Gesar was waving his arms in a spell-bound wonder at his own litany, and then stopped. There was silence as he looked over the watchers. He smiled. "Oh, dear," he said, "I fear I have lost my audience."

The pathos of the moment was not lost on Michael and almost in spite of himself he felt a stir of genuineness. Simply because he was still human, even Michael Pryor wondered, if only for an instant, about the reality of the soul, even his own soul. But in that moment's pause, the competitive reporter in him also saw a chance to leap into the arena. He, perhaps better than most, knew how to save the pathos for later analysis. There was immediately something happening in his inchoate thoughts, a connection he was making that he somehow had to voice. And he had to voice it here in this pause.

"Let us accept the 'science' for now, this SAEI," he called toward the stage. "I would be concerned about the technology. You called this, after all, a 'saved' soul."

Gesar looked at him with dark eyes and tilted his head in a seriously inquiring way. "Yes?" he said back with an inquisitive tone.

"So are you also talking about 'healing' this soul? Accepting for now the technology you have for acquiring this information," Michael Pryor asked, "is there also a potential technology of using, and indeed abusing, the information you gain from your . . ." he paused, found a word, "auroscopy?"

"Hah!" Dr. Richard Gesar erupted with a smile. "Auroscopy. What a nice word. I wish I'd thought of it, Mr. Pryor."

Michael might have felt exposed, maybe did feel a little surprised that this master of science and faith had reacted so greatly to what Michael vaguely meant as a derisive term. But in the next moment, he felt proud of his verbal construction, reminding himself that some creative thought went into reporting and that was something the video faces just didn't have.

"An incisive question, too," Richard Gesar was going on, his face thoughtful. He looked out over the group. "Ladies and gentlemen," he said, "the technological details about SAEI, this 'auroscopy' as Mr. Pryor calls it, and about the acquisition of this information—at least as much of those details as we are willing at this time to divulge—will be broadcast to you on band 2 at the closing of this conference. It is somewhat technical, but you may each make of it what you think best." He paused and looked at Michael. "But as I understand Mr. Pryor, the further question is, what shall we do when we know the state of another human's soul?"

The *tulku* paused and looked at his cupped hands as they lay on the podium, as if contemplating the possibilities that lay there. There was almost prayer on his lips, like tears in his eyes, as he looked up. "My friends," he said softly, "with any new discovery, and with any new technology, we stand before a set of choices that may change the world. When we first began to develop fusion reactions, we had to choose whether we would build bombs or create safe and abundant energy for all humanity. And we didn't immediately choose wisely. Whether it was the driving of automobiles in the last century or the channeling of water five millennia earlier, we had the opportunity to harm or to heal. With the discovery of genetic markers and the development of genetic therapies, we might have created a new system of healing or a new and ever-more horrendous system of discrimination. But this is our moral burden, not the burden of science and its technology. Here, today, we speak of the science and the technology, and, as Mr. Pryor so profoundly suggests, we stand again at the threshold of great moral choices, based upon a new and powerful understanding of our own souls. But if we can understand these things, both in the realm of technology and morality, and if we are wise, then the knowledge of our spirits shall at last open doors that have been shut against humanity since the Garden of Eden. For if we are clever, then we may not only know the spirit, but we may touch it and move it. And if we are wise, perhaps we shall even help it and heal it, as we have learned to reset the broken arm or the chemically imbalanced brain. Perhaps, therefore, also with auroscopy, we shall learn the truth about ourselves and use it to set ourselves free. Perhaps," he paused and seemed almost to be praying, "perhaps the wounded souls of humanity shall at last know peace."

6

DESRA'S DILEMMA

Desra was angry and on her way to her boss's office to tell him so. It was evident to any imbecile, she was telling herself as she stomped through the brightly lit hallways, that an injustice had been done. Her designs had indeed been adopted, she insisted, and yet she had not been chosen for the Japanese presentation. They had held their meeting, and each of the designers had been allowed his or her twenty minutes of presentation, but Kevin, in his classic, indecisive way, had pulled one of those "team" moves. "Let's try a 'team structured' model," he had suggested, with his typical, inane nice-guy smile. Following his pretense of a "Japanese team model," Kevin had said, "Let's pool our ideas and see what we can create from the totality of the creativity represented at this table," and Desra, like any designer proud of her own designs, groaned. For all that really meant was that Kevin had no ideas of his own but wanted credit for creativity, and it meant he didn't have the guts to choose between the models presented. Thus the "team" could steal any ideas it wanted and call it a "team" success. What a charade, especially when his preference had obviously been for Desra's own project, as he had directed the discussion toward her designs. Yet he couldn't just choose the stairstep style nor express any of the value in the work. It was as if he knew what was good but could not say it. He was so damned nice.

By the end of the meeting, Desra saw why. It was not Tharese, as she had feared, but Brandon. His own design carried only the slightest, superficial resemblance to hers, and yet Kevin had somehow equated the two. Brandon's styles built the condos into the hillside, and thus naturally used the hillside's rolling contours for variant spacing. Yet clearly they were indented much too far, Desra was convinced, and they would never be able to achieve the airiness necessary for a genuinely Japanese aesthetic. She had seen it in a moment, and Kevin's insistence that the two be combined somehow—indeed in a way that suspiciously resembled her own original design—could only have been an error of judgment.

Or intentional blindness. Desra knew Brandon had a Japanese language implant, and that, said Kevin, was a significant plus. As if having that damn chip in his brain made him an expert on Japanese aesthetics. Sure he could give us his five-year-old version of Nihongi—that was the problem with those chips, they can't be updated—but did that mean he knew anything about contour or nature? Desra alone, of all the designers, had taken the time to study Japanese nature paintings, had seen the grandeur of the rising hills and the smallness of the human figures. She knew the art and the feel, and Brandon only knew the lingo—and he knew that only because some technician had pasted it to his brain like a postage stamp.

Of course, Kevin's motives might even be worse than she wanted to believe. Brandon was always more than evidently demonstrative in his homosexual affections. He was as promiscuous as a teenager, and if they didn't have cures for all the diseases he picked up, he'd have been dead long ago. The damn queer!

Desra instantly felt guilty for thinking such words. But when you're angry, you let the feelings be free or they just build up and explode later. It was only healthy, she thought, to let your feelings run their course, as long as you don't hurt anyone.

Desra's justifications rang hollow, even to her. But she shrugged the feeling aside and concentrated on her anger. She wondered if she should just march right by Chris's desk and into Kevin's office unannounced. That would at least be good theatrics. But on the other hand, she could cause a lot of trouble for herself.

Chris, Kevin's secretary, was there at his desk, editing something on the screen in front of him. "I'm going in to see Kevin," Desra said, barely pausing. "Announce me if you want, but I'm going in."

"Well, he can't really be disturbed right now," Chris whined in his usual nasal tones.

"Is he alone?" Desra demanded.

"Well, yes, but he's exercising," he returned, "and I really can't . . ."

"Fine." Desra turned and strode boldly to Kevin's door. It would be useless to knock, since Kevin would be totally absorbed in his VR exercise routine.

As she pushed into the office, Kevin lunged toward her like a monster, and for a second Desra gasped in spite of herself. She had seen Kevin in his VR get-up before, and yet it was a shock to see him dressed up and waving his wands like a madman. Kevin's white body suit made him look ghostly, and the helmet he wore completely masked his face with a reflective shell, the inside of which, she knew, bore the images of the virtual reality he presently inhabited. The body suit gave him every sensation of pressure and pain that could accompany the images his visor delivered.

The wands in his hands were the real key to his exercises. The long shiny tube in his right hand thrashed through the air in whirling strokes, as Kevin leaped and danced wildly. The system of linked weights inside the tube gave him the illusion of every strike, made his "sword" feel like it hit flesh, even as the images of blood and carnage flashed to his eyes. The smaller tube in his left hand was his "knife," a lighter but similarly weighted tube he used to catch the opponents' attacks and strike with single thrusts in close quarters. Desra had once imagined the images and the feelings of fighting whatever "demon hoards" populated Kevin's exercise program, only to find out later that there were in fact no demons. As Kevin had described the images to her with matter-of-fact simplicity, the "demons" were actually normal people—women, children, old men—who fell before his blades bathed in gore and untouched by mercy. In this exercise program he was, after all, "the Wicked Baron," and the carnage of slashing and stomping was just part of the entertainment that helped to inspire a person to keep up the physical exercises. It was no different, Kevin had insisted, from doing dance exercises to upbeat music. It didn't hurt anybody.

Even so, Desra felt an autonomic shudder as she watched him lunge and twist his sword, wondering what sight and sound of flying flesh accompanied the act inside that mirrored helm. From the outside, the actions were almost grotesque, even without the context of mayhem. Kevin chopped and thrust, killing God knows who, while his feet stamped and kicked away whatever child or puppy clung to his feet in virtual reality. In a previous program, she knew, he had seen himself dancing and thrashing through the tentacles of some massive beast, but then, too, from the outside it seemed he only thrashed and leaped in meaningless wildness, like a killer gone mad. Apparently, that killer image had become real—or virtually real—in the new upgrades, and from within the helmet, Kevin's muffled voice spat curses, some accompanying bodily actions like grunts of exertion.

Suddenly, Desra felt afraid, as she should have been. Though her natural conscience had grown weaker over the years, sometimes still it whispered of intrinsic ugliness and corruption, as if there were, after all, standards of human character almost measurable, entirely apart from whether or not one's actions actually caused another person pain or disquiet. She could almost hear the whispers still of what it meant to be human, though she had practiced for years the art of denying any objective ideal of human nature, considering it important to remain "non-judgmental." But she also instinctively knew that, were she actually to accept the existence of standards of character, they would have to apply to herself as much as to Kevin. And that was a different kind of fear. So, finally, her instinct for self-preservation came to save her, both from the threat of objective morality and from the wild thrashing of Kevin in his VR world. Barely consciously, her various strands of uncertainty mixed into the genuinely troubling realization that she didn't know what to do next. With almost no hint of self-deception, she felt herself interpret the moment as a genuine danger of potential physical harm. How does one interrupt this flailing and fighting with the technologically animated air? Could he hurt her accidentally? Might he even hurt her intentionally in the confusion of his virtual dreams?

In the next instant Desra remembered her own victimization, and her indignation returned. It wasn't her fault she had to intrude. Whether or not Kevin could come out of his virtual trance, she had to face him and demand her right.

"Kevin," she called, trying to sound demanding. She had trained herself to be assertive, she knew the methods of self-presentation, and yet her voice sounded a little thin, a bit weak. Indeed, Kevin had evidently not heard her, as he went on thrashing against his images.

"Kevin," she called again, this time liking better the tone and volume. Hitting the right note somehow made her confident, and she took a defiant stance, waiting for him to come out.

Kevin stopped, with a muffled curse. Then he seemed almost to yell, "Who's there?" with an anger that unsettled her.

Desra was determined to be undaunted. "Kevin, it's Desra," she called back. "We need to talk."

Kevin cursed again and swung his sword in a sweeping arc that, for all Desra knew, decapitated one last child before he called "Exit" into his commlink, shoved back his visor, and tore off the helmet. Desra was almost taken aback once again when she saw his face, livid with exertion and eyes wide in a strange frenzy. His jaw was set so firmly that the lines were white with the strain. "So what the hell do you want?" he almost screamed.

For a second, Desra was truly frightened. Kevin was milquetoast, she knew, and yet here the livid face and rigid muscles, not to mention the boiling curses so uncharacteristic of this indecisive "nice guy," gave her a sudden, complete sense of impending violence. It was the same triangular face, the same shock of dyed blond hair that stuck straight up from his high, vertical forehead, and yet it wasn't. The same Kevin who couldn't face down his own employees in a meeting now seemed near to latching upon Desra's throat. In that moment of fear, she was frozen. She could not know, of course, that Kevin always had a hard time "coming down" from the vigor of his exercise and that his own anger was mostly inadvertent. Had that evident rage lasted in Kevin's pale blue eyes much longer, Desra might have yielded to an instinctive desire to run. But she saw his face cool, watched him take a few slow breaths. He had practiced in the company's mandatory yoga and meditation training and quickly recovered his calmness. Just as quickly, she felt herself winning.

She took up again her sense of injustice. "What the hell do I want?" she yelled back. "I want to know what the hell you're doing sending Brandon to Japan with my designs. You screwed me over, Kevin."

Kevin was already nice again. Still breathing hard, he smiled and raised his gloved hands palms outward as if to ward off her attack or to gesture for peace. When he spoke again and she heard the common, syrupy niceness returning to his voice, she congratulated herself instantly on having stood up for herself and faced down the bully.

"OK, Desra, OK," he said, turning his face sideways a little as if to cock his ear her way, "I know what you want, and I'm sorry."

"You should be sorry," she glared back, feeling she could now safely be angry. "You know you took my ideas and made out like it was a group project. And then you send Brandon in my place to Japan."

"Now Desra," Kevin shook his head, "you know I recognize your abilities. Don't be angry."

But Desra had him on the ropes. She had the upper hand with her quasi-moral claim. She decided to let the anger roll a while. "You're such a wimp, Kevin, that you couldn't just admit you like my designs. I'm the one who did the research, and I'm the one who should receive the recognition."

"Now, we're a team here, Desra," Kevin tried to say, but she cut him off.

"Don't give me that team crap," she insisted. "You know as well as I do you only use that to keep from making any decision you think might hurt someone's feelings."

"There's nothing wrong with being sensitive," Kevin said with a little whine that made Desra think he was backing down further.

"And I can't believe you'd send someone else, especially the gay guy . . ."

"Now, you shouldn't talk like that, Desra," Kevin interrupted, and Desra at once knew she'd made a strategic error. Kevin's whine had not been backing down, but rather an assertion of morality. With a fear she knew better than to betray, she suddenly realized that she had indeed made reference to Brandon's sexuality and that could cost her the moral advantage.

"Brandon's a good man," Kevin was saying. "He does have good designs of his own, and he can adapt to suggestions. And he knows Japan."

"He doesn't know shit," she spat, but it was already too late. She had lost the upper hand.

"At least he knows how to play with the team, Desra," Kevin said, smiling at her. In the comfortable position of his own niceness, he easily turned away and began stripping off his gloves and vest. "You're too caught up in your own advancement, Desra. You're forgetting that the needs of the company outweigh the desires of one member. We might say you have too many designs of your own." He smiled genuinely at her over his shoulder.

"Very funny, Kevin," she responded. "But my designs—"

"Your designs are our designs," Kevin insisted. "Boy, am I sweaty."

"Come on, Kevin," Desra heard herself pleading. She tried to recover the issue of her rights and the injustice of having her ideas taken into the group and the project given to someone else. But Kevin seemed no longer to be interested, though he was ever so sympathetic.

"I understand your feelings," Kevin was saying, "but you're just so hung up on self-assertion here. Brandon has the language, and you don't. He can take your designs or anyone else's and make a good presentation. Could you?"

He came up to her, his chest bare, his hand extended toward hers in peace. "You need to relax more and get your exertion out in less agonistic ways. Desra, you're the one being harmful. Whatever Brandon may do in the privacy of his life doesn't hurt anyone. It's like VR exercises. Let it all out with less anger."

As if in a trance, Desra realized Kevin was leading her toward his door. He was still talking about "proper forms of self-release" as his hand pushed the panel lock.

Desra tried a last shot. "Kevin," she whined, "this isn't right. I worked so hard."

"And I recognize that work, Desra," Kevin responded with unchallengeable sincerity. "This deal isn't over. You know you're the first one I'll call for further design ideas and adjustments. No one can replace you," he smiled, and Desra heard a threat.

In a second, Desra was outside the office, and Kevin was closing the door. "My protest is not over," she said back to him.

"And I understand completely," Kevin returned, and the door was shut.

"Damn." Desra cursed herself and began to stomp away. She felt like a fool. Chris seemed to look at her with some mixture of curiosity—like, "Whatever could have happened in there?"—and mockery—like, "That's what you get for ignoring the gatekeeper." She turned her face away but couldn't help feeling Chris's gaze follow her, seeing her foolishness hanging on her like cheap clothing. To ignore Chris, she turned her mind to her anger and to her strategic errors in the argument she had lost, errors that still, somehow, had to be Brandon's fault. She tried hard in her rage, however, not to think of references to Brandon's sexuality, somehow trained to know she was guilty of a sexual prejudice, yet simultaneously angry enough not to care. Thus, in the privacy of her mind she wrestled for words to condemn someone as spineless as Kevin, and someone as—she came up with *maladjusted*—as Brandon and decided people so sick should just turn themselves in to be euthanized. "What a waste of humanity," she declared to herself.

But by the time she reached the end of the hallway, she was blaming herself for the errors in argument, for an imagined failure to be more self-assertive, and finally for not having learned Japanese. And by the time she was at the elevators, the real issue was implants.

This was a point she could win, at least in her private self-justifications. So Brandon knew Japanese. It was just a chip, an outdated one at that, stuck somewhere on the outer rim of his left brain like a leech. It was like a drug, a dangerous drug, one that still sometimes did more damage than good. These damn chips never were quite as good as real learning. Sure they were quick; sure they were thorough. But they had no life, no creativity, and above all they showed nothing of the strength and self-discipline necessary for real learning. Michael would back her up on that, for he had always said the same about those video jerks with their clumsy vocabulary chips.

Not that she needed Michael's support. It wasn't as though she had learned such things from him or had gotten her principles from him. Desra was the creator of Desra, she told herself, and she could choose to have a Japanese language implant if she wanted to, just as she could learn Japanese if she wanted to. The issue was independence and self-direction, and she didn't need Michael's permission or self-righteous judgments.

In this way, by the time Desra's elevator landed at her floor, the entire direction of her anger had changed. She couldn't have admitted it, but Michael had become the easier target, someone she could blame—somehow—without the danger of prejudicial errors and without the discomfort of blaming herself. In shifting her anger to Michael, her self-assertion had become less focused on her architectural designs than on her right to determine for herself what plan of life she would follow. The issue was that she would choose her own principles. Michael couldn't tell her what to do; he had no right to judge her, whether she chose to learn Japanese, get a language implant, or play the goddam oboe. In the process of such thoughts shifting the blame to an absent lover, she had also pretty closely justified to herself the legitimate use of language implants. After all, it wouldn't hurt anybody.

7

MICHAEL'S VISION

Michael had called Desra with his news, but she had not been home. He had had to leave a visicom recording for her. It would have been a great surprise for her, he thought, to learn that he had received a special invitation to stay at Sandia for the night and tour facilities the next morning. It had come as a shock to him as well, but he had accepted the invitation immediately, recognizing a tremendous opportunity for a developed article, a full expose. Melanie, who had as usual been working late, had agreed. With typically peppered speech, she had declared she could save him the cover spot a week hence—"and replace that piece of shit Esther is working on"—if he thought he could produce that quickly. Of course, he had insisted he could, and though it would be difficult to round up the extra research, he was happy to get the spot. Desra would have been happy for him, too, especially if her own project that day went well.

Yet, while Desra's interest in his own luck was somewhat on his mind, Michael felt his own growing interest in the woman walking beside him. She was the attractive blonde who had overseen the address equipment at the press conference, and it was she who had come up to Michael after the meeting to announce the invitation. She had done it without ostentation, asking him quietly off to the side, as if she knew the singular invitation to "Mr. Pryor" might offend the other journalists present. Indeed, Michael later learned from her that she had been explicitly instructed by Richard Gesar to make the invitation as tactfully as possible.

The woman's name was Petra Ericksen, and upon closer contact, it became clear that she spoke with an accent. The short blond hair seemed almost silver or white, though it retained a faint golden glow where it flowed back from her high cheekbones. Her skin was very light, almost pale, though it gained a deeper color, a living pink, in contrast to the white lab coat she still wore. Her eyes were the color of the sky, almost with the whiteness of high clouds, and her nose a thin ridge, yet slightly bulbous and turned up at the end. Michael thought it might be the only mar to her perfection—that and the fact that she never smiled.

Dr. Eriksen, as she introduced herself, was Swedish, originally from Stockholm, but she had come to the United States to study biophysics at CIT Pasadena. She had given up the second year of a post-doctoral research grant in Atlanta to work with "Dr. Gesar," as she called him. Her qualifications were, of course, more than sufficient, but the excitement of the project for her, she admitted, was the combination of this work with certain forms of esoteric Tantrism with which she had nurtured a long fascination and invested more than a little practice.

"You'll have to tell me what that means," Michael said pleasantly. "I guess I haven't done my homework, and I don't have a dictionary in my head, you know." He wanted to sound humble.

Dr. Ericksen nodded. "In fact we *do* know, Mr. Pryor," she said. "We did some of our own homework on the reporters before you all came. It was no accident that you were chosen to stay with us for the evening. Dr. Gesar appreciates your work and your skeptical attitude. You had earned his respect before you asked your question in the press conference, and it was a good question in its own right."

Michael walked silently down the front hall of Building 973 from where it left the reception area and moved along the windows toward the southeast corner of the building. He had no response to such praise and realized none was necessary. Mostly he wished they could get beyond their respective titles. He wondered if he should invite her to call him *Michael*.

"But you asked me about Tantrism," Dr. Ericksen resumed. "The word *tantra* refers to an esoteric, mystical form of Indian practice. I should think you would know something of it. There are many books . . ."

"I'm not much of a reader," Michael joked. Dr. Eriksen didn't smile.

"You can find schools or tantra in both Hinduism and Buddhism," she continued coolly, "though the best teachings derive from the Tibetan Buddhists. The most basic idea is that tantra makes the most use of the spiritual energies that fill us and flow through us." Her hands drew lines up her abdomen. "These energy streams are the power that awakens us to new understanding, to new levels of consciousness. All religions know they are there, but some are more clear than others about focusing and using such energy to awaken the soul."

Michael was not as interested as he should have been in the religion lesson. He kept looking at the soft bit of blond hair that molded itself around her left cheek. He liked how she had drawn lines along her body.

"So how did you get interested?" he asked her.

As if feeling his admiration, Dr. Ericksen pushed the hair back from her face and might almost have smiled. "I have always had a mind for mathematics and research," she said, looking straight ahead. "But I also seemed always to know there had to be something more to myself than my own research could detect. I knew myself as a spiritual being even as I studied myself like a machine. It was tantrism, both Tibetan and Hindu, that gave me the strongest sense of myself. I had only hoped somehow I would find in my science a confirmation of what I felt when I meditated or performed Kundalini."

"Kundalini?"

"It's a form of practice that searches out the alignment of the *chakras* and strives to harmonize their flow." She again attractively pointed along her abdomen. "Spiritual power is here," she said, "and it rises like a blooming flower to explode in enlightenment over one's head. Kundalini aligns the energies of thought, breathing, sexuality . . ."

"Sexuality?" Michael liked the direction the discussion was taking, but he wondered if he was being too obvious.

"Of course," Dr. Ericksen responded easily. "Sexual power is a great energy in the body, and there is no reason to exclude it from spirituality. Indeed, many tantric practices harness this energy especially and turn it from its common use for self-gratification to a form of enlightenment."

Michael realized his own interests were more on the common end of the scale, and he found humor in the fact. He put a finger to his lips and rolled his eyes a little, to express to himself his unashamed embarrassment. He kind of liked the common end.

At that moment, Dr. Ericksen looked at him, and Michael caught the soft blue gaze. She looked at him sternly yet with a hint of humor, as if reading his thoughts, and he let his easy embarrassment become a full and ready smile of his own. He knew that she knew she was attractive, and it must certainly not have been the first time a man had enjoyed her looks. As he looked at her, she finally smiled, if only barely. Then as her gaze dropped, Michael saw her eyes catch the twist of his own smile, and he felt self-conscious.

"Don't get your hopes up, Mr. Pryor," she said, as they reached an open space where the hallway opened into a broad seating area with wide glass windows and sweeping views of the mountains to the east. At the corner, Dr.

Eriksen turned and continued, expecting Michael to catch up. Past the open space, they passed a doorway labeled "Meditation Room."

"The sexual practices of tantra are for spiritual growth, not for entertainment," Dr. Eriksen began. "They are the work of two people seeking insight and purification of the self, not merely orgasm." She continued walking to a hallway junction and a simple door marked "Private." There she turned to Michael and added, "Indeed, it is beyond seeking merely love."

Michael stood with her at the door. As she leaned in toward the retina scanner, he almost decided to take the serious and unsmiling tone of her conversation as a kind of challenge. Fine, he might have thought, let us dispense with friendly banter and be serious. Ultimately, he was sure the seriousness of Dr. Eriksen's voice was no match for his own seriousness when he chose to ignite it. She could smile if she wanted to, and Michael was aware that his own smile was not attractive, and the ever-present suspicion that it made him different, even threatening, reminded him that this was work. Fine. She was beautiful, and maybe he was ugly. But those facts gave him a strength of determination, a place to stand outside the niceties of everyday conversation, and thus lent a hard edge to his questioning. His job was to question, and he knew that an age-old, tiny but tiring anger at the beautiful world helped him do it well.

"Well," he began, "I wouldn't claim to be one who has seen spirituality beyond love, or even love beyond the orgasm. But sexuality *is* an interesting aspect of this practice, interesting not just to me but to a hell of a lot of readers. Maybe they're all interested merely in orgasms, but I can be certain that they would love to know how much sexuality figures into this spiritual health Dr. Gesar is preaching. Tibetan Buddhism is his primary, original religion, isn't it? So does he engage in sexual tantric practices? Is he engaged in them now? I might even ask if he engages in them with you, not that I'm probing into your sexual—er—voyage of self-discovery. But a guru who preaches sex, especially with his staff, as a means of 'spiritual awakening,'"—his fingers marked the quoted words—"is hardly a new or surprising bit of cultic hanky-panky. I'm sure my readers would find it, shall we say, at least slightly suspicious and would love to know exactly how much tantric enlightenment you two have experienced."

Petra Ericksen coughed a derisive laugh and pushed on through the door. Michael followed past a couple of plain doors that opened on either side of the unadorned, white hallway. Before the last door on the right, she stopped at last but stood silent as Michael came up beside her. As they stood by that door, she looked down the hallway away from Michael to where a bright red exit sign glowed. There followed a silence that seemed to Michael full of mystery. Had he discovered already a chink in the armor of God? Was he already getting secrets that would add rumors of simple self-indulgence to the news of ever-so-grand discoveries in science and religion? Then his guide faced him, and it was clear in her eyes, and with a thin-lipped almost-smile of confidence that bordered on arrogance, that the answer was no.

"Such things strike you and your readers as 'suspicious'"—here, she marked the quotes, having clearly added Michael to the list of suspicious people—"only because you fail to understand the spiritual ideals and practices of tantra. Also because your own traditions regarding sex remain either so brutishly egocentric or so absurdly puritanical."

Michael couldn't miss the judgmental quality of the last statement, and he might even have had a flash of reflection about it. He would have had no trouble insisting that his own sexual practices were neither brutish nor egocentric, although his yet-undeveloped capacity for honest moral self-analysis would not have gone deeply enough to explain why. The criticism of the "puritanical" was probably a notion he would have agreed with, perhaps even with a brief hint crossing his mind of his own brother and sister-in-law, along with their outdated view of marriage. But no moral analysis got very far, as his probing investigative sense looked instead at Dr. Eriksen's assertions as a form of self-justification. He let the scar on his lip twist a smile upward into a smirk.

"So while others foolishly have sex or foolishly don't," he interpreted, "you seek spiritual ideals through sex." He didn't wait for her to agree. "And what are these spiritual ideals, Dr. Ericksen?" he asked.

"Enlightenment," she answered quickly, "but not such an enlightenment that demands distance from the world. It is a wisdom that sees through appearances and recognizes the emptiness of our bodies, ourselves, our pleasures, and our pains. But it is a wisdom that does not deny those appearances or run from them. It is a wisdom that sees through appearances while embracing them fully. Escaping the temptations of the world by locking yourself in a monastery is a weak spirituality; seeing beyond the world while engaged in its most powerful sensuality—that is wisdom, that is awakening, that is inner light." She leaned her forehead again toward a retina scanner built into the wall by the door, but paused to look back to Michael. "Can you understand what I have been saying?" she asked gently.

Michael almost retorted with something harsh or sarcastic. He couldn't help but guess why she had said *can* and not *do*, and he heard her soft voice loaded with a kind of spiritual superiority he disdained. He looked hard into her shining eyes and steeled himself to face them with equal self-assurance. "I think I do," he said.

"Good," she answered with a slight nod, "for we're here. Dr. Gesar will see you now." She turned her eyes to the scanner beside the door. Michael heard a recorded voice announce her identification. There was a delay, but no words passed between Michael and his escort as they waited, until suddenly, without warning of approaching footfalls, the door pulled open.

"Ah, Mr. Pryor," Richard Gesar greeted Michael with a bright smile. "You are exactly on time, thank you. Please come in." Gesar's form bowed slightly and stood aside to admit his guest. Michael stepped in, instantly aware of cool air and the sweet smell of incense. The apartment's lighting was soft, reflected from the off-white walls from vapor lamps behind wooden shades. Sparse furniture—several chairs with short tables between them, a desk against the far wall, and a large bookcase clogged with colorful bindings—was arranged in a room apparently designed for quiet conversation or solitary reading. A doorway opened into a dark room to the right, while an arched opening to the left was brighter and seemed to enter a small kitchen area. In the corner of the far wall, a sliding glass door opened to the outside, the screen shut against the insects, but inviting to the cool air of early April.

Michael's host was dressed now in a long robe of deep crimson, sewn with a metallic thread that described flowing lines in an indistinguishable shape. He was unencumbered at the waist, yet the robe hung straight and heavy, with a kind of rich thickness that seemed, with its color, somehow warm. At the bottom of the robe, white socks and sandals barely showed beneath the swaying folds.

"Petra, won't you join us as well," he was saying to Dr. Ericksen, who still waited at the door. "We will have some tea perhaps."

"*Nen, danket,*" she responded. "*Det har varit an lang dag; jag vill fa lite vila.*" Michael wondered only for a moment if the statement were somehow about him. Then she turned to him and nodded graciously. "Good night to you, Mr. Pryor," she said. "Perhaps I shall see you tomorrow." Michael nodded, and she was gone.

Gesar closed the door with deliberate slowness and turned to face his guest. He was nodding. "Petra is a wonderful aide to our projects here," he said, as if by way of explanation. "A sensitive spirit and a fine physicist." He winced slightly, and a curious smile seemed to tempt his lips. "But she is slightly lacking in a sense of humor," he added.

Michael tried not to show too much agreement, but he involuntarily smiled crookedly. Somehow this man was disarming, in spite of Michael's conscious effort to keep his critical wits. This was, after all, business.

Yet the *tulku* didn't seem to think so. Like a slightly nervous host with a distinguished visitor, he quickly directed Michael into the room and pressed him with questions about his welfare here at the institute. "If you find the room too cold, I can close the glass. I like the freshness and am somewhat used to the cool air. I trust your meal was acceptable. Our cafeteria is nothing special, of course. I'm sorry I was unable to invite you here for something more personal. Would you be comfortable here, or would you prefer the stuffed chair? I can bring the rocker from the bedroom. I confess I like to rock while thinking; it is not altogether a very Buddhist mannerism, I'm afraid."

All these things Gesar said with a kind of giddy energy, like a child excited with a new opportunity. Yet he did not seem rushed or thoughtless. The questions came at Michael as sincere inquiries after his well-being and almost shy presentations of his own thoughts. Michael found himself responding with faint bows and an equally shy insistence that his needs had been quite adequately met. He even said *sir*.

But Michael Pryor was no amateur, nor was he a magazine social editor. He had made his name in reporting by being harsh, by taking no compromise, and certainly not by being gullible. He was known for being willing to press hard questions. A dozen pretenders had fallen to his inquiries, or at least to his sarcasm.

At the same time, this interview was perhaps his greatest yet. This was Richard Gesar, known already as anything but a charlatan—peacekeeper, advisor to presidents, somehow for thousands of people a symbol of spiritual awakening and deep, inner goodness. Now he was Doctor Gesar, scientist and inventor, one who might reveal the depths of our own souls, and not as mere wishful self-appreciation, but as alleged scientific fact. Face to face, this same Gesar was also gentle and shy, like a child.

As the tea was set, Michael steeled himself. He had read about dozens of bourgeois mystics who burn their sandalwood in modern apartments as if the scent alone could enlighten. As such, the wise leaders, sacred or enlightened as they seem, eventually show themselves to be self-satisfied, self-focused, self-indulgent. When pressed for insight and understanding, they dribble spiritual platitudes and self-help gibberish, bent into aphorisms modeled on the most recent translation of the *Daodejing*. "They inhale incense and exhale nonsense," Michael said to himself. That was a good line, and he made a mental note of it.

So Michael gritted his teeth for confrontation, exposure. Yet he couldn't quite escape the feeling that there was something unusual here, exemplified in the mere fact that he *had* to steel himself. He was disarmed, and not only because the *tulku* had insisted he bring no recording devices. "I have no recorder," he repeated to himself and tried to be suspicious. Yet why did Gesar ask him, Michael Pryor, when there were easily half-a-dozen other interviewers more popular and more congenial than he? Michael could not figure it out but could only insist on being suspicious.

He sipped his tea. It was very hot, with any flavor in the gently green liquid hidden by the stinging heat. His host was turning the hot cup between his hands. Michael felt from the inside the way the scar on his lip turned his offered smile into a sneer, and the feeling reassured him.

"I don't suppose I am here just for tea," he said easily.

"Yes, of course," said Gesar, "and I do not intend to keep you from that work. But as you have seen, I am excited about our news and about our work here. Do excuse me." He leaned forward as if to whisper a secret. His dark eyes sparkled, as he seemed to press a childishly delightful grin into a thin-lipped smile. "I am being so very un-Buddhist about all this."

Michael smiled in spite of himself and did not feel the tug of his scar.

Then Gesar leaned back and sat erect, yet not stiffly. "I can calm down," he said with a new tone. "I know we have much to discuss."

"Indeed," Michael responded. "I do have a number of questions about this technology, especially about—"

"But—do pardon me for interrupting," Gesar broke in. "But so much of the technology is in many ways uninteresting. Oh, not for me, of course, nor for some others like Dr. Ericksen or a handful of our colleagues. But I have tried to convey much of that information on the release chip, and any more detail would be quite unfruitful, I assure you. I don't mean to be insulting, but—"

"I do understand," Michael said, strangely glad to interrupt in return. "You mean that very much technological detail would not be very helpful for the average reader."

Gesar smiled, but with less glee. "Of course you understand me," he said. "I could, but simply do not desire to, give a lecture either on *chakras* or on photon emission. All such relevant material I would like to release soon in the relevant journals, of course."

"Of course," Michael nodded, congratulating himself that here, already, was a hearty suspicion. "You'll give us the details later and in other, more technical journals that, probably, none of us will ever read."

"Exactly," the man answered. Michael was surprised that the man did not seem to catch his suspicious tone.

"But my technological questions, even for one relatively ignorant, seem significant," Michael went on, aware of the slight haughtiness in his own voice and the pretense of self-deprecation. "For what we laypersons would be interested in might concern some of the details of *how* the proper information on bodily energies can be picked up, how it can be detected, and so on."

"Of course," Gesar began solemnly.

"There are at least two issues," Michael pressed without letting the man speak. "First, how intrusive is this study? I mean, if you must push probes into the brain, one might find the procedure a trifle invasive."

Michael had almost hoped to rile his host a little, but the sparkle seemed at once to leap back into the dark eyes. Gesar threw his head back and laughed aloud. "Indeed, indeed," he said, laughing, "and the great irony is that we do in fact push probes into the brain." He laughed some more.

"Not exactly, of course," he finally said, with the laughter still in his eyes. "I told all of you a little about the line of energy along the *chakras* from the base of the spine to the crown of the head," he explained, drawing the imaginary line up the torso with his two hands pressed together back to back. "And key points here, here, here, here, here, here, and up here," he designated the spots, "are focal. But the energies, especially in those untrained, are faint and confused, and we have indeed inserted 'probes,'" he wiggled his fingers to mark the quotation, "as far into the stream as we dared. It did, in some early cases, have us pressing micro-wires into the space just inside the cranium. That is not exactly into the brain, but . . ."

He let his words trail off with an oddly humorous smile. Michael somehow again felt disarmed by the humor of the man before him—and by his honesty.

"Then this isn't exactly a home pregnancy test," Michael put back.

"Well, not yet," Gesar responded. Michael noted a perky interest jump back into his demeanor. "But as we isolate more and more the measurable vibrations, I do not see why we cannot design our instruments to be more and more precise and therefore more and more sensitive. I do believe we shall someday be able to gather precise measurements at skin level, and most logically at exposed points, such as here at the neck or the lower spine, or perhaps here at the top of the head."

"Soon?" Michael asked.

"I cannot say," Gesar responded, looking straight at Michael, though with a thin-lipped seriousness. "It depends on how our work so far is received, I believe."

"By the scientific community, or by the public?"

"Both," the man answered. He paused, as if collecting his thoughts. "Certainly," he nodded, "much of how we advance will depend on what other researchers do with our ideas. We have no intention of keeping this discovery to ourselves, and if other experts—technological, medical, spiritual—find new ways of tapping into this information, we will be quite grateful, and the advances in this spiritual science will be tremendous." He paused again, and this time looked down at his hands as they rested in his lap. Michael felt himself waiting for words.

"The real significance will lie in how these ideas are received by the world at large," he whispered with a solemnity Michael almost felt in the air. "Do you not see it, Mr. Pryor?" He was not really asking a question, Michael knew, and the squint of the man's eyes was not due to the query or to any uncertainty but to whatever vision the *tulku* was seeing.

"It is a world of peace and wholeness, Mr. Pryor," he finally whispered. "I can see, literally see, Mr. Pryor, how the souls of men and women suffer on this earth. I can see how uncertainty and fear breed hunger and how hunger breeds pain. We know, don't we, Mr. Pryor, that the pain we cause one another is only a reflection of the pain we cause ourselves, that the health we cannot find within becomes an illness we foist upon others without. So if we can show that man, that woman, that the hunger and fear are here within, and if we can show them how to change the flow of life from fear to wholeness—"

"From blue to red," Michael inserted with only a hint of a question in his voice.

A smile passed like a breeze on Gesar's lips to respond before he went on. "If we can so teach wholeness," he said, "then we shall also teach love."

"So we have at last," Michael looked steadily at Gesar, allowing the instincts of his provocative manner to flow, "a divine aphrodisiac?"

The *tulku's* brows arched up, but he only smiled gently and rocked for a moment in his chair, until Michael wondered if the rocking were an affirmative. Finally the man spoke. "You tease me, of course, Mr. Pryor," he said softly. "You know as well as I that *love* is an equivocal term. But perhaps your question points up a valid issue. Let us then drop the term *love*. What we find when we find our own healthy souls, when the aura flows forth its deep vermilion, is perhaps more than love. It is truth. Yes, let us say *truth*. We shall, Mr. Pryor, see and know our own souls as whole, as one, and we shall learn that the truth is not in some distant realm or otherworldly dream, but here inside us. This has already been taught by great teachers in all traditions, that when the truth is known here," Gesar touched his breast, "then we replace ignorance with knowledge, and with knowledge comes the understanding that greed and hatred are useless. What is there to demand when we have all truth within us? What is there to detest when the same truth is shared by all? With our science we shall at last verify the wholeness of the self, and with such confidence in the glory of the divine, we shall create at last a unity of the world hitherto only imagined."

Almost in spite of himself, Michael felt the attractiveness of the teacher's words. Surely they were not new but had been dreamed and sung about by a thousand flighty poets since the beginning of human self-awareness. But the master claimed to see, to know, and to make us all capable of seeing and knowing the truth of ourselves. With such an awakening, what wonder might be possible, what unity proven, and hence what reconciliations made real.

At once, Michael thought of his own brother and the spirituality he had seen there and so long resisted. Even there, he thought, if we could replace faith with sight, if he could see the health of Daniel's "Christian soul," might Michael himself slowly discover the value of his brother's faith? Might he be able to let go a little bit of his disdain and skepticism and find unity?

With a slight shock Michael heard his own thoughts, almost a jealousy of his brother's faith, a long-hidden longing for what it meant. Yet that same flashing thought, like a jealousy of spirituality, reawakened Michael to his own well-practiced self-assurance and reminded him of his role in this conversation. With an effort, he recovered his general suspicion and pressed on to his second question.

"But aren't we faced with great potential for cultic manipulation?" he asked, steeling himself to be unconcerned whether he offended his host. "The people who hear your report and read my article will want to know how you differ from a thousand other gurus and shamans who have promised spiritual wholeness and led their masses to the desert somewhere to starve, while waiting for some Christ to return. How can they trust that you are any different?"

Gesar smiled, and his smile was less romantic and more personal. Somehow he seemed to be looking more deeply into Michael than he had during all his musings about world holiness. "The real question, is it not," he nodded, "is how can *you* trust me?"

Michael felt startled, as if the teacher had seen something in him he had barely seen himself. Had he really deeply, secretly wanted something his brother's faith represented? Did this *tulku* really call him, Michael personally, to a spiritual response? Michael felt more than heard these questions in himself. But no lip quivered or eyelid fluttered, and he stared back into Gesar's dark eyes until the man went on.

"I mean, of course, that you are yourself, through these interviews, going to play a part in answering the question you ask," he said, and with an invisible sigh, Michael felt released from introspection. "How they shall trust me is partly dependent on how much you shall trust me, for you are, in a sense, a *de facto* liaison for us all here. Why do you think you are here taking this interview?"

Michael realized he was right. He barely heard the next few sentences that explained how Gesar hoped Michael's own writings would help to introduce these ideas to the world, that he had been chosen precisely because he was a skeptic. There would be other writers and news reporters, Gesar was saying, but the choice in every case was based on the need to allay the suspicions of the public and to let them see that here was something different, something good and true.

"In the end," the man added, "I ask no one to trust me but only to trust themselves. In the end, it shall be their own souls that convince them. 'Be lamps to yourselves,' the Lord Buddha said, and my hope is that this technology, this teaching, will make that possible because it is in this light that they shall see light, and it will be the wholeness of their own souls that shall delight them and, therefore, convince them. I have some hope, Mr. Pryor, that it will begin with you."

Dr. Gesar paused. Michael found himself staring into his host's dark eyes as if into the eyes of God. There was indeed a kind of calm serenity there, a peacefulness that seemed at once warm and possible. "What is so bad about peace of mind?" it seemed to ask, and the *tulku* smiled.

Michael once again strove to awaken. Surely the speech about peace and hope had to be but one more invitation to some self-denying spirituality, and Michael felt the threat he had always felt, that rude violation by the preacher who thinks somehow you must look into your own soul for your own weaknesses that the preacher is all too happy to reveal. For Michael, even when confronted with his brother's gentle hints of some absurd need for Jesus, it was an intrusion, even an insult. "You lack this great blessing," it proclaimed, "and I have it to give." Michael felt himself stiffen, and he wanted to sneer, "How dare you step on my conscience! How dare you try to sell me your God!" It was a hardness of heart that Michael felt within himself as confidence and courage, strength of will and autonomy. Yet he also knew it was a strength better left hidden, for only the weak, he told himself often, fight a defensive war.

Michael quickly settled himself. Instinctively, his professional skills worked their well-trained magic, moving him from the simple rage of self-protection to the easy creation of a probing question. Feeling the sneer on his lip, Michael let his gaze solidify with a pressure in his eyes like a headache. "Are you asking me, Dr. Gesar," he said calmly, "to be the spokesperson for your cult?"

"Oh, yes, would you?" Gesar replied with a serious look. Then he laughed.

Michael was disarmed, almost embarrassed. He might have wished it had been the laugh of the maniacal villain in a bad movie, or at least some obvious dismissal of a genuine challenge. But the *tulku's* laugh danced with a kind of delight in the air of the quiet room. His eyes glittered with frivolity, like the eyes of a child at a birthday party. In spite of Michael's desire to doubt, he could see that his host genuinely enjoyed the humor of the moment. Michael felt a strange warmth in that glittering delight, as if, somehow this divine teacher was enjoying the presence of Michael himself. If he had had time, Michael might have felt loved.

"And is this not the reason I have asked for your help, Mr Pryor?" the master was saying. "Certainly I have all the spokespersons I need for my 'cult,'" he went on, "but I do not necessarily have anyone who will challenge what we do, challenge me personally." He paused. "I want your skepticism, Mr. Pryor."

Dr. Gesar stood and glided easily toward the counter that separated the small living room from the even smaller kitchen. He poured himself some water. "Actually," he started again with a softer and yet more serious tone, "I'm surprised you didn't see right away the great benefit our work might have for a skeptic like yourself."

"How's that?" Michael asked.

"Consider for a moment," the *tulku* said softly, "the possibility of looking into the soul of the latest teacher or minister to see if their spiritual warmth is real or only a show. How might we, you and I, reveal the charlatan and the false guru, if only we knew how!" He returned to his seat, sat, and sighed.

"And yet," he began with renewed earnestness, "I might wish that we, you and I, could also be more positive. For while the deceivers of the ages have occasionally succeeded in leading some astray, the true prophets and sages of a hundred generations have also failed to lead the world to the light. Oh, they have succeeded in various ways, hinting and whispering and pointing vaguely toward the glory we all intuitively feel, while leaving still so many in darkness where they languish or, indeed, become the victims of deceivers who prey upon their native hunger. Less important than catching the liar is creating a land where lies are no longer needed. Better than catching a thief is creating a land so full of bounty that no one desires to steal. What if we could all bring light with us into those dark lands where we fear to be misled? What if we could all pick from the tree ourselves the fruit the charlatan pretends to sell? If there are lies, Mr. Pryor, then we must, by all means, avoid them. But if there is truth, if there is bounty of spirit, would it not be a thing worth knowing?"

Michael was listening. Strangely enough, he was listening, even with an unexpected sense of hope. To know truly, to see directly the truth of one's own soul—this could awaken new life and heal wounds he barely acknowledged. The divisions, the suspicions, and the mistrust were burdens, burdens he knew, though a day ago he could never have allowed himself to say so. Even now, here in the privacy of his thoughts before the *tulku*, he could not exactly attach those words to his feelings, and yet in that moment, it might have felt like hope—hope that love might not be fleeting, hope that his brother might be right.

Then it was gone. As soon as he was aware of his unnamed hope, Michael closed down and recalled that his job was to mistrust. Thus, instead of his thoughts flashing through introspective self-challenges or the challenging faith of Daniel, he turned his thoughts purposefully to article deadlines and research sources. He was to be a skeptic? Fine, he would show them skepticism. He would show this Tibetan guru. He would show his brother and his brother's Christ.

Michael rose to leave, and Gesar looked surprised. Had he been able to be more honest with himself, Michael might have admitted he was slightly afraid, worried that this guru or Daniel's Christ might yet threaten his autonomy and self-assurance. But short of that insight, he was mostly aware that he needed more information, more data, to see for himself and to challenge the assertions of truth and love.

"I can see, Dr. Gesar, that I have much work to do," he said with a calmness that carried no hint of confession. "I need to study your technical information but also to study your religion of *chakras* and peace." Michael heard his own voice spit the words.

"Of course, Mr. Pryor," Gesar nodded. "I'm sure I can explain—"

"But I do not want to learn these things from you," Michael spoke with habitually acerbic tone. "Nor from Dr. Eriksen," he raised a finger as if to pre-empt an offer.

The *tulku* smiled at Michael but did not rise from his seat. His face remained calm and bright, and Michael might have appreciated the honest look in his eyes, but Michael had by now set himself to doubt and scrutiny. Gesar cocked his head to one side slightly and nodded. "Of course, Mr. Pryor," he said with only the hint of a smile. "You must be a lamp to yourself."

For a second, the two men looked at each other in silence. Michael's anger against the *tulku's* attractiveness was not truly a match of powers, though Michael might have imagined it so. Certainly at this point, his gifted anger did in fact save him, though he could not honestly have understood why, and he could not know that it was more grace than strength that allowed him to hold onto his doubt and rebellion for the rest of the evening. Gesar offered Michael another hour of his time before he needed to sleep, and Michael therefore sat back down and began his questioning. He asked whether followers who were "lamps to themselves" could really avoid being swept away by a charismatic leader. He asked if there were independent labs testing Gesar's findings. He even asked if the spiritual master was having sex with Petra Eriksen. All through the interview, God smiled and nodded but kept a determined seriousness that seemed precisely the attitude Michael needed to see. By the time he had to leave, Michael's mind was focused on how to write an article that would confront the dangers of cults and pseudo-science, even as he found himself insisting on the need for new information and a new line of skeptical inquiry. In spite of himself, that focus was the only way he could escape the lingering but necessarily unspoken sense of hope that all the teacher had said, all the promise of enlightenment and peace, just might be true.

8

BIRTHDAY

Michael waited as patiently as he could for the old elevator to complete its climb to the fifth floor, where Daniel and Helen lived. This old building—it still used fans for ventilation and hot wires for electricity—had booths only in the lobby downstairs, and the inhabitants and their guests had to phone in there. Daniel always smiled his strange, shy way when the subject of living arrangements was broached, as if he were a little embarrassed, yet not because the conditions were sparse or carried some implication of poverty. When one mentioned Daniel and Helen's home, he smiled more like one receiving a compliment.

Strange, Michael thought. He knew Daniel was not terribly rich, but he also knew the couple could have afforded more. That would be especially true if Helen were to look ahead, maybe pursue some further training in order to get better employment. But there was always that odd hope of theirs in the background, some pitiful assurance that they would conceive. For a second, Michael felt their sadness.

But why don't they get on with things? His next thought brought him back to their peculiar impracticality—and that in turn brought him to their faith. There was always that oddity about Daniel and Helen, a silliness, in fact, that floated around them like the playful atmosphere in kindergarten. It was at once pleasantly innocent and slightly naive, and Michael himself never knew quite whether to feel envy or pity for his brother and his wife. Religion was OK, of course, he added to himself, as if he knew he had to, but it can become an obsession. If Daniel and Helen would just use its reasonable comforts and not try to build their lives around it.

The ding sounded as the elevator breathed to a stop on the fifth floor. The shiny aluminum doors seemed to hold Michael back with a purposeful delay, saving him, perhaps, from some mechanical danger, or just letting him look at himself before he had to be sociable in a foreign context. As he looked, Michael automatically patted himself all over as if to check for lost items. But his hands had been empty since he left home, empty even of a present. He had been busy, he reminded himself, and refused to feel guilty.

Michael stepped into the carpeted hallway and turned left without thinking. Guilt, after all, was what apparently drove Daniel. Guilt was *his* problem. To Michael it seemed that Daniel had never reconciled himself to the decision about their parents; Michael had seen the hesitations from the beginning of the process and had known it was necessary to take control. Daniel was the elder brother, and for that outdated reason, he seemed to want to take responsibility. Yet Michael knew he himself had been the one to press subtly for the euthanizing of their mother and had only let it seem like Daniel was making the decision. Thus he had decided to feel noble, both for having "taken care" of Mother and for letting Daniel think himself a responsible son. Michael knew words, and he knew how to use them when it was necessary.

It had seemed to work, at least until their father's death. Dad had been silent throughout the whole process of his wife's sickness, and he had waved away their questions about what to do with her, how to "take care" of her. Thus the sons had taken over; thus had Daniel seen himself called to step forward and make decisions. Thus he had taken responsibility, and Michael knew—hell, everybody knew—that the injection was the compassionate choice. Michael slapped his hand on his leg as if to prove the point, and then wondered at his own vehemence.

Then something had happened. Naturally their father had become somewhat morose and withdrawn after the loss of his wife, but then, one day, it seemed he was coming out of it, talking happily again. Then, the next day, he and Daniel were notified that their father had turned himself in to the clinic and volunteered to take the drip. He had only been sixty. Michael had been shocked, but he had known enough to put a bold face on it and declare for everyone's sake all the lines about their father's dignity and choice. But to Daniel, their father's death—he had once called it suicide—had come like a horror—or worse, proof that their mother's euthanizing had indeed been an evil. "See," he had cried, "Father knew it too. But we were all so damn well trained." It was the only time Michael had heard Daniel cuss.

Daniel had never recovered, never understood the need and compassion of the two deaths. Michael had naturally felt some regret, but there were well-known loss strategies, and he knew how to find them with a simple search. He also knew when to drop the grief strategies and get on with life. Mother and Father had lived their lives, and now he was living his. There was no guilt in that.

Number 506. Michael stood before his brother's door, surprised to find himself almost angry. He had done what needed to be done with Mother, and Father's choice was his own. Damn it, Michael felt comfortable with himself, whatever guilt Daniel wanted to harbor to feed his archaic religion. Daniel could believe whatever he wanted, but Michael didn't need it. Oh, he knew he'd have to face some of his brother's friends' religious chatter and self-righteous moralisms, but Michael decided, as he had a dozen times before, simply to walk away from such nonsense. It wouldn't be his fault if this was going to be another fifteen-minute visit, even if he didn't have a present for his brother.

He heard voices just inside the door. For a moment, as the pneumatic locks hissed open, he felt conspicuous. But anger helped, and Michael straightened himself and raised a hand to knock. The door opened.

"What a shame you have to go, Morris," a woman's voice sounded. "I can't tell you how much your company means to me personally."

The woman stood at the opened door but turned sideways to the hall. For a second, Michael admired the silhouette. She was short, perhaps a little rotund, though not fatty, and he noted easily the shape of her body beneath the simple dress. Her face was turned away, addressing someone behind her, and Michael could see only her long, straight hair, almost black, but shining. It seemed to flow from her like a polished ebony waterfall, and Michael found himself wanting to peer behind the cataract.

Then Morris appeared at the end of Michael's field of vision. He was a medium size, perhaps a little short and heavy. His round face was clean shaven. He was perhaps in his early thirties, with light hair and a broad smile. With a practiced, fluid motion, he was swinging a light jacket over his shoulder as he passed the woman at the door. "Somehow, Marta," he said, "I don't quite think you're sincere. But Jesus loves you just the same."

"Same as what, Morris?" the woman responded, but he was not listening. He was calling behind him, "Come one, Millie. I can't be late for the meeting."

Morris moved to go, and his eyes flashed past Marta and caught Michael. In that instant, Michael probed the man's eyes, almost greenish, but storming, as if with anger. Yet Morris's smile remained broad, and in the moment he saw Michael, his eyes lit up.

"Oh, hello!" he said, with an almost bubbling happiness. "Excuse me, I guess we're barging right through you. My name's Morris, Morris Hobbes."

Michael took the offered hand. "Uh, Michael," he said, "Michael Pryor."

"Oh, the famous brother," Morris announced. "Daniel speaks of you often, and with some pride, you know. You are quite blessed to have him as a brother."

"Er, thanks," Michael said, unsure exactly of how one accepts a blessing. Physically, at least, his response was to back away to let Morris pass.

But the man's handshake clung like his smile, and Morris followed him out. "In fact," he was saying, "from what your brother tells us, you are quite a personality. A writer, is it?"

"Well, yes," Michael answered, "but just for a periodical."

"But still," Morris urged, "Daniel says you are full of fascinating ideas and perspectives on life. I had hoped to meet you someday and talk." Finally he broke the handshake and looked at his watch. He stared at the watch with what seemed to Michael genuine disappointment. "I do wish we could stay and talk," he said, "I really do. But Millie and I . . ." He turned and called, "Millie."

Michael looked past Morris to find another young woman moving past Marta with a gentle squeeze of her hand. "This is my wife," Morris was saying, turning slightly to bring her up to their conversation. "Millie," he said to her, "this is Daniel's brother, Michael. Remember, we've talked about him."

"Oh, sure," Millie said, smiling at Michael. She seemed almost wildly cheery and warm; her head tilted a little sideways as she smiled with her jaws apart, teeth showing white behind bright red lips. Blue eyes were fixed genuinely on Michael, although he couldn't help noting the distracting deep color of her eye shadow and liner. Her blond hair hung to her shoulders in a soft, but careful curve. "Michael Pryor. Why, you're something of a celebrity. Pleased to meet you."

Michael responded automatically. "Nice to meet you both," he said. He was already allowing himself to feel annoyed at being blessed.

"I was just saying to Michael . . ." Morris started toward his wife and then shifted. "Do you say Michael? Or is it Mike?"

"Michael." Michael tried to smile, but felt his scar wrench it into a sneer, and Morris caught the twist.

"Of course," Morris responded quickly, then resumed to his wife. "I was just saying that I wish we could stay and talk some. I'd love to share some ideas. But I have this prayer meeting to go to at church."

"And God does insist you're on time." This intrusion came piping in from behind, and Michael realized the other woman, Marta, was still leaning against the door, listening to the conversation.

Morris rolled his eyes, chuckling softly. "Michael," he went on, "it would be nice to meet with you some time and talk, if you're of a mind to."

"Sure," Michael responded immediately, and just as quickly regretted the insincerity of small talk. But it wasn't his fault. It came somehow with all the "sharing" and "blessing" that was somehow supposed to mean something to him. It came in this peculiar desire to talk about real ideas, which meant getting a sermon. Why couldn't these people just be straightforward? "Call me some time."

"Seriously?"

"Sure," said Michael again, with an impatience growing in his voice. "Just call *The Tempo* and ask for me. We'll arrange something."

Morris nodded, pressing his lips together. "Great," he said. "I'll get the number from Daniel." He paused, then added, "If you're serious."

"Sure," Michael said a third time, though by now he was looking through the doorway for some sign of Daniel.

"Well, great," Morris repeated. "And we really do have to go. We were supposed to be at the meeting a little while ago, but I think we can phone straight in from here. Oh, nope," he nudged Millie. "We gotta go home and get our Bibles. I should have thought ahead. Well, gotta go," he finally said, "but I will call, you know."

"Sure," Michael said for what seemed the thousandth time.

As the two disappeared down the hallway, Michael suddenly felt like he had entered a zone of calm. Without any intentional exaggeration, he breathed out a sigh. "Whew." And then, self-consciously, he looked at the short woman in the doorway.

Marta raised her eyebrows, and raised her hand in front of clenched lips as if she were holding in a howling laugh. As he watched, the laugh coughed out like a burp and her face brightened with a private glee. "You look like you've been punched in the nose by a nun," she laughed.

Michael laughed back. "I think I have been," he said.

"Well, come in, Michael Pryor, celebrity," Marta said, pressing her back against the door and motioning him inside with a flip of her head. "Quick, before he comes back."

Michael moved past her and smiled genuinely, but Marta looked past him out into the hall, as if alert for an enemy. She closed the door and leaned against it as the locks hissed shut. She wiped her brow in mock relief. Michael smiled.

"Marta Sanchez," she finally said, looking up into his face. "And you're Daniel's brother."

"Michael," he said, with an easy nod and a fleeting fear of smiling awry. "Pleased to meet you, Marta Sanchez."

"Well, Morris is an easy act to follow." She smiled back brightly. "Unless you're a chainsaw. Come on," she said to him, "Daniel's in the kitchen."

She led the way, and Michael stepped along slightly behind her, noticing her figure and the rhythmic swish of hair across her back. Though shorter and heavier than Desra, this Marta had an attractive form, a smoothness that intrigued him, and a lightness in her step that attracted his eyes to her legs. There was a fluid grace, a kind of beauty in her figure that was imaged again in the soft, but pretty roundness of her face, again unlike the fine, but chiseled features of Desra. And it had been readily apparent that her humor, though sarcastic, was lighter than Desra's. Marta's curious lightness and heaviness made Michael smile, and he shrugged away a hint in his mind that comparisons with Desra were unhealthy.

"Little brother's here," Marta announced as they stepped into the kitchen, and Daniel looked up from his conversation. He had been leaning against the counter, holding a glass containing his favorite mixture of fruit juice and ginger ale, talking with the Meyers—or, rather, listening to the Meyers ongoing lament about their son. They were nice enough people, Daniel always insisted, especially Reuben, who showed, in private conversations at least, a kind of quiet attentiveness to Daniel's own chatter of optimism about children in particular and people in general. But when the two of them were together, Reuben and Alexis seemed to have nothing positive to say about their own child, Andrew, now age fifteen, who apparently had never read a book nor done a math problem correctly. Daniel used to think they were exaggerating, but in fact he learned they were not, or at least not much. The delicateness of Andrew's education, they insisted, continued to worry them, even though the school he attended had disability specialists working on his case. Above all, it seemed to worry them that someday Andrew might find out that there were people who still expected him to read and do arithmetic, insensitive to his special needs. "God knows what that would do to his self-esteem," Alexis Meyers would say, and Daniel would nod and say, "Hmm."

So when he saw Michael, Daniel brightened. But then he always brightened when he saw his brother, and he saw in Michael's eyes a similar shine, perhaps in spite of himself. He shook his brother's hand forcefully, as was their tradition, and with a strange pride he introduced him to the Meyers and to Marta. Alexis and Reuben were "pleased to meet" him; Marta said, "Heck, we're old friends already."

Michael suffered through the introductions with good humor. For five minutes he went through basic descriptions of his work and travels for the guests, though with a conscious and careful effort, he avoided entirely his recent trip. All he'd need, he figured, was to mention God and souls to these people, and he'd be tied to a chair with a feeding tube down his throat.

It became evident rather quickly that the Meyers weren't yet done with their lamentations. Thus Daniel found himself once again under their eyes, somehow the target of Alexis and more the distant savior of Reuben. Daniel would have preferred to talk to his brother, almost about anything, as he had always found such a strange delight in Michael's presence. Michael was for him almost like Helen, a kind of living reality, an assurance that people could be human with one another. Although he shared very little philosophically with his brother—certainly he shared more with the Meyers and even Morris—any time Michael would visit, it felt like a promise that distance between them could be overcome. Daniel tried again to find something new in the Meyers' woes.

Michael felt relieved to be cut off from the conversation. He smiled at Marta, hoping to revive the earlier shared humor. "Are they from the same kennel as Morris?" he asked dryly.

Marta pressed her lips and shook her head as they slipped farther away. "Morris is annoying," Marta said easily. "These two, I just can't figure out. Or they can't figure out what sheet of music is on the stand."

"What do you mean?" Michael asked, genuinely curious.

But Marta waved him away. "I don't know," she said. "I confess, I don't listen much any more. Daniel listens. He's a great listener, somehow patient as Peter. He's a remarkable guy, your brother. A good man. You must be proud of him."

Michael found himself a little stunned. He was not surprised when people said Daniel was proud of him, but he had never wondered if he should be proud of Daniel. The idea was somehow brightening, even if he didn't quite know what Marta meant.

And somehow, that brightening also made Marta more intriguing. He looked at her again and smiled at the dark eyes.

* * *

Michael slipped into bed silently, though he needn't have been so careful. Desra never woke up. He felt he had to be careful to avoid having to explain why he had spent four hours at his brother's home—a new world's record.

The beginning had been clumsy, of course. Michael had for a short time pursued with Marta the usual questions: "What's your line of work? What do you do for fun?" But she had easily slipped past all that; indeed, she had not seemed very interested in his work either. But somehow, like magic, she had stumbled into some turn of phrase that brought up paradoxical language. That had turned them to the idea of paradox in general and suddenly to science fiction and time-travel. Michael had no idea how it had happened, but as if by grace, he was suddenly laughing and agonizing with Marta over the outrageous moves by certain science-fiction films and novels that seemed utterly to ignore the paradoxes of self-caused or past-resolved problems. What sense can it make, they had laughed together, to have to go to the past for an army when in the present the lack of army was caused by taking the army from the past.

They had been arguing whether time travel only into the future escaped all such paradoxes—he had argued yes and she had said no, since it could still not be explained what had happened to the matter of the traveler's body, nor how it could disappear or reappear into the universe—when Daniel had at last stepped up. Michael remembered with a strange new warmth the smile Daniel had given him. "You're still here?" He had laughed, and maybe it was that warmth that made more conversation possible, as he felt genuinely Daniel wanted him there. Helen, too. Or maybe it had been Marta's presence, with her pretty face and easy laughter. Something had kept him at Daniel's apartment far longer than normal. It had been a good evening.

Somewhere in the conversation, when only the four of them were left, Michael described his talk with Richard Gesar, and had even found himself trying to express a vague sense of possible hope. He had somehow felt more optimistic, less threatened, than ever before, and he wondered if it was because Daniel was really listening. Of course, "those Christians" hadn't responded optimistically to the Christ-less *tulku*, but Michael hadn't expected too much reception. In the end, he had actually been impressed that Daniel's primary comment was not about how evil or misguided the Tibetan monk might be but simply to note that other theological perspectives and interpretations should be researched, as well as other medical theories. Michael had been silently impressed, inasmuch as his brother's comment had matched his own determination. Daniel had even helped Michael by suggesting he talk to a famous television preacher who was coming to the city.

"Maybe you can make the connections to talk to David Roberts when he's in town," Daniel had said. "There's a guy who can talk a lot about the soul and peace of mind, certainly in a Christian context."

Marta had groaned aloud. "Better an insane Thomist than a wise televangelist," she had cried out with humor in her voice.

"Do you know any?" Michael had laughed back.

She had faked head-scratching cogitation. "I think I do," she said. "I'll get back to you with contact info."

Michael didn't realize she was entirely serious. At that moment, it hadn't really mattered to him, for Marta had said she'd call him sometime, and Michael hoped she would. And even as he slipped into bed with Desra, it didn't bother him that he was thinking more of Marta than the woman whose smooth, sensuous form he so easily embraced.

9

DESRA'S CLOCK

Walmart was not crowded, but by late afternoon, most people were thinking about going home, not shopping, especially on a Friday, and especially since shopping was so unnecessary. Physical stores were, after all, forms of entertainment, more than any truly needed outlet, since anything could be purchased by computer and beamed into one's home or some nearby phone booth. Yet stores continued to exist, sometimes open only during the Christmas season when the practice of wandering along aisles of merchandise remained part of the experience. Last week perhaps, with Easter chocolates and Oestre flowers tantalizing shoppers from the shelves, there might have been some traffic in real, physical stores. But now, with the Spring holidays past, there was almost no reason for people literally to "go shopping," and those who ventured to do so were few. Nevertheless, each person seemed in Desra's way, standing somehow right in front of the very piece of merchandise she wanted to see. Even the sales personnel, usually behind their counters watching videos, were for some reason out in the aisles, as if they could be of any help. If Desra wanted to see and touch a piece from the catalog, they were there at their controls to have it beamed over. But why did they have to stand there in public with their archaic "Want help?" Desra didn't want help. She was shopping.

Desra shopped because she enjoyed it; lots of people do, she insisted to herself, which is why stores continued to exist. There was nothing wrong with taking the time to wander these lanes of merchandise just to relax. No, it wasn't exactly exercise, but it was a proper therapy, she asserted silently. People need to get their minds off their problems and do something else, something physical, with seeing and touching. It's therapy, and cheaper than some babbling counselor, although, Desra realized immediately, her health insurance covered psychological counseling sessions but not shopping. Nevertheless, she insisted, there's something about touching merchandise. Why else would we wander these foreign aisles?

Desra smiled ironically at her own mental language. "Foreign isles," she punned and thought of Japan. Her ire rose like bile in her throat, but she stepped away from the feeling and let it settle. She knew how to relax, knew she could just watch her anger mindfully and let it sink. Still, it made her angry that this nonsense about sending Brandon to Japan was even possible. Her design, her research, her thought . . . and so the bile rose. No, she insisted, she would not be angry about that decision but would let it pass. It was more aggravating that it should make her angry in the first place. There were levels of anger, weren't there, and the complexity of anger meant that a person can't be expected to stand aside calmly and just watch anger with mindfulness. She heard "Damn it" in her own thoughts, like a mutter, almost unspoken. But she refused to think it; she could control herself. Besides, she was there to shop.

She liked being able to handle things, weigh the objects she liked. A projection on the screen at home just wasn't good enough sometimes. Sure you can see an object from all sides, but you can't shake it, test it. And who knows what they really send you, what kind of sound reproductions and dependability statistics. To get a really good product, to test it yourself and know you made the right purchase, you've got to feel it. OK, sure; for everyday things, when you are just buying what you always buy and don't need to compare or critique, then you just push the order in and get the stuff beamed home. But really to know what you're getting, to be knowledgeable and careful, you have to do what she called "real shopping" in the store, never from the screen at home where you can be so easily deceived.

She stopped to handle a briefcase. Hard shell, but light weight. The one she owned was soft shell, and she wondered if the hard case was safer. Some cases these days could have a video screen built into the exterior, but Desra found them too fragile. This one had a lock, but not one of the standard fingerprint locks. This one had one of those voice activated locks they're building into all the cases nowadays. Desra grimaced. They're a fad, she insisted, and she was sure they never worked right. She had watched with some amusement an embarrassed new applicant trying desperately to get his lock open at the front desk one day. "Looks like he's whispering into its ear," someone had said. "Alternative sexualities," she had said, and earned a laugh.

Still, the color on this case was good, a rich earth color, brown with a hint of red, yet not some putrid purple. Her soft shell case was black, and black just had no personality. Color could be important, especially if the image one portrays is subtly changed. People want to see a sign of personality, but with sobriety and control. She knew there were statistics about how others respond to the colors in presentations and sales catalogs. "Color is strategy," she thought, and the color on this one was good.

Desra put the case down forcefully and walked off. "To hell with them," she growled in her mind. "It's what I want that counts. I don't buy things or do things just so others will accept it. To hell with them. I do my own work and like my own work. Self-confidence. That's where the story starts and ends. They know my work is good. And I know it. Self-assurance, that's the market tip. Self-assurance, self-reliance. I don't have to care what they see in me. It's self-confidence that presents the image. 'Like what you like.' When they look at you, they want to see a self-confident worker. That's what they really want to see, not some damn briefcase."

Desra walked on. "It's about me," she thought, "about being myself and being comfortable with myself. I know I do good work, and I know how I do it. I like who I am."

Then she saw the clocks. On a vertical shelving system, an array of twenty different clocks was arranged to give maximum display. No two clocks were alike. Some showed digital time, and a couple had round dials that imitated the old analog face. Certainly all had voice activation, and probably they all projected. Some would have audible readout. She picked up a clock with a round face and two large bells at the top, as if it still used the vibrator to make that old obnoxious ringing sound. She found it amusing. She smiled.

But in the next instant, the irony hit her. There was an alarm clock, after all, in her brain, sewn into the neurons themselves, and it was a startling irony to have found, even for a moment, the fleeting thought of the quaint clock interesting and attractive. It was funny, yet also something worse. She felt the haunting thought growing somewhere near that time chip, as if it grew from the silicon itself, and with a hidden mental desperation, she pushed it away. But the haunted feeling remained.

She slammed the clock onto the shelf harder than she had intended, and she tried to laugh mentally. "I don't need a clock," she said aloud, trying to regain the humor that had preceded the tension. "It's cute," she insisted aloud but to herself, like a demand, "and I could buy it just for that."

Desra marched away. "I do what I do, and I'm good at it." The idea was there; she insisted it was true. "I like who I am," she knew, and that included the alarm implant. It was no error, no compromise. Hell, she could have it taken out if she wanted to, no matter what they say about the dangers of such late removals. "The issue after all isn't *what* I decide, but *that* I decide it. If I am satisfied with myself, I can implant a dozen alarm clocks and then go buy a dozen more, if I want to."

Desra marched around the store. The statements of self-worth and personal empowerment were truths she had known forever, it seemed, and yet somehow the truths still only made her angry. "People don't understand how difficult it is to wake up," she asserted somewhere in the middle of men's wear. "It's genetic." The world meanwhile is merciless. Out there—she waved a hand toward the world—dog eats dog, and the cat sneaks ahead while they are fighting. There was no greater evidence of the sneak than her loss in the office.

And the thought of that loss brought Desra back where she started, even as she came full circle to stand once again before the business-like briefcases. Color strategies and presentation formats, voice locks and entertainment media built into the imitation leather sides. The game was not so easy. Choices had to be made, and she knew in her own defense that the only difference between a carefully selected briefcase color and a Japanese language implant was a matter of which tools one is willing to use. It is not a question of compromise, but only a matter of what is at stake. Desra thought of herself surpassing them all in language development—and differential equations too, if she felt like it—and she saw them squirm.

She humphed aloud, and then suddenly felt self-conscious, as if others might have seen her gestures and heard her grunts. But the few people in the aisles didn't notice. No one cared. And in the anonymity was strength. "To hell with them," Desra thought. It doesn't matter what they think or say. She was strong, self-assertive; she knew her own mind and knew when to apply the available tools. Liking oneself is, after all, the real issue, and compromise can be tolerated if it is self-defined. "Compromise," she asserted silently, "is no compromise, if it is on my own terms."

Desra had made a decision, and it was justified, and she knew it. Yet the anger somehow was unassuaged. She would get the Japanese implant, it was just strategy, and yet somehow "they" were to blame. She could not name the guilt, however, neither in them nor in herself, and with a second's struggle, she focused again on the briefcases. "I don't need their colors or their locks," she thought to herself. "I can do it myself." Ten strides away, she found an alarm clock that "amused" her. She bought it—"for fun."

* * *

Michael was concerned, maybe even annoyed. He had not spoken to Desra all day, having left before she awoke and having called her a few times on the phone without getting an answer. He had even left video messages. Nothing. At the office, they said she had merely checked in earlier and left before noon. She hadn't said where she was going, but she certainly hadn't come back home. At home, Michael had cooked a dinner, a pre-made lasagna Desra especially liked, and he had set the table and taken out some red wine. By 7 p.m. she was long past due—not that he was trying to control her schedule, but it would have been courteous for her to tell him she would be late.

Michael, sitting at the table, poured himself a glass of the wine that had been breathing for half an hour. He leaned back, looking at the prepared table, savoring the slight dryness of the wine. He smiled. Of course he had gone through some effort to prepare the meal for Desra, but he also realized he did so out of a slight feeling of guilt. He realized he hadn't learned yet how her project meeting went; he had sort of forgotten to call her during his extra day in New Mexico, and today she had just been mysteriously unavailable. For the most part, he really did want to hear her story, knowing the project was important to her. At the same time, he had stories of his own to tell, and he wanted her to be interested in his experiences with Richard Gesar, his special project, and even the party at Daniel's place. He had gone into his own office today and gotten a lot of good writing done, and he imagined he would share with Desra some harsh skepticism about "God" and some slightly unkind jokes about the party. But Michael wasn't sure he would tell Desre about Dr. Petra Eriksen, unless he really stressed the "Doctor" part. He was pretty sure he would not tell Desra much about Marta. He felt a strange bit of guilt.

Michael had, in fact, spoken to Marta earlier that day. At the office, he had received an unexpected call, and with the appearance of her fingerprint identification, he had answered with more excitement than he had expected. It was a short call, yet it was amiable and complemented by just a bit of strangely winsome humor. She had called, it turned out, to offer him a real contact with "a crazy Thomist," if indeed he was interested. In fact, Michael wasn't sure he was, but he did enjoy seeing Marta through the video link, and he took the contact information partially just to keep talking to her. Dr. Paul Wacker, university philosophy professor and, yes, crazy Thomist. Michael had had to tap a side screen on the terminal to look up exactly what a Thomist was, though once he saw the reference to the philosophy of Thomas Aquinas, the epithet was obvious. He had laughed when she told him he had to memorize a least a few words of Latin for any interview with Dr. Wacker to go well, as, she quipped, "a few Latin words are the *sine qua non* of any truly erudite conversation."

An hour after disconnecting from the call with Marta, Michael
had realized he was thinking more about her than about Desra. Thus his
twinge of guilt.

Michael had always considered himself capable of honoring, and
willing to honor, his sexual relationships with exclusivity, if that was what
his partner wanted, even without the pretenses of marriage. Though Desra
would be the first to insist their relationship was an "open commitment," he
had always taken a fair amount of pride in the fact that he had consistently
been true to each of his lovers so long as the relationship lasted. Yet most of
today he had found himself thinking about Marta.

Surely, he thought with another sip of the wine he had meant to share
with Desra, it was no "infidelity" to have found Marta interesting, or even
a little attractive. And she had not been—let's face it—one of those very
attractive women. Certainly not like Petra Eriksen. Rather Marta had just
been funny, thoughtful, provocative, delightful. No, it was not guilt, Michael
decided; for the bare idea of a sexual relationship with Marta, practically
a nun, was ludicrous. Michael laughed aloud, swirling the wine. Yet the
thought was there, like an island on the horizon. Maybe it was possible to sail
there, or at least a little nearer to the beach. Then it was indeed guilt, but just
for a moment. With more violence than he had intended, he threw into his
mouth the last bit of wine in his glass. "Where the hell is she?" he said aloud.

Desra came home nearly an hour later. Michael had eaten dinner and
cleaned up, even finishing the entire bottle of wine. He had watched news
programs on the wall and had decided, not quite consciously, to think mostly
about Dr. Petra Eriksen. Thinking about her seemed safest, almost certainly
because she represented the sheer simplicity of lust. For relationships, he
knew—indeed, he prided himself on it—required some degree of principle,
even if they were the changeable and merely temporary sort Michael understood. After all, promises and vows like the kind Daniel and Helen make
are ridiculously impractical. Statistics proved as much. And if principles are
invented by the individual, then they are also unmade by the individual.
Moreover—Michael was arguing somehow with one of the relatively unknown news reporters—if one is driven to change one's principles, it is not
his fault, but the fault of those who change the environment. He could,
therefore, imagine a sexual connection with "Dr. Petra Eriksen" and be sure
it was Desra's fault. No doubt the wine helped him reach that conclusion.

Consequently, as Desra's name appeared on the phone and the booth
began its customary humming, Michael was more than ready to greet Desra
with a kind of cold interest. As he waited for her to materialize, he was sure
he would be properly interested in the affairs of her job and properly show
concern for where she had been all this time, but without giving ground on

it being her fault that dinner was past and their evening together spent. He did not count on the fact that she would arrive more angry than he.

And then Desra was home. For a moment, the numbing effects of the transport left her still and dizzy just outside the booth, and as Michael approached, she held up a hand to demand some time to recover. After a few slow breaths, she looked up at him, and her eyes were fiery. The recovery was quick enough, but then she was snarling. Her own intervening hours since shopping had been spent over an unsatisfying dinner and a few drinks. Like Michael, she had found herself feeling strangely exposed—the word *guilt* would not have occurred to her—both for having purchased the clock and, as time wore on, for being late. Had she been open to the possibility of guilt, even a guilt as mild and evanescent as Michael's, she might have been able to find a valuable softness in the exposed weakness. Indeed, she had imagined, if only for a moment, a conversation that revealed her disappointment about the Japan project and her own feelings of inadequacy, and she had imagined that Michael might simply take her in his arms silently and let her cry. It could be, she imagined, like trusting a dangerously revealing secret to a friend, and finding in time that the weakness and ensuing trust had made the friendship deeper. And yet *inadequacy* had suddenly come back to her as the problem for which she was herself the victim. "It was Kevin's god damn inadequacy," she had said to herself over the third martini, "that made nonsense of the whole work of education and creative effort." And ultimately, it would have to be Michael's "inadequacy" that made it a problem if she should decide to stay out and eat alone.

Thus it was that, when she felt herself weakened after her rematerializing, she looked up and saw a kind of concern in Michael's eyes—a concern that came to Michael almost in spite of himself—that flooded her with disdain. "Can you just stand back and give me a second, please," she said to him in a tone that belied the polite language.

Michael noticed the shopping bag in one hand, while her briefcase was in the other. "Been shopping?" he asked innocently enough. "Not really your business," she replied coolly and walked past him. For a second, Michael wanted to be angry, but it was clear even given the mental preparations he had been practicing that this was a time for diplomacy. Indeed, it struck him that this was a time for silence. He guessed that matters had not gone well at work the previous day, and as Desra put her things down in the living room and went into the bathroom, Michael felt himself at a loss as to what he should say. He knew intuitively what a relationship ought to be, at least while it is still alive, and he knew he ought to be trying to bear with her whatever disappointment she was experiencing. They had often enough before been able to share anger and disdain, point their shared sense of identity outward toward real or imagined enemies that helped them maintain a united front. He slid up to the closed door. "Kevin give you shit?" he offered.

There was silence. Then, as if he felt a palpable softening from beyond the door, he heard her sigh and respond, "Yes. Yes he did."

"Crap!" he said back. "What did the bastard say?"

More silence. A few moments later there was rustling and flushing. As the pause lengthened, Michael tried again. "Want to talk about it?" He smiled a little, feeling something of his own effort at compassion and a wan hope for a lightening of the mood. "You know, I had some wine here, but . . ."

The door opened and Desra emerged, dressed in her white, floor-length robe. "You know, Michael," she said with a kind of directness of voice that matched her glare, "I appreciate that you can talk about, well, whatever. But right now, I just want to lie down in bed and do some reading. I don't feel particularly well and, hell, I guess we've got tomorrow to share our news. So let's just let it go for now, OK?"

Had her voice been soft, Michael might have sensed that she was almost ready to let him back into their shared retreat. But her tone was still icy, polite for rhetorical effect more than a real kindness merely made edgy by weariness. At the same time, he had not entirely lost the caustic feel he had practiced against Desra for the last hour, so as she looked up at him he felt his heart harden, even as he felt he was, at least partially, willing to love.

There, for a moment, the two of them might have been able to fall in love. Desra was weak, broken by her disappointment, and deeply, in some hidden corner, longing for an acceptance Michael could have provided. Michael himself, had he been willing for a moment to cherish guilt and understand his own need of love, might have been able to see past her wall into her vulnerability. Had he not been practicing distancing himself from Desra, a practice moved by the mixture of careful anger and lust for another woman, he might have found compassion; and had Desra not so well practiced her own isolation, she might have accepted it. Love was there.

But Desra's tone had indeed been dangerously, intentionally ambiguous. She had deeply habituated rhetorical skills for setting up an argument such that, no matter what the other person did, she could win. If Michael were to press the conversation, it could be an imposition, but if he didn't, it could show his lack of concern. Yet something in Desra wanted him beside her, to share something of the anger she felt. There simply was an injustice, she might have said to herself in a clearer state of mind, and we all desperately need someone to share our burdens with us. Thus there were seconds of softness in her mood that would have liked simply to accept the love Michael offered, even while she herself found it necessary to be angry at that love. It was the need for a lover one could hate, even as one accepted and relaxed at last into the embrace. If Michael's had been a more genuine love, she might have broken, might have let him love her while she hated him. But as she looked into Michael's eyes, she saw too well the imperfection of his love, even without knowing what it was she really wanted. "Just leave me alone," she said, slipping past him to the bedroom.

Michael's own mixture of emotions settled over the next hour. Thoughts of what exactly his love for Desra required of him—knowing it was, after all, built upon a realistically temporary foundation—were mixed with thoughts of Petra Eriksen and Marta Sanchez. Inevitably, there were comparisons and fantasies of both love and failure, and even those terms took on different meanings at different stages of the internal conversation. But he was self-aware enough to know comparisons are always problematic and fantasies are for children. Eventually, then, he managed to laugh. "Yes," he mocked himself, "I'm a real lady's man," and he found he could settle his honesty back into a softer unhappiness with Desra's oddity, a distancing maturity about Petra's sexiness, and a more quiet fascination with Marta's unexpected attractiveness. These images reinforced one another, and as the wine and his practiced anger slipped from his blood, analytic skills took over, and Michael considered the women and their effect on him from a more philosophical distance. He decided coolly that he could ignore Desra completely if he had to, simply by returning to work. And with that return to work, he could decide with quiet insistence that he would look up Marta's "crazy Thomist." Strange as the man might turn out to be, Michael decided, he would sift through the professor's ashes for the gems, or at least satisfy himself that there were only ashes. As if unconsciously frustrated with his inability to peg Marta, he concluded with the force of self-determination that he would understand, and unhesitatingly evaluate, her Professor Wacker.

And he would do the same with Petra's "God."

10

MICHAEL'S WORK

"Nice piece, Michael," Lewis called as Michael passed by the cubicle.
"Thanks," Michael responded with a smile that became a sneer.
Nor was the sneer merely the effect of his physical deformity; he had been
strangely annoyed all morning by his colleagues' friendly congratulations
about his article on Gesar Tulku. Of course, he too thought it a good piece of
work, both in structure and balance of critical approach, but somehow the
applause this morning was strangely, well, warm, like he had just had a baby.
He felt like he was supposed to be handing out cigars.

Michael had taken Monday off, felt he deserved it after working hard
on the Gesar piece, as well as on a few side bits on other issues, including the
re-emerging clan fighting among the Wahabi factions that had grown up in
Arabia since the kingdom fell. He remembered struggling with that essay,
especially trying to keep straight the clan distinctions and the breakdown in
Saudi unity that had been evolving since the collapse of oil decades ago. The
logic of the piece, of course, had been simple, as sub-group conflict always
was, and it had been easy to turn his acerbic wit against the rivalries and
too-subtle rationales of their violent us-and-them thinking. But the names
and divisions, and especially the need to actually get in touch with the
principals by long distance had made the research difficult. He could have
merely used the taped material gathered from other sources, but that had
never been Michael's way. But getting through the Arabs' own confusion
and their barriers of mistrust in search of even a vague quote had almost
been futile and probably not quite worth the trouble.

Yet it was to the Gesar article that the people around him were responding. "That stuff from Albuquerque," Beth had intoned as he had
stepped from the booth, "that was really nice." Maybe she had expected him

to be groggy from the gas, but *nice*? The only thing worse she could have said was that it was cute.

So Michael had fumed all morning, only finally, after some decaf and another strange barrage of "compliments," to find an invitation on his computer to see Melanie. "At last," he had sighed, "I can expect some sanity from the insane." So he hurried on, trying to avoid eye contact with his "nice" co-workers.

"What the hell is wrong with the Mickey Mouse Club?" he threw at Melanie as he kicked the glass-paneled door closed, nodding toward the room behind him.

"They think you've fallen off your perch," she said back, almost off-handedly, as she turned to light a cigarette.

"What does that mean?"

"It means this." Melanie leaned back in her chair and stretched out for a hard copy from an erratic pile behind her. The top piece—the most recent printed for her by the staff, who found it strange that anyone read from paper—fell onto her desk and she flipped through quickly. "Here, I underlined it," she said and began to read. "'One can have one's doubts about visible souls, but there is a genuineness about the photographer that can disarm even the most determined skeptic.' End-quote." She looked up and blew out smoke. Her blue eyes shone with a kind of conqueror's mirth. "Some people assume this is autobiographical."

Michael was given pause. Had he written that? Of course, he had, and he knew what he meant, and yet taken by itself, it did seem strangely generous. He felt himself stiffen and the training of acerbic wit began to form words of response. "Autobiography is masturbation," he said, "and autobiographers . . ."

Melanie laughed and waved him away with her smoking hand. "Oh, stop," she commanded. "You don't need to defend yourself to me." She drew deeply on her cigarette. "I know you better than they do," she stated easily, brushing aside imaginary interlocutors. Then she tapped the page in front of her. "I also underlined this. 'Yet in the religious smorgasbord this is only another variation, whatever its 'scientific' spices. New recipes attract the well-fed gourmands bored with the usual gravy and meat substitutes.'" She smiled again. "It's a good piece of work," she finally said, "and *auroscopy*. That was a coup, coining that term right there on your feet. We got everybody with that move. Everybody creating copy on this guy is using your term. Nice." Melanie paused again; Michael let the word *nice* go by. "But," she continued, "the Mickey Mouse Club out in the world, maybe even just outside this office, wants a convert. Maybe you could try floating back to your desk."

Michael coughed a laugh, but also realized as Melanie tossed the pages behind her that he had been dismissed. He stood his ground. "Actually," he began simply, "I don't think I'm done with 'God' yet."

Melanie eyed him skeptically. "You're looking at more on this story?" She asked. Then it was her turn to snort. "You sure you aren't a convert?"

Michael humphed. "Only when *he* floats off the damn floor," he smiled. The *damn* felt foreign to Michael, but he liked inserting such words with Melanie, like speaking her language. He salted his language generously with expletives as he described the invitation from Richard Gesar himself to come again and be a skeptical observer. He also described his potential contacts with David Roberts, famous—at least in his own Christian circles and on his own television program—theologian and evangelist. He did not mention he hadn't actually made that connection yet, and he did not mention Marta's Thomist.

Melanie gave an exaggerated thoughtful frown. "You know as well as I do," she spoke matter-of-factly, "that it doesn't matter whether you've got leads or invitations or divine commands. And really, I don't care whether you are some wild-eyed, guru-chasing chavie or not. I just need news. So tell me, news man Michael Pryor," she added a dramatic pause, "is this news, or is this just this week's moon-landing by a lunatic?"

Michael sneered a smile. "Nice line," he said. "Can I use it?'

"Sure."

"I guess it depends on what happens outside Albuquerque," Michael was thinking out loud. The question was what Gesar and his cult of lab assistants were going to do with their development. The *tulku* was sure, of course, that his discovery was the doorway to some new age, to the development of a science of the soul that could cure humanity. Every discoverer of any new enzyme was sure this one would end diabetes or make chocolate cake into health food. Michael realized, even as he said so, that the next issue had to be technological, not just descriptive. "What will happen," he asked Melanie rhetorically, "if the president of the U.S. or of the Pacific Union goes to this guru and gets his soul-photo taken? What happens if 'God' here begins to change the souls of war-mongers into the souls of peace-makers?" What if he could change a depressed soul—like Michael's father's—into a satisfied soul? Michael felt the challenge of the almost-conscious thought. "Would it be news then?"

"You think this is where it's going?" Melanie raised an eyebrow.

"It might," Michael responded, with a bit more hope than he really knew how to feel. He couldn't yet pause to think about his father.

"If you get ahead of it," Melanie was saying, "and if it goes as you suggest, we'll be up on the event before anybody sees it coming. It might be worth the risk."

"No risk," he said. "I've got other work I'm doing, and, as I said, I have an invitation from God himself. I'll start raising issues, bring in the big Christian gun, and fire away. And if 'God' does start talking to presidents and warlords, we'll be there."

Melanie nodded in a slightly side-to-side motion. "So you'll get him?" she asked.

"I'll get 'em all," Michael asserted with an artificial oath. "No easier way to find the holes in religion and politics than to put two spiritual and powerful people in the same room."

"Hmm. OK," Melanie finally said. "Go ahead and push this thing farther. Poke into what your Buddha-buddy hopes to accomplish, see if there are political connections, bring in your religious critics. If in two months he's still popular enough, we can produce a full bio and a full analysis of his spiritual whatever-it-is and any political connections it might have." She paused to puff again, leaning back and putting the instep of one foot on the edge of her desk. "It won't lead, unless something big happens, or if the alternatives are dull. Might be enough to take over Jennifer's bit on comets and shit, if you play up the science, world salvation, snake-oil angles to hint at political power. Wanna do it?"

"Of course," Michael responded emotionless. "Jenny isn't going to like this," Michael stated, knowing he didn't really sound concerned.

"To hell with Jenny," Melanie responded, saying the name with a falsetto mockery of the diminutive. "The stars and comets will still be there in two months. Let's see if we can shed some light on your guru before his star fades from public view, eh?"

Michael smiled and let his half sneer be a silent assent. He was halfway out the door when Melanie added, "See what we can do to convince the skeptics." As he looked back at her, she was already back to the work on her desk.

The phrase bothered Michael the rest of the morning. It had certainly seemed that Melanie's desire had been more to expose a charlatan than to "convince skeptics." Given the mood he had been nursing, one that fed his natural mistrust on the milk of his colleagues' compliments, he had been most inclined to adopt the "inquiring reporter" image. It hardly seemed that the purpose of the biography and inquiry would be to convince skeptics, unless Melanie meant those skeptical of Michael's own investigative honesty. Certainly, it seemed to him that the point of the story would be to rattle the credulous, not to convert the skeptic. "Besides," he kept telling himself, "*I* am the skeptic."

So Michael spent his morning making notes and trying to make further contacts with the Christian TV-preacher and the institute in Albuquerque. It was easy enough to leave a message with the latter, but there was no telling how long it might be before anyone called back. He first called just leaving his name, and then a couple hours later asked on the recording if Dr. Richard Gesar or Dr. Petra Eriksen would like to reply to his article. When still no answer came, he worried that the special treatment he had received in Albuquerque had somehow been a show and they weren't even interested in what he had written. It would not be the first time that clever newsmakers had manipulated media writers; but it would be the first time Michael had been the victim. Yet even as he considered feeling used, he somehow couldn't entirely doubt that Dr. Gesar had shown genuine interest in his writing. Michael did have enough respect for the *tulku* that he couldn't totally question his honesty. It was a confidence that the *tulku* had genuinely shown respect for Michael's own honesty, and it seemed the man was open to genuine investigation. Perhaps Michael was a convert already.

Another event affected Michael's attitude toward the entire investigation. About mid-morning, while he was in the bathroom, a package came for him, through the mail. The sheer fact that it had been delivered by the U.S. mail was odd, and he didn't recognize the return address, although it was relatively local. The address had been written in a straight, bold hand with a broad marker, and the four-digit suffix to the zip-code had apparently been written erroneously the first time. It was crossed out and the new numbers simply written below.

It was a book. Michael could tell even before tearing at the brown paper. And that, too, seemed odd. Books and other written material especially were almost never delivered in print, especially to people who have to read for a living, and thus his first reaction was a strange annoyance. He assumed it was some kind of research material and wondered who the hell would send him this bulky hard copy instead of computer data. It was a small book, yet he didn't have time to labor through some unindexed text without search capability.

As he turned the book over in his hands, Michael was puzzled by the title: *Making Time*. In an instant's pause, Michael wondered if this were a book for the socializers. But it appeared to be an old sci-fi, time-travel story. With a broad smile, Michael realized even before opening the attached note that it was from Marta.

"Not sure she escapes the usual paradoxes, but a unique effort. Affectionately yours, Marta." Michael was, to his own surprise, unusually pleased at the gift. He found himself wondering, moreover, what the "unique effort" at solving time-travel paradoxes might be. With a curiosity almost exciting in its genuineness, he read the jacket copy. No clue there, he laughed to himself, and he was almost surprised at how pleased he was anyway. Despite having massive investigative work to do, including great amounts of reading, for a major article on the Albuquerque *tulku*, he found himself simply desiring to read sci-fi. It was mildly liberating.

As he dropped the paperback on the pile of notes before him, Michael considered Marta herself. With her, too, he felt an intriguing sense of honesty and straightforwardness that was likewise liberating. He had the peculiar sense that he could just talk to her, that his "investigative inquiry" mode could be relaxed. Perhaps he could just find out who she was and not "inquire" at all, maybe ask questions about the world and our place in it without it being a skeptic's investigation. It seemed like she would be the kind of woman who could tell the difference between learning and inquiring, between an investigation and a desire to understand. Maybe she was the kind of person who could overlook another person's failures to keep those distinctions clear.

Michael found himself wondering what a long and private, peaceful conversation with Marta would be like. Yet it was not long before the peaceful conversation became a romance in his musing. She was short and squat, compared to Desra, even more so compared to the gaunt beauty of Dr. Eriksen in Albuquerque. But Marta was an attractive woman. Her long hair flowed in Michael's imagination, wrapping the soft face like an adornment. Her dark eyes sparkled with mirth, and it was easy to let them sparkle with affection as well. He could imagine a kiss, a soft brush of hand on hand, and a curious and wonderful mixture of clever, almost caustic humor alternating with gentle thoughtfulness. He could imagine holding hands while walking in snow. With an unlabored smile, Michael realized he could not easily imagine sex. Nor did he try. And that was fine.

Marta was religious. Admittedly, her response to his news about the interviewing Richard Gesar had been odd, neither nodding smiles nor aggressive dismissal, but somehow Michael thought there was a connection between the spirituality of the teacher in Albuquerque and the Christianity of this pretty, young woman. Something about Marta made him think, perhaps for the first time in many years, that he could stand to hear again some of that tired Christian lingo he knew from his brother and from the million Christian stutterers in the news—or rather, "news"—industry. Surely, he could try to listen to her, and could listen to the *tulku* as well, perhaps as a way of listening to her. It was, after all, religion, whatever its stripe or name.

And even Daniel—now that Michael thought about it—had never been that bad. It had mostly been those friends of his, or the kind of literature he read or the news he listened to. Daniel had always seemed withdrawn, even held back, as if by a wall. Whether it was a wall of will or one of fear, Michael wasn't sure. Perhaps Daniel and his Christianity were not merely waiting to pounce on him; perhaps neither were they merely hiding from critique. Perhaps it had been Michael who had always been the belligerent one, opening conversations with antagonism or preparatory defenses. Perhaps Daniel had always wanted to talk religion but held himself back because Michael had always been ready to pounce. Or perhaps out of respect. For a second Michael wondered if all the "good news" was pent up in his brother like air in a balloon just waiting for Michael to need a new breath, and then, whoosh, out it would come, as much a relief to Daniel as a breath of salvation to his little brother. Michael smiled. Perhaps Daniel loved him.

For nearly a minute, Michael's fantasy saw himself as a believer. Of course, he had seen a thousand times before the ugly, mindless version of that fantasy, the one in which being "religious" looked a lot like being mentally deficient; but here, perhaps for the first time, he saw a vision of both thought and warmth that surprised him. It might have been that, for the first time, he saw an intellectual respectability both in Gesar and in Marta, and for that instant the barrier of his insistence on honesty began to open. Honest, thoughtful, *and* spiritual: that had seemed to him an impossible triad, and yet here were people who seemed capable of that. There was something, too, about Daniel, some strange hint that there was more to him than guilt and uncertainty. Marta had said he was a good man; Michael just now had called it love, and the idea was almost shocking.

Then Michael laughed at his sentimentality. Yes, yes. It was all very nice and furry, he told himself, and it was even good. He liked his brother and, yes, Marta was oddly attractive. And, yes, even the *tulku* had showed his intellect and warm humor in impressive ways. But none of that was reason enough to get soft. With a slight grind to his jaw, Michael heard again the cautiously condescending congratulations of his colleagues as they wondered if he could be a converted skeptic. He felt annoyance at being thought a believer in anything, especially if that anything were one more among the million self-comforting, pre-packaged spiritualites lining the shelves of the religious supermarket. Michael could believe the truth, he told himself, and could even follow a god if one would come to him and offer a bit more rigorous invitation than the promise of mindless self-satisfaction.

Yet the attractions were there, and Michael, with a kind of instantaneous decisiveness, chose to look at them again, from a distance. He realized he could bend, could choose to bend, and with that choice could easily begin to talk himself into warmth, whether it was Daniel's or Gesar's or some curious spiritual mixture. He *could*, he realized; it would only require looking in the right places and avoiding the wrong places, finding and focusing on those ideas and arguments that lead best to positive conclusions, seeking out only the most agreeable people, and running headlong from contention. He realized he could want Daniel and Daniel's God, or Marta and her God—wasn't it the same one? He could even want the *tulku*'s spirit, his peace and optimism—maybe again it was the same god after all. But Michael shook his head softly in the middle of his musing. No, he would not. There was more to the matter than his brother, a woman's touch, or even a famous guru's peace of mind. There was something more important than all of those relationships and states of mind.

But what was it? Michael wondered for a moment. It was a tremendous moment, a moment of twisting and convolution, with idea folded back upon idea, principle upon principle. He could, after all, find a way to believe that the "something" was just about anything he wanted it to be. He could twist his beliefs and self-concept any way he chose to become anything he wanted. The world was a wide-open range of brilliant possibilities, and Michael stood before that open plain in a warm sunrise. And yet he could not simply walk anywhere. There were paths, and perhaps among them was truth; and that was the one he wanted. He did not demand that he create the path, but neither would he condescend to follow a path of happy wishes, not even if they were his own. The path was too important; indeed, Michael himself was too important to allow himself to walk happily with pretty falsehoods. "I will not lie to myself, even to know love and peace," his mind raced. "Better die than lie for peace; better truth than love."

Almost angrily Michael punched in access to library records that would start his renewed research on Dr. Richard Gesar's institute and its finances. He would press for information about what the entire project would mean for the future, for political matters, for medicine. Hell, he would even look further into this new god's relationships with his co-workers, especially Petra Eriksen. What was God going to do with his omnipotence? How deep would his righteousness really go? Michael would find out.

Michael had his own righteousness to defend; he was self-righteous, in fact, and with a shrug he admitted it to himself. His taps on the keys were investigations into lies, he insisted, and if there were any to be found he would lay them naked in the light. The *tulku*'s enlightenment and Daniel's God would have to stand on their own merits; Michael would not buy from the spiritual supermarket anything unworthy of the dignity of his own soul. As yet he did not understand that something in that supermarket was needed to ground his assumption of his own dignity, nor could he truly explain what he meant by the term *soul*. But intuitively he had resolved that he would not lie, and only that resolution saved him.

11

DANIEL'S DILEMMA

Harmony Baptist Church lay, obviously enough, on Harmony Road only a mile from Daniel's and Helen's apartment, and they had actually been known to walk there on warm spring Sundays. Last Sunday, in fact, they had, like the majority of the church's membership, simply phoned in for church but decided the early April day was too inviting to ignore. On Wednesday, of course, Daniel had been at work most of the day and so had had to phone in, but Helen had ended work earlier and walked from home. She had arrived in the lobby of the church slightly breathless and windblown, her cheeks ruddy and her straight, almost-red hair a tangle across her shoulders. She had fair skin and a dash of freckles across the nose and cheeks just below eyes that seemed in a perpetual squint against bright sunlight. And when Helen smiled, her squint seemed to get even thinner, so that, when Daniel met her in the lobby, he could barely see the green of her eyes as she bubbled over with descriptions of the day and the evidence of spring buds on the hedge by the corner. Daniel watched her joy with a surprising ease, almost remembering how her beauty and goodness stirred hope in him. He knew again how good she was, to see beauty and joy even on the way to this difficult meeting, and he was reminded that he had learned to love only because she loved. Today, he almost felt it all again and almost could have taken her hand and with a sincere delight have said, "Show me." He was usually capable of simply enjoying his wife's joy, being infected by it until it warmed him to watch her be warm. But today, floating in the background of his enjoyment of her beauty, he felt a strange weariness, perhaps a hint of guilt that he had not shared the walk, or more likely an annoyance that such simple love had to be disturbed. Maybe it was just the pressure of the day, the disturbing news at work, and the uncertainty of this meeting.

Someone had died—or rather disappeared—in a "traffic accident," they found out today, and immediately all present had wondered whose machines or whose alignments had been out of spec. Probably a balance mechanism in a laser, someone had muttered, and it was an easy guess. That was usually the problem. Indeed the balances were notoriously touchy, notoriously apt to break down without warning. It had even been worse back in the early days of phone transport. But this time the phone line had been one Daniel had been working on in the past month. It was not his system alone, of course, nor could he be expected to predict every possible system failure, but Daniel knew he would be investigated, his work tried again, more nerve-wrenching "observations," the kind that require you to take a calmer before you began or your own nervousness will almost make it certain that you fail.

Now here he was walking with Helen toward the senior pastor's office, having come into church for counseling with the two pastors. Daniel had agreed some time ago to such a meeting, and at the time he had not dreaded it so much as he did now. He had always liked Pastor Ed Miller, a gentle old man with a tendency to look into the distance or stand silent in the pulpit for a full minute while the silence-loathing congregation squirmed. He tended toward gospel stories and made up new parables at the oddest times, launching once into a fantasy about dung beetles during a committee discussion of financial difficulties. Daniel found the man to be a little scattered, and yet some of his oddity was wondrously refreshing. He had learned, for example, that "Pastor Ed" had a broken window lock on one of the ground-floor windows of his office and for all these years had forgotten to have it fixed. Such absent-mindedness had become legendary, and yet Daniel had later discovered that Ed knew all about the window latch, indeed remembered it well, but somehow felt a charm in minor danger represented by leaving it unfixed. "There's something right about not quite being safe," Pastor Ed had said once, when Daniel had reminded him to get the window fixed. Thus he had been known for years to be slightly eccentric, and there was talk from time to time of urging, or rather insisting on, his retirement. But Daniel liked Pastor Ed, and so did the children of the church. Perhaps for the children's sake the church kept him around.

The other pastor, Jackson Hubble, was much more exciting, much more talkative, and overall just more interesting. He had a fluid command of language that his older colleague lacked, and his smile and waving gestures were equally easy and fluid. "Bubbly Hubbly" Daniel sometimes called him for fun, but only at home with his wife, and usually only after another particularly vivid and effusive sermon. Pastor Jackson knew how to speak to the modern heart, seemed to know intuitively—although Daniel realized the intuition was more a matter of research and careful homiletical training—how to awaken the desire for and comforts of love in people who seldom see the sky and never have to feel winter cold. It was indeed one of Hubble's sermons that had urged parishioners to walk to church if they could, or at least consider an outdoor stroll part of a "Sabbath experience." That suggestion had given way to the "listen to tapes of nature sounds" suggestion, and that one had eventually been replaced by visualization practices. But all such admonitions were inspired by sincere and thoughtful hopes for the worshipers' experience of peace and the love of God. As far as Daniel knew, only he and Helen continued to walk much; he wasn't sure if Pastor Hubble himself ever had. But then he lived in Clarendon Lakes, a full hundred miles away, so he had to phone in for every community event. That was already quite a burden of travel, Sabbath or not.

Daniel might have been more comfortable if he could have spoken only to Ed. But Ed had suggested that Hubble be present, since, as the elder pastor insisted, the younger man knew more about the modern issues, understood something of the complexity of the psychology. "He is so much better read than I," Ed had declared. Both Daniel and Helen had had to admit that that was so. Hubble was always ready to help with the pastoral counseling, especially in these personal and difficult matters.

And this was indeed a personal matter. Daniel's and Helen's inability to have children had surfaced again and again as a problem, not between the two of them—at least not for long—but as a consistently nagging question of what ought to be done. They both knew it was Daniel's problem, both physically and philosophically. The physical problem—how quickly the sperm cells died from Daniel's own body heat, and other such silly difficulties—were the easiest to understand, for there were many technological options that could overcome such minor physical problems.

But then came the philosophical ones. Of course we *can* enhance the sperm cells with genetic modifiers, and of course we *can* stir a few eggs and few million sperm cells in a test tube somewhere. But *should* we? Daniel was generally unhappy with the numerous articles written by medical "experts" and, especially, by fertility doctors, whose very livelihood depended on reaching acceptably positive conclusions. None of the articles he had read— at least none he had generally understood—had shared his assumptions, his concerns about the value of life, the haunted suspicion of divine providence. So whatever the reading list, Daniel remained reluctant.

At the same time, Daniel knew well that his own philosophical reluctance might have been rooted in a hiding embarrassment over his physical failure. Was all his thoughtful hesitation only the mask for some archaic feeling of threatened masculinity? He wasn't sure. For that reason, he was willing to bend, or at least to question—again and again—the wisdom of his philosophical hesitations. Consequently, at the very least he was willing to seek the spiritual advice of his pastors, people given him by God, he believed, for direction and counsel. After all, much of his worrying about fertilization technologies was bound up with his own peculiar theology, and that same "peculiar theology" told him his religious community and especially its leaders were meant to be guides and helpers. Of course neither pastor, especially not Hubble, would presume to judge him or Helen for any decision they made in their personal lives. Yet, oddly, Daniel might have welcomed some judgment, even more than he might appreciate Pastor Hubble's hints and urgings toward greater spiritual growth and a "closer walk with Jesus." So Daniel had arranged the meeting with Helen's knowledge and support. It had been her own argument that both his hesitations and the search for pastoral guidance were cut from the same cloth of "his own peculiar theology." She had been right, as usual.

Daniel moved with Helen past Lisa's desk into the senior pastor's office, and he watched with some gravity the closing of the door behind them. Both pastors were waiting, and with a few perfunctory pleasantries about health and matters of work—to which Daniel answered, "fine" in spite of today's announcement—Pastor Hubble led the way gently into the topic at hand with a pleasant segue through spring and new life to the possibility of children and the couple's hopes of life. He spoke with an easy tone that carried him through random chit-chat and the Sunday sermon. He had short brown hair and just enough beard to make Daniel wonder how he could keep it that way, so that he apparently didn't need to shave. He wore a denim shirt over a darker T-shirt, a costume that, like his voice, made him seem warm and informal. He could preach some encouraging messages from the pulpit, though Daniel wondered at times exactly how the man got to the encouraging parts from his chosen biblical text. Daniel had never attended one of Hubble's "Spirituality Evenings," where visualization, chanting, and other religious texts might be used.

"So I understand," the young pastor was concluding, "that both of you want to have children and that you both know what the physical issue is. Certainly there's no problem with attraction and interest, I imagine." He smiled warmly. "So the problems are not really so dramatic. Have I heard you right?"

Daniel nodded; Helen was silent. Daniel knew he would have to do most of the communicating, although she was easily more eloquent than he. Somehow she always managed to urge and encourage him but seldom to take control of a conversation.

"So the problem is motivational?" Hubble went on, raising his trimmed, arched eyebrows above an easy, well-trained smile.

"It's theological, isn't it, Daniel?" Pastor Ed inserted, leaning a bit forward over his desk. "It's theological."

The elder man had a thin face and a prominent nose, and a bright smooth rug of white hair always cut short like a thin fleece. He had tiny eyes that danced as he spoke, when he was not staring off into some more distant thought. At this moment, he was looking hard at Daniel, as if strangely excited by the prospect of a discussion. Daniel smiled. "As you know well, Pastor," he said.

"Hopefully, some theology is behind our motivations in general," Pastor Hubble came back from the side. "That's as it should be, of course. Motivational theology." He paused, letting the term find its echo. Then he put a finger to his lips as a sign of thought. "And so it's just a matter of seeing how our theology can be clarified."

Somehow that observation silenced Daniel and the other pastor, and both sat back. There was a quiet pause in which Daniel felt a strange mixture of a rising anger and the patient presence of Helen beside him. If there had only been an open door and no wife to serve. But then if there were no wife . . .

"I think, Daniel," Pastor Hubble was saying, "we can go straight back to the roots of our faith, to our theology of grace and love. 'There is no condemnation' here," he said, easily interweaving scripture with his point of counseling. "We are free in Christ, and we are called to life, to life in abundance, overflowing, poured into our laps." He smiled. "And we could say that having children is indeed a God-given abundance, poured into the lap."

Daniel looked at his wife; she stared at her hands in a faint humility, her pale cheeks bright with a soft blush as she smiled. Daniel smiled, too. He looked at her and said, "We need little convincing of that."

Daniel saw in Hubble's face a momentary flicker of uncertainty, as if the young pastor had suddenly become uncertain what the question was. Daniel felt briefly sorry for him, then in the next instant, he felt an odd satisfaction, and right after that he felt guilty for that satisfied feeling. He took a breath and tried to restart the conversation.

"I don't have to be convinced, Pastor Hubble, that children are good," he said. "I mean they are something we can create, some-*one* we can create and love. They are people we can serve, a way we can teach." He paused. "You know what I mean?" He paused again. "They are part of . . ."

"Certainly," Hubble interrupted, buoyed again with a confidence that helped him finish Daniel's sentence. "A child is part of yourselves, an integral part of your lives and, I might emphasize, especially part of Helen's experience of who she is. For women there is undeniably a fulfillment in motherhood that no man can comprehend."

This time it was Daniel who felt uncertain what the question was. He knew what the researchers had long said about the psychology of motherhood, and it did not fall mute upon his ears. But he did not need any psychologist to tell him what motherhood meant to Helen, and he frankly didn't care much about what motherhood meant to "women." He wanted to answer, but Helen saved him.

"This isn't about me, Pastor Hubble. Remember? Theology?" She was smiling. All three of the men laughed amiably at the reminder, and Hubble nodded. But Helen went on. "Daniel's concern is about God and his role in all this. I guess he—we—had wanted it all to be God's will, God's work."

Daniel felt a flush of gratitude for Helen's willingness to bring the conversation back to what he understood the matter to be. He loved her so.

"Children *are* a gift of the Lord," Pastor Ed inserted suddenly. "I suppose one might understand such a verse in two ways. In one sense, *gift* simply suggests the beauty and wonder of what is given; in another sense perhaps it suggests that it must be given, not taken." The elder man looked down at his hands, then out the window toward the spring sunshine. He nodded, as if suddenly in another conversation. Then, after barely a second or two of silence, he seemed to remember the room. "You two, if I understand you, have no trouble with the idea that God might give you children, you know, the easy way."

Daniel nodded. He might have tried to expand on the idea, but Hubble was ahead of him. "Oh, then the issue is faith, after all," he said.

Daniel nodded again, wanted even to cry out that it was so, but was constrained, perhaps by the presence of his wife or of the feeling of formality around him. Or maybe he was suspicious.

"Faith is nothing more and nothing less than letting God into our lives," Hubble was saying. "A gift of the Lord is as often our own work as God's, and it is an act of faith on our part to let God work in us by working through us. Don't you think?"

Daniel wasn't sure. He had heard such things before, thought them before. But he had never been sure what it exactly meant.

"You know," the elder pastor suddenly grinned and cocked his head to one side. "I wonder what the etymology of the word *gift* really is in this context. I wonder if I can find that." With an almost amusing interest, he swiveled in his chair and reached toward his computer and its digital reference materials.

Hubble smiled at the older man benignly, then turned back to Daniel. "The issue here is fertility," he asserted, as if everyone had to be reminded. "And fertility is an old, old issue in the Church of Jesus. Look at birth control. You know that even the Catholics gave up their constraints on that a couple of Popes ago." He smiled as if the phrasing had been humorous.

"God places the means to control our own bodies into our hands, and our faith is shown in our use of what God gives us. Surely you would not refuse to go to an orthopedist if you broke your leg, just because health, too, is a gift of the Lord."

Daniel knew this argument, too; Helen had used it herself and it perplexed him. They were right, of course, and Daniel knew he could draw no line between fertility and any other issue of health, and he knew that he could not deny the value and goodness of medical care.

"I cannot imagine that you would want to assert," Hubble was continuing, "that no one should ever make use of the gift of medical knowledge. That, too, is a *gift*," he kept emphasizing the word, "of the Lord, and it is sheer legalism to try to assert that such a gift ought to be left on the shelf."

"Agh," the older pastor suddenly groaned from the side of the conversation. "I guess I should leave my etymology search on the shelf for now, too, eh?" He smiled as he swiveled back into the discussion. "But what are you leaving on the shelf, Jackson?" he asked Hubble.

"It's Daniel, Ed," Hubble corrected curtly but politely. "Daniel seems to want to leave all the centuries of scientific and medical knowledge on the shelf, unused, as if it were somehow an evil, or an intrusion into God's work. But surely," he turned back to Daniel, "that is not what you mean to say."

"No, no it isn't," Daniel confessed, almost feeling as guilty as if it had been. "It isn't that fertility is some divine command, some matter of God's law. No, I'm not trying to be 'legalistic.'" Daniel wiggled his fingers in the air to mark the quoted term. He somehow felt less horror at it than Hubble apparently had. "But it just seems that it was a place where God lived in my life, a place where I could be quiet. I mean, I don't want to say it must be left on the shelf, but somehow I wanted to leave something there, leave something on the shelf, hoping God himself would take it down when he saw fit."

Pastor Hubble was nodding thoughtfully, though it seemed to Daniel not so different from shaking his head. At the same time, Pastor Ed, Daniel noticed, was nodding in a strangely different way. The former said, "But," and the latter said, "Hmm," and went on without waiting. "I see what you mean. But it isn't so much a cure on the shelf, but an apple on the tree."

He sat back and smiled, as if he had found a pleasant truth. "Yep," he said, "it's an apple."

"Well," Hubble inserted himself and paused, as if to stop the present, "if you're referring to the apple of Eden, then you're back to sounding legalistic, as if Daniel and Helen's desire to have a baby is akin to the mythic desire for the forbidden fruit. Surely you don't mean that. I mean, you yourself said children are a gift."

"Of course, of course." Ed laughed and waved away the objection as if it were irrelevant. "But the point isn't always about the sin; sometimes it's about apples. I mean, it could have been a coconut." He sat back again and nodded to himself, apparently musing as if no one else were there. Yet he spoke to Daniel, "So of course you're right, Daniel. It's just a shame it is such a burden. But then," he scratched his chin distractedly, "but then maybe it has to be."

The silence was awkward for a moment, a moment that seemed much longer than it truly was. Daniel wanted to ask Pastor Ed to explain, for it sounded like the elder man might truly be on Daniel's side, though it wasn't at all clear why. At the same time, Daniel had the haunting suspicion that Ed might really make no sense, and it would be worse to find that out in the further explanation than to suspect it now. Daniel wondered for an instant if he owed it to himself to ask for explanations and to try to see the sense behind Ed's gentle distance. In the next instant, he wondered if he owed it to Ed to let him explain, and if it was in fact more of an act of unbelief to let Ed leave himself looking confused. In the gap of Daniel's hesitation, Hubble responded.

"We're not just talking about whether the hairs on our heads are numbered here, Ed," Hubble said with a soft smile to show, it seemed, that the younger pastor had no doubt the older man was indeed confused but accepted anyway. "We're talking about something genuinely practical. We're talking about a wanted child."

With a start, Daniel realized Hubble had somehow looked past whatever connection Ed Miller was trying to make or had simply pushed it aside for something more "practical." Daniel wanted to go back to Ed's idea, wanted to grab it, to see if the coconut of Eden had to do with his own desire to let God live in his life, even if it meant not having a wanted child. Was it that somewhere, anywhere, we must let God be God? Somewhere, anywhere, we must bow to what God has done and refuse to take what we want? But what if what we want is good, even very good? And what if God has not commanded "Thou shalt not eat of it"? Daniel was confused. The child of the love between him and Helen was not Eden's prohibition, yet it was a somewhere, anywhere, in which Daniel could rest and admit that he, himself, was not God. He wanted Ed's agreement more than he wanted Hubble's confidence. He wanted even more to sort out his own confusion. And he wanted to love Helen.

Then Daniel realized that Helen was crying softly, wiping almost unnoticeably at a dangling tear. Even more valuable than some resolved confusion of his own, he realized, was the love of his wife, and for her he wanted resolution as well. He looked to Ed. If only Ed would explain, would balance for him a trust of God and a love of life.

But Ed only sat forward and frowned gravely, as if trying physically to move from his theological musing to the seriousness of Hubble's insertion.

"What we have here, Ed," Hubble went on at last, "is some confusion of faith and effort. It is no affront to God if we use what he has given us. We trust God as surely and completely when we go to the dentist as when we sit at home with a toothache." Hubble smiled at his own earthy example. "Let us give Daniel a reason to see that he and Helen can go on with life in the name of the God of life. Let us declare the peace and gentleness of God here in the very comforts of what God gives us to live with. Let us call them to abundance, and not the petty sacrifice of minor missions and allusions to mythic sin." Hubble paused again, as if to let the sermon point be felt. Daniel felt it and wanted there to be peace, especially for Helen. He wanted to hear Pastor Hubble, even though it also struck him as strange that the pastor continued to speak to Ed as if Daniel were not there.

"There is no affront to God," Hubble was going on, "if we take and enjoy what he has given us. And there is no affront to God if we stretch out for that fruit, not forbidden but supplied, that hangs within reach. And there is no affront to God if we build a ladder to take those fruits that are out of reach." He paused again to give his image force. "If there is any affront to God, it must surely be in the refusal to yield to the law of love."

Daniel felt a shock. It was the shock of guilt. He knew it rather well, and he knew that he knew it. Yet it came as a surprise as he felt Hubble's reference to love as an intentional reference to his own failure to serve Helen's desires. She had always been willing to yield, to take seriously his own reservations, however confusedly theological or physical they might be. She had never coerced, never played his guilt against him. But Daniel felt it keenly, felt it ironically from the pastor who spoke of helping them find peace. He sensed, but could never have expressed, the oddity of a legalistic law of love.

Hubble went on, making references to the myth of Eden and the tree of knowledge, noting how knowledge had indeed been not the curse but the salvation of many. He noted that the Eden story of sin was less significant than the implications for stewardship suggested by the command to "till the garden and keep it." Hubble suggested that the call to peaceful labor was more the message for those already in the bosom of Christ than any guilt-laden repetition of the Fall. Ultimately, he said, such references help no one move on in life, take up their works of love, as Christ took up his, and follow him to heaven.

Daniel let it go by. He heard it all, and some of it was actually directed to him, although Hubble still seemed to speak directly to Ed. Ed seemed to have fallen silent, looking away at times. Whether distracted or tired or convinced unto agreement, he seemed unwilling or unable to respond. Helen, too, was mostly silent, although she had stopped the soft crying and had reached to touch Daniel's arm. Daniel himself felt a variety of pains, intermingled and wearying. Somehow the reference to love and to work had mingled in him his concern for Helen and his concern for the emerging danger at work. There was all around him a sense that he had failed, that he had done damage to those he loved or to strangers to whom he, like the Samaritan, wanted to give of himself. Love and labor, confused and tormenting, mixed in his mind like twin commanders, insisting, twisting his arms.

Yet it could not be stopped. Daniel might have known that even before he came today, might have felt it in the emerging interplay of his love for Helen and his solicitousness about work. He was weary with the struggle to maintain some obscure principle for which he admitted he had no foundation and for which he could find no help, not even among those whose principles might have been similar to his. Somewhere in life there was supposed to be a gap, a hole into which God could climb. Not that God needed holes, but that somehow Daniel himself needed God to be someplace where Daniel could find him. He needed one part of his life he could say he was trusting to divine wisdom. There needed to be at least one tree the fruit of which he would not eat. But such obscure connections, perhaps which even Pastor Ed didn't understand, were by now too belabored, buried under the mixing mud, balm, and poison of love and fear and theological insight. Daniel knew he would have to eat the fruit.

Daniel was well aware of his choosing. As if from a comfortable, observant distance, he watched himself weaken and knew the moment he gave in. He felt the resistance disappear, or more accurately, felt himself turn from the face of God to the love of wife and fear of loss. The burden of the freedom of Pastor Hubble's loving God was too much like the burden of loving his wife, and Daniel allowed himself to worship the idol painted like love, even though he knew, somehow, it was an idol. In the midst of his sin he knew it was sin, and he called it by name.

Nevertheless, he smiled, and over the next several days he continued to smile as he acquiesced and made appointments with doctors and fertility experts. When his guilty mind wandered back to the choice of sin, he focused all the more on the routines and requirements of phone repair and lab work. And he focused all the more on his love for Helen, insisting on it as if to convince God that this love excused the choice of mistrust. It was good love, proper love, both in his heart and in the gentleness of their bed, with Helen quiet upon his shoulder after love making. Oh, the love was good, and he sincerely thanked God for it, and as if in trade, he determined to trust God to resolve the questions at work. Thus he knew peace, the peace promised to him by Pastor Hubble, the peace that insists that God is love, defined however we choose, with God's love placed carefully into selected pockets like a dollar in change. So Daniel rested. But in his rest he knew his sin, and he cried out for forgiveness.

12

PROFESSOR WACKER

It seemed that no one at the University of Madison—once Michael got through the various voice responses and spoke to a real human being—had even heard of Professor Wacker, although his name, voice ID, and teaching credentials were all given in the directory. Michael had left a message and called back at the time specified in the directory. The professor had indeed been in his office, but the face on the screen hardly ever looked up at Michael and in the end didn't seem to take him seriously. He had emphatically declared that there could be no useful discussion over "some damn video machine" and had insisted that if Michael really wanted to talk he had to "stop by." Michael wasn't sure it was a good idea; the professor had certainly seemed strange over the video with his constant turning and moving about the cluttered office, while his gray and indecipherable hair flew around him. "But I'm only here until 3, you know," he closed. "I've got to drive home."

Michael phoned into the university at two, and even knowing the office number of the hidden professor, he became lost in the labyrinth of passages in the basement of the Vishal Armandi building. He had inquired at the Department of Philosophy, but the secretary had been out and the student helper there had only looked at him strangely until Michael had mentioned Wacker as "the crazy Thomist." "Oh, yeah, the crazy guy." There was no sign the student knew what a Thomist was. "Guess I don't know him, but he's here somewhere." Michael had named the office number and asked for directions. The episode left Michael wondering if this professor might be a rather ridiculous source, and whether the new generation of philosophy students might be having some trouble with communications skills.

In the end, Michael found the professor along a back hallway that led to an emergency exit. Once he had found the right hallway, Michael found Wacker rather easily, as the door was standing open and sounds of mutter and shuffle were emerging dimly from the clutter. His was the only door in the entire basement, including the door to the philosophy office, that had been open.

"Professor Wacker?" Michael inquired through the opening. It was the same man he had seen on his monitor during their video conversation. He was easily over sixty, certainly not young, and yet he seemed spry and quick. His gray hair was thick and wild, not as if it were never combed, but as if it were ruffled and flung by constant motion. His face was wrinkled, even furrowed in the brow and around the eyes as if he were squinting, yet the skin didn't seem fatty or wasted. The eyes were difficult to see, undistinctive, and the nose large but not bulbous. There was no beard or mustache, but a light scratchy stubble surrounded the mouth and seemed to jump and shift with constant expression. He puckered strangely sideways as he motioned for Michael to come in.

"Yes, yes," he said, "I'm Wacker. Look, I cleared a chair for you. Michael Pryor, right? Do sit. Sit."

Michael sat. The office was not as cluttered as he had seen it on the video, but the relatively neat piles of paper on the desk and bookshelves were not apparently in any ordered system. Books all around the room were mostly shelved neatly, although here and there one lay on its side atop of the shelved books, and a small pile lay on the floor by the professor's desk, as if he had just selected some for referencing and failed to replace them. Michael admitted to himself that he had not seen so many books outside of an old library for some time. Who needed books anyway, when any book worth publishing appears first for download? And binding was so expensive. But then none of Dr. Wacker's books exactly looked new.

"So. Marta," the professor began, and Michael thought for a second that he was being addressed wrongly. "How is she?"

"Well, I've only just met her myself," Michael began, almost apologetically. "But she's fine, I think. Healthy, pleasant."

"I confess, I don't remember too well myself," Wacker nodded, frowning with thick lips. Then he tapped some papers on his desk. "I did just look up her grades, and that always helps me remember. She's a fine young woman, and one of the few capable of thinking. Can't imagine that'll get her very far." He lifted one corner of his mouth in a grin that made his right eye wink. "Pretty, too, as I recall. Now there's a combination."

Michael smiled and nodded, only to wonder for an instant why. But his professional focus returned quickly. "It was Marta who suggested I talk to you. As I told you during our video conversation, I have been working on a story and have some need of a cynic." He smiled, hoping the professor would find the suggestion inviting.

"Marta didn't call me that, did she?" he groaned, his mouth moving back and forth as if the teeth behind were grinding. "Agh!"

Michael paused, afraid he would lose his conversation. "I don't think she meant that you are, well . . ."

The professor waved him away. "Oh, don't worry. I know what she meant, and that's fine. It's just that the Cynics—the real Cynics, the Greek Cynics—were practically ascetics, denying the pleasures of life so they could achieve personal peace and independence from the world. Lord knows, I'm no ascetic." He paused and pursed his lips, then almost smiled broadly. "Nor do I carry a knapsack and a walking stick." There was another pause, and Michael, not at all clear on the historical references, merely waited, hoping the man would go on. He finally did: "But then, I suppose Marta was just using the word the way most people do, and for that matter, yes, the Cynics were well known for diatribe and satire in their efforts to argue with almost everyone. I suppose I seem that way to some people, although, Lord knows, I am not cynical about everything—just about things that are stupid."

Michael smiled crookedly at Wacker's blatant insult; it was strangely refreshing. But Michael was also moving into interviewing mode. "If not as a Cynic, Professor Wacker, how would you describe yourself?"

"Oh, Lord!" he exclaimed, throwing his head back as if in early exasperation. "I'm a Kierkegaardian Thomist, with some Socialist Christian Luddite mixed in." He shrugged, and then as he noticed Michael tapping his pad, he pointed to the device and said, "Just tell them I'm Amish."

Michael looked up to see the man's eyes twinkling, his thick lips curved back in a curious grin that showed no teeth. "Amish?"

"I'm joking," he said almost impatiently. "Want some chocolate?"

"No, thanks," Michael said automatically. But the professor swiveled to stretch over to a bookshelf, where he retrieved a small foil wrapping. Bringing it forward, he unwrapped it as Michael looked on.

"This is exquisite stuff," the professor said. "None of that cheap crap, mind you, but the real thing. Dark. Rich. You really should have some."

Michael nodded, feeling a genuine ease in accepting the treat. The pieces were small triangles, almost black in their smooth shimmer. He bit the chocolate and was somewhat startled by the bitter depth of flavor. Indeed it was not "cheap crap." Michael looked at Wacker, who was smiling like one who had just shared a good joke with a friend. "This is wonderful," Michael said honestly. "Guess you're *not* an ascetic."

"Epicurean in the classic sense, perhaps," Wacker returned, enjoying Michael's humor.

"Shall I add that to the list of Thomist Socialist Christian?" Michael asked calmly with the hint of a smile.

"Sure, sure," said the professor. "But we may have to debate where it belongs in the list. Epicurean Thomistic Socialist? Socialistic Epicurean Thomist? Certainly not a Thomistic Socialistic Epicurean."

"Certainly not," Michael feigned seriousness.

"But never mind." Wacker waved away the humor with a sudden impatience. "Nobody understands the word *Epicurean* anymore anyway. They think it means self-indulgent, even gluttonous."

There was a pause, and for a moment it seemed an uncomfortable one. Michael looked to his electronic notepad and saw his list of questions, although he remembered them well and didn't really need to look. Wacker meanwhile seemed happy to suck on his bit of chocolate, although his eyes scanned the room as if he were remembering duties that lay in the piles he'd collected.

"Anyway," he finally leaped back, "this isn't about Marta, is it." He stated more than asked the point.

"No," Michael answered. "It's about Richard Gesar. You might have heard about his alleged discovery of aura and colors of the soul."

"Oh, yes." Wacker nodded. "I confess, I didn't read the whole story anywhere. Looked up a bit more after I talked to you and looked up your story. I suppose I saw enough in all the bits of news. It didn't make much sense to me, I'm afraid."

"Well," Michael continued, "that's what I would like to hear from you. Why didn't it make sense?"

"Well, it's nonsense," the professor shrugged. "Can't make sense of nonsense, now can we?"

Michael found himself stumped. Not much to write about here, he was thinking. "Surely," he began aloud, "there must be more to the entire set of discoveries than—"

"Yes, yes," Wacker waved away the protest. "Of course there is great science and discovery and all that. But that doesn't mean it makes any sense. Listen, and think it through."

The professor took a deep breath and scratched at his mop of white hair. "The Big Bang started this universe sixteen billion years ago, on a Tuesday afternoon, I think, unless you follow the Bible and then it was on a Sunday." He paused and Michael looked up, finding a twinkle in the man's eyes as he waited for his humor to work. When Michael smiled appropriately, the professor went on. "You have learned about the start of the Big Bang since you were five years old, I suppose."

"Sure," Michael said.

"Prior to that moment, there was no universe, no natural laws, no space or time. All the known features of this universe, including its most fundamental structures were non-existent prior to the Big Bang, indeed prior to so-called Planck Time, some 10 to the negative 40 seconds *after* the primary event. Or so they say."

He paused again, and Michael wondered where all this was going. He wanted to ask what this had to do with souls and auras, but when Michael only nodded, Wacker went on. "Universes in general, the scientists tell us, bubble forth out of some ten-dimensional ylem, each with a random structure that explodes into an order we recognize, or else it flops back into obscure nothingness. Our universe, then, has bubbled forth out of the original nothingness to become what we know, and the rest, they say, is evolution according to the natural laws that just happen to have taken form at Planck Time." He paused again, then nodded, and said, "Fine.

"But it makes no sense. Scientists can talk all they want about the beginnings of space and time and then about events *before* that moment. They can say there is a ten-dimensional something that is really nothing and that it bubbles fourth without cause, as if any bubbles any of us have ever seen have *ever* been uncaused. They can talk and talk all they want, but that doesn't mean the idea makes any sense."

For a second, Michael felt afraid, as if he'd stumbled upon some backwoods Bible-belt believer who still believed the earth was six thousand years old. "Are you trying to tell me, Dr. Wacker, that the scientists are wrong about the age of the universe?"

"No!" the professor complained. "When did I say that?!" He settled back into his chair. "Shoot, you know I've looked at equations as best I can, and I don't see any reason to deny what the theoretical mathematical models say. But when the scientists try to tell the rest of us what those models mean, then they begin to enter crazy-land. If they really wanted to be honest, why don't they just spread their mathematical equations all over their computer screens," Wacker leaned forward into Michael's face and spoke with slow and forced deliberateness, adding, "and shut the hell up?"

Michael didn't know whether to laugh or argue. He smiled crookedly and felt his usual ambiguity of humor and disapproval. He started to tap in some notes but realized that all this was merely preamble.

"I've got a four-sided triangle at home," Wacker said calmly, as if changing the subject to a familiar chat. "I call him Howard. He sits inside a timeless, spaceless void and sings to me every Sunday at noon." He stopped and looked again at Michael, who had given up taking notes. And the professor added, "Agh!"

This time Michael did laugh. Professor Wacker's analogies were entertaining, though perhaps not totally revealing. He wanted to press for clarity, just to understand the difficulties of the argument. He did realize with some relief that the professor's point was not to dispute scientific claims, but to challenge the way words are applied in the description of what the science means. On that point, Michael could readily agree, and indeed he felt a little annoyed that he had not realized for himself that the issues with Gesar might be conceptual. At the same time, he also realized that, at this point, he had little to write about, as he could hardly report on Wacker's wandering analogical arguments. No wonder the professor's colleagues thought him a loony.

"So what do I write here, Professor Wacker?" Michael asked directly. "What do I ask Dr. Gesar next time I see him?"

"Ask him what the hell the word *soul* means," he replied. "If this is a science of the soul, ask him if that soul is material. If the soul is not material, ask him in what sense his work is 'science.'"

"OK," Michael was getting the man's point, "but certainly Dr. Gesar is smart enough to understand that this soul is not just some physical stuff. Maybe he'll say it's a kind of energy, like the electrical characteristics of the brain."

"And that's fine," Wacker responded with a shrug. "So then ask him if the electrical circuitry in the light switch has an aura, too. Don't you see? Maybe, sure maybe, he has discovered something wonderful, like the signs and wonders of the Bible. But then again, if it is such a wonder, it seems likely it couldn't really have been discovered this way. Or, if it really does yield itself to probes and picojoules, maybe it's not so wonderful."

"Let me get this down," Michael wanted to say, but he just typed.

"I don't doubt there are states of the brain, there are electrical impulses and currents and synapses, and blah, blah, blah. I don't doubt such phenomena can be found, measured, and studied by sufficiently subtle instrumentation. But is this the soul? Is this the *imago dei* self, or the eternally reincarnated Atman, the very substance of eternal Absolute Being? What the hell does this even mean, "a picture of the soul"? An eight-by-ten color glossy, with six free wallet-size added free!? Try suggesting that if there's a picture, it isn't a soul; and if there's a soul, there ain't no picture."

Michael found himself fueled for argument after all. "But surely your entire objection depends on what you think a soul is. Who is to say what a soul really is in the first place?"

"Agh!" Wacker yelled at him, almost making Michael think violence would follow. "First of all, don't you ever say, 'Who's to say?' Damn it! It's bullshit rhetoric, and you of all people should know that. Who's to say? *We're* to say. We have to say. Your physicist of the soul has to say. We, right now, are doing our best to say. And we must, because there's no one else. Not the dogs and cats, not the lab rats and the finger-spelling chimps. It's us. We've got to define what we mean. Either we define our terms, however tentatively, or we shut up."

Dr. Wacker took a deep breath as if recovering from his own tirade. "OK," he breathed, "enough of that. Now . . ." Wacker looked away and pressed his lips together in an unreadable expression that seemed like exasperation. "Let's agree that your Dr. Gusher—"

"Gesar," Michael corrected.

". . . is in fact trying to say what the soul is. He *has* to say what a soul is in order to make sense of his claims to have produced a visible aura of it. So we—I mean, you—need to ask directly, 'What *is* this soul you claim to see here?' If what we're seeing is an electrical current, then he has invented the volt meter. Ta-da! But no doubt, he thinks he's done much more than that. So ask, 'What specific religious doctrine are you espousing in this designation of souls?' This isn't some neutral claim or some universal observation. The very word *soul* is loaded with connotations and theories, and it needs, it demands, specification. Ironically, this guru's own traditions—some kind of Buddhist, isn't he?—his own Buddhism should insist there is no soul, that there is no unchanging eternal self that is the essence of our individuality and our shared natures. Maybe that's what he claims to find. But meanwhile, your scientist, like so many others, is merely riding a wave of incoherent pseudo-philosophical pseudo-religion. People hear the word *soul* and say, 'Ooh, ah, sure, that makes sense.' Make them ask, make them demand explanation. This is no game."

A sudden seriousness had descended over the professor's demeanor, and Michael was slightly daunted. He typed a bit more and then looked up to see his host glancing off behind the door. Michael tried to follow his gaze.

"It's just a clock," Wacker pointed. "I'm trying to figure out when I had better go. I told you I had to drive home."

"I don't mean to keep you," Michael started to pack up, but the professor waved him back.

"No, no," he said, "there's no rush, I guess. I mean, it's not as though there will be heavy traffic on the roads."

Michael was curious. "You actually drive? A car? Doesn't it pollute?"

The professor laughed. "There's an old thought," he shook his head. "The exhaust coming out of my car is cleaner than the air you breathe in a smoker's room. Or certainly cleaner than the smoke you probably breathe for recreation." He paused and let the hinted insult work. Michael found it humorous. "And Lord knows there's something about those damn transporters I just don't trust."

"Accidents," Michael asserted more than asked. "It is strange to imagine simply having one's atoms dropped out into space."

"Actually, that's not it for me," Wacker said, rolling his lips and glowering. "It's more a question of identity. I mean, who is it that steps into that booth, and who is it that steps out?"

Michael wasn't sure what the question meant.

"Look," the professor prefaced, leaning forward and tapping an open palm with a forefinger as if to begin making a point. "When you talk to someone, say you talk to me, on the videophone. What do you see and hear?"

"Well, I see you, and I hear your voice." Michael shrugged.

"Sure, that's the answer," the other replied, "but it's wrong. What you see is not me, nor is it even, to be a bit more precise, my face. You see a thousand little squares of color, glowing electrochemically on the inside of a piece of glass. It isn't my face, but an electronic reproduction of my face. Don't you see?"

Michael didn't particularly like the rhetorical question, as if he were being accused of sheer stupidity, but he nodded anyway. "And the same is true of your voice, I suppose."

"Of course," Wacker sat back but then leaned forward quickly to strike his emphasis. "The real point is to ask then what happens when you transport, when you travel by phone. I mean, there's a classic epistemological problem with seeing and hearing in any case. Even now, it can be argued, I don't see your face but only my own reconstruction of your face as mediated by optic nerves and brain cells. Fine. Maybe that's unavoidable. But now think about phone transport. What is the you that steps into the booth; what is the thing that steps out? Is it still you?"

"It's me," Michael asserted, ready to argue. The point was intriguing, even if purely academic, like the tree that falls in the forest with no one to hear it. He was finding the professor's intensity almost humorous, so he continued. "It's my atoms in my original pattern. There is no distortion, unless of course there's an accident."

"Oh, really?" Wacker sat up straight. "Tell me how a cancer operation works."

Michael frowned. What was the point? he wondered. "Well, that's the wonderful side-benefit of the technology, as everyone knows. If a tumor is discovered and isolated by ultrasound—at least insomuch as I understand it—disintegration and re-integration can be used to break down the body and reassemble it without the growth. I understand there's less success with fully metastasized cancer, but—"

"Right, right," the professor interrupted. "There's my point. If we can and do reassemble people differently from how they went in, what's to keep anyone, everyone, from being reassembled differently every time they go see Mom in Poughkeepsie? Who knows how many times you, sir, have been readjusted to make you the fine upstanding citizen you are?"

"Well, my good professor Wacker," Michael tried to sound good-natured, although he felt his smile twisting, "I do think you're a bit paranoid. You don't fear technology so much as some great conspiracy, eh?"

To Michael's relieved surprise, the professor suddenly laughed aloud. "Agh, I'm just a crazy old philosopher," he grimaced. "Ask anybody." But then his face went serious. "Then again, don't let's be naive. There are reasons to put chemicals in our water, especially if it's 'for our own health.' Meanwhile, all technology needs to be viewed with some suspicion. It is not neutral, you know. Technology changes what we feel about life, about space and time. A thousand miles is a matter of money when you transport; it's a great amount of time when you drive. In an age when we were all on foot, a thousand miles presented a great and glorious mystery. You are changed by teleportation not only when some bureaucrat decides to add a chemical here or there, but also by the fact that you get used to having your body broken down into bits and reassembled, and by the fact that you don't ever question whether it is still you or not. You become used to thinking of yourself as atoms in arrangement, instead of an integrated self. A Leibnitzian monad. A transcendental unity of apperception. A unique soul made in the image of God." He paused again to let the litany echo. Then he looked Michael in the eyes. "You are less than you could be, Michael Pryor, for every time you release yourself to a technology that reduces you, physically and conceptually, to a collection of atoms."

Michael was torn. Clearly the professor was a bit crazy, and yet Michael felt a stir from the professor's words. Certainly Michael's own sense of himself had always been rather grand, a kind of arrogance he held onto consciously, while all the world around him seemed to preach a vague humility that had, in the final analysis, no foundation. In the place of mutely demanded humility, Michael had always retained a sense of glory in his own integrity. For all his cynicism, Michael had no doubt of his own mind, a kind of startled understanding, that he was, as he would simply put it, *someone*. He was a person, whole and uniquely conscious. It was perhaps one of the benefits of having been unpopular or unattractive physically that the reality of his own awareness was strong. Therefore, at the professor's words, he felt a flush of assurance that this was exactly the status of selfhood

Professor Wacker was describing with heavy philosophical lingo. And with that assurance came the suspicion that there was a threat, the possibility of the loss of that integrity. It had never occurred to him that the manipulation of his body could be stretched into manipulation of his mind.

At the same time, Michael felt a countervailing flush of defensiveness, a sense that he was being accused by the professor of some wrong, some failure to see. Wasn't this all just a kind of paranoia? Weren't these assertions of monads and being made in the image of God all parts of religious doctrine? Michael wondered if he were being challenged to believe in God so he could believe in himself, and with that suspicion the urge to respond rose in him like quiet ire. Moreover, he was trained to argue, and in the end, that course won out over consideration of his own soul.

"Surely you overstate the case, Professor," Michael asserted calmly, taking on the reporter's air. "Surely whatever soul there may be is as integrated after the process as it was before. If there is any such *imago dei* at all"—Michael almost laughed, noting he had, after all, used Latin—"there is no reason to believe that it is less than it was for being transported by laser." He paused to grant stress to the gentle but intentional accusation in his next sentence. "That is, if you're going to believe there is any such soul at all."

Wacker furrowed his brow even more deeply, so that his eyes seemed to disappear, and sniffed. "Yes, yes. *If* you're going to believe. But that brings me back to my point, doesn't it?" Michael wasn't sure. "You're the one who came in here to talk about souls, and I did. If souls can be studied with energy beams and particle analyzers, then, yes, they might be the kind of things that can be broken into atoms and sent dancing down optical wires. But then they must also be the kind of things that can be added to and detracted from, mixed with and changed by other beams and currents and chemicals and bites of three-day-old of cranberry sauce that wasn't refrigerated properly. That, or the soul is a mystery, a ghost, a phantom we never understand and yet one we all know well. For the mystery is I, and I am I as God is God." Wacker raised a cautioning finger and added, "Except by grace."

Michael had no idea what that meant, nor even how to look it up. But there was no time to consider it as Professor Wacker continued. "But even this greatness of soul," he said with a peculiar intensity in his voice, "is threatened, not by technology *per se*, but by belief, by gullibility, by acquiescence to technologies and philosophies—and techno-philosophies, I might add—more than by laser beams or aura projectors. We resist technologies because they change us from the inside out. They change how we understand ourselves and the world. I do not avoid the teleporter, Mr. Pryor, because of what it will do to my atoms, but because of what using it will do to my conception of myself. And the same goes for your Dr. Gusher—or whatever—and his soul machine.

"Don't pretend it cannot occur, Mr. Pryor. Of course there *may* be conspiracies, and the technologies we put in place today can be used a million ways to Sunday by tomorrow. Someone has to be worried, if only to cry in the wilderness at those who have forgotten how. But in the end the greater evil lies here," he tapped his own skull, "and here," now tapping his chest. "This is where we will remember or forget who we are and what we are, the glory of being ourselves and the shame of being sinners. This is where the true disintegration will take place, and here the reintegration is much more difficult, perhaps impossible. *That* is what I'm saying, Mr. Pryor. Tap *that* into your computer. Or," he hurriedly added, as if coming to the insight himself, "or scratch it on stone with a stick. Whichever method of writing you choose, you will be changed in how you understand words and thoughts and ultimately yourself. So be careful."

Michael felt a little angry. His usual argumentative nature bristled, and he felt himself reaching for response. He might have wondered if it were self-defense, a response to the suggestively accusative tone of the professor's declarations. But Michael responded with an easy *tu quoque*. "And yet here you are," he spoke with a harsh tone. "You use these lights, this internal air conditioning. You drive a car, and I suppose you think yourself somehow superior to those who don't, but it is hardly evident that cars are non-technological just because they're anachronisms."

The professor rolled his eyes and suddenly stood up, as if angry, and for a moment Michael thought he had scored some kind of bullseye. But Wacker just shook his head and began gathering papers and books from the various piles. "You haven't been listening, have you?" he said almost casually. "I'm not terribly surprised, although I might have hoped for better."

"What is that supposed to mean?" Michael insisted.

"It means you haven't been listening. Am I speaking Portuguese?" Wacker paused in his gathering. "I'm talking about habits and changes in consciousness. I'm not talking about lists of rules regarding whether one can or can't use a car or a teleportation booth or even a pocketknife. I'm talking about how we change our ideas and beliefs slowly, and possibly irrevocably, by participating in and using the techniques and technologies around us. I'm not talking about outlawing cars; I'm talking about knowing what using the car implies and, even more importantly, what it presumes. Because as you go on using the car, it will change your way of thinking to conform to its presuppositions, unless you are very, very careful. And the same is true of your holy man's wonders of the soul."

Michael could barely follow the references to habit and the implications for Gesar's view of the soul. The flurry of the professor's activity distracted him. "Are you leaving?" he asked, dropping the flow of argument.

"No, I'm getting a haircut," Wacker snipped. Then he seemed to calm down. "Listen," he said more softly, more directly. "I'm not surprised that even you, whom I take to be pretty intelligent, don't see my point. We're a well-trained people—trained not to expect systems of ideas and behavior and, yes, uses of technology, to be interwoven and integrated wholes. We're trying to make sense of reality here, not just have good experiences or be nice neighbors. Few people seem to realize that."

The professor seemed on the verge of leaving, as he stuffed papers into a battered briefcase and took a small jacket from a corner hook. But Michael couldn't give up. "But maybe it's just you that don't understand. That's possible, you realize."

"Of course," Wacker replied as a soft blue hat emerged crumpled from the briefcase, "but how shall we tell unless, in some sense, I'm right?" Michael wasn't sure what he meant, and he would have asked, but was given no chance. Wacker moved to the doorway and pointed to the switch on the wall. "Do be so kind as to kill the lights and pull the door closed as you go, won't you?" he said with easy, though questionably sincere politeness. And he left.

Michael was a bit stunned. For a moment he merely looked about the room. Here he was, a reporter, left in the professor's room after having had an argument with him. With the lights blazing, papers strewn about the office, he wondered if he should just "investigate." He wondered next if anything could be found in this mess, or if indeed there was anything *to* find. Was there anything in any of this man's ideas? Michael wondered, and then noted again the oddity of being left behind in this man's private office and being merely told to close the door when he left. At last, Michael laughed. He sat back in his chair, balancing his notepad on his lap, and laced his fingers behind his head. He realized that he had, in fact, just had a really enjoyable time. Almost as payment to his host, he decided he would try to consider the professor's ideas and see what he could distill from the mash to inform his promised discussions with Dr. Gesar. As for Wacker himself, Michael decided he liked him.

13

THE PREACHER

While Professor Wacker had been hard to find sequestered in his dim corner of academia, the Reverend Dr. David Roberts was never hard to find, nor, as far as Michael could tell, did it seem the man was ever alone. In contrast to the good professor, Dr. Roberts seemed to have no time to talk, certainly no "office hours" for consultation. He barely had time to talk to an eminent member of the press, at least not one-on-one. He did offer individual interviews for Christian videos in which he related his "spiritual journey," or he pretended—Michael interpreted—to be responding to an interview when in fact he was preaching some moving sermon with personal meaning. Most of the time, the reverend gave press releases or had his PR staff do so. So it was a rare chance that Michael arranged a brief interview with the great preacher, having discovered—notably from a press release—that the man had come to town for one of his famous gatherings.

Roberts's great meetings, or "Ministerings," as they were billed—another verb made noun made plural by writers with no sense of grammar or poetry, according to Michael—were massively attended by the Christian communities of the large cities in which they were invariably held. Michael had watched videos in which thousands upon thousands of believers crowded the auditoriums and stadiums and sang simple songs to Jesus, while they held up their hands and swayed like palms in the wind. Apparently a few "seekers" also attended, since there were inevitably a few dramatic conversions and even an occasional miracle.

Michael had also read the standard critiques that accused Roberts of salting the crowd with "converts," instructing them to come forward at the right moment to find God. Interestingly, Roberts himself never denied using such tactics and even confessed as much. He had done his research, after all, and so he knew the psychological patterns of need and response among the urban population to whom he preached, and it was hardly a manipulation, he contended, to acknowledge and soften the modern seeker's common fears. "No one wants to be the first to stand," he once noted with a smile, and so he planned his rallies and evangelistic meetings with tactics designed to help people do with ease what they wanted to do anyway.

Such clear planning and execution had been key to Roberts' dramatic popularity. There had never been any intention of hiding the businesslike research and planning he had put into his ministry from the first days until now. From the beginning of Roberts's "Valley Church" to the national and international work of his "Minsterings," he had simply gone to the people to find out what they wanted in their Christianity. They want "a religion less dour but no less honest," he had discovered, "which brings people to Jesus without the demands of a religiosity that makes them pretend to be someone else." So Roberts had given them Valley Church, a product created for its market niche. The work had grown from there, described as a wondrous, "miraculously" successful ministry. All was clearly documented in the autobiography Michael read, an autobiography written when the preacher was thirty-eight years old. Michael was cynical: "What's a thirty-eight-year-old doing writing an autobiography at all?"

Yet the success of Roberts's Ministerings was indisputable, and as Michael Pryor walked into the Civic Auditorium that Thursday, he saw clearly how the planning of the young preacher thirty-five years before had culminated in the remarkable flurry of planning and organization he saw before him now. From the desk receptionist—young, pretty and with an almost delighted dance in her voice that made one want to smile along—he had been led with startling speed to one of several floor directors whose only job, it seemed, was to stand ready to coordinate other coordinators and to handle any unexpected need. The next level of coordinators—each recognizable by the red and gold badge that said, "Ministering: Today!"—seemed charged with merely standing by one of dozens of small groups of workers. These, Michael learned from his guide, were part Civic Auditorium staff and part Dr. Roberts's own technicians.

Michael's guide was Joy, a small, young woman with red hair so curly and thick it seemed to explode from the brown elastic band that gathered it at the back of her head. Her eyes were green, even bright green, and her smile faultless. Yet her manner was erect and professional, taking over the job of watching Michael with a forthrightness that seemed almost haughty. She had taken him into the main auditorium and checked in there with what seemed even a higher-level coordinator, one of three or four who literally stood still in control booths spread around the floor. These, through their various electronic connections, brought and sent the various coordinators of all levels to their needed spots, with no one showing the slightest sign of haste. From the control booth, after a very quick and apparently gentle conversation with his microphone, the young man she spoke to pointed Joy toward a knot of people on the stage and encouraged Michael to "Have a blessed day."

Even before Michael saw the gray-haired preacher in the group on the stage, he could tell that this, finally, was the true center of activity. In his imagination, the auditorium had already become a giant spider web, spread asymmetrically across the floor and even across the ceiling, with all threads ultimately linked to this man in the center. Here, too, the small group of coordinators seemed unhurried, yet Michael noted that the group was never the same people for long, as information and direction came and went again at the same easy but obviously efficient pace. Thus the nexus had its hub, and the web, Michael thought with a cynical grin, its spider.

As if clairvoyant, the "spider" turned just as Michael and Joy reached the circle of coordinators and advisers moving across the stage. He met Michael's eyes over the crowd, and with an easy gesture, he parted the circle to let Michael approach. Michael knew the man's looks already from the videos: a tall, straight man with a strong build that held up and filled his fine blue suit with a kind of royal stature. The hair was graying, but not silver, more a badge of the dignity of gathered wisdom than a sign of age. His mouth was large and wide, but it moved with fluidity as he smiled and spoke. And the eyes, set in a face at once bright but aging, were blue and clear, happy and open. Michael at once saw his own reflection in those eyes and felt some of his cynicism muted. Those eyes met him as if they saw a friend arrive.

"Mr. Pryor." Dr. Roberts came forward with an outstretched hand. "How nice of you to agree to meet with me in the midst of all this set up. A bit muddled for an interview, I'm afraid."

"No, sir," he started to respond. "I'm thankful to you that I could be given a moment in—"

"No, no." Roberts was laughing into an interruption. "Don't thank me yet. You'll see we haven't much time, and I'm afraid you'll be disappointed." And as if to prove his point, he turned at once as a young, dark skinned woman strode up. He spoke to her in the same easy, economical forceful-ness. "Ah, Roopa," he greeted her by name, "go with Maxwell here, won't you, and check the status of the technical difficulty they were having with the video feed. See if you can get that split screen part cleaned up, OK?" Then, without hardly a breath, Roberts turned to another man, addressed him as Hsin, and asked him to take over Roopa's direction of the recording equipment. "Thanks, Hsin," he said sincerely, and the trio walked off without evident hustle.

He turned back to Michael with an easy smile. "Come with me," he said, "and we'll take the walking/talking tour." Then quickly over Michael's shoulder, he added, "Thank you, Joy."

Michael turned to thank his guide, but she was already retreating, and by the time he turned back to his host, Roberts, too, was moving away. Michael caught up and walked beside the reverend across the large stage. Movement about them ranged from technical lighting and computer-coordinated camera sequences to spots of tape on the floor that marked the speaker's position or to the selection of sandwiches for the coordinators' lunches. Roberts made a couple of nods toward workers, patted the shoulder of one man taping down an electrical line, waved and called greetings to two others he knew by name. Somehow at the same time he began to speak of God and God's work, indicating with apparent awe the great accomplishments of the laborers in the auditorium. He seemed to see them not as an example of coordination and economical precision but as a miracle of divine work.

"All this," Roberts was saying by the time they reached the stage wing, "is in hopes of finding one person, one soul to call toward God, or one body to strengthen in his name."

"A lot of production for one soul," Michael observed.

Roberts smiled, clearly aware of the hint of mockery in Michael's voice. "Of course it seems that way," he agreed, "but compare it to what God himself has done for even one sinner, and you see that our efforts here are negligible."

Michael was about to suggest that God might surely find easier ways to call sinners, when the two came to a door. They passed through it down a hallway where electricians wrestled with bundles of colored wires, overseen of course by a coordinator whom Roberts knew by name, and through another door to a small communications room. There a young, dark-skinned man sat, glancing across three small computer screens and occasionally, with a tap on the screen, tossing a line or a page over to a printer behind him. The man started to rise as he recognized Roberts.

"Sit, sit, Desi," the preacher assured. "We're just gonna sit and chat a minute." Then he added, "But would you be so good as to get me a drink of something, maybe a cola? And Mr. Pryor?"

Michael realized he was being offered a refreshment, and he stumbled for a second. "Um, could I just have some water?" he requested, and then, as if it suddenly occurred to him to test the situation, he added, "with some ice, if that's OK."

The preacher looked at Michael and smiled, as if he somehow felt that Michael's request had become a subtle push. But he turned at once to Desi, who was already at the door. "Thanks, Desi," he spoke toward the closing door.

More pleasantries followed as the two men settled in large leather chairs that flanked a small table. Michael described his news "magazine" and some of the stories he had done in the past, careful to choose those he thought a religious leader might recognize. Roberts did indeed seem to know something of Michael's work, whether from genuine interest or as part of a preparation for this meeting. But the man smiled genuinely and listened with interest as Michael acknowledged that he had a reputation for taking something of a skeptical view on some issues in the past, especially where they otherwise dealt with recognized servants of humanity.

"Indeed it is difficult," Roberts finally agreed, lips thin, eyes thoughtful, "to find the evident difference between true service and self-service. And especially among the religious," he was shaking his head, "this is an infamous problem."

Michael smiled as best he could but knew it would look like a sneer, "Well, I fear I also have a somewhat suspicious nature." Of course it was hardly a fear.

Roberts laughed aloud. "I believe you do," he said with a genuine mirth that took away any hint of insult. "And that's OK. It's OK." Michael wondered if he was trying to sound assuring. "You can be free to inquire here all you like. This is a good ministry, an honest ministry." He paused. "I'd be the first to leave it if it wasn't."

Michael thought to protest that he wasn't, after all, here to question Pastor Roberts about his "Ministerings," but he decided quickly to let the protest fall as he took out his notepad. He had found over the years that unsolicited self-defenses were often the most revealing. So he merely commented, "Well, it is difficult for an outsider to see the difference between the authentic believer and the 'self-serving' charlatan."

"Yet in a way, that's how it should be," Roberts said, looking away as if to a distant thought. "True spirituality is, after all, a relation to God in Christ, not a relation to me or to you, or to your readers, for that matter. So it's not surprising that we mere spectators cannot see the relation between God and the individual soul. The scriptures themselves advise us to test the spirits but not to judge one another."

Michael ruefully thought that testing the spirits sounded like something one did at a bar. But he understood the man's meaning and saw it was a way to get to the issue. This, after all, was not supposed to be about Roberts' ministry so much as about his view of the work of Richard Gesar.

Michael went on. "But surely there must be some evidence, some way to know the difference between God and fraud."

"Nicely put," Roberts winked at him. "And of course there are manifestations of the spirit of Christ in our lives. That's entirely what we preach here. Not only are we to make some verbal declaration of belief. We are to follow Christ, to know Christ, to live Christ." He made a fist and shook it with each crescendoing verb.

Michael felt himself annoyed. He wasn't all that interested in Christ, and he wondered if he would have to wade through this preacher's "message" to finally get to the issues at hand. He was a seasoned-enough debater that he could see ahead the development of this discussion onto the lines he was searching. He was ready to press toward questions about auras when the door swung inward and Desi appeared with two tall glasses.

Thus the conversation was interrupted, and again Michael noted how easily and sincerely Roberts acknowledged his employee. As Desi returned to his computers and began moving icons about on the screen with his finger, there was an awkward silence in the interview as the two men sipped their drinks, Michael's with ice. Roberts looked quickly at his watch, and Michael realized he had better rush on.

"Dr. Roberts, you speak of 'Christ in our lives' as perhaps real evidence that something genuine is taking place spiritually. We might suppose that in many religions there are similar, shall we say, 'manifestations' of spiritual genuineness. I guess what I want to know is what you think about these manifestations of spirituality in general." He used the words carefully, looking for a transition out of Christianity and into something more universal. He felt like his prior talks with, and research on, Gesar had given him a vocabulary useful for avoiding the Christian focus. "Do you think spirituality could be something, well, measurable?"

"Ah, yes." Roberts nodded and sipped his drink again. "Yes, I remember now what really brings you here." He seemed to peer into the glass thoughtfully. "I have done some reading about your Buddhist scientist," he said, nodding, "and I confess I am somewhat torn about it all. But," he paused again, and this time looked up toward the ceiling. "But how can I explain?" There was silence, and Michael let it linger.

"Well," the preacher started at last, "we think and teach that true Christianity happens here," he pressed a splayed hand to his chest, "here in the heart. It is first and foremost an experience of peace, inner peace, an assurance that all is well with one's soul.

"You see," he went on without a pause large enough for questions, "it is simply a fact that we are alienated from ourselves and therefore from one another." Michael wasn't sure of the *therefore* but couldn't interrupt what was beginning to look like a sermon. "Life in Christ is the reunion of our souls with ourselves, becoming what we truly were meant to be. Our work of ministry is exactly that, a ministering to the broken, that they become whole. Wholeness here," and again he pressed fingertips to his chest.

"Jesus said," he was continuing, "'I come that you may have life, and life in abundance.' It is life overflowing, bubbling over with fullness." He was smiling, his hands moving in slow outwardly expanding circles. "Our good news overflows with blessings, promises of redemption and reward and fullness of life." Here his gaze seemed to drift to the other side of the room, sweeping the ceiling, as if seeking a window to look farther. Then his eyes shot back to Michael's, fastened on, gazed deep. "And this is life," he said, quoting again, "'that you know God and the Son whom he has sent.'"

Michael didn't know the Bible verses, and wasn't sure if the *you* had been specifically meant for him. But he felt uneasy, as if there had been a direct confrontation with some religious call to conversion. As his training moved him, he felt his resistance rise.

At the same time, he was honest enough to realize that this was somehow different from what he had known in the past, what he had heard of the Christianity his brother tended to preach. His brother's morose weariness, his sense that somehow faith had to involve moral repentance or at least a careful conscience seemed to be missing here. This message was positive, a call to "life" rather than a fear of death. In one way, that rang for Michael with a vague tone of possibility, if not because it seemed true, at least because it was not so damned depressing. Indeed, it sounded surprisingly like what Dr. Gesar himself might say. For those same reasons, Michael's suspicions rose in another direction: this sounded like a sales pitch.

If Michael Pryor, at that moment, had had the time and the spiritual sensitivity to question himself, he might have found himself wrestling with ambiguities deeper than even he could handle. It flitted like a shadow across his awareness that there were two very different pulls—maybe three—tugging at his thinking heart. Somehow the buried and almost always unspoken love for Daniel moved there, wanted something in that relationship that was kept distant, made impossible. And Michael's thinking heart knew it was religion, this Christianity. He resented its intrusion, resented its attacks on his personality and action, and resented especially the feeling it gave him that it was his own fault that the barrier stood unbreached, even thickening. It was always somehow part of the dreariness of his brother's religion that Michael was always made to be the bad guy, the opponent, the one unrepentant. With Dr. Roberts, the story was a bit different, less demanding, less angry. And yet for that very reason, it seemed suspect. Had Michael had, or taken, the time for introspection, he might have wondered how he could resist both calls, or for that matter if somehow both could be true, or indeed if he had merely misunderstood one of them. Had he known the sayings of Jesus, or had his brother been by him to quote some, he might have been challenged by the peculiar accusation once leveled against Pharisees who would neither dance nor mourn. But at the moment, he was interviewing, and Michael Pryor could avoid the harsher introspections that scripture or his brother might have forced upon him. He could once again take refuge in his job, where the dominant question for his professional and agonistic mind was clearly his evaluations of Gesar's work, and, increasingly with Roberts, evaluations of religion as business.

"So how shall I understand your faith," Michael began, hoping not to emphasize too much the first-person pronoun, "as different from Dr. Gesar's enlightenment?" He sat back, taking a thoughtful pose in order to avoid seeming too argumentative. He added, "Or different from any self-help technique or even a promising business venture? Surely if I could just medi- tate or make a really good investment in bonds or pork futures, I'd have the same kind of hope for 'abundant life.'"

Michael enjoyed his own ability to mix comments and questions, to hide as he did here, a criticism of business religion with a question focused on his professional interview. He also worried that he had sounded too criti- cal, and he knew his crooked smile would not help. Yet he really didn't care if he sounded a little cynical. Cynicism and challenge were his trademark, to put the opponent on his guard. And besides he *was* cynical. He looked to his right and noted with a hint of satisfaction that Desi had stopped his computer tapping and had looked up at them, his eyes curious.

But Roberts smiled genuinely. Michael had hoped to find some agita- tion in that barely wrinkled face, some nervousness in the hands or tremble in the voice as the man started to respond to the hinted accusation. But the eyes softened, and even their blue color seemed to become more gentle. Yet the smile did not land on Michael directly, it seemed somehow circu- itous, an inner amusement first and then a sort of kindness. Had Michael known the Bible verses about loving one's enemy and heaping coals of fire on one's opponent by being kind and gentle, he might have understood the preacher's smile as both acceptance and challenge. It was a winning smile, but again, equivocally, both the smile that ought to attract and accept, and the smile of one who feels himself the winner. "A winning smile is a winner's smile," Dr. Roberts had said in one of his famous sermons—Michael had read a short on-line collection—and again Michael found himself compar- ing it with Richard Gesar's implacable equanimity.

"Well," he started with a thoughtful musing, "if I understand the sci- ence of your Gesar Tulku—that's his name and title, isn't it?" Michael noted that the preacher must have done some homework, and also noted the personal pronoun that made it seem Gesar was Michael's own teacher. "If I understand him, he may be looking for this inner peace, maybe even finding it. But isn't he still finding it, so to speak, out there"—he waved a hand into the distance— "instead of in here?" His hand touched his own chest. "And Michael," the preacher seemed to whisper his name, as the gaze came back to earth, "if I understand your Dr. Gesar's philosophy right, I would have to tell him that the real abundant life is not in what we do but in what God does for us. It lies not in ourselves, but in Christ. Jesus is the way, the truth, and the life."

Here was a verse Michael recognized. He finished it as a question, "And no one comes to the Father except through him"?

Roberts nodded thoughtfully. "Our life," he seemed barely to say aloud, "is in God through Jesus."

"Only in Jesus?" Michael pressed the point. He knew well enough the exclusive claims of this religion. While there was something in the claims that troubled him, there was also something in them, at least when his brother declared them, that seemed forthright. This was again an ambiguity, a paradox he had examined, if only superficially. What was a savior who had been a man who was God and who came only to a small group of people at one specific time of history? It was like a revelation of a mystery, a peculiarly exciting story if one could take it seriously, with its own hint of possibility, like finding a treasure map with an X marking the spot. Yet it was also an absurdity, he thought, only to be tossed away with a cough of disdain. Moreover, it was also an issue in his present work, a way to challenge both this Christian preacher and the Tibetan *tulku*. So again, he came back to the point of the interview. He swallowed his own uncertainty and focused on Roberts' response.

"Jesus," the preacher was saying, "is Immanuel, God come to us, to dwell with us and in us. Some may say they can rise to the heavens and bring God down, or others, perhaps like the man you're studying, may say they can make God here on earth. But we say 'Immanuel, God come to us,' and therefore Jesus is indeed the way to God. Thus is Jesus our way to God, our way to life."

Michael caught the shift in emphasis and pressed it. This would work. "So do you mean Jesus is *the* way to God—or to life or whatever? Or that Jesus is *our* way to life?" He paused to let the distinction vibrate in the air. "Is then perhaps Jesus *your* way to life, just as some Buddha thing is Richard Gesar's way, and some kind of nature prayer is somebody else's way? These are, after all, the kind of things, I think, Dr. Gesar would tell me." He almost left it there, focused still on his professional work. But he couldn't quite end his critique either. "I mean, is your religion really about Jesus, or is it about 'us'?"

"The real issue, Mr. Pryor," the preacher said, pushing his gaze straight into Michael's eyes, "is whether he is *your* way to life." Michael should have seen that coming, and he felt the move set him back. "I do not press people to demand proofs and arguments, Mr. Pryor. The question is not just about who Jesus is but about who you are, what you will do with this Jesus. So I urge people not to debate but to have faith. Faith, Mr. Pryor. That personal inner assurance that Christ is in us, bringing us to God, our Father, our Dad, in heaven. Faith, Mr. Pryor." Again his fingertips went to his chest. "Here."

Michael felt the challenge had become personal. It struck him like a strategic attack, like a tactic that trained preachers like Roberts would know well. Indeed, he had performed the move very fluidly, and Michael felt himself in the unfortunate position of needing to defend himself. Yet it was also his own fault. He knew he needed to get back to Roberts's interpretation of Gesar and the wonder of auroscopy, but he could not quite avoid his own attacks on the preacher's views. Now the tables had been turned, and he was at a point where even self-defense would have been loss. He had learned in conversations with his brother that turning to defenses of why he doesn't need God were counter-productive. Besides the fact that Michael could never quite define what it means to be "good enough," he found he easily began to resent a religious view where self-justification is a sin.

So Michael turned again to professionalism. It was his own tactic, his own effort, perhaps barely conscious, to turn away from the disadvantage of religious introspection. He was not entirely self-deceived, indeed he was proud of his self-awareness, and he knew somehow in the unspoken recess of consciousness that he was avoiding a question of his own soul. But he also knew he had not always avoided it. Hadn't he on occasion tried to listen honestly to his brother's assertions? And he was sure that his own honesty was somehow itself "good enough," in that he was at least willing to let himself hear the question. There was always time later for such philosophical self-indulgence. So meanwhile, he decided, even if it was to avoid his own soul, he had a job to do. He went back to the interview.

"But faith in what, Dr. Roberts?" he asked as segue toward his more pressing professional concern. "You talk of faith in Jesus, others of faith in Allah or the Buddha. It is precisely what makes the work of Dr. Gesar so intriguing that he claims to find, indeed to measure, this faith in all religions." He paused for emphasis, but not enough to allow response. "Would you admit that non-Christians have as much faith as any Christian?"

Dr. Roberts pursed his lips and scratched at his barely white hair, looking thoughtful. Finally he nodded. "Well, certainly," he said, "in some sense everyone can have faith. But faith in Christ is not something I'm willing to say is measurable, whatever science your Tibetan friend may claim to have developed."

Michael realized the preacher had not really answered his question, but he let it go, hearing in his words a peculiar and unexpected echo of what Professor Wacker had said. "Do you mean to say you doubt that Gupta's science can find the soul?" he queried.

"Well, I confess," the man responded with a smile, "I don't understand what that 'science' really does. Of course I've tried to read a bit about what the man is doing, and certainly I laud his attempts to know and understand the deeper spirit of humankind, but the 'science,'" he said, indicating quotation marks, "is certainly beyond me."

"Well, me too." Michael smiled back. He felt a genuine relief at escaping personal introspection. For some minutes he and Dr. Roberts shared what seemed an almost congenial humor about the mystery of the *tulku*'s work. The two men played on words and winked at their own misunderstandings as Michael tried to explain what he knew of the "science." But in the end Michael brought seriousness back in, strangely comfortable with the hope that he was now on Roberts's side. He tried using Wacker's complaint.

"But you'd say, then, that it is perhaps a mistake from the beginning to try to measure faith like a physical thing?"

"Yes, of course, that seems problematic," the preacher responded, "since faith itself is the work of God. And who can measure God?" Michael thought at last that he might have found the religious reasoning behind Wacker's philosophy. And he might have believed that Wacker and Roberts were somehow alike, if the latter had not gone on. "And the faith itself is not something seen or heard, nor is it an object of our analysis, whether physical or philosophical. We feel Christ here." Again the preacher grasped at his chest. "We don't think Him here," he said, moving his hand to his temple.

Somehow Michael felt Wacker never would have made that distinction. Neither would Gesar Tulku. So which was it? Did the two Christians agree, or did the two philosophers? Or were they all different? Suddenly for Michael there were too many positions, and he wasn't sure he could sort them out. There were faith and philosophy and science, relations between minds and bodies and spirits, and Michael wasn't even sure what the preacher before him was really grabbing at in his chest. Yet that was where the distinctions lay; Michael was certain of that.

"So what is . . . this?" Michael clawed at his own chest and tried not to sound annoyed.

The preacher repeated his gesture, so natural and smooth it was for him. "This is where we know God, where we know that God loves us and sent His Son into our hearts."

"We don't know God here?" Michael pointed to his own temple.

"No, no," the preacher responded quickly. "We only think God up here," he smiled and added his own helpful image, "and we maybe try to see God here," he pointed to his eyes. "But we feel him down here." Michael would have pressed, started indeed to note that the verbs changing from *know* and *see* to *feel*. But the preacher was quicker. "Christians understand what I mean," he asserted gently.

That gentle assertion was the usual trump card, and the statement annoyed Michael. It brought the issue all over again to the personal and even accusative nature of faith. It claimed, "Of course *you* don't understand me— you are not a believer." Michael could only admit that was true. But he would not be bullied, and he still had his earlier question to readdress. He strategized and realized he could use his own faithless status in the argument.

"But Dr. Gesar's experiments do seem to *see* something, indeed to measure something," he asserted to force a confrontation. "It strikes me that if I were to take one of his scans, I might find that my aura is blue as the sky—blue, that's bad—which by his calibration means I am indeed a heathen. And then he'd be right, wouldn't he?"

"Well, Mr. Pryor, I'm not really here to comment on the status of your soul," Dr. Roberts said, as if with a humility that belied the many comments already made about the status of his soul. "But it is possible," the preacher went on, "that some of what science tells us can awaken us to our need for God. Psychology succeeds at this much of the time. So if in fact your aura were to show blue—using your *tulku's* calibration—then perhaps it would mean something. Perhaps not. But there might be value in it, if perhaps we could convince even a skeptic like you of your need for Christ." He smiled genuinely.

Michael had hoped the preacher would be unable to resist. He pressed on. "But if those same tests showed a skeptical heathen like me before and after my conversion to, say, Buddhism, wouldn't that show that Buddhism is just as much a true religion as your Jesus?"

Dr. Roberts was silent, with a kind of vacuous gaze. For an instant Michael was sure he had won. At the same moment, he felt an old tinge of guilt, as if even the desire to win had been somehow misdirected, a wrong choice. Michael thought of his brother.

"But Mr. Pryor," the preacher began, "Jesus is not a religion. He is a person."

Michael forgot about his brother and felt annoyed again. He had given the preacher an easy way out. "Jesus is a person, Mr. Pryor," he was saying, "and what we have here in our hearts is a relationship, not a religion."

Michael was stymied, or maybe just exhausted. Though he tried to bring the issue back to exclusive emphases on Jesus, he couldn't seem to restate his challenge the right way. By now the preacher was moving fast, going over the same ground. "Jesus is the Truth," he would say, but that did not seem to mean that the Buddha was a lie. "Jesus is the healer of our hearts," he would say, but that did not mean the physical heart or even the physical brain. "It is like pineapple," he finally asserted, "rough and thorny on the outside, but full of sweetness within, and one needs to have eaten one to know what it tastes like." With that, Michael realized he was back on the defensive, back under the demand that he had to be a believer before he could know what believing meant.

Dr. Roberts looked at his watch again, and Michael realized the interview was essentially over. "So what can I say, really?" he asked aloud, and he realized that this rhetorical question might mean to the preacher that Michael was defenseless against the fact that he was indeed an unbeliever. But that fact gave him one last approach. "I guess it's true," he prefaced, "that I don't feel what you feel, and at least so far I have not seen what Dr. Gesar might see if he looked into my soul with his machine. But I suppose I could participate in Dr. Gesar's tests, and I imagine my aura would be as deep a heathen blue as you can get."

"And coming to Christ," the preacher inserted, "would change that."

"Dr. Gesar would be the first to agree," Michael responded. "But I also think he would say that I could convert, not to Jesus, but to Islam or Buddhism, and then find my aura to be deep and red, as fully red as Dr. Gesar's," he paused and felt the final attack, "or even yours." He smiled his crooked smile. "What would you say then?"

"Well, Mr. Pryor," the preacher started, touching his watch. "I can hardly claim to know what God thinks of your soul," he started, and Michael saw he would simply stop there.

"The real question is," Michael emphasized as directly as he could, "whether what Dr. Gesar measures is really the soul. Because if he accurately finds the spirituality in your soul, then he must just as accurately find it in everyone's. And then it is not God who declares whether we have true faith. It is Dr. Gesar's science."

"Well, Mr. Pryor," Roberts started again, "I see your point. But I trust you see mine as well." Michael did not, but the preacher went on. "So if you see your Dr. Gesar again soon, or if you write your article for your readers, let it be clear that I continue to teach Jesus Christ and him crucified. I teach a living relationship with a living God. A God who lives in my heart." He paused for his usual emphasis. "And He can live in yours."

The words seemed final to Michael, yet hardly helpful. He felt as if the prepackaged sermon, as moving and even challenging as it might have been, certainly did not answer his questions. It seemed only to avoid the hint he had just dropped about the color of Dr. Roberts's own spiritual aura. Yet the finality in the man's voice told Michael he would get no more.

As if on cue and by demand, a knock on the door stopped what might have been left of the conversation. Without waiting for a response, the knocker pushed the door in. It was Joy, Michael's coordinator-guide. "Pastor Roberts," she imposed, "I think they're ready to try those satellite links again."

"Thank you, Joy," Roberts said easily. He rose to go, offering Michael a handshake. "Mr. Pryor," he intoned in his deep voice, "I do hope some of this was helpful, helpful on many levels. There are many mysteries. I by no means claim to understand all that our spirits feel. And if having your aura measured by a Tibetan guru can bring you to Jesus, I applaud the man's work. I can see that you take these matters seriously. Perhaps that is enough for now." He smiled with genuine compassion.

Michael instinctively fired one last question, making his hint explicit. "But would you be willing, Dr. Roberts, to have Dr. Gesar measure *your* aura?"

Roberts smiled easily and shrugged. "Of course."

"And when the color came back?" Michael spat quickly, trying to get in the last point. "If it came back red, that might show your own faith, but wouldn't it also show an acceptance of Dr. Gesar's ideas? And if blue, wouldn't you risk sounding like an unbeliever, having to say your own heathen soul must be a mistake as measured by Gesar's science?"

"I have every confidence in my faith, Mr. Pryor," he said, and his clawed hand patted his chest. His final words were to Joy: "See to Mr. Pryor's interests here, won't you?"

14

WOMEN'S PRAYERS

Marta seldom felt the need for comfort. Even when she did need it herself, she found herself giving comfort to someone else. It happened at work all the time, like the time she mentioned to Todd her sense of being alone even among friends, and she spent the next hour helping him look for "a real relationship" within the long list of lovers he proceeded to describe. By now she rarely hoped that her colleagues at work would be the kind of people who would understand and be able to help her.

"Now, old Father Aloysius," she mused to herself, as she sipped the tea Helen had just brought, "there was a listener." He had been a great old-school Papist, raised somewhere near the Poland-Ukrainian border, his father having barely survived the re-capitalism movements seventy years ago. She had learned—he hadn't told her—that he had struggled greatly to weigh the moral imperatives of serving his father and joining the priesthood. Somewhere in all those struggles, apparently, he had learned to listen to what others had to say. What a confessor he had been!

But Father Aloysius had been dead now these eight years, and in the moments that Marta watched Helen return from the kitchen, she considered his replacement, Father Dave. Nice guy. But no matter what you said, he could recall a time when he had a similar quandary and how much he had learned from those days. He was terrible at absolution, but he could always report which contemplative technique had helped him. Marta smiled to herself.

Helen sat down. Marta genuinely loved Helen, having found in her a strange warmth and friendship she couldn't quite comprehend. They didn't talk philosophy or even theology, but they were women together. Helen had the sometimes-frustrating habit of simply shaking her head and being silent when Marta would offer some problem or personal turmoil. Or she would reach out and take Marta's hand so briefly it was nearly a tap, again without comment. Yet Marta realized this was not merely Helen's inability to speak, for she was genuinely thoughtful and careful of speech. But rather Helen just sometimes seemed to know that any response would merely be more argument. At those points, she would just let Marta be and would choose to be with her.

As Helen settled to her tea, Marta began, describing Todd at work and even a bit of Father Dave, just as she had been thinking of them. Helen enjoyed the stories, but felt the disappointments behind the words. Marta's view of Helen had been, in fact, very accurate. She was indeed thoughtful, and Helen knew that she could, if required, analyze in detail very complex matters. Thus Helen's apparently non-responsive approach was not indecision of any kind, but a curious manifestation of something like humility. It was not that Helen felt she was less than intelligent, but she did always seem to feel that others, somehow, already knew what she wanted to say. With both Daniel and Marta, she just always was sure that they, somehow, already had good ideas, and that even if hers were also good, they wouldn't add much. Far from any problem of self-esteem, she listened with a kind of curious contentment, a simple willingness to let others speak, and to let them struggle and try. She would simply be there.

And with Marta, there was something else. She had once listened smiling to Marta ramble about some Greek philosopher's analysis of friendship, and she had known at once it was accurate. No, it was not that Aristotle—or whoever it was—had been right. What did that matter? It might have been Plato or Descartes or some other Greek. Helen didn't really care. But she had seen at once that Marta herself had been trying to express her own fondness for Helen, and that the love between them meant something also about the health and wholeness of their individual lives. So what did the philosopher matter? That conversation, she had known intuitively, was about friendship, and so Helen had let it be. Today, as Marta talked on and on about the last celibate priest and about her colleagues, Helen knew in the middle of each sentence that the real story was about loneliness. She touched Marta's hand.

Marta felt the touch and knew its meaning. Inside Helen, she knew, was this love of friendship, and it blossomed above Helen's own worries like a crocus peeking through late spring snow. Marta stopped talking. It was all evasion anyway. She knew herself, and knew she had come to talk about someone else, a different man. But it was difficult, and when she felt Helen's knowing touch, it embarrassed her. It troubled her, too, that she found it easy with Helen to lose sight of others' sorrows.

"So," she said, waving away her narrative complaints, "tell me how you're doing. We *are* talking baby this time, aren't we?"

Helen smiled. "Oh, I think so," she said, but she turned her head away a little, and Marta knew it was not so simple. Strange: she found it easy to listen and care for people she didn't want to help, but found it difficult to comfort her friend, whom she loved.

"But you know Daniel," Helen was saying. "Even if we go all the way this time, he won't be happy." She paused. "He's doing it for me."

"A good man, doing something for me?" Marta tried to be funny. "Sounds great."

They laughed a little, but Marta knew it wasn't that easy. And Helen could have explained it. Sure, it is good to be loved, she could have said, and it's good to have a husband who will give and live to love his wife. And Daniel was indeed such a man. Yet in her woman's heart, Helen's own love wanted even more to be the giver of gifts. Even the greater gifts of love were somehow laced with sorrow when the beloved giver is himself not at peace. The desire to give and the desire to receive, love that loves so much it sorrows at love that gives out of love and not desire—complex indeed, she knew. Yet she did not bother to explain it; Marta understood already.

"But it's not that Daniel doesn't want a child," she decided to insert, instinctively offering explanation as if he needed defense. "It's just, it's just this whole fertility process, the manipulation, he calls it. You know how he is. Somehow he just wants God to do it."

"Sounds like old Daniel needs a little biology lesson," Marta quipped naturally. "I think, outside of the Jesus example, it's Daniel, not God, who should be doing it." The humor was only a temporary cover. Helen replied that she and Daniel had no trouble with that part of the deal, and with girlish shyness the two hinted at sex and joked for a few minutes. Marta delighted that her friend could so innocently enjoy this fleshly delight, and she urged on her friend's playful self-indulgences with her own wit. Helen understood, and could have explained if she had chosen, the simplicity of sexual joys and the warmth of her husband's gentle passion. She could distinguish it properly from the desire for children and the ensuing frustration. But Helen caught herself suddenly embarrassed—not about sex but because she suddenly felt her friend's sorrows, saw the juxtaposition of Marta's loneliness and her own delight in her husband. Helen fell silent and touched Marta's hand.

It is difficult to know when some silence is enough silence. Perhaps friends know. But even if they do not, for friends the silence is needed and is somehow always enough. Helen felt it and drew herself back to talking about Daniel. "Daniel is just so complicated," she said, as if the discussion had never strayed.

"Or just so simple," Marta responded. "I do envy you your love, Helen," she said with easy openness. "He is a good man."

"But he is always so unsure." Helen sighed. It was not as if she needed some domineering man to run her life, nor a caricature of masculinity who never cried or felt lost. She was sure her criticisms of her husband were not attacks. As a young bride she had fallen into that trap and found a peculiar solace in the complaining game, the temptation to connect with other women by finding fault with men. But she remembered having found such genuine heartbreak in Daniel, such a softness of spirit in his uncertainties, that she could only find guilt in her own complaints. After a time, she had been forced to choose between her relationship with her friends and her vision of her husband's heart. The cost of friendship had been dear, and she wondered if Daniel had even seen it occur. It didn't matter, for she had learned to change her own heart, learned what it meant to choose to love her spouse. In time, God, she believed, had given her a new friend. With Marta, Helen felt safe, safe to express her worries and even dissatisfactions without contradicting love.

"But his unsureness is his simplicity," Marta was already saying. "I think Daniel's troubled precisely because he loves, loves both you and God. But as the world is a broken place, there is often no peaceful union between the two. It is not wrong to be unsure, Helen. Only the foolish and the arrogant are sure. Daniel is certainly neither of those."

Helen agreed. "Never arrogant," she said, "and only sometimes a fool." Again, the two fell silent. In those moments, as the mind races its way through connections too rapid and imprecise for consciousness to follow, Marta's thought discovered Michael, and felt the thought of him as a pique, even a flutter. She knew it was there, but even her usual honesty couldn't quite name it. Instead, she translated it and hid it behind family relations and general curiosity. She hesitated, hoping not to bring the flutter into light, as if it were a secret threatened by being broadly known, or as if it were a shadow that would vanish in too much light.

"But wouldn't he have been more arrogant and less a fool when he was a boy," Marta asked, knowing she was not quite being honest. "Wasn't there always the protective older brother in him?"

Helen frowned a denial. "Not really," she said innocently. "I get the impression he was always a little timid. I don't know, kind of soft. He tells me it was always Michael who ran ahead brashly, climbed trees too high, planned the small deceptions of the parents." Helen smiled to think of the stories Daniel had told her, with his usual gentle charm, conveying a hint of gentle envy of his little brother. It felt ironic that Daniel was clearly the better man, and yet the little brother seemed to have the boldness and self-assurance.

She considered her husband's peculiar innocence, until at last she realized Marta's question had really been about Michael.

With a snap of understanding, Helen looked up at Marta, who glanced down at the table. The bittersweet realization struck Helen that her dear friend was in love with her husband's brother. It didn't come in those words; it came as a feeling of love in herself, a feeling of the good of love. It was a special goodness she spontaneously recognized when she saw it in her friend.

Helen touched Marta's hand, and Marta knew that her secret was revealed. She felt herself blush.

"Well, yes," she said aloud, "I have sort of been thinking about Michael. He just, maybe, intrigues me a little."

Helen laughed softly. "It's just like you, Marta, to fall for somebody like Michael."

"I don't think I've fallen for anyone, Helen," Marta retorted with feigned indignation. "I'm not the falling kind."

"Call it what you will, girl," her friend replied. "But you might be wise to keep your moves restrained for a while."

"Oh?" responded Marta with exaggerated curiosity. "Would he spurn my advances?"

"Quite the contrary, my dear," Helen answered with a slight attempt at an accent. "I think he would readily accept your advances." Helen had hoped to be funny but instantly felt she had said more than she should have. Just as she saw the innocence in her husband's uncertainty, she perceived the lack of innocence in his brother. That made Michael a problem, a curious object of love, pity, and fear, like a lost dog that might bite. She had seen it always in her brother-in-law's words and manner, not in the scar of the lip, but in the too-quick reply, the too-easy self-acceptance. She could have named it, but she never had chosen to. Even now, with Marta, there was no need to offer a label for Michael's tender lostness.

At the same time, Helen felt instinctively the quandary of her own general reticence. For just as it was too easy to say too much, it was possible to say too little. As the quandary worked its way through her feelings, she stared at her hands. If she had been more analytical, she might have recognized her perplexity as a problem more with the world than with herself, for she knew the same feeling—that she could neither speak nor remain silent—when she spoke with Daniel about his worries. Do you share the fears and uncertainties silently? Do you question them? Offer assurances? Surely it would be enough just to speak the truth, but as usual Helen felt her friend already knew what Helen might say.

"You know," Helen started, automatically reverting to the world and the feelings she knew best, "I think Michael is really a good man, a good brother to Daniel. He seems genuinely to love us, I think."

"When he seems to think of you at all," Marta added.

Her friend nodded. "When he seems to think of us at all." There was a slight pause. "And he does, you know, already have a, er, a . . ."

"A girlfriend? A mistress? A paramour?"

"Yes." Helen nodded and smiled at the options. "A paramour," she copied Marta's affected accent.

"I think I knew that," Marta said, finding her normal calmness and inner resignation. "I don't think I'll fight her for him."

"She does have sharp fingernails, and her arms are longer than yours."

"But I've got bulk," Marta replied with an expression of sternness.

Then Helen let herself say what she couldn't quite avoid: "And he doesn't share your faith."

Marta pretended shock. "What? He's not Catholic?"

Helen smiled. "Nope," she shook her head. "Not Catholic."

"Oh, no! He's a Baptist?!" Marta cried, and they both laughed. Marta felt a strange relief, like the secret had been loosed and she herself had been freed. Her friend understood her and spoke truth to her.

Helen experienced a similar relief. Whether she had spoken too much or too little, her friend was still her friend. Once again, conversation became possible.

"I guess I'm just lonely," Marta confessed. "Probably more lonely than really interested in Michael Pryor." She knew it was true. She knew moreover there was something wrong with her loneliness and something right about it. Somehow, she thought, her principles and devotion to God should be enough in some purely theoretical way. Yet clearly it wasn't. But neither was it weakness of character to crave warmth and companionship, even sex. Marta's religious anthropology, her philosophy of what it meant to be human, would allow a clear expression of both the glory of spirituality and the value of physical pleasure. She could have explained it; she had thought through these ideas explicitly many times, even tried to explain them to colleagues who, in the end, could not understand. For many of them, loneliness didn't seem to have anything to do with sensuality. Sensuality, for them, was only sexual. Spirituality, for them, was even more mysterious, perhaps like a not-very-interesting hobby. Certainly spirituality didn't have anything to do with loneliness, for loneliness in spirituality, like loneliness in a sexual relationship, could only mean it was time to drop the old gods and seek a new one. But Marta experienced loneliness in both spirituality and sensuality. Sensuality, at least in her virginal fantasy, was more about closeness than sex, and so was her religion. It was no accident, as she understood her theology, that faithfulness was a virtue in both religion and in marriage, and that her religious tradition had a long, thoughtful history of describing some of the saints' spiritual life as being married to Christ. But Marta was neither wife nor saint, and loneliness somehow haunted her in both worlds. She had long felt this way. Though the feeling of loneliness was unsettling and unsatisfying, at least it made sense to Marta. Indeed, it was exactly because she understood it and could explain it that she found it bearable.

But with Helen, Marta knew it wasn't necessary to explain loneliness. Both understood already, though no doubt in different ways. Marta smiled up at her friend. "I guess being Catholic doesn't mean I'm a nun," she said.

As if to confirm her understanding, Helen touched her hand again.

15

ACTS OF GOD

Michael was no expert in the science of optics or brain physiology, but he was familiar with how people work, and by all observations, the work of Dr. Richard Gesar was remarkable. It had taken some time to get a specific invitation back to Albuquerque; the *tulku* and his staff had been uncommonly busy. The previous press conference had, as Michael should have expected, resulted in a barrage of visitors to the labs by other researchers of brain physiology and electrophysics. Like all good scientists, they had simply wanted to see the work themselves and then to replicate it. By no means, Gesar had finally told him, was this an intrusion or an effort to steal his research. It was the nature of science: there is no scientific discovery until scientists anywhere can find the same results using the same methods.

Those methods still stumped Michael; indeed, they still seemed to stump some of the other experts who had come to the Albuquerque labs on very short visits they had crammed into their own busy schedules. Dr. Andre Thorne, MD, Ph.D., professor of medicine at the University of Arizona Medical School, had told Michael he was sure something was being measured, but he wasn't sure what it was. "Surely it's just electrical signals in the brain," Michael had suggested, but the professor had shaken his head. "It isn't exactly in the brain," he had replied, "but below it, somewhere around here," he touched the base of Michael's skull at the back. "Lower than the cerebellum, but higher than the medulla oblongata. It might be a pulse that travels between the two, but not on any neural pathway." The doctor had then looked at his watch and asked Michael if that were enough.

"Well, no," Michael had said.

Dr. Thorne had smiled. "For me neither."

Dr. Thorne was one of a dozen experts who had sprinted through the labs of "God" for a day or an hour since Michael's news article—and many others—had made bold declarations about Richard Gesar's discoveries. Michael had not met all of the scientists, but he had tried to. His own two days in the labs had been a flurry, or rather a mixture of flurried activity and mute waiting. "You have ten minutes to talk to the physicist from Fermi Lab," someone might say, and twenty minutes later, Michael would be back in his room again sifting through notes. That particular scientist, a Dr. Margherita Valsky, had largely agreed with, and yet essentially contradicted, Dr. Thorne. "No," she had said, practically echoing the brain expert, "ees no event in brain at all, but only point of measurement ees in brain."

Michael had nodded and reached for the back of his neck. "Around here?" he had asked.

"No!" the physicist had practically yelled at him. "Ees out here, seems slightly outside, above skull altogether."

Perhaps Michael had not understood her through the accent.

By Friday, Michael's second day at the labs, he was beginning to wonder if he would see Dr. Gesar at all. He didn't mind Petra's company, nor was she uninformative, but even she was often distracted. Lunch was brief, and she had only been able to tell him small bits about the early days of the research, how Dr. Gesar had been "visionary" and "driven," though never anything other than calm and focused.

"How many of you were there at the beginning," Michael asked, "following this vision of Dr. Gesar?"

"Just three," Petra replied calmly, "and I wasn't one of them. Not at the beginning. Richard was something of a renegade student at MIT, you know, inasmuch as his first dabblings into Aura Enhanced Imaging, what you've called auroscopy, was too speculative and strange for many researchers. At first Richard's PhD director, Dr. Andrei Kirkovski, tried to dissuade him from this work—thought it was a waste of his talents. But Kirkovski eventually saw the merit in what Richard was doing, even if he could not fully appreciate the spiritual meaning." She slurped at her bean soup.

"What does Dr. Kirkovski think of the work now?" Michael asked, watching the pretty woman eat. "I might like to interview him."

"That would be difficult," the woman replied. "He died a few years ago. Richard can see souls, but he can't bring them back to life."

Michael recalled that Gesar's previous mentor at Stanford—Beslow, wasn't it?—was also dead. "How did Kirkovski die?"

"Dr. Kirkovski was already rather old when Richard moved from California to Massachusetts," Petra said, finishing her soup. "After Richard finished at MIT, Dr Kirkovski made an extensive effort to record all his work, leaving the field of bio-spectrography with a fine legacy of research, mostly applicable to the study of crop disease. His vision was failing even as he retired, in spite of the corneal reconstruction—I guess it was something about the retina. Anyway, within a few years, with all his work recorded, he nobly declared his work done and insisted the world needed room for new work in the field. He applied for euthanasia when he was eighty-three. I understand Richard tried in vain to persuade him to join us in his last years."

"So he and Dr. Gesar were in contact in those last days?"

"Oh, yes. Even across the distance between MIT and New Mexico they remained in contact. The two were quite close, right to the end of the elder man's life."

Michael felt slightly disappointed. He had almost hoped to discover some angry scientific falling-out that would open up a point of disagreement or skepticism about the discoveries of Dr. Gesar. It was unfortunate the two men had gotten along; it was unhelpful of the the elder scientist to die.

"What about the other members of the original team?" Michael pursued his inquiry. Dr. Eriksen had moved on to her soft dessert, a vanilla pudding she seemed to sip from the spoon. He watched the way the spoon slipped past her lips, the movement of her cheeks as she drew it in.

"Ah," she paused, bringing a napkin to her lips. "Tanya Devereuax came with him from MIT, drawn by the master's charisma, even before she finished her doctoral work. She left us a couple years back, to return to her studies, though I don't quite recall where she went. I heard she went on some spiritual journey and ended up in a convent on Iona." There might have been a hint of disdain in her voice, but Michael didn't care. Petra took another sip of pudding and wiped her mouth again. Michael watched.

"And Dr. Valeratswamani, or 'Dr. V' as we call him, is still here. His specialization is spectro-mechanics. If you want to know about how the machinery actually works—or what is wrong when it doesn't work—he's the authority." Michael made a show of noting Dr. V's name, asking Dr. Eriksen several times how to spell it, though he was confident that this particular line of inquiry would not be very helpful. The show of interest was to keep it clear to the lovely woman in front of him that his questions intended to be challenging and that he was quite consciously looking for avenues of investigation. He wanted to convey to Petra that her own perspective was not enough, and that he would not be distracted by her beauty and sexual attractiveness. She wiped her lips again.

"When did you join the team?" Michael asked her.

"I thought you already had my biographical info," Petra inserted, with her bright blue eyes lit up.

"Didn't read it," Michael lied.

Petra Eriksen sat back, as if gathering her thoughts. She still wore her lab coat, her name tag pinned above her left breast. "If you had read the material," she began with a vague hint of impatience that Michael took as playful, "you would know I joined the team only three years ago, coming from a very different street." She paused. "Or down a very different road, I should say. While most of the people working on our project are scientists converted to Dr. Gesar's vision, I was a convert pulled into the science."

"Meaning?"

Petra Eriksen breathed deeply; Michael watched her chest rise and fall. She looked at him, and he snapped his gaze up to meet her face that, for a moment, seemed girlish, as if it embarrassed her to talk about herself. "Meaning," she began, "I had had my own career in brain-chemistry research but left it years before I met Richard. I left that work out of a kind of despair, that for all the study of the brain I had pursued, I couldn't find what I was looking for. It was as if—" she just stopped.

"I have heard it said," she began again, "that people who study psychology do so because they are the ones most in need of analysis." She smiled again. "I studied the brain and found a grand, complex machine that was still, all the way to the bottom, a machine. And yet what my brain craved was something else."

"What?" Michael asked.

"Value," she replied. "A sense of my own transcendence. I had had dreams as a child of other lives, other ways of being, and I couldn't help but believe there was more to this than this." Petra ran her slim, white hands up and down her body. "This body," her hands still moved up and down, "is vital and powerful and animal and sensual." Her polysyndeton climbed in intensity. "And it is capped here," she said, indicating her head, "with nature's greatest invention. And still—I felt then and still do—that there is a great mystery in this axis, this movement, from sex to belly to head."

Michael watched her hands draw a line between her breasts to her head. Her voice seemed more like song than he had previously heard it, ringing like Daniel's voice would ring when he spoke of worship.

"So you found God?" Michael asked, intending to sound a bit demeaning.

The beautiful blond woman laughed softly. "No," she said simply. For a brief moment, Michael felt he should not have mocked, yet his flash of worry held no sense of guilt or offense. He wanted to dig at the ideas before him, yet he did not want to offend Petra Eriksen, whose autobiography had become for him a kind of sensuality.

"Oh, the old Scandinavian Lutheranism was fine for some," she finally volunteered, "and, to be honest, my work here helped me find more value there than I found on my own. But my path to spirituality could not be through something as tired as a cloud-man with commandments. I had begun with my own sexuality, and through it I found, not God, but the tantras. And from the tantras, I found Dr. Gesar. And from Dr. Gesar, I found a place for my old research." By the end of the story, she had again built a kind of rhetorical line that lifted her tone and her smile. She met Michael's eyes. "You see?" she said. "That's my story."

"And did you have sex with him?" Michael asked the question almost before he thought it. In one sense it was clearly part of the investigation, a question that might come down to issues of professional ethics and a form of harassment. But Michael's own swiftness in the asking surprised him, and with a little introspection he could have seen the connection with his own desires.

Dr. Eriksen's smile was cool, more polite than friendly. "Actually," she said softly, from a distance, "I read his book on *The Liberation of the Chakras*, and I practiced over the next year at the old Gelugpa center in Santa Fe. And I had sex with lots of people. Still," she paused and looked at Michael, her head slightly turned away. "Still, I can't help thinking that what I mean by the term and what you mean are somewhat different."

Michael found her answer funny. "You're probably right," he said, yet he realized she had not quite answered his question. Before he could repeat it, Dr. Eriksen's eyes turned to something behind him, and in the next second, they were joined at the table by a messenger. He was young and a bit rotund, his slightly fleshy face made more round by thick sideburns tumbling down his cheeks. He smiled at Petra, and Michael felt a small flutter of jealousy. Petra's cool response, though, left Michael feeling strangely reassured.

"Mark?" she said to the young man.

"Doctor," Mark began, "I was told I'd find you here. Dr. Gesar says he could meet Mr. Pryor at 2 o'clock, if you're done with him. He said that still leaves you a little time to finish what you have to do." He stopped in a short, uncomfortable silence. He kept looking at Petra. "Oh," he finally interrupted his looking, "he suggests meeting in Lab 4. You'll show Mr. Pryor the way?"

"Of course," Dr. Eriksen responded, cool and distant. "Thank you, Mark." It was a dismissal.

Dr. Petra Eriksen and Michael Pryor cleared their dishes to the recycler by the kitchen sink and left the small common area that functioned as a kind of cafeteria. "This way," Petra said as they emerged from the glass doors and turned left. Soon they passed a door on the right that said "Lab 4," which Michael's guide indicated with a nod. "There," she said, "so you can find your way."

They continued past an office on the left labeled "Archives" and down a stretch of blank hallway that brought them back to the junction where Petra had led Michael on his first visit. Michael recognized the sign that said "Private" and watched again as she activated the retinal scanner. The door's lock clicked open just as the door behind Michael also opened. Two young men walked from the Meditation Room and strode past smiling at Petra Eriksen.

"Coming through?" Petra's voice called. Michael passed again into the white, somewhat dim hallway that led to Gesar's room. Then Michael realized that the 2 p.m. meeting with Dr. Gesar was still ninety minutes away. With almost naive curiosity, he followed his hostess down the hall to one of the doors that opened on the left.

"Want to come in?" Petra offered, as she pressed her thumb to the door lock. Curiously, she suddenly seemed to Michael a bit warmer, yet Michael couldn't help feeling that she was straining to be pleasant, at least not so professional as she was to the world around her.

"Uh, sure," Michael said.

Michael passed through the doorway and set his recording tablet on the table by the door as she went on into the small living area. "Nothing here really to offer a guest," she said.

"You keep the rooms nice enough for impressing us important people without being ostentatious," he offered, trying to be friendly.

Dr. Eriksen removed her lab coat and laid it neatly across the end of the small, beige divan. Her shoulders were bare; a simple dark, thin-strapped blouse clung to her. Michael admired her. Then she came close and reached past him to push the door closed. Michael felt her closeness, and she began to unbutton his shirt. Michael's hands went to her waist and the hem of her blouse, and all qualities of the investigative reporter melted away.

* * *

The walk from the private rooms back to Lab 4 was strange. Dr. Petra Eriksen seemed strictly business once again, merely his guide through the bright hallways of the Sandia extensions, commenting only generally about what went on in each of the labs and rooms Michael might not already have seen. As they were a bit early, they stopped for a short introduction to the Archives room where the physical evidence of previous experimental evaluations was kept, along with backup electronic files of research notes collected over the years. Michael was invited—in a cool and utterly efficient way—to browse files of past research before he had to leave the next day. He was prohibited only from searching one particular file that linked personal information of all research subjects with their specific findings. "I'm sure you understand," Dr. Eriksen said matter-of-factly, "that we hold the results of our studies in confidence with respect to the name and personal data of the subject. As subjects of the study, they are only given a number, as you know, and all our statistical data refers only to numbers, never to names." She paused and then repeated, "I'm sure you understand."

What Michael didn't understand was the woman's distant coolness. She had returned to the business-like demeanor that was her natural state. Even while Michael more or less pretended to look at graphs and numbers in a few files, he wondered about her, wonder what sex meant to her. He could allow himself a bit of judgment about her oddity, that she was some-how both sensually needy and yet unable psychologically to bond. There was no opportunity, of course, to actually speak to her about such things. And Michael's speculative examinations of her were only part of his wonder because Michael was also wondering about himself. Very quick, very brief thoughts about his relationship to the beautiful stranger and to Desra appeared at the edges of his consciousness. He pushed them away or rather displaced them with thoughts about Petra's and Desra's personalities. He allowed his almost-sexist guesses to eclipse what might have been more fruitful speculations about his own moral ideals. At least here in the Sandia hallways, he wanted to look away from that mirror, feeling in that flight that he had to concentrate on whatever clues or words he might get from the woman beside him. At the same time, Michael was self-aware enough to know that questions of his own principles could not be avoided. He would get to those later, he had decided, if not quite honestly.

Outside Lab 4, Dr. Eriksen stopped. "I will leave you here," she said easily. "I believe Dr. Gesar is inside. We are a few minutes early, so if he seems busy, perhaps you might just wait until he sees you. He will keep his promise to speak with you at 2." She turned.

"Petra." Michael stopped her; he felt oddly to be without any words that didn't sound either adolescent or condescending. "Will I see you again?" he finally asked.

"Not soon, I think," she replied coolly, yet without rancor. "Some of my own work has been delayed these last few days, and I must return to it this afternoon. But I'm sure we'll see one another in the future." Michael wondered if he was supposed to try to kiss her goodbye, but she walked away.

For a full minute after she disappeared around the first corner, Michael stood silent, puzzled. He found it easy to emphasize the strangeness of the woman over her beauty and sexiness. Yet that emphasis was itself a strategy for distancing himself from responsibility. Having had sex, he wanted to step back and make it into an aberration, an oddity, an event as strange as the passionate-yet-distant woman herself. Even so, he could also feel a hint of thrill in the promise of the future she had alluded to. With better mythic images, Michael might have felt what the allure meant, something like the taste of fruit or candy that, once experienced, would be part of him forever. He might have recognized desire that is keen, even painful when barely out of reach, forgotten or disdained once fulfilled, but still there on the edges of one's mind at all times. Even in terms he did know, he might have felt something of the fear of the narcotic drug; he had no categories to consider fearing the succubus.

Yet for Michael Pryor in that moment, there was also still some honesty and the slight shadow in his mind of what he had chosen. Michael briefly felt confused about himself. Guilt whispered in his ear like the call of a savior, the only voice that could outcry the call of the siren. Desire, delight, fear, guilt, and transcendent hope barely mingled. With more time, Michael might have tried to sort them out, or see their interwovenness. He might have wondered if anyone, even God, could sort them out.

And then the door behind him slid open, and "God" appeared. "Mr. Pryor," Dr. Gesar said at once, "I hope I haven't kept you waiting."

"Er, no," Michael stuttered with an unexpected feeling of discomfort. "Not at all."

"I was just imagining you might be standing here wondering whether I really exist. I have been rather invisible during your visit."

"Actually," Michael returned, "I've had some opportunity to speak to other scientists and colleagues of yours. And Dr. Eriksen has been showing me around quite well." He thought he might blush and therefore probably did.

Michael wondered if Dr. Gesar had seen the blush, but immediately the man turned back into Lab 4, gesturing to Michael to accompany him. "I know," he was saying, "you have been doing your homework, and perhaps some of this will seem redundant, but I wanted you to see this lab and a reading in progress."

Michael had to hurry to keep pace with his host. Right at that moment, he felt less than confident about his homework, no doubt partly because so much of the information gathered in the last day or so had been quite technical, and perhaps partly because of the lingering stirrings of his moral senses. There was no time to sort through such things as he moved forward to catch up with the *tulku*.

"You may have read already," Dr. Gesar was saying as he walked, his lab coat fluttering behind him, "that the simplest method of photon generation can go back easily to x-ray characterization and the movement of electrons across energy shells. Here is where that begins." Without slacking his pace, he pointed to an array of tubes and lasers that seemed to wander down the long, stainless steel bench beside him. Here and there a technician bent over a spot, watching some dial or checking some alignment of materials. The work space had parallel benches on either side, so Michael and his host seemed to be walking down a canyon of glittering and glowing fixtures of metal and glass. There was no talking other than the *tulku's* own voice, yet he seemed to be speaking loudly over a deep, low hum that made the room feel vibrant. Ahead, at the end of the lab, was a glass wall, and beyond that a separate space that held a strange apparatus and a single, reclining chair. It reminded Michael of a dentist's office he had once visited as a child, back when doctors still had to repair teeth with foreign materials.

"Don't be intimidated by all the lights and bells," Dr. Gesar said with humor in his voice. "All this," he waved his hands at the room, "can finally be made much simpler, much more compact. But this is how we test it and refine it." He stopped at the end of the tables and looked at Michael. "You'll see."

"So what we're looking at in this room," Michael was trying to remember some of the technical language he had learned, "is for creating photons?"

"Well, yes," Dr. Gesar said, "and deciphering them. And perhaps much more, as today we shall see two very important tests, not just one."

Michael waited for an explanation.

"For you see," the man smiled with a twinkle of mirth in his eye, "I'm just not scientist enough to care about the photons as such. You should know me well enough by now, Mr. Pryor, to understand all this as merely a tool for understanding something much more interesting." Michael felt for a half second that he was supposed to know the answer to this riddle, but Dr. Gesar looked past Michael and, with an air of delight and kindness that seemed to Michael wholly genuine, said, "and here it comes now."

Through the glass came a small band of people, all but one dressed in the formal white coats of the technicians in the room. The other person was a man in his mid-thirties, hardly good looking or particularly well built, shuffling as he walked into the room. He wore something like a hospital gown; his head was shaved. He seemed uncertain or afraid, or at least nervous. Dr. Gesar waved to the man with a kind of happy movement that seemed to Michael almost boyish. The man perked up, smiled in return.

"No doubt Dr. Eriksen explained to you," Gesar was saying without looking away from the man in the glass room, "that we know our subjects by their test number. This is number 413." Dr. Gesar paused and looked over at Michael. "Actually," he said as if revealing a secret to a friend, "his name, like yours, is Michael." He turned back to watch the subject being seated in the chair, and the array of machinery being rolled up beside him. "He's a good man, I think," the *tulku* was saying, "but you might say he is no one special. He works for a merchandise distributor scanning in and phoning out orders." The man paused. "He is also lonely."

"Lonely?" Michael asked.

"Yes. We found him through an online dating service. Our ad had many responses. Michael here seemed a good, healthy test case precisely because he is, well, simply a good, common person." The *tulku* mostly kept his eyes on the subject in the glass room, occasionally nodding with silent assurances.

"But lonely," Michael repeated.

"Ah, yes, lonely." Dr. Gesar seemed to take a deep breath. "I suppose there are finer technical terms for his condition," he said, "but such descriptions would only seem to diminish the real experience of Michael himself. What can I say? He is lonely. He doesn't think of himself as special, nor does he present himself in manners that might make him seem especially attractive to friends or lovers. In our interviews, he expressed a sense of having tried to be more socially active, only to fail in ways that seemed embarrassing, even though for most of the psychological team, the events he described seemed rather common, even trivial. But Michael here—our Michael—is unhappy and wants a kind of acceptance he does not feel." Once again Richard Gesar looked over at Michael Pryor. "We want to see if we can help him."

As the *tulku* looked back to the man in the glass room, Michael himself felt strangely lonely, as if the man beside him had touched him and then gone away. Michael hurried to regain his interviewer's composure and looked for a critical question.

"Seems a rather unsanitary set up for sticking probes into someone's brain," he offered. "Your surgeons are hardly ready."

Gesar laughed lightly. "But you see we are also experimenting these days with external reading, using probes outside the skull. People are not very likely to take an aspirin if it has to be given through a hole in the cranium."

Gesar laughed at his own joke, his small eyes glittering above round cheeks that reflected the lights of the lab. It occurred to Michael that there was something wrong with the aspirin analogy. Before he could quite grasp what he wanted to ask, his host pointed him again toward the procedure before them. "Now I urge you to watch this," Dr. Gesar was saying, "not because you will actually see much going on, but just so you can describe our process in your own terms. What you see at first is simply the placement of the receptors on Michael's scalp and the directing of photon receptors around his forehead." Michael followed the narration as the actions before him played it out. The voice of Gesar was slightly lilting, as if he slipped into an Asian accent as the procedure in front of them drew him in. His descriptions, too, became lilting, as if he were describing an artistic performance.

"Now," he was saying, "the tubules over Michael's head are beginning to create a resonant field into the crown *chakra*. There, the glowing peak of Michael's soul will feel that resonance, attempt to sing along, as it were, or to dance with the dancer it meets. The steps, however, may or may not match, as when the masterful dancer and the novice meet. Then the steps of the one will have to conform to the other, primarily the teacher to the student, so that the dance may proceed. But some day, it shall be the student who conforms to the step of the teacher, that the dance may be a dance indeed."

Michael almost felt he could see that dance, as the other Michael closed his eyes and settled back into his chair. The attendants meanwhile seemed in unison to step back a single pace, as if they were guests at the performance. Yet no music came through the glass.

"More prosaically," Dr. Gesar continued, "the input field will descend to resonate with the ambient field, dropping electrons into any lower field, thereby producing photonic energy. The song, in other words, moves to harmonize with the melody it finds, and in the harmonization we read the divergence of notes. Those changes appear, then, as a color in the photonic spectrum." Dr. Gesar fell silent, exhaled audibly, as if he'd been holding his breath. Michael saw him staring, as if entranced, into the room where the other Michael sat quietly. To Michael Pryor, it seemed almost a look of love.

"But I'm sorry," Gesar then said, turning to face Michael, "I seem to have mixed my metaphors horribly. Of course this is a scientific experiment with measurable and reapeatable results. There is no dance or music."

"Yet music is itself often quite mathematical, isn't it?" Michael found himself asking.

"Indeed it is," Gesar smiled up at him. "Indeed it is. 'The music of the spheres' the ancient cosmologists used to call it, talking about how nature itself exhibits beauty in the orderliness of God's creation." He smiled back at the other Michael. "Perhaps then we have seen the science of music after all." As if interrupting himself, Gesar inserted, "And here is the music."

Below the pane of glass that separated Michael from the room before him, a small panel came to life. The small screen glittered with the subject number and an array of numerical readouts in florescent green, alongside a small patch of color about five centimeters square. The square was a soft blue.

"Here is Michael's soul, Mr. Pryor," Gesar began to explain. "A some-what troubled soul, at that. It is imprecise, but the blue color corresponds quite well with what Michael has told us of his own disquiet and loneliness, his lack of consolation and companionship, whether human or spiritual. This Michael has few friends and no God. We predicted from his own statements a blue color, perhaps on the order of 500 nanometers wavelength. This is 515."

Michael found himself mesmerized by the soft blue glow. If it was a soul, it was alive, and its shimmer, its vibration, was not merely an effect of machinery. Yet in the next moment, Michael felt a surge of indignation at his own credulity. What was the question he had to ask? Michael struggled to regain his sense of analysis and critique. It was strange to him how difficult it was to find distance, find the right question. For help he recalled some of the arguments of Dr. Wacker.

"But wait," he inserted to give himself time. "You tell me I see here the dancing of Michael's soul. Fine. But what—or who—is actually dancing?" Michael paused again, calling up an air of criticism. "Perhaps it is music, but there's a lot of difference between the song of the wind, the song of a bird, and the song of Beethoven. Surely if we're looking at something physically measured, then we're looking at a physical phenomenon, not a soul or a spirit or a ghost. Or if we're truly talking about ghosts, what can it mean to measure it with colors and numbers?" He felt a surge of strength as hints of argument came back to him. "Are we really looking at something in the soul of a man or at the electrical impulses of a machine?"

Gesar for a moment remained silent, perhaps because there was a small flurry of activity in the glass room, as attendants moved to work on the subject, pulling back from "Michael" the shining arrays that had come down across his forehead. But Michael Pryor fastened upon his own resolution to engage Gesar and turned to him. "If we are talking about the brain, then surely we are just measuring something like the wind. If it's a soul, how does it have measurable energy? The lights in the ceiling have photonic energy; do they also have a soul?"

Gesar looked at Michael with a smile that seemed intrigued. "That is a fine question," he said softly. "Rather Cartesian." Michael felt immediately a sense that he had heard a dismissive critique, even though he was not entirely sure what it meant. Was it like a Thomist? Michael felt himself hesitate in the silent pause, trying to remember if he had previously revealed the source of this argument, mentioned explicitly the visit with the "crazy Thomist." But he said nothing, perhaps embarrassed to use arguments that were not his own or perhaps hesitating out of fear, a strange paranoia, as if he were a reporter being specifically quizzed about his official sources. Or perhaps he felt that, in fact, he didn't really understand these ideas—Cartesian or Thomist—and that confessing ignorance would leave him exposed.

"We measure an energy," Dr. Gesar started again, "but not the kind we might expect. We must broaden our definitions, Mr. Pryor, and learn to see what has yet to be revealed. Before Galileo brought forth his telescope and pointed it to the moons of Jupiter, no one could imagine seeing those bodies in their evident orbits. But once he had the instrument, he could point it heavenward and see for himself. Moreover, he could then hand his telescope to anyone and let them see as well." He chuckled softly. "How perverse might someone be," Dr. Gesar said to Michael without looking at him, "if someone were to disbelieve in Jovian moons and simply refuse to use the telescope offered him?"

Michael felt both challenged and annoyed. He felt the ambiguity of the *tulku's* words like a call to personal faith, an invitation like others he had heard that seemed at once to call a person to hopeful love and to criticize him for resistance. Michael felt his hackles rise.

"And are we then just supposed to trust anyone who claims to be Galileo?" he asked. "How do we know for sure the moons of Jupiter are there, around Jupiter, and not painted on the end of the lens?"

"Oh, look!" Gesar suddenly said excitedly, and for the instant Michael heard it like a command. But Gesar was pointing into the glass room, at the other Michael. "I told you, Mr. Pryor, that we had two tests being run today. Here comes the second."

To Michael, it seemed hardly different from the first, as another array of tubes and silver bars were arranged around the subject's face. Yes, the array was slightly different from the first, but to Michael's untrained eye, there was no clear evidence of why or how.

The attendants bustled around the other Michael, moving electrical leads to new machines. There was also an odd change in the chair itself, as the subject leaned forward and a long pad, lined with wires like a many-tentacled sea creature, was slid in behind his back. Michael heard no sound until again the technicians stepped back in unison to watch the dance. Michael had to ask what was happening.

"Ah, yes, Mr. Pryor," Gesar began, as if realizing Michael was there. "We have seen Michael's soul. Yes, very good. But to know Michael is not yet to love him, is it? Or might we say, to love him is not yet to have compassion. And it is above all both wisdom and compassion that we must cultivate, not in tandem, but in unison."

"I have no idea what you mean," Michael confessed with a slight disdain in his voice.

"Of course," Gesar responded. "The language of compassion and wisdom is my language, I suppose, and not yours. But we understand, don't we? We understand that our subject number 413 is not merely something to study, but someone to help. We shall see in a moment or two if we can both know and help our dear 413."

Michael felt driven to quiet by the *tulku's* soft intensity. Once again machinery around them hummed, and the Michael behind the glass sat back quietly. Again a minute passed in a palpable tension of expectation;

perhaps that other Michael shuddered, shivered slightly, but made no noise Michael Pryor could discern. Then Dr. Gesar nodded and smiled in the translucent reflection Michael could see in the glass. The machinery was withdrawn, and all the wires removed from the subject's head. Liberated, the experimental Michael behind the glass sat up, as if from a brief, quiet sleep.

"You see, Mr. Pryor," Dr. Gesar spoke into the quiet, "we have hoped that resonance works both ways. We can see how the decaying electrons produce photons for us to measure, but might we also see if the lower energy level can be moved, or enticed, or invited to partake of the higher. What if, Mr. Pryor, what if the sad and silent soul can be helped toward God?"

At once Michael found the phrasing both troubling and puzzling. Before he could clarify his own thoughts, Gesar nodded to the panel below the window. There again were the luminous numbers and the softly colored box. The box was now a slightly deeper shade of green and the number indicated with nanometer units read 558.

Suddenly, for the first time since Michael had entered Lab 4, there was a murmur of voices around the room as the few technicians saw their own readouts and seemed happy with the results. One voice softly said, "Congratulations, Dr. Gesar."

Michael looked at Gesar for explanation, but the man was still looking into the glass room, watching the other Michael becoming free. He smiled and waved slightly at the man, and Michael almost got the impression the scientist was going to cry. But he kept smiling and watched Number 413 leave the room before turning to the Michael beside him.

"This is a good day," he said. "A good day. The numbers are perhaps not all we might want, but they are a good indication for a good day."

Michael looked into the man's round and happy face and felt an odd happiness of his own, as if he had heard an innocent, contagious laugh. His eyes asked for explanation.

"What is science, Mr. Pryor?" Dr. Gesar asked rhetorically. "It is uncovering. It is seeing what we have not yet seen. And what is technology? It is learning to use science in a way that moves the world, changing reality through our applied knowledge. And what is compassion? It is the turning of knowledge and technology to the benefit of the human condition, to the alleviation of the suffering inherent in our nature. It has ever been the goal of religion to ease sorrow, to call the spirit toward a higher light. So it is the compassion of religion that is the key that will unlock science and technology and open for us a door of spiritual health. We have here the beginning of a hope for a medicine that will cure the human soul. God is within us all, Mr. Pryor, but locked away, shut behind our own cares and worries, our reasons and calculations. Desire and delusion beget themselves in an endless and tragic play, while only a few, those mystics of discipline and insight, have managed to cultivate the liberating divinity that is our true essence. They, Mr. Pryor, the mystical, spiritual geniuses of all the ages and all the religions of the world, have pointed us toward that divinity and found dozens, even hundreds of ways to bring us there, one by one, step by step. But it is a slow and demanding walk, a narrow way, and few there are who find it. But having seen it, having pointed to it like a star in the sky or like a moon of Jupiter, they have promised us all that it can indeed be found, that it waits for us within our own selves. The great spiritual masters of the world have pointed toward a day like today, when we can begin to offer the wholeness of divine life to every human soul."

The *tulku* sighed again, smiling at Michael. "Of course," he said with a kind of happy, but deliberate calmness, "I should be speaking like a good scientist, with restraint and uncertainty. These results must be verified. They must be repeated. How many times was cold fusion declared a reality before it was truly a technology? We must be sure before we make promises. But can we also speak like poets and dreamers? Might we be forgiven for singing a brief song of hope, a song that describes, however unclearly, a coming Day of the Lord, that *olam ha-ba*, the *satya-yuga*, the day when the grass itself is enlightened?

"Peace, Mr. Pryor." Gesar met Michael's gaze. "Peace of mind for any who will find it. And with peace of mind, the end perhaps of rancor and disputes among those who suffer desire and delusion. Peace of mind, Mr. Pryor, and peace on earth. Peace on earth and goodwill to all."

The *tulku* turned back to look at the empty room before them, and Michael instinctively followed his gaze. "Look, Mr. Pryor," God said, "the chair is empty and inviting."

16

PEACE OF MIND

Michael Pryor was happy with himself. Two days after his interviews at Sandia, he was back home and had pounded out one of the better articles of his career. It was clever and critical, he thought, almost heavy handed in the use of quotations and assertions of the ideals of Dr. Richard Gesar, all carefully led by "he says" and "he claims." He had carefully read some classical discussions of mind/body dualism—he had learned why Gesar called him Cartesian—and he had insisted that critical, philosophical minds still required convincing. At the same time, he had given the science its proper place, offering the imprecise and puzzled endorsements of Gesar as he had heard them from the scientific community, making it clear that those endorsements, "if we should call them such," were "hesitant."

He considered his article fair and positive. Michael had described carefully the experiments on "Michael" as he had witnessed them, and he was careful to make his descriptions of the apparatus in Lab 4 somewhat confused and embellished. "If Gesar believes the mechanics of the project can be miniaturized," he had written, "it will need to be done with tremendous technical care and will in itself require another technological miracle." Indeed, Michael had somewhat overused the word *miracle* he thought, but had smiled to himself in its use, hearing himself scoffing the word rather than suggesting real amazement. "If Gesar truly believes there will be peace on earth," he had written, "it will take more miracles than we have seen so far."

Michael had said nothing in his article about Petra Eriksen, except to mention her obliquely, along with others of Richard Gesar's staff. He noted their almost slavish devotion to their "god," and the way they seemed to step away as he walked by, as if they were not worthy to be in his presence. Michael could hint, in that context, that if there were any falsification of data in the extensive number of ongoing experiments, we would never know it, as the entire body of followers seemed a mix of scientific precision and careless credulity. He had allowed himself to comment unkindly on the "faith of subject 413," who would place his happiness and wholeness into the hands of "angels in lab coats," when "a good meal and a little human companionship would have done as much."

Michael's general satisfaction, however, could not entirely hide a lingering feeling of deception, perhaps a hint of fear, as if he had a secret that could betray him. It might have been rooted in his transient fling with Petra Eriksen, but that was an idea he could dismiss too easily. Sex, at least in his own conscience, had long been made an amoral issue. If there were any concern about betraying his commitment to Desra, that had been weakened by the growing feeling of coldness between them. She had become more distant, staying away from home, barely talking to him when she was there. She had asked nothing at all about his new interviews, and the selective bits of information he had offered—with characteristic scorn and disbelief—had been met with shrugs and barely polite excuses for having to leave him home alone. Again. And it wasn't as if Michael were having an affair with Dr. Eriksen.

Or was he? There was something nagging Michael about his sexual activity, and yet he knew it shouldn't. Sex, after all—as Michael had insisted more than once to himself and to amiable company—was something like playing tennis. No one really cares whom you play tennis with, though for a time one might decide to practice in strict company. It simply is not a moral issue. "What if you want to play doubles?" Desra had interjected in one of those conversations. Everyone had laughed. Michael, too, had laughed, although he had never "played doubles," nor was he particularly comfortable with the idea. Yet his own analogy spoke against his discomfort, as it spoke against his nagging sense of guilt. He wondered for a moment if the guilt was Marta's fault.

Marta was at that moment walking beside him in the afternoon sun. The lakeside path through the Harrisburg Forest Preserve was relatively quiet, and they were on their second circle around the water. With his work behind him and a sunny day ahead, and with Desra distant and Petra a spectre, he had called Marta and invited her out. The walk had been her idea.

"What made him so interesting was his bizarre notion that people should *not* love God," she was saying, "and once I figured out what he meant, it made a lot of sense." She had been talking about "Professor Wacky," telling Michael how she had met the man and come to discover what she called his crazed insight. "In the end," she added, "it helped me understand how to be Christian and how not to be."

Michael had already told Marta almost every detail of his own meeting with Wacker, and she had laughed through much of it. Before that, they had talked about the science fiction book she had sent him. He had admitted not finishing it, although he had felt an interesting desire to lie. Yet a strange respect for Marta had intervened, and he had confessed where, in the midst of a chapter on the official legislations that prohibited meddling with the past, he had lost interest. She had acknowledged the tiresomeness of that part of the book and then proceeded to tell the rest of the story, entirely giving away the ending. He had found her innocent carelessness entertaining.

"There was something in Wacker's ideas," she was going on to say, "that he called cultivated madness, something that made it easier to claim a strictness of character that includes a resistance to normality. I've never forgotten it. It was liberating."

Marta felt she had been chattering through most of the walk, some of it sheer blather and nonsense. She was strangely nervous around Michael, and she knew that he could see it, too. And that made her more nervous. She wished he would find some long speech to give and let her rest. Her wish made her smile inwardly at her own girlish feelings.

"I can sympathize with the desire for resistance," he said, as if answering her need. "I guess I've always felt a certain disdain for conformity and normality." Michael found himself wanting to tell her about the scar on his lip and his smiles that became sneers.

"But resistance needs reasons," Marta said into his brief pause, still unable to bear too much silence. She let a habit of philosophical argument come to her rescue. "The point about Wacker's notion of cultivated madness is that the cultivation is what makes the madness possible. 'Cultivation' here," her fingers put quotation marks around the word, "doesn't refer to the madness. One does not cultivate madness for the sake of madness. Cultivation refers to the character of the madman. And here's where Wacker's Thomism comes in. In any good Virtue Theory of Ethics, one is supposed to cultivate character based on adherence to ideals. Given such character, one can depend on principle, and with principle, one is free to be wild and to resist any conformity that principle does not demand." She paused for her conclusion. "Resistance without principle is adolescent," she said.

Michael acknowledged her argument with a mocking nod. "Impressive point, Dr. Sanchez," he said. "I see what you mean. Is that last line a quote from Professor Wacker?"

"No, it's a quote from me. Pretty poetic, ain't it?"

"I'll quote you in my next article," Michael said.

"Just get my name right," she responded.

They paused. Marta held herself back from nervous chatter. She knew she had to shut up, yet she was afraid to. Michael was less aware of the tumult in her heart than she thought. His reticence was due largely to an odd combination of thoughtful listening and peaceful enjoyment. It was his job to listen and to analyze, and he was finding he enjoyed hearing Marta speak. He knew he was avoiding thoughts of his other women, yet avoiding those thoughts was also peaceful. He might have thought that, one day, he could sit down quietly and think through the lines he had to draw between love and lust, between self-control and faithfulness. He had the mind and heart capable of the struggle, but as yet he could not take it on, could not yet imagine that it would end in failure. In his peaceful listening, he vaguely knew he was hiding from the tougher discussion and was not yet able to consider the struggle of the moral soul and its failure as the call of grace. So he was quiet.

"How is your next article going?" Marta finally spoke.

"Well," Michael said, "I finished my last piece about 'god.'" This time he put the quotation marks into the sentence, partly because he felt he had to, for Marta.

"Tell me about that." Marta looked up at him with an honest curiosity. "I'm interested in these things, you know."

Michael knew she was; yet he didn't quite know why. In his still-confused hope and sense of desire, he instantly made the barely conscious decision to tell her all he could about Dr. Gesar and his experiments. He could even make it sound better than he had written it, like there was the possibility of peace, maybe both "on earth" and in his own heathen soul. Much to Marta's relief, Michael spoke rather fluently about the science he understood—or could at least restate—and the hopes for reading and helping those whose souls are troubled. He did his best to hint that "even skeptics" might find room in their world view for deeper awakening and that there could perhaps follow some "resonance" that might make love possible. The long story was overtly focused on Dr. Gesar and his labs, but hiding inside the story was a vague hint about himself and the possibility of knowing a different kind of woman.

Marta said little. At first, she was just relieved not to be speaking. Then she fell naturally into her analytical self, reacting at points with simple interjections, giving voice at other points to more elaborate thoughts. "Really?" she said here. "You were satisfied with the evidence?" she asked there.

Michael let the story flow to its end. Where he had been critical and doubtful, he let his voice carry that critique; where he had found himself strangely hopeful, he allowed himself, with Marta, to let that come through as well. Somehow, by this lake, he felt both skepticism and hope might be natural to him. When the story ended, he wagged his head a little to suggest ambiguity. "So there is god's promise to the world," he said, "and maybe it will amount to something." He looked over at Marta. "And maybe not," he added.

Marta was nodding slightly, not in agreement but in evident thought. "Well," she said after a little pause, "let's hope not."

Michael was surprised. "What do you mean?"

"Well," she began, "we've come full circle, haven't we?"

Michael looked up and noted that they had in fact made their way back to the gate building where phone booths allowed entrance to the Preserve, with the payment of the appropriate fee.

"Not full circle around the lake, you buffoon!" Marta laughed. "We're back to talking about resistance. Don't you remember my earlier brilliant argument?"

"'Resistance without principle is adolescent,'" Michael quoted with his own pretense of seriousness.

"The point was that there have to be standards," Martha said. "Cultivation is required to make the madness possible. Otherwise, it's just madness."

"I still don't know what you mean." Michael could see she was quite serious.

Thoughts ran through Marta's mind, analyses she followed intuitively. That seriousness was the feeling within the ideas, an emotion that captured the importance of the issue. There were, for her, times like these when the feeling and the idea were natural comrades, somehow complementary aspects of her whole life that made sense of the world. Yet she was lonely and she knew it. For a second she knew that this kind of seriousness had deprived her of friends and the potential of love. It was threat within honesty, and there the wholeness broke. Desire and idea clashed. This, too, for her was common, intuitive, but difficult. It meant decision. She decided to insist on truth over peace.

"Rebellion without principle is adolescent, Michael Pryor," she said, her dark eyes intent on Michael's, "because we justify our rebellion only by having a place to stand. Without a place to stand, there is no reason to rebel. No reason to conform, for that matter. Why do you think I can be Catholic, arguably one of the most conformist institutions in history? It's because I know why I rebel and therefore I know why I conform."

Michael waited. It was clear to him that she wasn't done.

"In the same way," she continued, "if your *god*," she seemed to spit the word, "is going to measure and even heal our spirituality, it can only be because he knows what spirituality ought to be. How does he know what spirituality ought to be, Mr. Pryor?"

Michael was stopped. He felt the question enter him—the question he had almost felt back in Lab 4. How had he not asked that question? At once he saw that she was right, and yet, at the same time, his own argumentative tenacity could not quite give in.

Michael let himself sneer. "Surely he understands peace of mind, the presence of God, whatever you call it. Of all people, Miss Sanchez, I would have thought that you would find some sympathy with the idea." He sounded accusative.

"Ha!" she yelled in response, throwing her head back, her hair flying around her. "Sympathy with an idea? Are you even listening to what you're saying? The sympathy and the idea are two very different things. You need to decide which one you're listening to."

Michael couldn't help but smile. "Damn!" he thought, watching the fire in Marta's eyes and catching the nuance of her thought. He caught the harshness of Professor Wacker yet with its own softness and beauty he somehow loved.

Marta saw his softening from confrontation to puzzlement, maybe vulnerability. With his change, she too was changed. Suddenly she was self-conscious.

"Listen, Mr. Pryor," she said, her voice and eyes almost playful, "I'm not preaching asceticism or even celibacy." She paused involuntarily. She hadn't quite meant to go to that idea, but there it was. She began to walk again. "I'm not saying that our ideas and our desires are enemies," she said as he kept pace with her. "I'm Catholic, but I'm not a nun." She smiled at the ground, hearing the same words she had spoken to Helen. "But we do have to be thoughtful about what we like, about our peace and happiness. Otherwise," she paused again, almost afraid of what she had to say, but too honest not to say it, "otherwise we are victims of every delight, taken by warm smiles and nibbled ear lobes. We must know why we delight and what we desire and if our desires are the right kind. And that includes the spiritual peace of your god." Marta knew it also included her own desire for love, even love for a man she really shouldn't love.

He touched her arm, stopping her. Michael felt an odd mixture of anger and fascination. How did she know? How did she see through him? It was like revelation to think of his questions for Gesar, his affair—so it was after all "an affair"—with Petra, and even his disregard for his brother's religion as all part of a single piece of cloth. It was all sewn together somehow, and Marta had tugged a thread. He could not know the way her words tugged at threads in her own heart, hurt and helped as she said them like a confession. Yet her vulnerability somehow came through to him like an epiphany, dispelling momentarily his need for self-assurance and self-defense. He wanted to look at Marta's eyes and to confess something—something about Petra, about Desra, about Marta herself.

"Miss Sanchez," he said, looking at her with a smile of innocence he almost couldn't stop. "You are an amazing woman." He stopped before the truth and didn't know why. Then he said, "You see this scar." He pointed to his lip. "I've had this scar since I was six," he said, "when my brother and I were foolishly playing sword fight with real kitchen knives. No, don't laugh at our stupidity. We were dumb kids."

He continued. "The point is, I could have it fixed, made good as new, even better. But I haven't done it. And I won't. Because for these twenty-some years I have used it to confuse people. I smile, but I also don't. I like people, but I also threaten them. At times I've been a little unhappy about it." Was this the confession? Having no experience with the experience, Michael couldn't tell: it wasn't, and yet it was. He forced himself to go on. "But then I grew to say, 'To hell with them. Let 'em squirm.' So I smile, and people don't know if I'm smiling, and I just let people be uncomfortable with me because I'm uncomfortable with them."

He stopped. Marta's brow was creased, her eyes bright. "And what has this got to do with anything, Mr. Pryor?" she asked, sounding almost happy.

"I have no idea," he said, and they both laughed. "But I'll tell you this, Miss Sanchez," he went on with an unaccustomed feeling of lightness, "I will think over what you say. I may not agree with you in the end, but I will think things over. And some day—"

Marta shushed him by placing a finger on the scar on his lip. She had not meant it to be sensual, but it was, and she felt it meant more than she had intended. "Mr. Pryor, people may not be able to tell if you're smiling or not because they are looking at your lips. They could tell if they'd look at your eyes. I've been able to tell."

He smiled, eyes and lips. "I believe you truly can, Miss Sanchez," he said. Without thought or plan, he asked, "Can I kiss you, Miss Sanchez?"

"Don't be ridiculous!" She laughed and turned as if to walk on. "But you may hold my hand all the way to the phone booths," she said politely.

"I'll take it," Michael replied, and he did.

17

REVISIONS

Michael was watching the news. Lyle Littleton, whom Michael considered one of the better video newsmen, was reporting from Riyadh, standing for his face shot in front of the Farm Palace where, for the first time in a decade, talks were to commence between the Faisali and Abdullahi factions. There would not be a great deal of interest in the report, Michael knew, as the lingering power of the Saudi family in Arabia had, since the death of oil, been focused more on maintenance of past glories than on world-changing policy decisions. Even for Michael there wouldn't be much reason to focus on the rivalries among the Saud family factions. No, this report, like those on other channels, wasn't so much about the Saudis as about Dr. Richard Gesar.

Dr. Gesar, the peacemaker, had been part of the story since Michael had first heard of the man. But this time the issues were religious as well as political. Forever, it seemed to Michael, the legitimacy of the House of Saud has been dependent not only on political might but also on religious orthodoxy. As the third and fourth generations of kings in Arabia fell from world power into personal bickering, that did not change. Each faction's power rested, at least partially, on being able to convince a chaotic array of clans and zealots that it would support Wahabi orthodoxy as well as Arab sovereignty. So, as the children and grandchildren of greater kings spent the dwindling resources of ancient oil money on military might and personal finery, they accused one another of heresy or apostasy until it came down to a series of challenges of spiritual purity. And how better to measure spiritual purity these days than to speak with Dr. Richard Gesar?

It did not bother Michael that he was not reporting on these events himself. This was fanfare, the kind of reporting done with thirteen-second shots in front of famous buildings—like the Farm Palace—and then one minute and seventeen seconds of clips shot by someone else. There would be no probing of ideas, no critique of speeches. That would come later, and that kind of reporting job would be open to Michael.

Michael also didn't need to be in Riyadh because he had already done more for this story than any of the Lyle Littletons of video news could imagine. It had only been two weeks since his article had aired, and at first there had been little reception. But then came the invitations to Dr. Gesar, asking him to visit, asking for spiritual advice, consenting to be studied. Readers were responding to Michael's article and seeking to be included. This would not have been surprising if the requests had come from the usual collage of happy Christians, religious spiritualists, and shamanic wannabes that Michael so easily associated with religion in America. Instead, within a few days of his publication major religious figures—a known American Catholic bishop, a politically engaged French Buddhist, a widely published Native American elder—asked to be studied by Dr. Gesar. Downloads of Michael's article skyrocketed and news reports of the *tulku* making trips here and there began to appear. The news of the spiritual advisor trips and the downloads of Michael's writing went ahead in tandem. His editor, Melanie, was ecstatic.

The first national leader to call had been James Nmboko, the congenial and generally admired interim leader of the Republic of Congo. Then came a handful of British MPs, perhaps trying to satisfy what seemed to Michael the laughable clamour of noisy neo-pagans. Then it was the fiery, strangely political Buddhist monk of Myanmar, the Venerable Anandatamana, who had Dr. Gesar visit him, along with a small attachment of technicians and boxes of equipment. In each case, the leaders were consenting to the auroscopic tests in order to prove to a skeptical populace their devotion to spiritual ideals. They were willing, it seemed, even to be changed in the process. Whatever their auroscopic color might have been when they started, by the time Dr. Gesar left, there was a general sense that each leader had a somewhat gentler public image, moved, it seemed, to soften his voice and offer peace to opponents.

In all these cases, Dr. Gesar had himself been interviewed, but only in passing. In every case, he spoke little of his own work and discoveries but spoke instead—rather effusively, it seemed to Michael—of the leaders and their spirituality. He spoke with hope of people becoming more at peace with themselves and therefore more at peace with the world around them. He spoke of them as pioneers in the discovery of a new world of spiritual wholeness and draped them with saffron scarves that represented spiritual initiations into higher levels of awareness. Whether it was through the photonic resonance of his technology or through the effects of his own wise counsel, every leader he had met for the last two weeks had come to regard Dr. Gesar as a personal guru and to regard his role in politics as one of spiritual mentor. At no time had Dr. Gesar himself said anything about what actually had taken place that made a difference.

With the Saudi situation, Michael felt he might be watching for the first time the direct process of spiritual peacemaking. Of course even here there was, on one level, simply the need of a political leader to show followers that he was, after all, a good person. Certainly each Saudi prince would only benefit by being proven a good Muslim in the depth of his soul. But in this case the two most powerful contenders had even agreed to let the spiritual truth arbitrate their political differences. In a corner of the world locked in petty war, the better man would win, and Dr. Gesar's technology would determine who was the better man.

"Better by what standard?" Michael asked aloud.

But soon it became evident that the standard didn't matter, not even to Michael. As Lyle Littleton cut to the live feed, Michael watched the two Saudi contenders emerge from the Farm Palace entrance, smiling. Places had been marked for them in front of the massive pillars that supported the front rotunda of the restored palace. They stopped, and as they spoke, the TV's male-voice translator gave Michael the English with smooth and fluid intonation. Mirza Salman ibn Saud spoke first.

"My brother," he said, gesturing to the man on his left, "and I have come today to announce peace between us. We have been guided to this decision by spiritual wisdom and the example of the Prophet, peace be upon him. For we have found in one another a dedication to peace and purity, recognized now, as we have both seen, as something we both crave. I confess to you all that, at first, upon seeing the depth of my brother's soul, I could not help but be skeptical and even angry. For I knew his zeal well enough, but it had always seemed to me a danger, rather than a spiritual reality. But later, when I had been awakened to my own soul, I could suddenly see his heart for Allah with my own. Therefore," he stopped and smiled at his newly-anointed brother, "I have no longer any dispute with Abdul Sayed ibn Saud. I say to you among our followers, who likewise seek to emulate the Prophet, peace be upon him, and to bring glory to Allah, you should likewise seek unity." The English translation continued over the muted gutterals of Arabic, noting that the details of shared government had not been clarified, but, thanks to their experiences of the past days, the two men were, resolved to work together, "*Inshallah.*"

As if on cue, Mirza Salman stepped back and his cousin, Abdul Sayed, stepped forward. His voice, higher in pitch, was matched by the translation software as Michael listened. "What we have seen in these days," he was saying, "is the brotherhood of our shared faith and the devotion of our individual souls. I have seen in my dear cousin the spiritual strength of Al Ghazali, whom I have always admired. Indeed, for the first time I have even seen in myself the possibility of a deeper, more peaceful submission to Allah." The man paused as if overcome with emotion; one might have expected tears in his eyes. "When I found my own contemplative soul," he said even more softly, the machine translation softening in echo, "I could feel that peace at the heart of Islam. Having found peace in ourselves, we emerge with a peaceful understanding each of the other. How can we disagree when Allah alone is Allah?" Here, too, there was more expostulation, more idealization of peace and unity, until Lyle Littleton's voice came back over the continuing Arabic. Dr. Richard Gesar did not appear in the ongoing report. He didn't need to.

Michael called up another screen on the wall and told it to fetch pictures of Mirza Salman and Abdul Sayed. At once Michael could detect the changes: set and hardened faces had been changed into a softness that seemed out of place. If Michael didn't already know what had happened, he might have believed the men had been exchanged for imposters. But Michael knew: these angry rivals bent on war had been changed into men of peace The *tulku* had done it.

Michael said, "Back," and his wall returned to the news report from Riyadh where Lyle Littleton was delivering a monologue. "So perhaps there will after all be a peaceful settlement to the brewing civil war among the Saudis," he was saying, "and it seems to have been the work of Dr. Richard Gesar. We had been promised miracles," he said with a smile, "and this appears to be one of them. This is Lyle Littleton, Riyadh, Saudi Arabia."

Michael recognized the reference to his own words. "It wasn't a promise!" he said to Lyle Littleton on his wall. "It was sarcasm." It was ridiculous, he thought, that an intelligent man like Lyle didn't realize his reference to miracles did not mean an appeal to God but just that something was impossible. OK, there's the "miracle of birth," he thought, and all that metaphor of wonder. But how could people think he, Michael Pryor, had meant that Gesar really was, in any way, performing miracles? It was almost funny. And then, suddenly, it wasn't funny.

"Richard Gesar," Michael said to the wall. "News."

Immediately onto the wall there flashed up a scroll of more programs like that of Lyle Littleton's. News agencies and TV networks apparently had been feeding material from Riyadh, though most of them, like Littleton's said, "Just ended." But as those scrolled away, a few listed at the top of the wall showed programs still going on—USNews, BBC. Then, at the top of the listing, there appeared a video article from *MN Magazine*, "Gesar's Arabian Conquest." Always such hyped nonsense from Murdoch, Michael thought, but he'd look at it anyway. Before he could call down the file, another appeared: "Gesar Successful in Arabian Peace Plan." This was *The London Times*, and it seemed clearly less extravagant in tone than Murdoch; yet even with *The Times*, it was Gesar and not the Saudis themselves who took the focus of the headline. Michael started to call out the download of *The Times* article when another headline appeared, and then another. Suddenly his wall screen was scrolling downward like a cataract as articles and video clips came online. Many were sloppy news agencies, even personal reports by people unknown but to themselves and whose opinions were probably equally important only to themselves. But flowing with the waterfall of news reports were major presenters: BBC-US, MSNBC-US, *Newsweek*, *Seattle Post*. Michael knew these reporters' names; many were reputable, some even with referenced sources.

"References," Michael called to the wall. The scrolling was replaced by a relatively stable list. There were only a handful of writers and reporters who would note their sources. Why bother when almost no one cared to look for them? Yet still there were some who wanted to list their sources. Not that these, Michael humphed, were the nobler, more honest writers. Rather they were, for the most part, those who listed sources because they hoped that someone else would list them as well.

"Reference Pryor," Michael called, and at once, under each of the news programs listed was his own name. One by one, he called them out, and soon it became all too clear that Michael had somehow become practically and inadvertently a disciple of the *tulku*. One piece, perhaps the most glaring, referred to "what Michael Pryor called Dr. Gesar's miraculous work." Others, too, made reference to "miracles," or played up allusions in Michael's work to angels and divinity. Every one of the articles and transcripts he expanded was effusive about Gesar's work and made it into "works of God." The worst perhaps was one that called the work of Gesar divine "as Michael Pryor predicted."

Michael was livid. He had predicted nothing, certainly not miracles. For fifteen minutes he fumed and cursed at "a world gone mad." It was a world of the ignorant, a world of thoughtless readers, or rather of no readers at all, who could not understand the difference between the amazing or remarkable and the truly impossible and nonsensical. It was a world for which the word *incredible*, like the word *miracle*, had ceased to be a challenge and had become high praise.

"Miracles indeed!" Michael said aloud. It would take a miracle to get people to read thoughtfully. Michael felt with some satisfaction his own disdain for a mass audience that was, in fact, the source of his own success. That irony tugged at Michael for only a moment. He liked disdain. It had always been for him a form of self-defense, and as he had learned to think and to write, he had found his disdain repeatedly justified. In this case it was again true: people really are fools; they really do willfully misunderstand and allow habits of self-indulgence to make them see and hear only what they already believe. Michael humphed in disgust, condemning, as much from arrogance as honesty, a world that could not hear him speak the truth.

Yet there was a pause in his inner tirade, a reward perhaps granted to him for having practiced some insistence on seeking unpleasant truth. Had he actually been practicing that search as much as he thought he had, he might have responded to the call to turn his disdain inward, might have seen that judgments and self-defense were themselves another kind of spiritual self-indulgence. The hint did occur to him softly, like the brush of a feather; he almost allowed himself to see how the subtler evils of self-love slide so invisibly from the good and honest assessment of a genuine virtue to the aggrandizement of oneself and the belittling of others. Had Michael been as honest as he thought he was, he might have faced this revelation as an opportunity for guilt, perhaps even gratitude. But Michael could not yet be thankful, for he had no one but himself to thank.

Although he didn't know it yet, there were ghosts of love in Michael Pryor, visiting spirits that could make even his arrogant honesty into something salvific. Almost by accident, and not wholly with kindness, he thought of his brother. "If anybody should believe in the *tulku's* miracles," he thought, "it would be Daniel." At once Michael knew his sarcastic thought was untrue, and he felt for a second time that strange, subtle intrusion of the possibility of guilt and gratitude. Of all people—and the realization surprised Michael slightly—Daniel would see his laser repairs as a matter of science and miracles as a matter of God. How strange, he thought, that his brother, Daniel, given his Christian assumptions, would deny Gesar his "miracles," presumably because God alone does miracles. No, Daniel—and with him, probably, his wife, Helen, and the remarkable Ms. Sanchez—would not accept the "miracles" of Richard Gesar. "How remarkable!" Michael said aloud as his conclusion came to him. The fools on the TV screens believe in miracles not because they believe in God, but because they don't.

With this almost peaceful thought, Michael returned his attention to the news wall. He read for ideas and what to do about them. And then he did make a prediction, not about miracles or the Dr. Richard Gesar *Tulku* at all, but about the next news trend. It would be an interview, a direct interview with the Saudi princes or with Richard Gesar himself. It would be an interview by someone important, a recognized face, someone trusted and attractive.

"News specials. Tonight. Richard Gesar," Michael called at the wall, and the display changed instantly. At the top of the list was D'Bon Sanders sitting face to face with Dr. Richard Gesar. The picture was not a construct from stock photos but a real image of the two men in conversation. No doubt, Michael thought, they were recording it even now and would edit it for tonight's program. The listing said 7:30 p.m.

* * *

On camera, D'Bon Sanders seemed thin in the face, but the wire-rimmed glasses he wore for televised interviews tended to make him look a little rounder and certainly a great deal more intellectual. His dark skin and eyes were framed by close-cut, slightly greying hair that added to his look of respectability and fatherly wisdom. The one earring stud that glistened in his left earlobe was a mark of progressive style. Otherwise, he tended to wear the same grey-colored suits, though he was also known for his bright, multicolored ties that carried a slightly African tone into his on-screen persona. It was, of course, mostly about persona after all. Even the greying hair and the glasses were not, Michael suspected, really based on eye-sight or age. After all, almost any vision problems were corrigible, as were grey hair and baldness, for that matter.

Michael held a begrudging respect for Sanders, who seemed aware that much of his job was that of an actor. At least Sanders didn't seem to take himself too seriously. On camera he had to play his part, that of the thoughtful, inquisitive, honest searcher. He had perfected the thin-lipped, nearly-frowning look that showed a real effort to understand while also engaging a critical mind. The only thing better was when he would raise a slightly closed fist to his lips as if holding back a question that simply had to be asked. D'Bon Sanders was good.

So the 7:30 p.m. interview with Dr. Richard Gesar went to him. Michael felt only a bit slighted, only barely sensed that Gesar's TV interview tonight was somehow leaving behind the less impressive and more incisive interview Michael might have done. There might have been a moment when Michael could have imagined himself as the interviewer, the show broadcast onto millions of screens, the newsman almost as famous as the man being interviewed. Sometimes video reporters—including Sanders—were hired to give messages of alien invasions or global disasters in popular movies,

proving themselves in Michael's opinion, to be truly actors and not reporters. Michael almost laughed aloud.

Of course D'Bon Sanders was doing the video interview with the
tulku. This was going to be an advertisement, not an interview. Even so,
Michael had to watch.

During the perfunctory introductions and the connection of Gesar to
recent political events, Gesar looked uncomfortable, glancing at the camera
as if shyly embarrassed to be so visible. Sanders referred to the program
as a "rare live interview," and that seemed evident in Gesar himself. Yet
intent on his replies to Sanders' questions, Gesar seemed to abandon his
self-consciousness.

"Some have deemed your accomplishment here, Dr. Gesar," Sanders
was saying, "a miracle." Michael bristled. "How do you describe in your own
terms what we have seen today?"

"Well, of course it is a miracle in a way," Gesar said, "for it was an event
rooted in the souls of two human beings whose decisions will change our
world in a miraculous way." Michael snorted at the equivocation, and yet
Gesar's speech flowed into a statement of hope and purpose that transfixed
Michael almost against his will.

"I do not pretend to speak for God." Gesar smiled at Sanders' next
question. "Or for any such Being greater than ourselves, whether within
us or without us. For however this Greater Being has managed to create us
through the miracle of evolution, we are here now, in this world, with the
remarkable capacity to choose a health and wholeness for ourselves that can
bring health and wholeness to others."

"Yet these things would not have happened without your own input,
Dr. Gesar," Sanders inserted. "Tell us what you have done to bring these
changes of health and wholeness."

"The world turns without us, Mr. Sanders," Gesar replied gently. "We
cannot know what would have happened without us. We can only know
what we hope the world will do with us. My addition was only to urge upon
the two men a growth they themselves had already chosen. These leaders
were both Muslims—a word meaning 'people who submit to Allah'—long
before I entered the conversation. They submitted themselves to hope—that
is, to the possibility that God—call God what you will—is as much in the
other as in ourselves. They submitted themselves to the hope that they could
find the glory of God, the *baha'u'llah*, everywhere, even in their own breasts.

"Do not laugh, Mr. Sanders. It is the greatest act of bravery to find
God within ourselves. For once found, we discover the possibility—no, the
necessity—of living up to the greatness that fact entails. If the divine spark

within myself, Mr. Sanders, should meet and recognize the divine spark within you, how could we not find ourselves at peace?

"The Hindus have known this for millennia. With hands united, bowing deeply, they greet one another, not as people, but as divine beings. The Buddhists of China insisted that there is no *icchantika*, no one who is without the inherent perfection of the Buddha Nature. In the West, has it not always been declared that all people are made in the image of God? There is nothing new in this technology, Mr Sanders, that has not already been declared in the world's great religions, namely that we are all of the divine essence. It is the recognition of this fact that is the miracle."

"But surely, Dr. Gesar," Sanders said, emerging from his thoughtful pose, "such statements underplay your own role in the way these men have discovered, shall we say, God."

"Call it what you will, Mr. Sanders," Gesar responded. "The technology of finding the harmony of the soul, of aiding the seeking heart, is something we—not I, Mr. Sanders—we have been allowed to contribute. Certainly we hope to share this technology more and more as the months stretch out before us. But again, the point is that the men who made this discovery of God found peace, not only in themselves, but between themselves. How much might we all hope, therefore, that the next step in our human journey will be to discover the same spirit that is *baha'u'llah* in the Saudi is the *shekinah* in President ben David of Israel? What if Premier Zhou of China, were to discover the beauty and wholeness of his soul, his own Buddha nature? Might we hope then, that there would be peace between nations?"

"And peace within nations," Sanders offered, as if helping Gesar along.

"Indeed." Gesar smiled broadly. "It was the great insight of Confucius in particular that the wisdom and virtue of the leader must of necessity filter down to the people. And that is why, to bring the discussion back to the events of today, both Mirza Salman and Abdul Sayed have pledged to bring this healing to their people."

"But doesn't that raise a problem for us?" D'Bon Sanders said, raising a finger gently as if to intrude with a challenge, his face with a carefully grave expression. "Have not both Mr. Salman and Mr. Sayed offered to fund your work and to help import your technology to Saudi Arabia for further testing on the general population? Doesn't this raise a conflict of interest, if you come to bring, as you say, peace, while you gain from it personal reward?"

Michael was surprised and impressed. He had not expected a challenging question from Sanders, and this was one Michael himself had not quite thought to ask. But then he had had no knowledge of the promises of the Saudi princes.

Dr. Gesar reacted only with a smile and a nod. "I understand your suspicion," he said easily. "But you know, the days of great Saudi wealth are long past, and their pledges of support, as you suggest, are not quite as great as you believe. They did offer to fund further research in America, but I politely declined. What I did accept, however, was the offer to bring the technology of the soul to the people, to allow every man and woman to know his or her own wholeness. This is not, in my view, the support of my research or of me personally, but the support of the people. It is no more and no less than the supply of food or health care to the people of a nation, a work surely we might hope to see accomplished by any magnanimous leader. What if Saudi Arabia could be the first nation on earth to be populated entirely by people who know that Allah dwells richly within them? What if China were next? Or the United States?"

These rhetorical questions were followed by a series of technological questions and assertions, a banter between a reporter clearly being fed technical questions through an implant and a scientist answering with confident optimism. How shall this technology make its way to the common person? Can it be made inexpensively enough to make it as available as, say, a retina scan? Can the technology of enhancing the aura truly be available to every citizen in a modern nation, or will it remain a luxury for those with wealth and leisure? They were almost good questions, and Michael was almost satisfied that they were the right questions. But any concern that the questions might have been deeper or tougher, might have questioned the metaphysics of souls and the epistemology of peace of mind—those questions that a Professor Wacker or Marta Sanchez might have asked—were eclipsed by Gesar's hopeful answers. "This democratization of a technology of the soul is, after all, like the medical and pharmaceutical advances of the past," Gesar said with a somber smile, "advances that have, even after a slow and tenuous beginning, revolutionized our hopes for health. Of course there is still research being done on the technology itself, but the motivation is clear and hopeful. Yes, the technology must make its way to the fingerprint and retina of every person, just as inoculations against smallpox or the availability of antidepressants have only in the recent past become a human right." Gesar looked past D'Bon Sanders to a distant vision. "The red soul, Mr. Sanders, is surely as much a human right as clean water and meaningful work. Perhaps within the year, we shall be able to say, 'Don't be blue' to those who labor and are heavily burdened, and it shall be like transporting food to the hungry across the span of a continent. With this technology simplified and streamlined, it will be made possible for all people. The goal, Mr. Sanders, is nothing less than peace on earth and goodwill to all people."

There was silence while Sanders looked into the face of Richard Gesar. Normally, even a second of silence on video was a form of death, as the common viewer's attention span would hardly survive a moment without entertainment of some kind. But the silence felt right, somehow contemplative, even to Michael.

"Peace on earth." D'Bon Sanders finally breathed. "Great minds have spoken of this ideal for centuries, and always it has eluded us. Religion has often been both the source of promise and of failure. Yet here we are on the edge of this renewed hope, and you are saying that it is finally to religion we must return?"

"It is religious, Mr. Sanders, but it is not religion. It is spirituality. It is the wisdom of the sages that has taught us to breathe deeply and pray profoundly. It is mindfulness of the masters, the contemplation of the saints, the dance of the mystics."

"What shall you have for the angry atheist?" Sanders reflected. "What for those of us who have no God?"

To Michael's surprise, Gesar laughed. "Our concern, Mr. Sanders," he replied, smiling, "is not with the atheism, but with the anger." Gesar seemed amused by his own wit. "If the atheist will consent to know his own soul and is at peace with himself, and therefore with the world around him, then what need does he have of us? If his soul is red, he has found God already, though he has no need at all of the term. If he already loves art, if he loves his family, if he loves humanity and is at peace with his own being, then by all means, let us let him be. For like all true spiritual physicians, we come to heal the sick, not the healthy." There was a pause, a softer smile. "I make no one worship any god he does not already have, Mr. Sanders."

D'Bon Sanders was quiet. Micheal might have wondered if the speaker in his ear was also silent, but even Michael's own thoughts were still and quiet. As if to fill the void, Dr. Richard Gesar started again. "Mr. Sanders, let us be clear that neither Mr. Salman nor Mr. Sayed is a convert to any particular faith, certainly not to mine, nor even to my particular science. They became great men today because they found what was already within them. They found what was within them because they looked for it. All I do is help people find what is already there. It is true that, once that center, that heart-mind of perfection is uncovered, people become open to possibilities of service and peace that are the mere extensions of inner divinity. It is true that I can myself help direct them to that goal. But again, this is not about making converts to my brand of Buddhism any more than it is about gaining donors for further research. These men found Allah. The Tibetan might find the crown *chakra*, the Hindu the *Atman*. You, Mr. Sanders, might discover Christ. When the soul is healed, and its deep, blood-red energy revealed, then it is up to the new teachers of faith and peace, the new Buddhas of our age, to point the unawakened ones to the paths before them. I know this path only because I have already been there. But I am not the first, nor am I the last. The Buddha was there, certainly. And Christ was there, and Muhammad was there, and Laozi was there. Each became nothing in order to point others toward everything. That is all I have done, Mr. Sanders. My hope is indeed that the discovery of self and the ensuing movement of peace can begin to spread from the few to the many. Peace between nations, Mr. Sanders, and peace across backyard fences. How can there be any argument against this?"

The interview was essentially over. As if coming from his own trance, D'Bon Sanders offered Dr. Richard Gesar his thanks.

Immediately D'Bon Sanders reappeared on camera, full face, the body only slightly turned, set up for the common editorial conclusions. For a moment Sanders seemed thoughtful, and Michael's normal cynicism consciously noted that the pause gave Sanders time, not to gather his own thoughts, but to sort through the expressions and gestures suggested to him electronically. But Michael was also gathering his own thoughts, and he shared the silence with the on-screen puppet as if the peace Gesar had promised were already achieved. As Sanders began to speak, Michael realized he truly wanted to hear what was next. More miracles? Peace? Sanders was asking the questions. "Technological marvels," Sanders declared, and yet it was not clear what form those marvels would take. "Personal and social healing," was mentioned, and Sanders' nods and thin-lipped seriousness were enough affirmation. "Lofty promises," Sanders announced, and Michael wondered what exactly those promises had been. Had he missed something in the interview?

"Apparently we shall hear more of what Dr. Gesar has to say in his next interview, this time with Christian television personality Reverend David Roberts. That meeting is scheduled for Saturday, May 20th, in Anaheim. Watch for coverage of that meeting on Dr. Roberts's own channel, streamed as an optional selection on this station. Until then, this is D'Bon Sanders . . ."

Gesar was being interviewed by Roberts? Why had Michael not heard of this? If anything, it was his own idea, and yet somehow the connection had been made without him. Michael felt almost angry. Of course a major video interview would be done by someone like Sanders and not by a mere writer like himself. He understood that the connection between important religious figures like Roberts and Gesar could happen without him. But he could not quite escape the feeling that he needed to be there. There were harder questions to ask, he was sure, and something made him want to ask them. "Too many rhetorical questions," Michael said to himself. "How can anyone argue against peace?" Michael paraphrased, and for a second he hoped that someone would. Someone should. He vaguely hoped that the Reverend Dr. Roberts, the Christian, would challenge Gesar. These two would be rivals, wouldn't they? The meeting would therefore surely be more like a debate than like a salesman being interviewed by an actor. For a saving moment, Michael wanted honesty.

"Contacts," he called aloud, and his computer's voice responded, "Contacts."

"What was that woman's name?" he asked aloud, knowing he could receive an answer. "She was the secretary or whatever of Dr. Roberts. I'm sure I have her information—"

"Joy Anderson," the computer interrupted aloud, "personal liaison."

"Audio contact," Michael said aloud, realizing in the next second that there could certainly be no connection this time of night. But the computer made the connection, and almost at once, the buzz of the connection was replaced with an automated voice. This was the general switchboard for "Dr. David Roberts Ministries," and Michael was invited to give a further contact request. "Joy Anderson," he responded. A clearly automated response told him that Joy Anderson was not available and asked him to leave a name and a message. "This is Michael Pryor," he spoke into the air. Suddenly he realized he didn't really have a message. "Yes, Mr. Pryor," the machine responded, as if recognizing him. "Nice to hear from you again. What shall I say to Ms Anderson?" There was a barely audible click as the machine listened.

"I have only just learned," Michael said, "that Dr. Richard Gesar is going to appear on Dr. Roberts's program. I was, er, hoping," he paused to find the right words, "to attend the program in person."

There was a whir and a click, as voice and word recognition software worked its way through the options. "Yes, Mr. Pryor," the machine repeated itself. "The program you refer to is for Saturday, May 20th, at 7 p.m. Your name appears on the guest list."

Michael was startled. "Er, thank you," he said to the machine.

A click. "You're welcome."

Michael had not even known the meeting was taking place, and yet he was already included. Had he missed the invitation? Was there merely a presumption that he, as much as anyone, would be part of the show? For it would be a show. Still Michael hoped for more. Ironically, he felt that somehow Dr. Gesar's presence would lend some substance to the Christian show and that the Christian context would force some disambiguation on the *tulku*. Could there be in this one place a combination of thought and feeling, the science of Gesar with the bubbly Jesus-for-sale of the television preacher, the doctrinal assertions of Christianity with the universal experientialism of auroscopy? Michael felt a strange mixture of hope and confusion. Had he known the history of religion better, he might have expected to find a unity of faith and understanding or feeling and reason as a kind of promised beacon illuminating a unity of truth and delight. But he was not there yet, so the moment of possibility felt to him like a vague uncertainty. The unity, the possibility, not of Gesar's all-inclusive peace, but of an honest inquiry that might somehow discover spiritual awakening, and the glory of spirit that could be the raw data of philosophical thought—this hope barely showed itself, just out of reach of his too-short arms. Vaguely, Michael knew there was more to reality and knew that he was not able to find it. He was not yet able to understand the unity of honest sin and healing forgiveness, nor could he even yet imagine the more abstract unity of truth and love that might mark one who truly is "made in the image of God," an image he had always taken for granted and never really understood. Had the vision been less of Gesar's hope and more of Daniel's uncertainty, he might have opened his eyes more fully. But as yet, Michael could not find the mirror of love and honesty that could point outside himself.

Yet even in Michael's unready state of soul, even from the blowing of an empty wind, the beginnings were stirred. At that moment the best kind of insight he could manage was to think, somehow, of Marta.

18

TRANSITIONS

Marta was alone. She was often alone. Sometimes, even when she was with other people—especially at work—she was alone. She could interrupt her isolated mind-discussion to carry on a conversation with Ben or Jason and then return to her own reveries later with minimal difficulty in picking up the threads of thought she had been following. So even when her loneliness was broken by the presence of another, she could return to it easily. But she was truly, physically alone.

Often the threads of argument ran through Marta's mind like a conversation of its own. Yet she was not two people. This was simply the phenomenon of reflection, aptly a metaphor for seeing oneself in a mirror. Or was it the other way around? Which came first, after all, she considered, the invention of mirrors or the discovery within the human mind of one's own voice? Had some primitive human first known himself by looking into the calm waters of an ancient pond, or by thinking and then suddenly knowing he was thinking? What was it like the first time to "hear"—she placed quotation marks around the word in her own conversation—oneself think? She tried to remember when it had happened to her as a child and called up dim memories—or invented narratives—of being a little girl in a park, watching people. That little girl, perhaps five years old, had seen an old man walk by, an old man who stopped opposite her at the edge of the play area and waved at her with both hands at once. "Why did he do that?" she had wondered, and then, somehow, she had instantly known that she could not know what the man had been thinking nor could he know what she was thinking. Suddenly, the little girl had become self-aware.

This was not a new narrative. Marta had often had these thoughts about thought, wondering about wondering. Not necessarily a common phenomenon for everyone, she added to herself. Perhaps there are thousands, even millions, who never realize they are beings of consciousness. Perhaps, she thought, there are many who simply have no souls. She recalled another, more vivid memory, when Jason Sanders had insisted that no one really has a soul. "Of course I don't *have* a soul," Marta had said, "I *am* a soul."

This night, Friday, her physical body was as alone as her soul was necessarily. In spite of four-day work weeks and the flourishing popularity of telecommuting, workdays still seemed like they should end on Friday and there should be some party or gathering or social engagement of some kind for a pleasant, healthy, and not-altogether-bad-looking young woman. She thought, of course, of Daniel and Helen, but how often could one impose upon friends? Besides, they were out on a date, working—once again, it seemed—on their relationship. Marta appreciated that. There were the Lambreys, an older couple she knew from church. Albert loved the Mass, and Mary Ellen loved her saints, while Marta loved the old couple for their love, whether they understood that love or not. Yet with the Lambreys she had never been quite comfortable, with so many years between them that Marta felt out of place, even though they accepted her like a daughter, or maybe a granddaughter.

Marta laughed to herself, alone in the warm evening. She was just alone, and that was OK. It was not—she felt herself beginning a formal discussion—that she wanted to be alone. Hadn't God said it was not good that a person should be alone? Yet this was the same God—if one was going to take the story consistently—who made the aloneness in the first place. Shall we say that a Creator makes a first effort and then sees it incomplete, acting then to fix His first oversight? No. Rather we might say the Creator makes the person alone in order to demonstrate the inadequacy of isolation, or perhaps to show the insufficiency of all the other options. That was, surely, the purpose of the naming of the animals: that some primordial Adam learn his need for Eve. Also that humans be given the honor of co-creation. The latter, indeed, suggests a basis for a kind of Aristotelian realism, something certainly greater than nominalism.

Different argument, Marta thought, and not one to pursue in polite company. Who indeed, of all the people she knew, would be willing even to consider such an argument? There were "scholars," but in her experience the time was long past that scholars, especially of antiquated religious arguments, took those arguments seriously. Scholarship was really about clarifying ideas that might have absolutely no relation to the scholar's own life. That's why one can be a Doctor of Philosophy in Religious Studies and not have religious bone in one's body.

"OK, OK," Marta caught herself. "That, too, is another argument." It is not good that a person is alone, she picked up her thread, and yet the same Creator in the same story made the man alone to learn the goodness of relationship, the relationship of equals. OK. Yet the presumed good of that relationship cannot be absolutely overriding. Her own tradition, Marta acknowledged with a slight swelling of pride, had found place for monastics, a few people dedicated to aloneness for the sake of service and devotion. The old tradition of celibate priesthood had been overruled by the previous pope, much to the delight of most of the church—much to Marta's own delight. For much Catholic celibacy had always been forced, she thought, and often therefore hypocritical. Surely the calling to celibacy had to be exactly that, a calling. It had to be rare, a special blessing. That's why there is a sacrament for it.

Yet another argument, one she had used on Daniel, annoying him greatly.

"I am no nun," Marta thought, as she often had. Yet God had given her celibacy, like it or not. Therefore, celibacy had to be good. People had argued for ages, it seemed, that all sexuality, whatever one's proclivities, must be given by God and therefore could not be wrong. These days it was the practitioners of incest. Marta had her doubts about such an argument. Those in her tradition who had argued for celibacy had never denied the overwhelming good of sexuality and, especially, family. There was no question in her mind that a consistent position could be made for the good of sex and its moral limitations. Indeed, even those who were always pushing the edges of sexual morality drew their moral lines. The difficulty, it seemed, was to do so consistently.

Marta sipped at a glass of red wine. She let it bathe the sides and back of her tongue, then drew in a breath over the wine to feel its slight dry sting, suck in the flavor before swallowing. The wine was deeply sensual, rightly so. She laughed in her mind at old Protestant arguments—some, still, in the more fundamentalist sects—that somehow Jesus would not have turned water into real, fermented, alcoholic wine. "Wine, yes," she said aloud, "and damn good wine, too." She took another sip.

The good of wine. The good of sex. Yet both can be abused, and both are limited. Not only, as is clear with wine more than sex, for the good of others, but even for one's own good. The limit of sex, like the limit of wine, is not only in cases of rape. Consent in sex is not license any more than the consent of the wine. "May I?" she asked the glass in her hand. "Thank you." She sipped again.

Fasting. It was like fasting. There is nothing wrong with food; nor is fasting about being obese or unhealthy. Religions all over the world have enjoined fasting at various times and for various reasons. Some, no doubt, imagine they cleanse their souls along with their colons, just as some think that calm in meditation is somehow a quality of enlightenment. How strange was the Buddha, Marta thought, utterly suspicious of sensual pleasure and yet unquestioning in the acceptance of his own mental calmness. Surely both are good, and both are dangerous. Surely at times we should fast from both.

So sometimes we fast from food because the labor of fasting is good. Sometimes we fast from company for the same reasons. Thus loneliness. "Maybe I'm fasting from sex," Marta said out loud, and then was suddenly embarrassed. She took another sip of wine.

"Maybe at times we even fast from God," her mind suddenly added. Thoughts like this just sometimes came to her, flew into the mix of argument and analysis with a new connection that made her pause, made her think about something new, something deeper. She moved on: "What is 'the dark night of the soul' if not fasting even from God? Not that we choose this fast, but that it is chosen for us. Yet even here, the fasting, the loneliness, can be right.

"*Dominus dedit, Dominus abstulit*," Marta intoned. "Blessed be the name of the Lord." With a last swirl, she downed the wine in her glass and looked at the half-empty bottle on the table. "I can delight in the pleasure God gives me within the limits he sets," she summarized, "and I can want the good he does not give. I shall not always have what I want, for I do not want what I want. I want more than I want, and I shall deny myself the good I want if it is not given, even if it be God himself." For a second she was shocked by her conclusion. Then she noticed the bottle beside her. She took the synthetic cork, inverted it and shoved it into the neck of the bottle as far as it would go. "Good wine," she said aloud.

* * *

It was Saturday night—early Sunday, actually—and Daniel was up. He and Helen had talked on their date, but it hadn't gone well. Back home, in bed, they had made love. Maybe made a baby. Probably not. After midnight, Daniel had still been awake, so he rose, turned on the TV, and tried to think.

Daniel was less trained in analysis than Marta, and yet, like Marta, he couldn't quite avoid it. Perhaps that is what made thinking things through all the more troubling, that it had to be done and he didn't have adequate tools to do it. It was like trying to fix a laser alignment without a micrometer, except that one can just turn off a maladjusted laser.

Daniel couldn't turn off his mind. Maybe it was the news of Richard Gesar that had troubled him, a story he might not even have paid much attention to but for his brother's involvement. He wasn't sure what actually bothered him about the stories except that there were too many gods. He had never doubted that God exists; the problem for him had always been that there were too many, and here was another. Because he loved God and was honest, every god invited him to love; and yet because he was a thinker—however reluctantly—he knew he could not love them all.

Laughter came from the TV late-night talk show that had appeared on the first channel. He could name or point to another program and the wall would fill up with the new picture, but when Helen was in bed and he couldn't sleep, he tended toward the talk shows for mild diversion. They were sometimes funny, not always vulgar. Still, he often felt a vague sense of guilt, since watching the shows was a waste of time. He had never fallen for the Christian notion that one had to commit every waking moment to God, as that was clearly impossible, at least for him. Indeed, in his internal wrestling long ago with the God of Islam, he had finally reached the conclusion that he could not do enough to be a Muslim. He had discovered in his struggle that it was a burden too heavy for him to bear, even if it was clear that some people—many, in fact—were sure they could. His inability to be Muslim did not prove Islam false—Daniel was smart enough to see the logic—and so his wrestled conclusions regarding one of the gods did not entirely settle the problems. It seemed they could not be settled. That was the point.

The talk show laughter—clearly choreographed as part of the program—indicated that the joke had indeed been funny. That was the blessing and the curse of such laughter. It's so damned planned. Maybe it's funny, and maybe it isn't, but we can create the laughter that makes it seem funny, and so it is. Convoluted as the ideas were, Daniel saw here—again, almost automatically—that there was a deep illogicity to the manipulations of entertainment. In his own vocabulary: it was simply a lie.

Still he watched the show, thinking his own thoughts, seeing through the lies on the screen and wary of the lies within. Helen, he hoped, was asleep. She had cried when he told her he had reneged on the decision to try in-vitro fertilization. He had tried to explain why he had changed his mind, but she had hardly heard him. He hadn't explained it well, though somehow it all fit together. Richard Gesar and the promises of peace were somehow like the hopes of having a baby. Somehow like late-night talk shows, too. They were all gods, and they all expected his love. It was not that the God he believed in was in any way threatened; Daniel's theology was clear enough that he knew nothing can threaten God. But his God, too, asked for his love, and if Daniel could not love all the gods, then he found it difficult to love any. That, too, made sense, though he could not say why.

A guest came onto the show, and with much smiling and bowing and applause from the audience, the man sat down beside the host and they began their banter. It would be general chat about what life was like for these unreasonably rich and well-known people, and it would be about the actor's new movie or the comedian's new special. There would be funny moments and a great deal of blather, none of it serious, all of it happy. These people were always happy. They didn't come on the shows to talk about the death of a spouse or the current famine in Eritrea. If they did mention the famine, it was to emphasize the great relief efforts the actor was vaguely involved in, maybe giving millions of dollars—a miniscule fraction of the actor's wealth—to have someone beam food to someone who would beam it to someone who might or might not get it to people in need. In any case, they would be entirely confident that they were solving the problem and, especially, that they themselves were good people. So even disaster was rendered happy.

Daniel put his thoughts together automatically: Am I happy? Do I love God? Am I a good person? All three questions rose together, yet for Daniel they represented a disconnection that a mind like Marta's would have been able to name. His ever-haunted sense of inadequacy, however, made Daniel wonder if he just couldn't find the right connection, or couldn't live it. It was hard to be a good person; he knew that from experience. Yet, as an honest man, he also knew his own experience of that difficulty would not be other people's experience. Perhaps others find it easy to be good, and therefore find it easy to be happy, and therefore find it easy to love God. Still, each of the *therefores* in the argument seemed wrong.

There was a new guest on the talk show, a woman who sang a song from her new album. The song was about love—no surprise there. Then she sat with the host, and the banter began again, this time about her expected new baby and how brave it was to interrupt her singing career to have a child. But "it was the right time" for her, she said. Apparently she was happy. Perhaps the baby was, too; the father wasn't mentioned.

"You don't have babies so you can achieve personal happiness," Daniel said to the woman on the show and realized of course that he had also said it to himself. That seemed an immediate and important truth, though Daniel could not at once have suggested why people *do* have babies. The negative point strengthened his sense of resolution; he wouldn't go through with the procedure. He would simply refuse to make happiness the condition of a new life.

"The kingdom of God suffers violence, and violent men take it by force." The Bible verse came to him out of nowhere, as if for no good reason. But what did it mean? Daniel had no clue, and yet he had tied the pieces together. Even as he had been pleading, explaining, arguing with Helen, he had said it and had not known what it meant. "I will not storm the gates of heaven to make God my friend," he had said. It hadn't really made sense in that context. Perhaps it still didn't. In his uncertainty, that was Daniel's answer. And for a moment, he rested.

* * *

It was Monday morning, and Desra had intentionally lingered at home. Then her phone buzzed in her ear, and she saw that it was the call she was expecting. Almost in spite of her interior insistence on confidence, she glanced over her shoulder toward the bathroom where the shower, presumably with Michael in it, was still running. That glance might have been a fact to consider, something that still, even now, might have helped her recognize her own struggle with her own choices. She might have paused, made a step back, even a little, from the great trudge forward that was her ever-so-confident self-making. Even a pause in that march, a look back over the shoulder to see if she just might have made an error, could have been liberating. But the backward glance was not part of her thought, even though it was part of her fear.

So Desra passed with determined casualness through the living room door as she responded, "Yes, this is Desra."

Business mode kicked in. Information about the Ise project was being offered, just as she had hoped. Kevin had been a little angry with her, of course, for calling Japan behind his back, even if she had hidden her motivations well behind questions about the drawings only she could answer. It had, after all, been her own design, and she deserved to be in on the project. That was a fact in her mind as truly as the geography of the Ise bay. When it suited her, she could explain why the designs were truly hers and assert with cool thought the details of the designs she had foreseen and planned for Toba Island. It was with that kind of assurance, both moral and geographical, that she had called Japan late on Sunday night—first thing Monday in Japan—to ask how the sunrise might reflect off the windows of the low-rises at different times of the year, and whether that would require careful use of non-reflective materials. She asked, or rather pretended to ask because she already knew the answer. Thus her intentional deception—not strictly or simply a lie—could generously be interpreted as a conscientious and even culturally sensitive way to be sure that those on the other end of the conversation knew that reflected light should be a concern. Of course, it also gave her the chance to begin speaking Japanese with her design counterparts in Kyoto. Almost offhandedly, the original conversation allowed her to demonstrate her knowledge of the designs and her new-found linguistic abilities, even as she was able to show a team spirit and an ideal concern for the health of the overall project.

Kevin, no doubt, had had his suspicions about Desra's motives, but she had no such doubts. In the end, calling Japan herself to inquire about something she already knew in detail had achieved its end: her direct involvement with the Japanese team. And that, she knew deeply and with common assurance, was for the good of the project and everyone involved. Let Kevin have his suspicions; she had done the right thing.

Here was the payoff. Shingo Nakamura was calling her to confer. To her credit, Desra was not immediately or directly aware of her pride, or even quite focused on the success of her personal strategy. For ten minutes, she genuinely interacted with Nakamura about serious issues of how the sunrise fell across the water, costs of the different glass materials, even how typhoons or tsunamis might affect the structural integrity of the glass. Eventually, they fell into some banter, particularly how much Desra had hoped to come to Japan and how sincerely she might trade places with him some day. Overall, it was a healthy thing that she could discuss the project itself and be drawn away from the meaning it had for her personally. Even at this point, a realization that such a project could have value in itself, apart from her involvement, could have been redemptive. "*Go kyoryoku arigatogozaimashita*," Nakamura said, and noted politely that her insights had been of great value, so when she said, "*Anato no seiko o kibo*," she almost really meant it. She could really, almost, have wished for the welfare of others.

But as Desra closed her voice connection, she saw Michael at the door, wrapped in a towel, hair still wet. He was looking at her curiously, with a slight smile, and she felt herself flush with a brief embarrassment. But Desra's thoughts were complex, mixing the intuition of relationship with the necessity of identity, so, along with the embarrassment, she immediately felt an accompanying anger at feeling ashamed. In an instant, she thought through the feelings of intimacy with Michael and knew there was something she could sacrifice to his love; yet she also knew her own self-determination, and she thought just as quickly of the work that required her to be the woman she was. "I am my own life," she had told herself often enough, indeed, had said so to Michael. Generally he shared that idea, so that the two of them, ironically in both cases, bonded over their insistence on being separate. Consequently, Desra had the ability to think of the bond itself, could have considered the possibility of the sacrifice of the individual to a love greater than both. As she saw Michael's smile, having loved him enough to know his smile was not a sneer, she had a chance to smile in return, to let the blush become a confession. Yet because she had never quite found it necessary to base her strong sense of self on something greater than herself—and because she had been practicing the arguments of self-justification recently—the more habitual argument dominated. Had she practiced instead an argument that found selfhood a kind of miraculous given, had she followed the logic of her own selfhood to its absolute ground, she could have risked losing herself, knowing her identity could not, after all, be truly lost. She might have let herself be guilty—of something—and might have let herself be forgiven by a lover, accepting being accepted, even as a greater thinker might have accepted being an individual, as a kind of grace. But Desra had never quite practiced that softening line of thought, and so she hardened.

"Eavesdropping?" she asked with an artificial insouciance. She knew quite well that Michael was innocent. But habit helped her decide which kind of argument to have and how to switch from defense to attack.

But Michael was a skilled opponent and did not accept the shift of focus. "Why didn't you tell me?" she heard him ask. She didn't have to ask what he meant.

"Did I need your permission?" she riposted.

"Of course not," he replied easily, "but I would have thought you might have told me what you were going to do."

Desra paused, unsure. Michael was as skillful as she; he had returned the thrust, making it a question of her choices. For an instant, Desra might have moved to his side and wondered along with him about her choices, not only of getting the implant, but of not telling Michael she was doing so. But uncertainty was uncomfortable, even painful. In the brief seconds of her silence, she felt herself losing something, something she had never quite thought to name or justify.

"I had to make decisions," Desra said, almost letting the inner struggle live, "and you just weren't here to consult." Both the move back to Michael's own inadequacy and the word *consult* were helpful. With a vague surge of confidence, she added, "God knows where you've been these days." She saw Michael stiffen and his eyes get a little darker. She instinctively knew she had moved the argument down the right path. When he said, "You know I've been busy with these interviews," she knew she had moved the struggle onto safer turf.

"Chasing your gods and girlfriends," she said with a smile that could almost mean she was joking.

"What?" Michael's response was louder, defensive, and for Desra that signalled victory.

"Listen," she said abruptly, as if offering peace instead of, in fact, moving to a safe distance after landing a blow, "what you don't hear when you listen to me on the phone is that I, too, have a great deal of work to do. You should have known how much the Ise deal meant to me. I can't help it if you weren't here to talk it over. But it's my career and my brain."

Desra stepped past Michael in the doorway. As she passed, he spoke softly, almost with a question in his voice. "I've never said otherwise," he said, a comment she might have construed it as apology or as defense, or even as weakness.

"It isn't what you say, Michael," she shot accusingly over her shoulder, "but what you do." In the silence that followed, she snatched her briefcase from the couch and walked to the booth. She placed her hand on the identification pad and keyed in the address of her office. That's when she realized she was shaking. The nervousness suddenly was to her a sign of her own weakness, both a fear and a hope that Michael would say something or just come up behind her and touch her. But as the booth slid open, she heard instead his footsteps stomping back toward the bathroom. At that moment, she might have felt she had won. Nonetheless, something like fear gripped her still--another call of grace she might have heard. But stepping into the booth, she turned to face the apartment through the aperture and once again held her image of defiance. Defiance was necessary. It had served her well. Yet when the door closed, she felt herself slump, exhaling audibly, releasing the tension. Almost by luck, she recovered to inhale deeply as the mildly palliative gasses hissed around her so she felt nothing as the lasers decomposed and mapped her body. But there was a tear on her cheek.

* * *

Michael was in some ways fascinated by Desra's choice. He understood it entirely, inasmuch as it revolved so evidently around the recognition of her work for the quality of which she was so confident. He had also just learned of his brother's refusal to do the in vitro fertilization procedure, and that, too, fascinated him. On the one hand, Daniel's issue had always seemed a peculiar moralism, maybe even a hang-up about some supposed evil of masturbation. Yet, in light of Desra's decision, Daniel's seemed all the more strangely principled—principled and yet strange. He felt he understood Daniel better than he understood Desra.

Michael was home alone, buying groceries. The recorder had, of course, the entire contents of his last several purchases, so grocery shopping was never a difficulty. He could compare what he was considering with what he had recently purchased, and the databases handled all the price comparisons and quality assurances, if he was ever hesitant. The hardest decision to make when buying groceries was whether to let the computer read his fingerprint or his retina. Voice recognition was moderately safe, of course, but for true security, it had to be fingerprint or retina patterns. For ease of use, fingerprint readers were still the most common, as Michael could simply lay his hand on the table in front of him, as opposed to having to lean the forehead toward an eye scanner. Michael didn't know the statistics, but he assumed most people appreciated the simplicity of hand scans. Whether hands or eyes, there was simply no other way to be secure when buying and selling. Indeed, there were probably no businesses or agencies anymore that allowed any other kind of transaction. Michael wondered how Luddites like Professor Wacker managed to avoid starvation.

Thinking about Wacker easily led Michael to thinking about Marta. He remained fascinated by her—and fascinated by his own fascination with her. She was certainly interesting, and he easily enjoyed her company. That made it possible for him to think of her sexually. Michael was not yet wise enough to wonder if that transition should have been so easy and automatic for him, or for any man. Yet his common, haunted honesty gave him a subtle uneasiness that might have been a vague stirring of genuine moral guilt, had his conscience been as well trained as his sexual interests. He did see his own thoughts move away from the sexualization of Marta as if by unconscious choice, and with a smile to himself he acknowledged the moral motion. Yet he did not immediately see it as rooted in his own moral principle but instead transferred the morality onto Marta. "She wouldn't have me," the projection declared, and Michael almost believed it. Strangely, for a man who could usually spot with ease the projection of moral blame, he could not see as easily the projection of moral value. Yet there it was, looking back at him from his moment of reflection. Maybe, just maybe, the sexualization of Marta was not just wrong because "she wouldn't have me," but because, well, it was wrong. Maybe, just maybe, Michael seemed to muse about there being actual principles of morality that were not his own invention. Principles of fidelity that he had invented, he realized, had made him proud of being the noble person he was; but principles of morality he invented would also make it possible to change them when he needed to, or simply desired to. Principles of morality he did not invent, on the other hand, would not make him proud. They would make him . . . guilty.

This idea made Michael stop scanning the "shelves" of the grocery store and think. He had always easily seen moral guilt as a feeling, one of those emotional flutters he imagined to be the standard feeling of someone like his brother. Surely that is what had led, once again, to Daniel's indecision about having a baby. Michael had heard about Daniel's change of heart through a random phone call from Helen. That was nothing new; Michael had long seen his own brother as wavering, not least about this fertility issue, and Michael had always supposed the trouble was rooted in Daniel's peculiar feelings of guilt. Yet, more recently, Michael had also seen in Daniel a resoluteness about life that was at least as much a characteristic of the older brother as any waffling of guilt. What was it, after all, that kept Daniel so strong in his marriage to Helen? What kept him so bound to his peculiar faith? It suddenly seemed to Michael that perhaps it was not just the burden of guilt, that vague and wavering feeling that seemed to change day to day in the case of artificial insemination but remained solid and almost absolute in his marriage and his religion. What if guilt wasn't a feeling? What if it was a fact? The reality of moral standards implied that an equally real moral guilt would follow a real failure to live up to that standard. Almost in spite of himself, Michael wondered.

Then there was Desra. A careful conscience would have recognized the movement in Michael's thoughts as one of the subtle moves of self-deception that still lingered at the edges of Michael's honesty. When moral guilt threatens, it is certainly a safety maneuver to think about someone who is guiltier. Desra hadn't even lived up to her own invented principles. Michael understood the pressure she must have been under, the almost unbearable disappointment about the assignment of her Japan project. Yet to get the implant so readily, and without telling him! Michael thought Desra had simply compromised and wanted to hide the compromise from Michael. What did that say about all their conversations about self-reliance and self-discipline? What did that say about their shared humor at the expense of the architects and news reporters who "chipped away at their own brains?" That had been her phrase—apt, and even quite clever. More than one college student or scientific genius had rendered herself useless by adding language chips and information data chips and calculator chips until the brain itself seemed to rebel. Such *wunderkind-wannabees*—another Desra coinage—had found themselves incapable of independent thought, of decision making, and sometimes even of forming a coherent sentence. "Nope, there's no substitute for making yourself yourself," Desra had said a couple of years previously, and they had clinked their wine glasses and smiled and made love.

Michael considered his shopping cart. He had yogurt and some cheap granola-like cereal, some wine, toilet paper, and a few kiwis. He loved kiwis.

Desra had also loved kiwis. He wondered if Marta liked kiwis. He realized it didn't matter to him whether Petra Eriksen liked kiwis.

"Hmm." Michael wondered if he had just noticed that there was more to his love of Desra than in his sexual interactions with Petra, and there-fore—that conjunction was important, he thought—more to Marta than to both of the others. If there was more to Marta, was there also more to her religion, or at least to religion generally? Possibly. Yet Michael was a man of his time, and he could not yet see any particular difference between those two questions. So, rather than think of Marta's Jesus, his thoughts turned to Richard Gesar, such that spirituality seemed, however vaguely, a possibility on Michael's psychological horizon.

Michael had been keeping up on the developments of the *tulku*'s au-roscopic science and had just finished an article on some of the changes coming out of the laboratories in New Mexico. Michael still had a kind of inside track, a certain priority of coverage—and readership, he was quick to point out to Melanie—about what was new from Sandia apart from what-ever political and social headlines the new god was making in the world. Most recently, as Michael had reported, the Gesar labs had claimed to have developed simplified tests for auroscopic color, tests capable of being built into some of the most basic identity readers currently in use. At the same time, the news from Albuquerque was that tests regarding the verifiable heightening of spiritual consciousness were proceeding with some success, and that with each success of "spiritual healing"—some unfortunate press-release verbiage Michael himself had avoided—there were better and better chances that "we can know what peace of mind looks like, and we can know how to help people find it." This line Michael quoted from Gesar himself had at once awakened in Michael both an instinctual suspicion and a pe-culiar feeling of hope. His suspicion had been that the intrusion of Richard Gesar's spiritual technology would violate the autonomy of the person, and the hope was that there could be, after all, peace of mind even for the likes of Michael Pryor. Gesar had, in the end, replied to Michael's challenges, claiming that any technological development was, in the larger picture, a technological augmentation of free choice, enhancing the individual's medi-tative and prayerful states rather than creating them.

For a few moments, Michael wondered. Spiritual realities and spiritual possibilities. If there was something to the former, did that mean there was hope in the latter? Might Michael, after all this time, submit to Richard Ge-sar's study and even accept his help, if that meant he might even embrace a religious view he was slowly, almost begrudgingly, beginning to respect? Could he bring his worlds together, marry the wisdom of the *tulku*'s spiritual technology and the wisdom of Marta's Christ to find a family like Daniel's? Why not? Why not?

Michael shook his head. "Nope," he said out loud. There was something still in him, some resistance to manipulation, that brought him once again to denial. "Let there be moral and spiritual realities," he thought, trying to be honest to his first considerations, "and I will follow where they lead, even if to guilt. But I will not be injected with some spiritual botox just to find peace with a fictional savior, even if it means losing a shot at love." In that thought, Michael was almost saved.

Then the phone buzzed in the ambient speakers, and the audio phone announced the caller as Professor Wacker. Michael responded, "Dr. Wacker, what a pleasant surprise." On the wall, Michael's shopping cart disappeared, and the grey disheveled hair and over-wrinkled, squirming face of Paul Wacker appeared.

"Yeah, hi," Wacker said quickly, apparently intending the greeting to be cordial. "I think we should talk again."

"Well, OK. Sure," Michael stammered, a bit off guard. "What's up?"

"Nothing," the professor replied quickly. "Or rather, a great deal, but nothing I choose to deliver through the walls."

Intrigued by the older man's manner, Michael couldn't help smiling. "Sure," he repeated, "I can make some time, but—"

"Nobody can make time," Wacker said. Wacker let the obvious point become clear. Then he continued, "You'll need to drive out to my place. Think you can do it?"

"Drive?" Michael looked quizzical. "You mean, like a car?"

"No, I mean like a golf ball," Wacker replied sarcastically. "It's not difficult. Beam your molecules into the transit station in Madison and rent a car. Tell it where to go, and it'll get you here. No skill or even actual thinking is required."

Michael again found the crazy professor unexpectedly disarming. He laughed. "I'll find some time and not pretend to make it," he said. "When do you want to meet?"

"Make it soon," Wacker said.

Michael waited, expecting directions or a specific date and time. Instead the professor seemed to change the topic. "You know," Wacker said, "I've been reading what you and the others have been writing about our semi-divine friend, the Doctor Richard Gesar." Wacker's words and his face showed a strangely calm wariness, a worried fear that did not seem related to the logical impatience of a jaded philosopher. "If what you say about developments is true," he said to Michael sternly, "then we're all in grave trouble."

19

WARNINGS

The last time Michael had driven a car, nearly a decade ago, it had been a whim, an adventure. No wonder, then, that this time he fell asleep at the wheel. He woke only when the car's alarm voice told him they were near his destination. It had only been a little over an hour's drive from the car rental offices, and he had slept for the last fifteen minutes, so the trip had not been arduous. Even so, it annoyed Michael to spend so much time traveling, only because the "crazy Thomist" liked to go places where there weren't people "zipping around in wires," as the man had said. In this case, it was Wyoming—Wyoming, Wisconsin. To Michael, it might as well have been Wyoming, Wyoming.

Michael had considered not coming at all. The intensity of Dr. Wacker's manner had made Michael accept the invitation to "chat," but then the stipulations arose that there could be no recordings and that Michael's travel by car would be lengthy, since "car rentals are rare these days." For what? Dr. Wacker was vague.

"Your destination is ahead five hundred meters, on the right," the navigation voice declared. Michael looked up. It was a farmhouse down its own gravel driveway connecting to the state highway. There was a line of trees on the north side, planted no doubt generations ago to serve as a kind of windbreak, but the trees didn't hide the house from view. Rather, the small, dirty white building seemed framed against a dark green background of trees. "Not exactly off the grid," Michael said aloud, but then he never did get from Wacker any of that old survivalist nonsense. Wacker wasn't hiding or amassing food and weapons for some dreaded apocalypse. Besides, Michael knew there was no such thing as "off the grid." The car's navigation system didn't even need buried wires for guidance any more; it was entirely navigated by geolocation: here's the road, here's where the car belongs on the road. Radar and cameras related the car to obstacles or other cars—though Michael had seen exactly zero other automobiles—and the computers did the rest of the driving. They even steered the car gently into the gravel drive and moved it slowly to the front of the house. "Stop here, I guess," Michael said to the car.

The home of Professor Paul Wacker was austere but not primitive, more evidently from neglect than from principled self-denial. There was a front yard of sorts, mostly sparse but verdant grass whose lands had long ago been conquered by invading ajuga and creeping charlie. The garage, in which Wacker presumably had his own automobile, was separate from the house, a single story with grey aluminum siding scratched in spots, showing the shiny metal beneath the paint. One large maple tree stood between the two buildings, this time of year well leafed out and dropping helicopter-like seeds in the breeze. A large straight pine with multiple dead branches down low and a wide shock of green branches high above shaded the west end of the house. In the middle of the yard, a small box held the well mechanisms. On the gently sloping roof was the common array of solar panels. There were no flags or emblems like those that might rise and flutter over some survivalist's camp. This was simply the home of a loner, and Dr. Wacker did in fact live here alone.

Michael knocked on the door. Silence. Indeed the whole world was quiet here, though not utterly lifeless. In the trees and in the air there was birdsong, and the light sway of the branches whispered and hushed. There was no rumble of other automobiles on the highway, let alone the murmur and hum of human voices like the noise of Michael's office, where individual voices and individual words disappeared into an impersonal vibration. The wind's soft voice barely hummed around the corners of the house, and the tall pine creaked a little, its top branches spread like a sail. Michael knocked again, still perhaps too timidly in the country quiet.

Nothing. Michael moved along the front of the house to peer into the large window, shading his face with his hands against the reflective glare. Dr. Wacker was stretched out upon a sofa. Michael smiled. "Figures," he thought, and went back to pound on the door without mercy. Even through the door, Michael could hear Wacker awaken, yelling an exclamation. Michael pounded again, more for annoyance than from perceived necessity.

Wacker was at the door. His hair was, if possible, more disheveled than usual, and his eyes winced against the daylight, as if he were awakening from a long night of celebration. Yet there was nothing groggy or unclear in his voice. To Michael's surprise, the man knew him at once and seemed to blame Michael for being late. "Ah, Pryor," he said, "'bout time you got here. Come in."

As Michael entered, his host disappeared through a doorway. "You'll need something to drink," he called back. "I have good water here, some ice. There's tea of whatever temperature. I've got cold beer. None of that cheap crap people drink for fun or inebreation."

Michael closed the door. "Sure," he said. "I'll try your beer."

"And you'll be the judge of whether or not it's superior, I suppose," Wacker said, already emerging from the other room with two beer bottles. "This happens to be Twice Born Amber Ale, which, in spite of its religiously inappropriate name, is pretty darned good stuff." He held out his bottle for a clink; Michael obliged, and they both took a swallow. "You know," Wacker went on, "I predicted back in my youth, at the end of the craft beer craze, that all the microbreweries would help us recreate a beer culture similar to the local pub with the local brew. There would be all these fine local beers that would restrict themselves to the local audience, creating, as it were, the classic relation between an ideal product and a unique location. In short, you'd have to go to Twice Born's pub to get Twice Born beer." Wacker took another drink. "But of course I didn't foresee the impact of teleportation technology on simple industries like distribution and logistics. Thousands lost their jobs, Mr. Pryor," he said with seriousness, "and no local brew remained local. Everyone could become a worldwide distributor, and everyone tried to be the next billion-dollar beer company. Those companies that couldn't manage it folded up. Those with a moderate success got bought up by Coors. Those with great success had to standardize their beer recipes to keep their million faithful drinkers faithfully drinking the faithful beer." Wacker took another sip. "You know," he suddenly brightened, "I have some mugs in the freezer that would make this even better." He deposited his bottle on an end table and turned back to the kitchen.

Michael surveyed the room: the couch and the mostly unmatching furniture pieces around the living room were simple and functional. The two chairs were a reclining chair and a rocking chair of an old-fashioned wood design. Beside each were standing lamps and small tables with short stacks of books. On one sat a small plate that once might have held a piece of chocolate cake but now only a dirty fork.

Michael felt awkward, as if he had invaded private space but equally wondering if he had entered the secluded lair of some dangerous madman. "You live a long way out here," Michael called toward the back room.

"*Long way*," Dr. Wacker said emerging again from the back of the house, "is a relative concept. Two hundred years ago, a trip of sixty miles might have required a week of intensive labor. Fifty years ago, it was barely worth a moment's thought to the average car driver. Today, once again, it's a 'long way,' ironically for the opposite reason of two centuries ago." As he spoke, he took Michael's beer and poured it into a frosty mug.

Michael took the mug. "You separate yourself from your fellow man," he said with an intended hint of accusation, "but not from his carnal pleasures." He held aloft the mug in salute.

"As you are a philosophical materialist, Mr Pryor," Wacker replied as he poured his own beer into a second frozen mug, "all pleasures are by definition carnal. It is only because I am not a materialist that I can speak of non-carnal pleasures; you cannot." He too held his beer aloft. "To your health, Mr. Pryor."

"And to yours, Dr. Wacker." They both sat.

Wacker smacked his lips and put his mug down. "Now that we both have our carnality properly satisfied, however temporarily, suppose we talk about something important."

"I presume you called me for a reason. Rather mysteriously, I might add." Michael drank deeply of the cold beer. It was indeed good, and with almost a sense of self-control, he set his beer down on the table beside the recliner. "What is it you think I need to know that made me drive this long way for the carnal beer?"

Wacker smiled genuinely, and Michael felt for a second that he might be having a beer with a friend. Then the older man looked at him sternly. "It's about technology, Mr. Pryor, technology of the soul."

"OK?" Michael responded, as if to hurry the interview along.

"No, not OK," Wacker shot back. "Damn it! The proper response is, 'Dr. Wacker, sir, your highness, there can be no such thing as a technology of the soul, since the one is purely material and the other immaterial.' Perhaps you don't remember our first conversation."

"Of course I do, but—"

"It doesn't matter," the professor waved him away. "I should apologize for that. I no doubt dismissed you too quickly, let it all go too lightly. You see, I didn't really take your information entirely seriously, and I made the naive assumption that you would either see quickly the sense of my logic or, like most people, you would be happy to ignore ideas and thought and consistency and just babble on your merry way. I can see now I was wrong, because there is a third alternative." He paused. "Perhaps after all there *is* a technology of the soul, and all this you've been writing is going to change the world dramatically."

"But if there is a technology of the soul," Michael said, trying to sound logical, "then your world view is false. You were wrong not merely to speak so briefly the first time, but indeed about the very nature of reality."

"Right," Wacker responded, so matter-of-factly that Michael was startled. Wacker reacted. "What?" he said. "You don't think a smart man knows he can be mistaken, perhaps utterly mistaken? Thinking is not the same as peace of mind; arguably, the two are directly opposed. You know this yourself, I suspect." Michael heard that as a compliment.

"I could be wrong," Wacker said, as if starting a speech, "and so any honest person has to think and rethink his positions. There," he said, pointing to the table and its books, "is the standard Rene Descartes, Daniel Dennett, a few evolutionary psychologists, even something by your beloved Richard Gesar. Down there," he said, pointing to another pile of magazines and papers, "are monographs on brain structure—I don't understand most of it, I confess—and on the tablet there I have a thousand more articles on similar stuff. I even have your additions, Mr Pryor, though they are flaccid in comparison."

"And so," Michael stepped in gruffly, "what is your new conclusion?"

"Admitting that I could be wrong," the professor said calmly, "I conclude nonetheless that I'm not. And if I'm not wrong, then there are other things going on, more dire than I had at first perceived."

"How's that?" Michael intended to sound skeptical.

"I've explained before the apparent absurdity of a technology of the spirit," Wacker said easily, without sounding defensive. "Consciousness doesn't come in pounds or inches or picojoules. We don't have half of free will or three quarters of a mind, though I have half a mind to get me another beer. Want one?" Michael wasn't sure if he was supposed to laugh, but the professor was apparently amused. Then he looked away. "Not the time for clever repartee, I suppose . . .

"Listen," Wacker said, "here's the deal. Let us suppose that every time we human beings change an idea into an action or a physical impulse into an idea, we do miracles. They don't seem like miracles because we do it all the time, thousands of times a day. But—let us say—being creatures made in the image of God, we are by nature creators, creators of a kind of reality."

"I don't know about the God stuff," Michael tried to respond conversationally, "but I see that we all create a kind of reality for ourselves."

"No, damn it!" The professor's exclamation startled Michael. "We don't create a reality for ourselves. We create reality. Reality is both the physical and the mental. Ideas—at least some of them—are facts. Indeed, only ideas can be facts. The fact of the idea can match, more or less, the fact of the matter—there's a pun there, if you want philosophical humor. When the fact matches the fact, we have truth. No idea can be complete truth, but some ideas are more true than others. And we must strive always to conform our ideas to the reality around us; it does not work the other way around."

"But surely we do change the world. I thought you said it works both ways."

"No, I said the miraculous interaction between the world and ideas works both ways, but truth only works one way. When we work the other way—which, again, we do so often, so commonly, that we barely notice the miracle—we change not the world into idea, but will into the world. Here we deal not with truth, but with goodness, as we seek to change the world to match ideas. Not just any ideas, mind you, but *ideals*," he emphasized the *L*. "Ideals are ideas we think are good. We change the world with good—and not so good—ideas, and the world changes us with facts, though we can get them wrong. Follow me so far?"

Michael thought he did, but it seemed a pointless argument. "Sure, Dr. Wacker," he said, with some emphasis on the title, as if to stress the possibility that the honorific could be mocked, "but so what? Suppose all you say is true. Fine. What do you want from me? Is this some philosophical diatribe, or am I supposed to ooh and ah about your worldview? Frankly, this is either the raving of philosophers who have debated this shit over and over for the last few thousand years or it is so obvious nobody gives a damn."

To Michael's surprise, Wacker smiled, held up a finger and said, "Exactly! Debated and obvious. The three-thousand-year debate changes nothing of what we all understand about ourselves. You do understand me. Good."

Michael felt more annoyed to have inadvertently agreed with the man's ideas. It felt like the praise he received when colleagues told him how much they appreciated his agreement with Gesar. He was going to object, but the professor went on.

"Let's assume the miracles of thought and action," he was saying. "Let's assume the world changes us and we change the world, yet there is more to these changes than the way sunlight changes the temperature of the roof or water changes a dying plant. Let us now consider the medium by which such human changes occur. Let us consider—"

Michael was done. "That's enough, Wacker," he interrupted and stood. "Thanks for the beer. I don't have time for the ramble. I regret the time I took getting here. If it hadn't been for Marta Sanchez's opinion of you . . ."

"Ah, yes. Marta. I'm sorry." Wacker held up a hand and apologized a few times as Michael stood. "Tell you what, Mr. Pryor," the man said. "You give me five more minutes, and if you're not intrigued, then be on your way. Five minutes."

Michael looked at his watch and pretended to push a button on the side. "Five minutes," he said. "Go." He sat back down.

"Five minutes," Wacker repeated. "OK. I forgot you have no training, or perhaps interest, in actually understanding what you believe." He paused.

Michael snarled a slight smile at the insult. "Four minutes and 45 seconds," he said in reply.

Professor Wacker took a breath. "Nothing has changed in this debate for three thousand years," he said, "except the technology that deals with the mechanism between world and idea: the brain. As the eye is the medium of sight, so is the brain the medium of thought and will. There are no colors like blue and red in the world, Mr. Pryor, but our eyes and brain translate certain impulses into these experiences. Let that stand. Yet if I poke your eyes out, you will not be able to see those colors nor invent them for yourself. Light waves are material, but colors are mental, and without the eyes, one cannot become the other, not even miraculously.

"The brain, then, is the analogue. You change the brain, and you change perception of the world. There is little debate about this, though exactly how a brain changes electrochemical impulses into ideas remains a mystery.

"But let us not forget the other direction, Mr. Pryor. The brain is also the mechanism whereby the will is changed into action and thus changes in the world. Once again, if we change the brain, we change what people can and cannot choose. With sufficient access to your brain, Mr. Pryor, not only can I remove your free will, I can remove your free will *and you will like it*. I can make you into a puppet of my will and make you happy about it."

The professor stared at Michael. Almost in spite of himself, Michael was intrigued. Yet he kept a poker face. "Two more minutes," he said without looking at his watch.

Wacker knew he had gained more time. But quickly he resumed. "We are in the midst of a tremendous new manipulation of the human self. The technology of the spirit—in one sense an evident oxymoron—is a technology of the brain that removes from people their ability to desire more than life. To desire more than themselves. To desire more than acquiescence to the moral standards of the world around them. It makes them happy, Mr. Pryor, and in doing so it removes their humanity."

Michael was strangely surprised by this conclusion, but he tried not to show it. "Oh, come on, my dear professor," he said with intentional mockery in his voice. "Happiness is hardly a problem. We all want happiness. You do."

Wacker coughed a laugh. "Don't insult me, Mr. Pryor," he said. "I am not happy, not in the sense being used here. Not in Gesar's sense. And neither are you." He paused. "Nor do you want to be."

Michael felt the point of that observation acutely. He knew both claims were true, felt indeed that sense of superiority he knew in his own dissatisfaction. Yet he had never heard it named. There was a pause, the ticking of a clock.

"Have I used up my five minutes, Mr. Pryor?" Wacker asked, cocking his head.

Michael smiled a genuine, if crooked smile, and didn't mind being defeated. "Go on," he said.

"Good! Happiness is the problem, Mr. Pryor. Satisfaction is the tool. You and I, people like us, aren't happy or satisfied because we want something more. In knowing we want truth; in doing we want goodness. Realizing these things exist beyond and outside us, we strive and wonder and struggle and are constantly dissatisfied. The very worst thing that could happen to us, Mr Pryor, is that we might become happy."

"So you're trying to tell me," Michael rejoined the discussion, insisting still on a cynical voice, "that Gesar and perhaps some other, unknown cabal of mystics in a cave somewhere or industrialists in a smoke-filled room, are plotting the take-over of the world by helping people find spiritual satisfaction? Isn't that what religion is all about?"

"No, it isn't," Wacker said matter of factly. "But that is a digression. Even the speculations on conspiracy are a side issue. We must consider the gravity of where this particular technology, conspiratorial or not, leads. Because this is not merely about world domination. This isn't about Sheikh Muhammad al-Aksa being followed by a million Muslims, or Mao Zedung being followed by a billion Chinese, all of whom have been tricked into some self-destructive vision. This is about taking the individual and, one way or another, killing him."

Michael rolled his eyes. "Now I think you're crazy again. Nobody is dying; nobody is being killed."

Professor Wacker laced his fingers beneath his chin. "Let me try it this way," he began. "If there were some new technology, some new way to boil an egg or make a phone call, you might use it or you might not. Right?"

"Of course," Michael responded. "Nobody threatens your life if you don't want a boiled egg or want to be phoned to another place. You are clearly an example. Do you think your life is threatened because you don't phone around like the rest of us?"

"No, Mr. Pryor, no," the man responded with slow words, "I'm not merely projecting my paranoia into some bigger picture. I'm entirely happy, and the world over all is entirely happy, if you don't want a new kind of boiled egg. I'm glad you choose to let me drive a car and not zap myself through phone lines. But suppose I have a broken leg or a severed artery and there's a technology for fixing it. Suppose I refuse that technology as if it were the boiling of the egg. Now what's your diagnosis?"

Michael shrugged, unsure where the professor's logic was headed. "I would suppose you're crazy, or maybe depressed. Why would any sane

person keep a broken leg when we can mend it easily? We've seen it often enough, that people could have children inoculated but refuse because
they believe some dire conspiracy will make their children into drones. Or
they could save their lives with a blood transfusion, but they refuse because
some outdated religious text tells them there's some mysterious morality
about blood. Some people, I suppose, are so depressed they can't even be
talked into taking antidepressants. Some people are so sick they can't in fact
be cured. So?"

"So what is your prescription, Dr. Pryor?" Wacker asked. "What should
we do with such people?"

"We give them therapy. We give them drugs."

"So there's the technology, right?"

"Yes," Michael agreed easily. "So what?"

"So evidently they are so depressed or ill they cannot choose for themselves to address their own illness," Wacker said straightforwardly. "So do
we take them away from themselves and treat them for their own good?
Or do we decide they have some inexplicable right to remain ill. What
is our option?"

"I suppose," Michael answered, predicting the line of conspiracy thinking, "that you fear we are going to treat them against their will. But we don't.
We let people choose illness, even if it means letting them die."

"Right," Wacker said, somewhat to Michael's surprise. Then the professor held up a finger. "But," he inserted, "we don't let people die, do we, Mr.
Pryor?" he said with a kind of pretended compassion. "That would be unkind." Michael was silent. He suddenly saw the direction of the professor's
logic, and it called up a mix of evident rhetoric and unpleasant memory.

"Mr. Pryor," Wacker said, looking down into his own hands as if
speaking to no one, "if people refuse to be happy, if they refuse the simple
technology of physical and mental health, it can only be because they are so
unhappy they cannot choose happiness properly. Therefore, in our compassion, we will find ways to help them make that decision. If they still will not,
then we must, in our same compassion, help them toward a peaceful death."

The logic of Dr. Wacker's paranoia—Michael mentally called it that—
was indeed intriguing, and yet Michael couldn't shake the feeling that this
carried some hint of global political conspiracy. For him, such conspiracy
talk was nonsense, the ravings of madmen and religious fanatics who live in
the mountains of Idaho, waiting for some nefarious apocalypse, wrapping
their cabins in tin foil to keep out the evil radio waves of some imagined
Big Brother. Michael had heard the professor insist it was not a political
conspiracy, and yet those were the only real terms Michael could apply. Still
spiritually unborn himself, Michael's categories for danger were limited,

narrowed by a world view still too much in the camp of Gesar than of Wacker. Even his own memories—of his mother's disease and especially of his father's euthanizing—were not quite honest enough to allow light to shine on this new way of thinking. Thus he didn't know what the right question was. Before he could form an alternative question that made sense of his doubt and his recognition of Wacker's point, the professor started one last time.

"Free will," Wacker spoke, "is the last mystery. In fact, it was the first mystery, as God in a wholly unimaginable act of love gave over omnipotence to the inviolability of the finite mind. You and I, Mr. Pryor, are holes in the omnipotence of God. As such, we cannot be violated except by our own act of will. Nevertheless, we can be asked—or seduced—to willfully submit ourselves to the ending of our wills, being made satisfied with the moral and intellectual life of the day. This evil, like all evil, must embrace a contradiction, namely that in the seduction of the self away from itself, the will must choose to relinquish itself to having no will. The great attraction is happiness and satisfaction. This is why merely traveling by phone or submitting yourself to cancer treatment that dematerializes the body and reassembles it elsewhere without the cancer cells is not enough. These manipulations of the self are merely the opening, the rehabituation of ourselves, the conditioning, as it were, of a people being trained for a greater, more final choice: *the choice to have no choice.* That choice must be made because to refuse that choice is itself a sickness that the choice would cure. Therefore the only alternative is death."

Michael had no idea what the professor meant, but he felt he could not be silent. Silence would have allowed his feelings about his father's death to speak. Silence would have allowed his confused thoughts about honor and sexual fidelity to speak. Silence might even have allowed him to hear his own mumbled confession of a vague attraction to the technology of the *tulku.* But Michael was not yet ready to hear what all these voices had to say. "But perhaps," he responded, "perhaps the result is not so evil. Perhaps after all, with the proper technology and the proper compassion people can find peace. Peace, not death."

"Here, Mr. Pryor," Wacker said, "they are the same thing.

20

MIRACLES

Michael carried the professor's concerns to church. He saw with some clarity the philosophical problem the "crazy Thomist" seemed to assume, and he could not quite deny that, in many ways, he assumed the same problem. He liked the professor for that, a kind of directness of language and argument, along with a simplicity of observation that he had not quite expected from a professional philosopher. But Michael could also not quite abandon his suspicions about religious belief, religious assumptions that somehow crept into the common-sense idealization of Wacker's understandings of mind and selfhood and free will and other abstractions that still seemed to Michael a distraction from getting on with life. Life was complicated enough, what with Desra's distant coldness, recurrent thoughts about Marta, and, of course, work. Michael had, after all, writing to do, and references to Rene Descartes just didn't fit into his observations. That's what this was about: observations, the cold, hard facts of what was going on in the labs of Dr. Richard Gesar.

At the same time, even in those labs, there was more than cold, hard science. Gesar himself seemed to base his works on religious presumptions, and his religious conclusions were interwoven with what he insisted on calling "science." Michael would have liked to have just been a reporter, but that option seemed closed. He had to be a philosopher. He had to think religiously. He didn't like it.

So here he was in church. The Reverend Dr. David Roberts versus his Holiness, the Tulku Dr. Richard Gesar. Of course the "versus" was not in the program, but Michael couldn't help but imagine it that way. In fact, he hoped for it. If there would just be a good fight, he thought, at least one or the other would have to be defeated. That would actually help.

Michael sat toward the front. He had arrived early and been shown to his seat with some formality, although without the presence of Dr. Roberts. As Michael watched the pre-show preparations, he saw the preacher looking at the marked spots on the stage floor. He saw, too, Dr. Gesar being shown those marks and being led through how the introductions would go, where he would enter from stage right, and so on. With no flood light, Gesar had noticed Michael in the front row and waved at him amiably.

Yet the show was not simply a debate nor even an interview. It was church. Much to his discomfort, Michael had first to sit through what seemed interminable hymn singing and prayers. The hymns were not what Michael expected, as he still had some sense that Christians sang long-outdated tunes and lyrics salted with *thee* and *thou*. These songs, however, were upbeat and active, vibrant even, led by a quintet of singers—notably racially mixed—accompanied by a band of guitars and piano and drums. The people in the audience—Michael decided against the word *congregation*—were on their feet most of the time, singing along, following the words projected onto giant screens at the front and onto small screens in the back of every chair. Michael felt strange sitting silent and praiseless; he felt even stranger standing.

Besides the singing, there were prayers, sometimes spoken into the amplified system on top of the continued humming of whatever chorus had just ended. Sometimes more formally the prayers interrupted the music and seemed less like praising Jesus and more like talking to God. Michael felt he could vaguely understand the latter. If there were a God, he thought, it would almost be necessary that God would hear prayers. Unexpectedly, Michael heard himself think, "So there You are," though he could not have called it prayer. Had he named it, he would have been closer to "religion" than he wanted to be. So he called it "philosophy" and thought again of Professor Wacker. He nearly laughed aloud and felt vaguely as if he had escaped some danger.

At last the program moved into content, or what seemed like content to Michael Pryor, beginning with a sermon-like presentation by Roberts. It didn't sound like a sermon, didn't involve any evident notes or a speech from anything resembling a pulpit. Roberts walked the stage, confidently knowing how far to pace each direction, when to turn and face the audience for a significant pause. It was well done, Michael thought, though not necessarily because of the content. Michael couldn't help thinking Roberts was to church what D'Bon Sanders was to the nightly news.

The content of the church production, unlike Sanders's news, was mostly about love. It reminded the people listening that love has two directions: horizontal and vertical. It emphasized that the world around us hungers for the horizontal, needs us to be that love in this dangerous and painful world. The listeners were told that love also is vertical, directed at God, and that there could be no successful horizontal love without the vertical. Michael doubted that, but he understood the message. At the very least, the preacher said, the horizontal love becomes tired and worn, losing its strength as do all things human, and Michael couldn't help but think of Desra. In the end, the sermon said, the love of God that informs the love of humanity is inspired first by another love, the love from God, the love of God for us. There were Bible verses and many references to Jesus, and the sermon ended. Or rather, it almost ended. It became clear after a short break that the sermon on love in Part One was meant to lead into the discussion of other kinds of religious love, whether they could be true love, whether God exists as part of all love. So the stage was set for the interview with Dr. Richard Gesar. Michael was ready.

Roberts provided the introduction, announcing some of the recent news events in which Gesar had played a major role. Roberts announced further that his guest was a highly respected spiritual figure, recognized as adept, master, sage, or minister in many different religious groups, not only in his own Buddhist tradition. "And yet," Roberts said, "there are matters of faith and belief that we all must question and face with honesty, and therefore it seems inevitable that we cannot agree with my guest on all points of religion. Nonetheless, or all the more," said Roberts, smiling at the clever juxtaposition of terms, "the conversation we're about to have can be, or must be, an honest one, so we might share our understanding, learn from one another where we can, and face our disagreements with congenial honesty." And Dr. Richard Gesar entered, stage right.

Gesar wore his common orange robe, but his feet were in white socks and tennis shoes, making for an almost comical sight. As he entered, he began walking straight toward his host, then seemed to realize there was an audience. He squinted into the stage lights and seemed embarrassed, smiled and almost stooped, seeming to shrink from the lights and soft applause. It was as if he was not used to being a celebrity.

Quickly, however, he recovered his focus on David Roberts, strode the last steps with confidence, and shook his host's hand. The seat was offered and taken. The conversation began with an introduction that repeated some of Gesar's accolades, including his title—naming him a *tulku*—and what that means. Roberts reiterated Gesar's recognition within other religious traditions, as Thera, or "Elder" in a Theravada Buddhist monastery in Sri Lanka, as "Master" of Taiji, as *curandero* or healer shaman among a group of native elders in central Mexico, and so on. "I believe, in fact," Roberts said, "that you have even been recognized by several well-known muftis, recognized scholars of Islam as a sort of honorary 'Muslim'"—the preacher marked the word with wiggling fingers—"and have been invited to Mecca. How did that happen?"

As the list of spiritual recognitions progressed, Gesar smiled gently, and Michael again noted the shyness of this great man. With the last question, however, he once again perked up, distracted from his embarrassment, it seemed, by the challenging questions. "Ah, yes, well, you see we had some rather fine meetings, Sheikh Daud ar-Rahman and Sheikh Ahmed Smyth-Anderson and I, and we thought long and hard about what it means to submit to God, which is, after all what the word *Muslim* means." The *tulku* smiled toward the floor again but looked up quickly. "There is no such thing, of course, as an honorary Muslim. One either submits oneself to that which is greater, or one does not. I struggle—which is the meaning of *jihad*, as you know—I struggle to make that submission, as I'm sure you do as well. In that sense, Dr. Roberts, I should say you, too, are Muslim, etymologically speaking."

Dr. David Roberts apparently accepted the spiritual compliment but gave a small laugh. "Still, I'm sure I shan't be invited to Mecca any time soon," he said. There was some laughter in the audience, although Michael wasn't sure who among the devoted flock of Roberts' massive congregation might have understood the interchange thus far.

"Actually," Gesar responded, evidently taking the joke more seriously than it was intended, "you might be surprised. I think we are entering a new era of tolerance and openness that might surprise us all. Certainly, I hope so."

"This gets us to two important matters, then," Roberts said, sitting forward in his chair as if physically entering a new conversation. "No doubt your hope is partly built upon your own work, your discoveries of auroscopy and your claims that there is an observable spiritual reality we all share and that you claim, shall we say, to augment. Your own work would seem to help us all submit to the same God, even though not everyone believes in the same God. That forces the second concern: how do you deal with the fundamental disagreement among religions? Evidently you would have us all be Muslim."

"Ah, yes," Gesar said, "I see your concern. But as our conversation just revealed, I am Muslim in one sense, but clearly I am not Muslim in another. I am a Buddhist." Gesar smiled. "Perhaps you know that," he said with a grin. There was some laughter in the audience. "I would in the same way urge that everyone can be Buddhist in one sense but needn't be Buddhist in another. I would suggest that everyone can, in the same way, be Christian in one sense but needn't all be Christian in another."

"But you must know, sir," Roberts responded with apparent force and seriousness, "that we here, most of us anyway, understand there needs to be a very explicit focus on Jesus as the way, the truth, and the life. No one, Jesus says, comes to the Father except through him. I raise this point for the sake of my listeners as a crucial matter of distinction."

"Ah, but you see," Gesar started, also leaning into the conversation with a kind of happy intensity, as if describing some new discovery or a glorious sunset recently seen, "I, too, believe what Jesus said. Perhaps you know I have had some fine conversations with the new pope, discussing these very matters, and wondering together about how Christlikeness is achieved and what it exactly means. To find Jesus is to find love, even as your own sermon just demonstrated. And just as we took care to define *Muslim*, so we must take time to define *Christ*. What does it mean but an anointed one? I believe," Gesar paused as if for effect, "that you, Dr. Roberts, are anointed."

Roberts sat back as if startled, but still smiling. "But I would never claim to be Christ," he said strongly. "No Christian would."

"Indeed!" Gesar said. "And neither did Jesus."

"Well," Roberts said, leaning forward again, as if to respond to Gesar. "Well," he repeated and stopped, momentarily frozen. Then, in a strangely sudden, yet slow-motion way, he began to change. Michael wondered at first if the great TV preacher had lost his temper and was about to get angry. His eyes grew strangely wide, more however with a sense of fear and surprise than anger, and his gaze fell from the face of his guest. Michael realized then that Roberts was not responding to Gesar at all, but seemed to be choking, as if struggling to swallow. There was a slow moan, almost a single, long musical note, but strained, barely escaping a closed throat. Then, as if slowly levitating, he barely rose from his chair, pushing himself up from the arms, until, only a little above the cushion, his right hand came up and grabbed at his chest. For a second he was poised as if in a delicate balance, and then, with a dull thud, he fell to the stage at the feet of the Tulku Richard Gesar.

The next ten minutes were a wild flurry of often careful, sometimes almost frantic, activity. The details of the medical emergency were something Michael learned only later, when reports were made available and the world was full of information, literally offering minute-by-minute replays of the events. Yet even from the front row of the auditorium, he felt distant from the action, sometimes unable to see anything at all through the wall of people on the stage. Yet he could not thereafter forget the events and was constantly asked what he had seen.

What Michael learned from later reports is that Dr. David Roberts had suffered sudden cardiac arrest, an utter electrical failure of his heart brought on, it was speculated, by a milder, relatively not-so-dangerous slowing of blood from the heart. What might have been, therefore, a mild heart attack became life-threatening. Worse than life threatening; it was a killer.

What Michael actually saw transpire was a series of fruitless attempts to save the preacher's life. Richard Gesar was the first to catch the victim, but almost immediately, there swarmed onto the stage helpers of various kinds. Some were clearly just concerned, gasping, huddling, crying, some pointlessly patting the man's cheek like some ridiculous fainting scene from a movie. Quickly however, there appeared a more efficient-looking medical team, two men kept on staff at the church to respond to medical emergencies that sometimes arise when there are several thousand people in attendance. The two men pushed aside the concerned crowd, and even Richard Gesar moved back, allowing the EMTs to do their work. They quickly saw the severity of the heart attack, one of them calling for a defibrillator.

That was the first two minutes, declared the later reports, and while one EMT ran for the electrical defibrillator, the other began CPR. Another minute. As crowds on and off the stage surged and moved in Michael's field of vision, he caught glimpses and heard pieces of dialogue that were again like scenes from a movie, with the machine charging, the EMT declaring voltage, the characteristic call of "Clear!" followed by the jump and thump of the body. Another minute. Two. The EMTs continued; a cardiac specialist named Dr. Arjun Rakur came up from the audience and was allowed on stage from the left wing. Another minute.

At that point, there descended a strange quiet, perhaps, Michael surmised, because those present and medically trained were realizing, as Michael was, that by this time there would be brain damage. Even if Roberts could be resuscitated at this point, he thought, there could be nothing but a short hospital stay and the mercy of euthanasia. Perhaps because this thought was occurring to others, Michael saw the crowd on stage thin a bit, helpers and staff of the church drifting away a bit, crying, trying to be mutually comforting.

Then Richard Gesar seemed to reappear. He had always been there, of course, but in the back. Yet in the eighth minute, the *tulku* stepped forward and touched one of the EMTs on the shoulder. He whispered—said Dr. Rakur's later report—"Let me see," and as if by some odd instinct of impending wonder, the medical emergency expert moved aside and the Tibetan master moved in. From where he sat, Michael saw Gesar kneel beside the body of Roberts, and with his eyes closed he began to chant. Closest witnesses could never agree on what he chanted, even if it was English or whether it was melodic. But something soft and fluid was on his lips, followed by a gutteral groan. The crowd stepped back as if afraid, so Michael saw clearly what happened next.

His eyes still closed, his lips still moving, the throaty growl still vibrating from his chest, Gesar leaned forward from his knees and laid his chest across the chest of Roberts. Michael caught words spaced out like a list, names or places or objects, magic words, words of some power Michael had never imagined. Gesar began to shake, almost as if he were laughing. Laughing.

Then Roberts gasped, caught air into his lungs in a wild, sucking swallow, and his immediate exhale was a scream. His eyes shot wide open, and with an almost supernatural force he pushed himself partly upright, as Gesar sat back. "What? What?" was all Roberts could say for those next seconds as his gaze took in the savage scene. Gesar relaxed onto his haunches and hung his head, apparently exhausted.

Some witnesses on stage said there had been a great heat from Gesar. Some claimed there was a light around him, a halo. Michael felt or saw none of those things, and neither did the cameras that were running the entire time. But the cameras were running, and within minutes the whole world was watching the *tulku* Dr. Richard Gesar raise a dead man to life.

BOOK TWO

The Vultures Will Gather

21

CHANGES

Michael awoke, rolled over and felt himself slipping again into sleep. He spoke to the clock, "Time." The digital readout was projected onto the ceiling: 7:45. He groaned, worried suddenly that he would be late for work . . . again. Somehow he had taken to sleeping later than usual. He closed his eyes, felt drowsy.

"Better get up, sleepy head," called a voice from the door. Michael, fully awake at once, sat up and stared. Desra was lounging against the doorpost, her blond hair straight and gleaming in the morning light that slipped through the darkened glass of the bedroom window.

"What are you doing here?" Michael asked urgently, more harshly than he intended. "Back to get some trinket you left?"

Desra smiled. "No," she said, "but if you didn't want me to visit, you should have changed the phone code." Her voice was almost pleasant, quite different at least from the last time Michael had spoken to her nearly five months ago. He felt his own sudden realization that he had wanted his tone to hurt her a little, that it would have been nice if she had gotten mad at him for his harshness. But she just smiled again. "If you don't want a morning visit," she said, "you shouldn't sleep so late."

Michael let his smile curl into the sneer. His parting with Desra had been anything but gentle and amicable. With the exception of a few signs of her returning to the apartment to gather "her things," he had neither heard nor seen any evidence of her existence. The month before she left for good, he had watched her descent into anger and irrationality, and, at least at first, Michael had responded with concern and efforts to console and encourage her. He had—at least in his own estimation—been sincere in his desire to help, though he had at the same time been annoyed that she had to have her crises at work and her various levels of self-doubt right after the great "miracle" that he and half the world, it seemed, had witnessed at the hand of Dr. Richard Gesar. She had continued to melt down that month, variously complaining about the stupidity of her boss, Kevin, and the ineffectuality of having "learned" Japanese—the verb she chose and that Michael had even adopted in order to sound like he was on her side. But her multifaceted dissatisfaction had also found its mark in him, noting his distance from her, his self-absorption, even his failure to dispose of a few pairs of dirty socks. Michael had finally "had enough," he told himself, though he knew some of her complaints about him were justified. Truth was, he didn't know what to do with his own dissatisfactions. So he had gone to work, followed the doings of Gesar, watched over and over the film clips of the miracle, buried himself in the multitude of naturalistic explanations and religious praises that poured out all over the newswall. When he was concerned about Desra, he was genuintely concerned, but he knew he was often pretending.

"So how's the Japanese?" Michael said, rising from the bed and strolling to the bathroom. "Got any new words?" Michael intended the mockery. Desra didn't miss it.

"You know," she said, as he passed her, "I should have talked to you more about those decisions. That would at least have been courteous." She paused; Michael peed.

"So are you here to apologize?" Michael called.

As he passed her again, she was smiling. "No," she said. "That wouldn't be helpful, would it?" Michael didn't respond, but proceeded to order his clothes, his back to Desra. What did he even want from her, he wondered silently. Somehow provoking her to anger would seem like a victory for him. But she was right, it wouldn't help. In a way, he knew he was the one who should be apologizing. That wouldn't help either, but for Michael's growing self-awareness, it seemed honest.

"No," Desra repeated to his back, "I'm not here to apologize. My own choices have made me what I am. I don't have to regret or apologize; I only have to move on, find myself. I have to be happy with myself."

Michael spun toward her, one leg in today's paper pants. He stared at Desra. She was indeed happy, happy with herself. He frowned. "You did it, didn't you?" he asserted more than asked.

"I did," she said, smiling even more broadly. "It was my decision and it has helped make me what I am." Michael frowned at the repetition and the bold happiness. "And I like what I am."

So that was it, Michael thought. Desra had chosen to undergo auroscopy and "the adjustment." Michael felt strangely disappointed, maybe even sad for Desra herself. But she was hardly unique in this choice, Michael knew. As the *tulku*'s popularity and authority took off, Michael watched the whole world hunger and thirst to become like him. And the technology was available to make it happen.

Michael had followed all the changes, had even written about some of it, although he was never quite satisfied with his own voice in any of his recent work. Melanie hadn't liked it much either. Michael couldn't find his own voice anymore, couldn't be sure what tone he wanted. Since the miracle, he hadn't been able to write well, though he had done his research, followed the interviews with both Gesar and Roberts. Michael had been at the press conference when Roberts declared his backing of Gesar, and since then the TV Christian preacher had been using his network, his influence, his audience, and his wealth to explore the spiritual reality of what he had experienced and what the world had seen take place on his own stage. It had been Michael Pryor who had asked Roberts, "What about Jesus?" He had wanted a damning response, something like blasphemy that Michael could pin on the man's picture, whether Michael actually believed in apostasy or not.

"I have not left my Lord," Roberts had answered solemnly. "I am truly a follower of Jesus and him alone."

"But?" Michael had prompted.

"But I am not going to limit God with my doctrine, Mr. Pryor," David Roberts had responded with thin-lipped sincerity. "'I have other sheep,' Jesus said, 'who are not in this fold,' and 'I will by no means cast them out.'" In the months that followed, Roberts had done more than merely "not cast them out." A master of marketing and television and mass appeal, the preacher had become a new kind of witness, an *advertiser*, to use Michael's own term. He had given other interviews—with more sympathetic writers, Michael noted—in which he expounded a theology of "grace" and a hope that all who came to find the deeper spiritual wholeness, a red aura, would indeed, "in their own time" find Christ. He had used his network to sponsor the "Don't Be Blue" program, both here and abroad, until auroscopy had become a common household term and the adjustment of one's aura as common as vision correction. Apparently now Desra had also had her vision fixed.

"So you're here to gloat," Michael tried. "Here to display your heightened spirituality." Michael wanted it to be an accusation, but he also knew somehow that it was just the truth: there in front of him was a happy Desra, while inside of him was still a miserable Michael.

Desra smiled sadly. "No, Michael," she said. "I only wanted to see how you were doing. And," she paused, "I wanted to let you know I'm OK."

"Hmm," Michael murmured as he slipped into his shirt, "sounds like gloating."

Desra almost laughed. "Still the same Michael," she said good natured-ly, "blue soul and all. But it's OK, Michael, it's OK. God is not in a hurry."

"God?" Michael responded? "Jesus! You sound like Daniel."

Desra nodded. "Actually, you're the one just like Daniel. Both of you stubborn as hell. But it's OK," she repeated. "It's OK."

Michael slipped by her at the doorway, still wanting to be angry, still afraid to meet her smile, afraid he did indeed want that smile, wanted to re-lax, wanted to stop arguing. "Like Daniel." But Daniel had his Jesus; Michael had no one. He rushed toward the kitchen for orange juice.

"You know," Desra called from the bedroom doorway, "it's a shame you got dressed so quickly. Maybe I could stay, and we could, you know, go back to bed for a bit. For old time's sake."

Michael stopped in the middle of the living room. It was not as though he had no thoughts of sex or lacked desire. But this offer from Desra seemed strange. He didn't mind a playful attitude toward sex, had many times insist-ed—mostly to Desra, in fact—that sex ought to be a morally neutral, shared entertainment. Privately, he had placed "healthy sex" somewhere between the spiritual exercise of Petra Eriksen and the equally spiritual prohibitions of Marta Sanchez. Yet, with Desra between him and the bed, the suggestion seemed almost too whimsical. Besides, he wanted to be angry.

"What old times are we talking about?" he asked with mustered scorn in his voice. "Those from two years ago, or those from six months ago?"

"Well, Michael," Desra said softly, "Maybe you aren't in the mood. Or, if I'm the problem, maybe you need to find someone else." Her smile came back. "You need to find some peace."

Desra passed Michael on her way to the phone. She paused and kissed him on the cheek. "Don't be blue," she said and went on to the booth in the corner. Michael watched as she fingerprinted her ID into the machine and stepped in. She turned and waved, the door closed and went black.

"Don't be blue," Michael said into the ensuing emptiness, his voice a huff of disdain. "Or maybe find someone else." He finished buttoning his shirt. He could follow neither of those options, apparently. Lord knows, he had tried both, though admittedly more the latter than the former. Within a month of Desra's departure, he had tried to contact Marta, wanting to tell her Desra was gone and he was, in some sense, free to form a new re-lationship. Perhaps—he had meant to hint—perhaps he was even willing to consider Marta's Jesus, maybe try to seek the spiritual side of life as he never had before. Surely—he had thought—surely that would be precisely what Marta would have wanted. She liked him—he took some comfort in that simple, if inexplicable fact—and if he would even try to be open to her religious sensibilities, surely she would leap at the chance to bring him into the faith and into her arms. Surely.

But after the miracle, when Desra had moved out, Marta had rebuffed him unambiguously. "No can do," she had said, in an almost joking voice. Then more seriously, "The world and my soul, as they are right now," she had insisted, "I just can't take unneeded risks." Michael had assumed she meant she was afraid of being hurt, of being loved and then abandoned. He had tried to assure her that he had perhaps—he had used the word *perhaps* and regretted it later—changed, and that he could be a new man, more devout and devoted. That turn of phrase had just happened, and he had instantly liked it.

There had been a pause in the video feed, as Marta smiled and almost winked at him. "You really don't get it, do you?" she had said. Then she had gone off into a long dissertation about the nature of spiritual risk, some reference to Soren Kierkegaard, and then—somehow—about how that obscure philosopher had "not really been interpreted fairly by either Christian or non-Christian philosophers." Michael was lost. Then, in the midst of her expatiation on all things existential, she had stopped abruptly and laughed. "*Factus sum insipiens,*" she had said.

Michael had laughed, too, not because he knew what she had said, but because he enjoyed her humor. "I have no idea what you mean sometimes, even most of the time," he had replied, "but I ike-lay your augh-lay." They both had laughed, a little.

"You know, Michael Pryor," she had finally said, "I saw the miracle on TV along with everyone else. You were there. Maybe you could tell me more. But right now, I need a man of God more than I need a man. I hope you understand." She said goodbye, and she had not returned any call since.

That was the other point, wasn't it? Michael mused in the quiet of Desra's departure. At least on one occasion he had thought to call Marta to assure her that he could be a "man of God," that maybe he was ready at last to seek a spiritual experience. He had, after all, been a mere ten yards away from a miracle, which placed a new demand on his life, on his conscience, on his soul. "What if?" he had wondered now for months: What if he, too, needed a spiritual healing, a new soul? What if Gesar could make that happen? What if? And Marta's Jesus was surely one of the options.

And yet. Every time that line of thought came through Michael's mind, the old bile rose up in him like the rebellion of an oppressed people. "No, damn it!" he would say to himself. "No. I will not embrace a lie to find happiness. I will not embrace Marta's Jesus to get Marta. I will not take on Gesar's spirituality to find peace. I would rather die in turmoil than accept their lies! I'm too important!" This was more true than Michael himself knew.

All that resolve, all that insistence on truth and integrity, left Michael alone. In his loneliness—a loneliness he almost couldn't confess, as it seemed a weakness, yet a weakness that was somehow right—his determination wavered. Off and on, he had wrestled with the call of Marta's God and wrestled with the call of Gesar's technology, still unable to discern the difference. Work had not gone well. Writing was stymied. The trust of his peers seemed strained until even Melanie's voice became strangely distant. Melanie's replies to his work and varieties of angry insistence had become critical rather than sympathetic. Or more accurately, Michael thought, her tone in general had changed the other way around, becoming less critical and more sympathetic, until he had realized that she, too, had embraced the spirituality of the day. Even Melanie had heard the call to peace, the lure of auroscopy, and the healing of the soul. Melanie had become nice.

So Michael had become truly, finally, alone. He was only Michael Pryor, and it was not enough.

So it was that, almost as an act of despair, he had finally, yesterday, gone to the clinic and done a test, and the result was clear. His aura was blue, blue as the summer sky. If Gesar was right, that meant that he was a spiritual failure. He needed God—or something like God. He had always needed a reality beyond himself, something more than himself, but that hole in his soul had become a scientific fact yesterday. It explained his dissatisfactions, his frustrations, his angers, maybe even his resistance both to Desra and to Marta. It explained everything. Michael had found out that his soul was broken, unenlightened or whatever, and the fact was proven both by his inner experience and by the *tulku*'s machines. Surely that meant both Gesar and Marta were right and he needed to be a man of God. Perhaps then he could find love, love of Marta, yes, but also love of himself. Perhaps he could yet find peace.

The discovery of his blue aura and his need of God also meant—or was supposed to mean—that there was the hope of a cure. What did it take? Most obviously, it meant that he could schedule an appointment *today* to go have his aura adjusted. He could be made spiritual. He could have a red aura. He could be happy. Surely that was a grand hope. For even in his more advanced loneliness, Micheal had not yet learned to distinguish between God and the peace of God.

Even so, there was enough arrogance left in Michael that he was safe. For still, for Michael, the "cure" promised in the spiritual healing of Dr. Richard Gesar seemed anything but hopeful. It seemed like a final and irrevocable loss. For Desra to show up unannounced after months of silence only made the whole matter more confusing.

The salvation of Michael's cynicism struck him. He had gone in to find his aura blue—faulty, weak, broken. The next morning, before he could even get out of bed, Desra had appeared. Was that a coincidence? Had she known of his test result and appeared to help him find peace? Had she become a missionary?

No, that was not the right question. Michael was used to missionaries; hell, his brother had been his personal missionary for a dozen years. The question was how Desra could have known he needed a missionary. Could she have been, in some sense, sent? Sent by whom? By God? That would sound like Daniel. But what could it mean that Desra had appeared spiritually red and happy in Michael's apartment the very day after he had shown he was not spiritually healthy? What could that mean?

Michael caught himself and laughed aloud with a humph. Some global conspiracy? Michael didn't believe in such things any more than he believed in Daniel's God. He tried to push the idea from his mind, but it resisted. It stayed. Michael wrestled with it, wanted to mock it, called it the lunacy of Professor Wacker. Yet the thought did not go away, and somewhere in Michael Pryor's rebellious insistence, he decided he would once more seek the advice of the crazy professor.

22

MILLER'S TEARS

Like his brother, Daniel Pryor had grown weary with resistance. Had the two brothers shared the same worldview, even the same language of love, they might have been able to comfort one another, to uphold one another. But as the little brother still could not see the suffering in Daniel's faith, Daniel felt alone. Helen remained as always his love and his life, a beauty he never felt he quite deserved. There, in that single figure, was solidity, a reality he could count on. It was for him as if all that "love of Christ" stuff he heard and duly recited took its only manifest shape in Helen. Her love stayed, lived, endured through all the folly and uncertainty Daniel called "faith." For Daniel his wife was like the recitation of a creed he didn't quite understand. But he knew intuitively that the creed contained the assertion that it was OK if he did not fully understand it.

But Helen was his wife, and all patriarchal presumptions aside, Daniel knew she depended on him as much, perhaps more, than he on her. She occasionally asked him for reassurances—how ironic, he thought—and sometimes she seemed to hold onto his arm as they walked through the world as if he were the steady hand and the steady gait. And when they walked this way, it felt to him like he was.

But that wasn't enough for Daniel, though he could not have told Helen this in precise, sense-making words. It would make her cry. He often made her cry, he knew, not because of cruelty or unkindness, but because he was not enough for her either. But that, too, was right.

Their interdependence was complicated by the issue of fertility. Like it or not, that was the place where Helen depended on Daniel simply to be male. There were a hundred ways to get babies these days, and for technology's sake the man was no longer really needed. But in Helen's world, where conceiving a child was the result of a mutual act of creation, most of those methods were not even options. Literally, other options did not seem even to occur to her. Once when he had mentioned sperm donors, she had burst out laughing, taking it as obvious that he was joking. Daniel had laughed, too, half worried she would realize he had been serious, half delighted in her innocent love.

So there was no one for Daniel to talk to—or almost no one. Daniel had arranged a visit to church just to see Pastor Ed—to see only him, choosing to meet on Pastor Hubble's day off. Daniel felt vaguely guilty for having intentionally circumvented meeting the younger pastor, as if he had somehow lied, just a little. He had not exactly said to anyone, "Oh, oops. Too bad Pastor Hubble couldn't be here, too," but Daniel felt in his honest soul that, if confronted, he would say something like that. Already he was thinking it, like planning to lie—and that was as bad as lying.

Daniel found himself at Harmony Baptist Church at noon on a Thursday, not only avoiding the younger pastor but even Lisa, the church secretary, who would normally be watching the front office. Arguably, Daniel was sneaking in.

So Daniel Pryor sneaked into the office of Pastor Ed Miller and found the older man sitting uncomfortably upright at his desk, looking out the window with the broken latch. Daniel called him by name, slightly embarrassed when the older man jumped, as if startled by an intruder. "Sorry, Ed," Daniel said genuinely, but the man apologized for his own inattention, offering welcome, bidding Daniel to sit in the big soft chair in the corner. Then the pastor turned back to the window, fell silent again, until Daniel felt strange, watching the older man's distractions. Pastor Ed had always been a little scattered, but this was something else. Daniel wanted to ask what was wrong, but that didn't seem quite the right thing to do. He noticed a book open and upside down on the table next to him—a real paper book about biblical archaeology. "Been reading?" Daniel broke into the silence.

Pastor Ed came back from his thoughts. "Oh, yes," he said. His eyes lit up. "I do like to keep reading books like that one. Wonderful to see the ever-growing number of artifacts from the Holy Land that are by now so common in museums that no one speaks of them much. Imagine," he said with new enthusiasm, as if he had stepped into another mind, "a clay cup from the first century! Jesus himself might have held it, might have drunk water from that cup."

Daniel picked up the book and looked at a picture on the open page. "The Holy Grail maybe," he said, smiling.

"Maybe not *the* Holy Grail," Ed Miller responded, "but if Jesus drank water from it, that makes *a* holy grail, eh?"

The two men smiled, as if there was finally something right between them, in spite of the tension around Daniel. The two men looked at each other, and Daniel saw in the pastor's dark eyes a kind of light—almost humor, a kind of wonder he might have called love. Daniel felt warm to see it, would have kissed it with innocence in another world. Here, in this world, it was just a moment of warmth, and then it was gone, as Pastor Ed's eyes went dark again, as if overtaken by some fear. The man swallowed, seemed to force himself to take on a deeper voice, and then looked at Daniel with a seriousness and solemnity that Daniel recognized as both necessary and forced.

"What can I do for you, Daniel?" he asked in a pastoral way.

Something seemed strange to Daniel, as Ed Miller sat forward and peered at him deeply. Daniel hesitated. In the pause a light came on in the pastor's eyes and his concern was replaced with a soft kind of mirth.

"Oh," he almost exclaimed, "and how is Helen? I trust she's doing well. Pregnant, I hope."

"Well, er, no." Daniel was slightly confused, not by the question, but by Ed Miller's awakening.

"Oh," the man said softly, frowning a little. "You know I've been praying for you these past months, but then God sometimes . . ." The older man's voice trailed away. Then, as if inwardly gritting his teeth, he looked at Daniel directly. "If you are still struggling with these matters, Daniel, perhaps we can consider some strategies of faith. I've been reading recently a book by that title, *Strategies of Faith*, and I think there's a lot to learn, a lot to hope for . . ."

"What's wrong, Ed?" Daniel asked, unable to stand the strain in the air any longer.

"Wrong? What do you mean?" Pastor Miller asked back, but Daniel saw fear in his eyes.

"What's going on, Ed?" Daniel repeated his question. "You're acting weird. You sound like Hubble."

Ed Miller gave an exaggerated frown. "I just want to be helpful, Daniel," he said gravely. "We are, after all, called to love, and love means . . ." He stopped and turned his face away, looking out the window. Daniel let the silence sit, until Pastor Miller coughed a laugh. "You know, Daniel," he said, without looking at him, "I never did get that latch fixed on the window, and that's OK with me."

"Is something wrong, Ed?" Daniel repeated, though by now he knew that, yes, something was wrong. There was some intrusion, some shift and spin of Miller's mood that was not merely the scatteredness of the man's usual humor. The question about Helen and the comment about the window, those were Ed Miller, but the look of concern and the pastoral voice, those were somebody else.

Ed Miller took a long breath, exhaled through his mouth. "Daniel," he started, "fact is, I couldn't help you even if you asked me to." With a sad kind of whimsy, he raised his thin, grey eyebrows as if simply asking Daniel if he understood. Daniel didn't.

"I don't know what's up, Ed," Daniel said softly. "Maybe I should just come back. I just don't have many people to talk to about the things that are going on these days—"

"Daniel," Miller interrupted. "I—I can't help you. Like I said."

"I don't know what you're saying, Pastor," Daniel started to reply.

"That's just it," Miller interrupted. "I'm not your pastor. I'm being terminated."

Daniel was stunned, partly by the ambiguity of the verb. "Terminated?"

"Fired, if you will," Ed said back, smiling his sad, distracted smile. "Forcibly retired, relieved of my post, sent out to pasture. Pastor pasture." He smiled weakly.

The information struck Daniel like a physical force. Daniel had come to ask about the soul, about spirituality, about what it meant to "know God." In the recent months his own angers and resistance had shifted with the news of the day, moving away from the problems of fertility to the "larger" problem. Why had he been so unable to trust God all these years, all these recent months? He wondered if, perhaps, he should find out the state of his soul. Deeply, deeply he had wanted to talk to his brother about it all, his brother who was, after all, something of a public authority on these events. But Daniel couldn't share with Michael any sense of doubt or hope or how the two mingle. He couldn't share either fullness or emptiness with Michael; it had to be with another Christian. So he had come to Ed Miller. But he recognized the problem in front of him, like a revelation. "You're blue, aren't you?" Daniel said to Pastor Miller.

Miller didn't answer but stared out the window. "You know," he said, "prayer is a funny thing. If you think about it, it's less like asking for something you want than it is giving up on something you want. Acts of faith and acts of despair are almost indistinguishable."

Daniel didn't know how to reply.

Miller continued, "You know, I think I've known Jesus a long time. I've known he was there, known to some extent who he was. I was even comfortable there, even when I wasn't. You know what I mean?"

Daniel nodded.

"But when you pray," Miller went on, "you have to let go. That is what I always thought it meant to have faith. But then you get caught, you know, caught in a funny paradox. Almost funny in a ha-ha kind of way. Because, well, what if you have to pray for faith? Don't you have to know God to pray to God to know God?" He looked at Daniel. "Yeah," he said, "I got tested. I was told it was a decision applied to all pastors in the whole denomination, so I got tested. And, yes, blue. Blue, blue, blue. I wouldn't have guessed it, but as soon as I heard the verdict, I knew it was true. It's always been true. I've never quite been ready to be a pastor, Daniel, never quite been ready to be Christian. I knew it; I've always known it. Now everyone knows it."

"Ed, maybe you're just misunderstanding this whole— "

"Doesn't matter what I understand," Pastor Miller interrupted. "Doesn't matter. It's a rule, it applies to all affiliated churches, even outside the country. Ever since the miracle."

"Ed," Daniel reached across the desk and touched Miller's hand. "I can talk to Hubble—"

Miller coughed almost derisively. "Hubble!" he groaned. Miller started to say something, then stopped himself. "But there it is, right? There's my anger, my uncertainty, my jealousy. It's all true. I'm blue. They tell me I'm not fit to be pastor. No, they don't say that exactly. They say, 'You can't give others what you don't have.'"

Daniel understood all too well. What could he give to Helen? What could he ever have hoped to teach his own brother about the beauty of God? The only thing worse than this lack of faith was knowing the failure caused pain to others.

"So I can't help you, Daniel." Miller smiled weakly again.

Daniel felt a resistance—his own barrier—to the obvious suggestion he should make. But in the face of love, compassion stirred and shook that barrier, made him look past it, like wishing death on a sick parent.

"Maybe . . . maybe you can just go ahead and, you know, get adjusted."

"Ha!" Miller's exclamation startled Daniel, but also relieved him. "Oh, no." The older man stared with a kind of anger Daniel had never seen. "There is no way I'm going to take that risk." Daniel was surprised by Miller's vehemence, but just as quickly the pastor sat back and spoke calmly. "I'm just, I'm just too old for that," he said.

Daniel wanted to ask what he meant, but the man went on. "Besides," he said with a tone of intended petulence, "I don't wanna. I just don't wanna."

"Then don't," Daniel responded, hearing bitterness in his own voice. He responded with a mixture of anger and love in which he could not have distinguished one from the other, nor did he need to try. His spit was spontaneous, full with a hope he could not have named. "Just don't," he repeated. "You're still pastor to me, damn it. I don't care what they say."

Miller pulled his hands into his lap as he sat back in his chair. "Damn it," he said with a soft mockery of Daniel's words. Daniel too sat back, feeling less sure, as Miller continued, "In the end it doesn't matter. I think I'm done here, and I don't have enough strength or enough reasons to fight. It's not like I'm being asked to sacrifice a child to Moloch or to dance naked under the moon." He laughed softly. "Actually, I might do that dancing thing." He paused, looked away. "Maybe when I get to heaven God will say, 'Go ahead, dance naked under the moon.'" He smiled again, more genuinely than he had all afternoon.

For a minute, Daniel felt confused. The odd thought of dancing under the moon struck him as both wonderful and incomprehensible—so much like Ed Miller!—and yet he was still lost in his deeper despair. Daniel wanted to respond, to offer hope, though he had little of his own. Yet wasn't this exactly the pastor's problem? Could he respond without presuming to know the answer to the problem they shared? Daniel paused, silent.

"So," Pastor Miller finally said with a sigh. "I guess you came to talk about your own worries, maybe the whole fertility thing again. I don't suppose I have any more answers than I did before. And now"—he breathed heavily—"now I don't think I can even pray for you, Daniel."

Suddenly, in the midst of Daniel's uncertainties about auras and spirituality and dancing beneath the moon, it was his compassion that won, leaving understanding for love. "I can pray for both of us," he said.

The prayer wasn't long, nor was it eloquent. He didn't try to salt it with biblical texts or some ideal order of praises and divine names. It stuttered and stopped, crept along with no content and then tried to say too much at once. It spoke of the need for wisdom, it presumed goodness, it expressed hunger and thirst, it gave up on everything it asserted, and it stumbled over the paradox of faithless prayers for faith. In passing, it made an anguished cry for the red spirit and its inner assurance, and it named that hope with the conflicts and confusions of a troubled theology. Jesus was an aura, but he wasn't; the Holy Spirit was the Comforter, but he was also perhaps a technology. The prayer whispered God's name and confused it with "adjustment," then gave up both for a God whose name Daniel didn't know and a Comforter he watched from far away. In the end, he was unsatisfied. The prayer couldn't do what auroscopy and adjustment could do, and intutitively Daniel knew that was right, even if it wasn't enough. Of course it wasn't enough.

So the prayer stumbled to its end, and Daniel's *amen* was echoed softly from the other side of the desk.

"Thank you, Daniel," Pastor Miller said with a soft smile. "That was kind, although I don't know if it changes anything of what I have to do."

"I'm sure it changes a lot," Daniel smiled back. "I'm just not sure what."

The two men smiled then looked away, each with a soft embarrassment at the reality of love. Then, as if the timing were obvious, both stood. Neither knew what to say, though it seemed to both that the meeting was over.

At that moment, there was a slight bumping noise at the closed door, and the troubled peace of their shared submission was shocked as alarm flashed in Miller's eyes and raced in his own heart. "Well, er, thanks for talking, Pastor Miller," Daniel said, perhaps too loudly. He moved quickly to the door. "I'll see you Sunday," he called, grabbing the door handle.

Daniel opened the office door, and there walking up, as if just coming into the outer office was Pastor Hubble. "Daniel," Hubble said quickly, perking up his head with a kind of happy recognition, "what a pleasant surprise. Here to see Ed, huh?"

"Yes, yes," Daniel replied simply. He wanted to say he was surprised to see the younger pastor, but he didn't want it to seem that he had intentionally chosen to come visit on the man's day off. "I was just asking some questions, as usual. You know me."

"Of course," Hubble said gently. "I think I do know you. You should know that you can always depend on Ed and me, any time." He put a hand on Daniel's shoulder as he began to walk past him.

Almost automatically, Daniel pulled the door closed, barring the way, acting on an instinct of protection against some force, without knowing what it was. "Um, I think Ed was going to pray for me a little," he said to the young pastor. "Maybe give him a minute. I need all the prayer I can get."

Hubble backed away, his eyes darker. "Don't we all?" he said. "Here, I'll walk you to the phone. I can talk to Ed later."

So Daniel walked to the phone with Jackson Hubble, and the two exchanged intentionally vague information about Daniel and Helen, about Daniel and Ed Miller. Daniel tried to hurry into the booth, used his handprint for ID and stepped inside quickly, as if escaping a trap rather than entering a small booth. He turned back toward Pastor Hubble.

"See you again, Daniel," the man said.

Daniel forced a smile as the door slid closed. As the calming gas began to hiss around him, Daniel knew he was afraid.

23

COMPASSION

For a while, Michael thought his fortunes were improving. It had been a rough few months: wrestling self-doubt, Desra's departure, the strange disconnection from everything at work. As the news of the miracle had come and gone, Michael had been there to report on what he saw, but he had hesitated, strangely unsure of himself. Within a week the world had been flooded with news stories and commentaries by every kind of expert in every field of science and theology, until Michael's own voice, his "expertise," he would have said, was lost in the din. Any information about Roberts or Gesar he had tried to dig up was somehow found before he got there by a researcher in some news office that fed the details to a famous face on the news. Michael found himself again left without anything to say. And Melanie saw it all, his hesitations and his silence, and cussed him out for it, too—until she got the adjustment. Then she was nice to him.

Melanie's adjustment had come as a surprise, but Michael couldn't deny that it changed her. She stopped whining and cussing about Jennifer, her lover, and let Michael know how happily and quietly the two had divorced, and how Melanie had moved on—and apparently moved in with another woman whom she loved. They were all quite happy.

Then Melanie began assigning Michael to stories about a series of famous people who had been tested by auroscopy and "discovered themselves," or, more dramatically, had found the nature of their inner dissatisfactions and come around. There were a couple of congress members, some significant priests in the Catholic Church or gurus from India, a star or two of popular music or movies, even the standing president of China, and Michael got to choose a few to interview. Not all of them, it turned out, were adjusted by the auroscopic procedure. Some merely discovered they were "already red" and spoke of how it opened their eyes to the wholeness of life. Others came to insight and enlightenment "the old-fashioned way," namely by meditation or peyote sessions or prayers to Jesus or submission to the will of Allah. But after only two such interviews and articles, along with research into half a dozen more, Michael had had enough. The story never changed: they were all happy.

"They're all so goddam happy!" Michael had said, hoping the Melanie of his past would laugh and cuss with him. She had smiled kindly.

"Maybe you're asking the wrong questions, Michael," she said with an air of helpfulness and guidance.

"They're the same questions I've always asked," Michael responded, as if to jolt her back to memories of earlier argument.

"What questions were those, Michael?" she asked him directly, taking a deep breath. She exhaled slowly, as if she were still smoking.

"I want to know if these people have considered what they're doing," Michael said with frustration. "I want them to ask themselves if they are any closer to understanding the truth about reality, or are they just being deceived. I want them to ask if they are really better people. I want them—"

"You want them to doubt," Melanie interrupted.

"Something like that," Michael said.

"Doubt like you do?"

Michael knew he was trapped. Was it just a matter of wanting other people to be as unhappy as he was? Was it jealousy, a vindictiveness that would desire other people's sorrow as a way of justifying his own? Michael didn't know. It might be true, and perhaps there was something genuinely immoral about it all. He knew it was possible, felt the sting of the sheer possibility of a moral guilt that could not be overlooked. Had he been in that moment in the presence of a prophet, or even his brother, Daniel, he might have come to light even then. But looking at Melanie's kind smile, he only felt again that he was in a trap.

"It's healthy doubt, Melanie," he had said, trying to escape.

"Is it healthy?" she had asked. The conversation was over. Melanie had given him time off, letting him later do one story about an interfaith building project in the Sudan but denying his request to pursue an article on correlations between auroscopy results and euthanasia rates. So he had little to do, leaving him time to try to catch a scoop on Gesar and the progress of his spiritual science, but mostly time to feel frustrated. Last week's visit from Desra hadn't helped.

Then Melanie had asked him if he wanted a front row seat at another interview with Gesar. Michael had jumped at the opportunity. "Hell, yes," he had said, thinking he might get back into the game. But the press meeting was not with the *tulku* at all, but with David Roberts, and was only one of ten meetings going on simultaneously, each interview given by a representative of a different religion. Disappointed, Michael took the assignment without protesting that the whole thing was a publicity event.

So Michael Pryor was once again at a press conference—in another front row seat—waiting for the announcement of some new achievement of Dr. Richard Gesar. When Roberts appeared on the stage, even Michael almost automatically rose to his feet. Some of the reporters even applauded. Roberts smiled broadly, his almost-grey hair dancing in the breeze of his brisk walking. Unlike Melanie or Desra, Roberts showed not even a small change in his demeanor. His smile and general friendliness seemed essentially the same as they were when Michael first met the preacher in his church. Genuine and friendly, Roberts thanked "Henry," the young man who checked the button mic tacked onto his lapel, pointed and waved at one or two faces in the crowd, and nodded with recognition at Michael.

"Thank you for coming out today," Roberts started with his speech. "Some of you know who I am," he said, pausing as a bit of pleasant laughter bubbled through the crowd of reporters. *Everyone* knew him. Roberts had been front page news for more than a month after the miracle, with everyone checking on his health and reporting any hint of damage or improvement. Roberts continued to make news as he joined with Gesar in various ventures, including using his vast network of churches and studios and applying his influence with politicians to get a hearing for the further trust and development of Gesar's ideas.

"In case some of you feel the need to ask me how my heart is doing, let me just say that I'm doing quite well, thank you. God has healed my heart," Roberts said as he pulled a pair of glasses out of his front pocket, "but I still need glasses to read."

There was more mild laughter. Michael scowled. "Get on with it," he heard himself thinking, but also felt in his mind the pin prick of an angry schadenfreude. He almost wished Roberts were not so healthy. In the months after the miracle, Roberts had also undergone auroscopy and was found to be a deep red, as truly spiritual as all his flock already believed him to be. In the series of interviews that had followed, Michael's only suspicion had been hidden in the desire to ask if Gesar had ever asked Roberts to give up his Jesus. Unexpectedly, that question had been posed to Roberts by Juliette Bryce on her popular morning show. "Not at all," Roberts had responded. "The matter never even came up." Michael coughed at his own memories of those interviews with Roberts. Sitting there watching the man amiably chatting with reporters about his health, Michael found himself almost wishing Roberts would just have another heart attack and put all the hubbub to rest. But Micheal caught his own thoughts and turned his attention back to the events. Even so, he couldn't quite forget how easy it would be to hate.

"Let me get to the announcement at hand," Roberts was saying, putting on reading glasses and spreading a single sheet of paper on the podium before him. "As you all know," he began, "this announcement is going out simultaneously through all the religious groups with which Dr. Gesar is affiliated. Yet this isn't really a religious announcement. Nor is it truly a technical one, as if he had some new breakthrough in his work. What Dr. Gesar has discovered so far is quite enough, I would say." He paused for effect.

"But what is new," he went on, "is, we might say, economic news. Dr. Richard Gesar has decided to release all patents and scientific claims about his work to the public domain." There were murmurs in the short, dramatic pause. Michael himself wasn't sure this was so newsworthy, but he realized he had never given any attention to the obvious economic questions: who holds these patents, who owns the technology, who's getting paid? He had more or less assumed all the research was already publicly funded, or funded through some system of grants. He knew Gesar had always had a trust fund, a sizeable trust fund, set up by a thousand different donors the day he was recognized at two years old as a newly incarnated *tulku*. Money had never seemed an issue. Now it had become an issue, but only to say it wasn't.

"The decision to make this bequest, this gift," Roberts continued, "was reached after we all agreed—unanimously, across all the religious beliefs and ideals we represented—that this technology was most truly the property, not of any one man or any one laboratory, but of humanity. Today's announcement is simply to make that ownership official.

"I don't presume to speak for anyone else," Roberts said, laying his left hand on his chest, "but I argued vehemently for this action, argued as a Christian. This is what Christ would have us do, Christ the healer, Christ the compassionate. You all know I have preached Christ and him crucified all my life, and I will do so till I die. Therefore, for me, this is a Christ-act. I preach compassion, I preach love, because He first loved me."

Michael didn't bother taking notes. There were enough recorders doing that; no word would be missed, no smile or gesture of nobility would be invisible. Michael thought he should try to look up the evident scriptural recitations, those words that slipped in and out of the preacher's speeches so naturally, maybe to see what they really meant. But in the next thought, he knew he would do no such thing; maybe Daniel could do it, but Michael could not.

The Reverend Roberts was taking another dramatic breath, as if gathering his thoughts. He changed tack. "Most of you know, I suspect, of the most recent technological developments in Dr. Gesar's work. Admittedly, there is nothing new in the basic concepts or technological details—or so I'm told. Jesus knows, I don't understand anything Dr. Gesar says when he gets into science mode." He paused again, for some laughter. "But the developments most recently have been simply in the areas of miniaturization and simplification. The result of that work, and the result of today's announcement, is that the auroscopic technology will be given away to every manufacturer of scanners and ID detectors across the planet. That means anyone who produces retina- or fingerprint-recognition devices will be able to build into their machines the capacity to read a person's aura. In this way, at every point in the day, at any place one shops or buys or phones him or herself across our world, a person can monitor their spiritual health. Anyone at any time can be reminded that wholeness is here for us all and can be encouraged to find that wholeness here," Roberts was tapping his own chest again, "here in our own souls.

"Listen," Roberts continued quickly, as if to drive to a point he had not yet reached, "this is the religious fact of the matter: When a person knows peace, knows the spirit of Christ within himself—I mean, of Christ or whomever—then there is peace here, and here, and finally, here." Roberts yet again touched his chest, but then his head, and finally, held out his hands, palms forward, as if granting benediction to a congregation. "It is through peace within that we come to know peace without, and when we act with peace, we heal the world.

"This is not news," his sermon went on. "The great religious teachers of the world knew this; Jesus knew it more deeply than anyone, I believe. But what has always been missing is the ability to make it universal, to make it real for everyone, and to hand it on to a world hungry for peace. Peace for every individual," the preacher made a dramatic closing gesture, "is peace for the world."

The speech ended, and Michael half expected some kind of applause. Yet he could not keep himself from demanding a question. Later he would admit that it should have been a question about the logic of this world peace, the logic of how religious experience leads to peace and what that peace means. But Michael, still unclear about whether his internal honesty was a search for truth or a form of the tacit rebellion that had served him well for so long, could only ask his own question.

"What if a person doesn't want to know his own aura?" he blurted, raising his hand slightly only by instinct.

The preacher smiled at Michael. "Ah, Mr. Pryor, my old friend, always the one with an incisive question. In fact, this question was raised among us at our meeting, raised indeed by Dr.Gesar himself. 'We must honor the integrity of the individual,' I think he said, 'and we may not force life on those who do not desire it.' Most of us agreed immediately.

"But, Mr. Pryor," Roberts was lifting a finger to show he was making a point, "it was, I believe, Anandadaupinka Thera, the eminent Sri Lankan Buddhist, who noted first the parallels. How long ago was it that people protested receiving immunizations based on irrational fears of complex disease or absurd conspiracies? We know better now, and children are immunized against a dozen diseases that have all but vanished from the earth. How long ago was it that some pregnant women protested against amniocentesis, when in fact we have learned to heal children even in utero, and when we can't heal, to offer painless and healthy ways to save the mother and relieve the child of a burdened lifetime? We know better now, and these simple tests are today easily built into the most rudimentary health checks for any woman and for any child. How long ago did people object to the universal testing of 'Likely Inherited Intelligence,'" imagining that these tests, like the old IQ tests of another century, were only the tools of barbarous and racist elites? We know better now, as we measure and understand the brain in ways that help us heal previously dangerous and painful learning disabilities and dysfunctions, so that today we heal children by the millions, and those we cannot heal, we ease into gentle sleep.

"Don't get me wrong, Mr. Pryor," Roberts went on. "Don't let's be rash or careless. Let us test the technology fully and carefully; let us use it wisely. Yet in another way, this is only—and I mean merely—technology, and like any new technology some will be afraid of it. But it cannot be stopped, as merely a means of knowing our world and knowing ourselves better. Don't be afraid, Mr. Pryor. Don't be blue." Roberts smiled.

Michael hoped that was meant to be funny. A few laughed, but Roberts went quickly on. "But in this technology, ladies and gentlemen, we're also talking about something much more than technology. We're talking about much more than a science for studying that obscure and suffering creature we call humanity. We're talking here about compassion, universal compassion. In medicine, in psychology, and now in spirituality, it is all the same: Those we can heal, we must heal; those we can ease, we must ease, and those we cannot help in any way, we gently help to a peaceful sleep. This is the way of compassion. It always has been. Only the technology has changed."

Roberts' speech had already turned away from Michael and toward the greater audience, and yet Michael couldn't help but feel his words like a kind of danger. Had the advertising slogan, "Don't be blue," been directed at him personally? Can compassion be a threat? A new question emerged from somewhere on the floor, asking when the technology would become implemented, when and where would we first see it brought into easy public use. Roberts continued his answers.

But for Michael the inner discussion had just begun. In his new and, for him, quite strange sense of personal uncertainty, his feelings of worry quickly became mingled with questions of doubt. What if it were true that he and a million others on this planet just needed to be shown the way to find peace? Maybe he was ill, like his father had been psychologically and his mother physically. It did make sense. We test and we heal, and wherever technology serves us to find and to create health for the suffering few, it is the duty of a compassionate world to give that love. We ease and we rest, and wherever technology fails to heal, the same compassion that would heal is the compassion of palliative care and, ultimately, of euthanasia. It was just technology, wasn't it? It was compassion, wasn't it?

But in Michael's new, emerging ability to know the reality of uncertainty, the ghosts of his family intruded. But what if he had been wrong all those years ago in the way he had acquiesced to his father's euthanizing? What if he should have protested his father's death, like Daniel had done? Must he think Daniel's protests were truly rooted in a failure to love? Somehow for Michael, that seemed impossible. Michael knew well, had known even back then, the logic of compassion, but could not, then or now, accuse his brother of lacking it. Daniel had protested. Should someone protest now? Somewhere in Michael the stirrings of honest guilt and the insistence on honest logic were wrestling. In the end, the honesty of both would be necessary to save him.

At that moment, however, the grace that came to Michael was to find his thoughts moving from those about his parents to thoughts about his brother. With those thoughts there sifted through his anger and uncertainty a whisper of love. Love, in turn, became in Michael a response of softening that was almost salvific, coming to him in the form of a resolve to talk to Daniel, to ask him what he thought. Perhaps he had never before in his life really asked Daniel what he thought.

24

LOVE

Daniel and Helen weren't home. The apartment was quiet, entirely dark but for the lamp that burned by the left end of the sofa where Marta sat with a book upside down in her lap. It was a history book, tracing changes in the Roman Empire from the time of Augustus Caesar to Constantine. As the context in which Christianity grew from a tiny Jewish sect to a world-dominating religion, the period was naturally of great interest. Much of the information, in fact, Marta had read before, but this author was supposed to offer a bold new thesis about the relationship between the growing Christian religion and the Jewish diaspora that would explain the tremendous success of the "Jesus Movement." Marta had gotten to the middle of the third chapter.

"Not so new or so bold," she had said to herself somewhere in chapter two. In a moment of self-amused distraction, she had wondered if it would have been better to have brought a novel, maybe science fiction. That thought had led her to Michael Pryor, to her Stoic resistance to her own emotions, and to the bubbling frustration and anger at a world, even at a God, that did not seem to want her to find love.

These thoughts were neither new nor bold for Marta. Any of the thousand variations on the philosophical problem of evil—why does the loving God fail or refuse to give us good gifts—had been common arguments in her philosophical oeuvre almost all her life. Although the questions arose again and again, each time with vigor and seriousness, she knew how to consider the ideas with honest frustration that neither allowed the sorrows of life to go unanswered nor allowed them to be anything but painful. She knew the difference between an answer to a philosophical problem and the satisfaction of a human need. Consequently any construction or reconstruction of her "answers" were painful struggles that had to hurt and yet could not kill. It was like dealing with a broken bone.

Her recurring thoughts of Michael were more like tending an open wound, a wound that came from no remembered injury. It was just there; it hurt, and if the wound wasn't kept clean and free of germs it might fester. Yet in another sense, the wound was the festering; it had often seemed to her over the last few months that if she could just forget that wound, it would heal on its own. But it didn't. So she had forced herself through another chapter of the book but could not stay attentive. The wound would not be forgotten.

Marta didn't know how long she had been crying. It didn't matter. There was no one near to hide it from. Daniel and Helen were "out," due back home perhaps later tonight, maybe not until tomorrow. They had gone out of town just to be together "somewhere else," still struggling, Marta guessed, with the decision to go through with in vitro fertilization. There had been some progress on Daniel's side, a certain unhappy willingness to "obey love instead of fear." Marta had heard Daniel's rationale from Helen earlier in the week, when she had also been told about the couple's plan for an early start to the weekend. So Thursday after work, they were away for the night, maybe for two. And in the pretended offer to "watch their place," Marta too had decided to go "somewhere else," even if it was only to their apartment. In her own apartment, even the walls seemed to tell her she was lonely; here at least she might remember she had friends.

It wasn't working. All she wanted was love, she said to herself, and then she laughed at herself for the obvious equivocation. Which love would that be, her inner debater posed, and there followed challenges about defining terms and specifying the natural value of each different kind of love. She laughed again. No wonder she couldn't find a man to love her.

But that wasn't really true. There were men who would love her, she was convinced. Arguably too many, depending on which kind of "love." The various good kinds of love were possible, she knew, and she again thought of Michael. He seemed to her a good man, an honest man, one whose wit made him clever and funny and interesting, but not self-satisfied. She thought— she believed—that he loved her, maybe even in the right ways. But that was the problem, wasn't it? Even if he did know the right love, did he know he knew it? For a moment, Marta's thoughts flashed with an obscure epistemological theory that declared the sufficiency of knowing truth, but insisted we couldn't know if we knew it. She smiled and wiped away a tear.

It came back to this: she was alone, and she was lonely. Part of the loneliness was physical. She sat on a couch in a quiet apartment, and she felt aware of her own womanhood. It was under the book, in her breasts, in the tension of her shoulders, in the wiggling of her bare feet in the soft carpet. She felt it in the wet tears on her cheeks that someone could kiss away, in the quiver of lips beside the tears. It was in the cool touch of the air-conditioner breeze that touched her arms, in the soft pressure of her own legs pressed together to hold the book in place. She knew sensuality even in the pages of the book itself, in the difference between reading a printed text and reading the same words on a video screen. She could feel the page, trace its smoothness, taste the crispness of the sounds it made when you turn the page. It was sexual.

Or almost. She began to cry again.

But the problem wasn't just sex, was it? It wasn't just the recognition of being a sensual person, a sensual being, and the desire to feel. There was supposed to be something about sensuality, about sexuality, that made it more than sensual. Something was supposed to make it intimate, and Marta understood—understood more than merely felt, for she was still Marta San-chez—that the opening of her femaleness to a man meant more than sex. It meant sharing, being possessed, being a willing vessel, and therefore—the logic of the *therefore* was crucial—it had to be an act of love, love in some greater, deeper sense than the senses alone can relay. A virgin in her thirties, she knew this, and the knowledge hardened her against the desire to be touched, though it lessened that desire not at all.

Still there was more. For wasn't the desire for the touch, for intimacy, even the desire to be made recipient of a man's seed—wasn't all that a sym-bol, a sign of something even greater? Wasn't there even a deeper penetra-tion to which every soul is female? For mustn't every soul open itself to the presence of the Divine Husband, willingly receive, even bear fruit that is both human and divine? Marta knew the imagery of the mystics, and she felt herself smile and blush at the thought of God, of love and of sex, all in the same mental motion. For she knew, looking as far back as Israel de-scribed as God's wife and the church as the bride of Christ, that the pictures were there. God's love was described in the metaphors of sex, or rather, as she mused, it was sex that was the metaphor and divine love the reality.

Marta sat back and wiped at her tear-puffy eyes. "Nonetheless," she said aloud, as if God needed to hear her prayer. Then she insisted, "Or rath-er, *therefore*." It made sense to her. "I know that the feeling is not enough," she said, knowing she was speaking to Someone, "and that knowing can make sense of feeling, especially when the feeling is lacking. Yet knowing is also not enough, though it can make the feeling's failure fit where it belongs. But sometimes, just sometimes, I'd like to know more than I know by feeling more than I feel."

She stopped praying. Could she stop long enough actually to analyze each term and make sure her prayers were all consistent? They didn't need to be, at least not right now.

And that's when the chime rang that announced a visitor. She jumped, at first thinking it must be Daniel and Helen returning early, then quickly realizing they wouldn't announce themselves with the chime. Marta felt exposed and quickly tried to brush back her hair and wipe furiously at her swollen eyes. She didn't know whether to call out that she was coming or tell the door to unlock—the apartment recognized her voice—so she hesitated, moved her book aside, straightened herself. By the time she had risen from her seat, the chime rang again. Then she was up, moving, still unsure how to respond, when the door, as if expressing impatience, clicked its lock, recognizing apparently, the handprint of the visitor on the panel outside. She was almost to the door. Daniel and Helen after all? No. Then who?

Marta knew who it was, even as the door swung in and Michael stepped into the emptiness. At once she felt anxious, and for a moment she stared with her cheeks getting red. Michael was as surprised as she. He had seen her in this apartment before, had met her here in fact, but then there were lights blazing in the hubbub of Daniel's birthday party. This was clearly different, with the room dark but for the single light by the couch, with a kind of odd silence hanging in the air. It became all the more odd that Marta herself said nothing. The two of them just looked at each other. For Michael, Marta's face was mostly in the shadow with the light behind her, barely il-luminating the side of one cheek, like a crescent moon at sunset. That same light came softly through her hair, making it seem glowing, and the little ambient light that reflected from the walls touched her eyes just barely, so they seemed to sparkle. She seemed in that moment angelic.

Michael didn't know that the sparkle and glow of Marta's face was due to the wetness of tears, but she knew. She could not know the sudden beauty he saw in her at that moment; indeed, for her the moment was fraught with the feeling of exposure. "Michael," was all she could say, as her wit seemed suddenly reticent. Yet in the full light of the lamp behind her, she saw in his face both surprise and delight. Recognition in those eyes seemed to Marta something warm and good, yet her disconcerted feeling intruded, made her look away, and in a motion of concern utterly unlike her character, suddenly begin to smooth her hair. With a kind of nonchalance she knew was less than genuine, she walked back to her seat by the lamp and picked up her book. "What are you doing here?" she asked without turning around.

Michael stammered. He had been genuinely happy to see Marta, and in that first recognition in the glancing light, she had been remarkably pret-ty. Yet her turn, her distance, at once bothered him, and he recalled that she had not responded to his attempts to contact her. He distanced himself from the vision and tried to remember why he had come. If she had no interest in him, perhaps it was because he was not yet ready for her.

"I, er, came to see Daniel," Michael said. "I should have let him know I was coming, but I guess I took it for granted that the old married man would be sitting home doing nothing on a quiet evening." Michael let himself simply be himself. "You know how those boring old married people are," he said with his common mild sarcasm.

"Actually, I don't know at all!" Marta wanted to say, but a pause by the couch with her back toward the door allowed her to recover, just to be herself as well. With a feeling of ease she would later recognize with thankfulness, her wit came back. "At most," she said turning back to Michael with a smile, "they'd be playing a rousing hand of mahjong, no doubt."

Michael looked at Marta silently, her profile now more illumined.

"I suppose you could close the door," Marta said with a slightly mocking tone, "unless you brought along a few other guests."

Michael smiled and hoped his smile wasn't too crooked. But it had been this woman who had said one should look at his eyes. He turned and closed the door, with his own back to the light, away from the image of Marta in the dimness, wondering what to do. In a bare instant of introspection, he sought out a rightness apart from himself. In the moment of not really knowing what he truly wanted, he could vaguely wonder what he ought to do. It was a healthy possibility.

"So Daniel isn't here?"

Martha had taken her seat, with her book in her hands, though he couldn't tell whether she was going to read it. He saw that her face was a little red, her eyes tired, as she wiped indelicately at her nose with a tissue apparently already nearby. "You OK?" he asked.

Marta intentionally ignored the question. At once she began to inform Michael coolly that she was "house-sitting," although that wasn't exactly true, hoping her easy banter would mask her nervous self-consciousness. She ended, almost too honestly, by saying that the lovers needed to be alone, along with a weak humorous reference to Romeo and Juliet.

"As I recall, that love story didn't end too well for the lovers," Michael responded, "though it could be worse. Could be Abelard and Heloise."

"Spoken like a true male," Marta replied, "for whom castration is worse than death." Then there was silence, and it was uncomfortable. Marta used it. "What do you want with your brother?"

How could Michael explain that he actually wanted to talk to Daniel about something serious, something spiritual, something Daniel seemed to know about. How could he explain his need to ask questions about Daniel's

Jesus? Michael realized that Marta could probably answer such questions better than Daniel, yet somehow he didn't want to go there with her. In Michael's religious confusion, he imagined Daniel was safer. But some habitual honesty helped Michael respond to Marta; he told her he had wanted to ask Daniel's opinions on matters dealing with religion. Trying to sound off-hand, he mentioned his work on the Richard Gesar events, pretending he was merely a reporter gathering information. He thought he should be maintaining a distance, an appearance of impersonal inquiry. But Michael was aware that he wanted to know something about his brother he had never before bothered to ask; Michael wanted to understand what drew Daniel and what held him. He might almost have said he wanted what Daniel had and what Gesar promised. He might almost have hinted that he wanted it in order to be able to be closer to Marta. He almost could have said such things. Instead he said only, "Too bad Daniel isn't here." And even with Marta in front of him, he meant it.

Marta saw that he did. She saw that Michael had softened toward his brother, perhaps had begun to see in him what Marta already knew. Marta saw that Michael loved his brother, and that made Marta love Michael more.

Another awkward silence fell. Michael was still standing in the middle of the room. Michael wanted to stay with Marta, and his old habits of lust remained, hinting to his psyche that there was sex in the air. Yet surprisingly, even to him, there was also a sense that he ought to hold back, ought to respect something. It was something about Daniel's home, something about Marta herself, that made him take the "ought" seriously. There was a law beyond himself that he could not have named even if he'd had the time to work up the vocabulary. But he knew it like the distant call of another voice, and the discomfort of the silence in these moments became for him a sense of danger, that he ought not to be there. He was aware of the door like an invitation, even a demand. He started to say, "I guess I should just go . . ."

Marta was going through her own struggle. She had a vocabulary Michael did not, but that did not mean she had the necessary resilience. She had recently been weeping over her loneliness, she had recently been thinking of love, indeed of this very man, with a kind of wrestling hope that knew the deceptions of hunger but could not deny its reality. Her struggle was greater than Michael's because she knew its true nature, knew its true name. As perhaps only those who truly resist temptation know its full depth and strength, so Marta felt the pull and reality of illicit longing. Marta, more than Michael, knew what it was to desire sin.

As Michael was turning to look at the door, Marta was setting aside her book and rising. On some level of her mind, where she could name the common forms of self-deception and self-justification, she thought she could be a good hostess, an honest friend, simply courteous, if she would offer Michael something to drink or a reason to stay. "I could get you some wine or something," she said as she turned toward her guest.

That's how it happened that Marta and Michael stood face to face in the middle of Daniel's and Helen's living room, suddenly each confronted with the nearness of the other. Michael found himself holding Marta's arms, and she reached back, her hands moving past his upper arms to his back, each steadying the other as if tossed on a windy sea. "Marta," Michael said to her too-near eyes, "I tried to call you several times." The delay with that moment of speech was an act of nobility. Marta, both stronger and weaker than he, merely pressed forward. "I know," she said and leaned in to kiss him.

Michael tasted her kiss like a newborn love and let it surge through him into his heart and, by the glory of biology and the shame of habit, into his loins. This was, for him, warmth and goodness, though not yet for him an entirely new thing, having had too many lovers already to know love as a surprise. Having tasted too much beauty, he could not be as thoroughly enraptured as he should have been, not awakened, though unquestionably he was moved, and he pulled Marta close, drew her chest to his chest, and sank into her. Any exit was forgotten.

Marta let herself be absorbed. Where the book had been, she felt an awakening, not something she had never explained and explored or felt. Marta had kissed a man before, but this pressure of chest to chest, of lip to lip, of breath sucked past breath, was a force she had not known before. She let it sweep her away. She let it draw her in, move her, excite her. She felt, as if for the first time, the presence of her own tongue, mingled as if by a macabre experiment, with the push of her right thigh against Michael's left. The kiss became many, barely interrupted breaths. She knew speaking would interrupt the feelings with reason, and reason would hurt.

But the danger could not be avoided. For Michael, untrained by virtue, or rather trained entirely by the common justification of indulgence, had forgotten the door, and in the vacuum of forgetting was swept up in the habits of what he had long called love. He yielded not to Marta herself—an act that might have been redemptive—but to the commonality of satisfied desire, as his kisses moved from Marta's lips to her neck, from her neck to her upper chest. Marta's head went back in weakness, and Michael felt it was an invitation. He turned from kisses to the buttons of her blouse and almost expertly worked through them. Each bit of skin exposed was fulfillment of expectation for him, as the love that might have been fueled by restraint became the desire that explodes from a careless spill. His hands drifted down to the contours of her waist and stroked with skill and honest delight the curve and fluidity of her form. He might have rested there, might simply have enjoyed that feel, that almost-love, like watching a sunset from a distance. But the habits of pretended love cannot be overcome so easily, and in a moment, the blouse was dangling from Marta's waist and he was at work on the back of her bra.

Marta felt Michael's hands down the buttons of her blouse and the coolness of air on her skin as inch by inch she was exposed. She felt her own emerging nakedness like a release of fire, like a gift she could bestow upon the world, or at least on this man. She felt beautiful under his hands, because she was. Yet she, too, had habits of mind and soul. She, too, had a mind, if not hands and a body, trained to reflection. In the delight of her own self-revelation, her own Eden-like willingness to be naked and unafraid, another part of her soul cried out to the God she had spoken to so many times. What Michael lacked, she could not escape, and a bare spark of a cry of denial escaped in the midst of her sighs of soft submission. "No," it said, though softly, only weakly, audible to no one but God.

Michael, unrestrained by any such intrusion, was on his knees, kissing at the belly below the exposed breasts. He was pulling at the dress, almost at the same time sweeping up the light form of his object of desire, to lift her from the floor and carry her . . . anywhere. He was a machine of desire, oiled and programmed for this production, and he felt Marta's hands on his shoulders, on his head, pulling him and yielding to him, as the only normal reality he knew. That she had even the slightest qualm was not even a consideration, and so it was not love.

Yet in one last gasp, as her clothing came undone, Marta did love, or had too many loves at once. Her inner truth called out for desire yet also for more than desire. "Oh, God," it said in groans too deep for words, "give me more than I want." So she prayed, even as she felt Michael's hands, soft and wonderful upon her legs.

Then there was a rattle, a scuffle, a movement at the door that had been forgotten by them both. There was a muffled voice beyond the portal and the click of a lock. The couple froze, bewildered, and in through the door walked Daniel and Helen.

Shock and silence—mere seconds that seemed like an hour of absolutely twisted bewilderment as every member of the group felt the agony of this strange discovery. Daniel stammered; Helen turned her eyes away. Michael stared stupidly at his brother and his wife. Finally, Marta burst into tears. "I'm sorry," she said aloud, though to whom it was not clear. "I'm sorry," she repeated and repeated, with a strange mixture of sobs. In a flurry she gathered her dangling clothes and half ran, half stumbled toward an open bedroom door. The door slammed. Michael stood alone in the center of the room, uncommonly speechless, feeling the weight of his brother's gaze.

25

UNCERTAINTY

Michael had had several days to prepare his defense, prepare for what he expected as the inevitable judgment from Daniel. Of course the kind of judgment he expected was colored by his continued misunderstanding of his brother, that same projection of his brother's faith he had misrepresented to himself for so many years. By the middle of the week, when the challenge had still not come, Michael felt a doubt. He might have thought Daniel was not going to be judgmental at all, would somehow let the whole episode fade. Or at least Daniel would only go cold, stay distant, increase that distance, and then there would be no moralistic confrontation. Michael had expected the call to judgment and felt the threatening expectation harden him, raise up again his own justifications, or at least the denial of someone else's. When the call did not come, he could interpret the silence as shunning. Either way, he could take some comfort in being the victim of another's self-righteousness.

Knowing his own guilt helped Michael feed that defensive feeling. He had enough integrity, even in his vague rules of sexual self-indulgence, to know he had done something wrong, though he was not quite clear what it was. He remembered with some genuine remorse the pain he felt for Marta as she ran away in tears. He could wonder with an honest fear where she would have run the next day if they had not been interrupted. Had they made it to that bedroom together, had they made love in that darkness, would it have created a relationship between them or destroyed it? Would it have created or destroyed Marta's relationship with herself? Could it have created one and destroyed the other? Michael didn't know. In that uncertainty, Michael felt guilt, not for knowing some breach of a divine commandment but for knowing he would gladly have had sex with Marta no matter what the answer to those questions.

So guilt whispered to Michael and fed both the need for justification and the hunger to be confronted. Deeply, somewhere, he expected that judgment from Daniel because he needed it, knew he deserved it, and could not entirely leave the evening to dim memory without some kind of challenge. It was a challenge he could not create on his own. Even though his sense of honesty helped raise the sense of guilt to a level of helpful self-doubt, he lacked the categories for a sufficient internal challenge. Being still his only standard for measuring himself, he vaguely hungered for the attention of Daniel's call. As it was delayed, he felt loneliness in the security of pretended innocence. So when the call finally did come, when he heard his brother's voice say, "We should talk," it was in Michael's mind both a call to resist those who would shove their moralistic God down another's throat and a relief that felt like liberation.

For Daniel the delay in calling his brother was rooted in his own natural and habitual self-doubt. He had given up years ago trying to have religious conversations with Michael, realizing that this silence in the later years was as much rooted in fear as in respect for Michael's autonomy. Daniel had always felt his brother was smarter, certainly cleverer, and could hurt him if Michael's back were to the wall. Daniel was afraid of him, and he couldn't help feeling bad about that. "Love casts out fear," he would quote the Bible verse to himself, and pray in vain for enough love for his brother to face him in honest conversation. "Do not worry about what you will say in that hour," more Bible verses said, "for the Holy Spirit will tell you what you are to say." So was Daniel's fear of Michael ultimately a lack of faith in God?

Finally Helen said, "You have to talk to Michael, because I can't talk to Marta until you do." But, in fact, Helen had met Marta alone the very next day, but that in Helen's mind hadn't been "talk." She had sat with her friend silently, like sitting with a friend when a loved one has died, and she had taken Marta's hand as if to console her. She understood that there might have to be a confrontation, although she wouldn't have called it that, inasmuch as she was, in her way, the "older woman," who knew something of love and sex that Marta did not. Yet for Helen, that role of "older woman" carried neither a sense of superiority, nor, as it did for her husband, a burdened sense of obligation. It was, for her, simply obvious that she had to have "a talk," like a mother might talk to a teenage daughter. No, it was more like an older married sister talking to the younger, although the conversation should carry some air of authority. Helen realized she didn't really know what to say, that the conversation might be difficult. But it had to be done, and, whatever family or friendship metaphor applied, it would be a matter of love.

Helen assumed the same matter of love would have to occur between Daniel and Michael, assuming her husband's version of the talk would be just as loving as her own. Consequently, she didn't even pause to explain what she meant by suggesting that the men's talk had to come before the women's. Daniel didn't ask. It was enough that Helen spoke the way she did, and so the invitation to Michael, weak and halting, was given. He prayed the Holy Spirit would give him eloquence. But in the end, "We need to talk," was the best he could do.

Daniel didn't really understand the Holy Spirit. In a deep Christian spot in his soul, Daniel knew Jesus and understood the Savior's peculiar love. There was, therefore, a final hope and a final solace that hid behind—or within—all the worry and uncertainty Daniel lived with daily. Yet those days, those daily days, were fraught with a theological doubt that Daniel had never been able to reconcile. Surely that Power, he had thought so often, would want him to be strong, would want him to be a good husband, a good brother. Surely that Power would want his brother to find grace, would want his father to find wholeness, his mother to find health. Surely that Power would do more than that Power does, whatever the promises of salvation, and so he doubted that the Spirit would give him the words he needed to say. He doubted and wondered in his doubt if the doubt itself created the silence. Michael had always been the cleverer man, the angrier man, and Daniel had never stood up against his words, never been able to speak a coherent gospel, not even to one he loved so much. He had little hope tonight would be any better, expecting again a silent Spirit, a distant Jesus. Yet he was here, at this kitchen table, with Michael across from him, looking at the older brother with eyes that held a dark brooding that Daniel feared. Yet love was supposed to cast out fear.

The greetings behind them, both of them expected a speech. Daniel spoke with the only honesty he had. "I don't know what to say, Michael," he admitted, "but I feel like I ought to say something about the other night."

Michael was prepared. He had a two-pronged response. That was not to say his speech was pre-packaged, and it was not at all insincere. He actually expected that his speech would be more honest than most of the speeches he had given to his brother. He was sure this one would be a little more to the older brother's liking, for it included confession of guilt.

But first came the moral argument prong. "Daniel," he started, "I know you have never liked the way I've lived my love life, and I understand why. You know I just don't see the world the way you do. And I'll tell you the truth, I envy your life some, your life with Helen. But I've never taken kindly to feeling like your morality could be forced on me either. You know that."

Daniel was already puzzled. This was not the way he had thought the conversation would go at all. He wondered if the Holy Spirit . . .

"But I know, too, that Marta is different." And Michael did. "If it's wrong of the Christian to force his morality on me, it was wrong of me, too, to push my morality on Marta. I know–I know I should have respected her more, even if I do stand outside your moral ideals—"

"Wait, wait," Daniel waved a hand at Michael. This was going too fast. If only the Holy Spirit would speak. "I didn't ask to talk to you about your morals. Do you really think I've always judged your sexual morals somehow? I mean, do you think I sit in my kitchen thinking about how immoral you are or something? Jeez, Michael." But that was all.

Even so, it was enough to puzzle Michael who sat across the table, silent, his eyes quizzical.

"Listen, Michael," Daniel tried to explain, "if there's a moral conversation to be had, it isn't between you and me. Heck, you aren't in it at all. It might be between me and Marta because she does share my moral ideals. But Lord knows, I don't think I can tackle that one either. Jeez!" For half an instant, he thanked God that Helen would do it and he loved her a little more.

Michael almost smiled, but at the same time was conscious of his sneer. Something about Daniel's words was strangely right, not because of the content, which admittedly he didn't quite understand, but because he suddenly saw Daniel strong. Michael wanted to hear what he had to say. "So why am I here?" he asked.

To Michael's surprise, Daniel laughed. He put his head in one hand, elbow on the table and frowned. "Truth is, I don't know," he said to his brother. "But you know, it's like in *Casablanca*: If you shoot my partner, I gotta do something."

"I think that was *The Maltese Falcon*," Michael responded, and they both smiled. There was love there.

Daniel's smile changed to something like a grimace. "Michael," he said, "Helen and I, we really like Marta, and it's just that . . ." Holy Spirit?

"I can see you guys do care for her, Daniel." This fact meant something to Michael. He wanted to add, "I care for her, too," but he held back. Maybe "*And* I care for her, too."

But Daniel was speaking, looking away toward the refrigerator. "It's like," he said hesitating, "it's like she's our daughter almost. I mean, clearly she isn't—not just because she's old, but, well, she's a heck of a lot smarter than we are. Maybe *sister* is better, kind of like you're my brother. I mean—" Daniel stopped, felt embarrassed, then almost sad, praying again for inspiration, though he did not have the faith to receive it. So he gritted his teeth and looked at his brother. Michael was smiling, his lip slightly twisted upward by the unchanging scar Daniel knew was also his fault. He gritted his teeth harder.

"We just feel protective about Marta," he finally said, "and we don't want to see her get hurt."

"I don't want to hurt her either." Michael meant it.

"But you would, Michael, you would. Don't you see?" He didn't. "Don't you see she's lonely and wants someone? Well, you could love her and all that, and maybe she'd even be happy, but she wouldn't be Marta."

"So this *is* a moral judgment," Michael's response was automatic.

Daniel frowned. "Yeah, I guess," he responded, "but it isn't a judgment of you. It's a judgment of Marta. She can handle it." Daniel felt himself almost angry, then afraid he might fail after all to love his brother rightly.

Michael nodded inwardly. "Nicely done," he thought to himself, strangely proud of his brother's response. Michael wanted to smile. He held back, realized that the sneering smile was both a bond and a barrier between him and his brother. For a second, he was muddled, but he also had habits of a probing questioner.

"So you think Marta is vulnerable, and you want to make sure I don't hurt her. Is that it?"

"Yeah," Daniel responded. Somehow that sounded right, like what he should have said but didn't have the words.

"Do you think she wants to be with me?" Michael pressed, knowing he sounded a little like a teenage boy asking about a girlfriend.

"I know she does," Daniel said with a wry smile. "But—"

"Do you think she is just so lonely she'll take anybody, and you're afraid I'm not good enough for her?" This was Michael being an interviewer. It felt easy to him, but also, back in his soul, softly abusive. This was his brother, yet he was being a probing reporter.

"It's worse than that," Daniel responded almost angrily. "She loves you."

Michael flinched. It was not that he had never been loved before. He was confident that other lovers, other women for whom he had cared genuinely and with whom he had shared more than sex had truly loved him. They had said so. When he had spoken of love in return, he had meant it as genuinely as they had. Yet with Marta it was something new. Later, he might have been able to explain it. But in Daniel's kitchen, there was only an intuitive sense that there is more to love when one is loved by someone who is good. The intuition was perhaps in Michael's heart already the saving sense that there would be more to being loved by Marta than by Desra, more to either than the love of Petra Eriksen, more to her love than the love of the local bed-hopping barfly. With time to think and a little training, Michael might even have been able to articulate the implication that the greatest love of all would be to find oneself loved by God. But at this moment, the other implication, one almost as important, was that Michael's own love of Marta would also be somewhere on that scale, somewhere presumably lower than it should be. So the intuition that somehow felt the value of the love of the lovely, had the extra benefit of the hint of guilt, and that love would be better from a better man. With more sincerity than he actually had planned, Michael felt himself move to his second prong of argument.

"I do see the problem," Michael said to his brother, more softly than he had ever spoken to him. Michael felt himself on the edge of a decision, a confession that would mean something to the world, to God perhaps, certainly to Daniel. More importantly, he wanted it to have that meaning, even though in his native honesty he also knew the desire was not unalloyed. Marta was in it, along with all the desires she suggested to his mind and body. Daniel himself was in it, along with the peculiar desire to be fawned over, welcomed into the fold like that lost goat or sheep or whatever it was in the old story. He felt that mix of desires pushed and fed with the simple fact of "being blue," and the growing sense that those with the red souls really did perhaps have something he did not. Perhaps even somewhere in that mix he did in fact hear the call of God. But that latter desire was dark and hidden, still too dim to show itself as the ground on which all the others could stand, the water in which all the others could be washed. Thus Michael made a spiritual confession that was good, or almost good, even if utterly wrong.

"I do care for Marta," he said to his brother directly, knowing it was true. "Maybe you don't think I do. And I think I do understand that there is something in your religion, in your spirituality, that makes me unacceptable. In the past that would have been enough to turn me away. I mean, I don't usually respond well to religious judgments." He smiled at Daniel and hoped his brother saw his eyes and not his lips. "But all the stuff I've seen in the last year, all the holes in the world I thought I could fill just by asking more questions, all that has gotten a bit shaken up. I've been close to Richard Gesar and his technology and his miracles. And you know I like being a skeptic. But . . ."

Michael paused, looking into his brother's eyes for surprise or encouragement. He saw a kind of alarm, a shock that Michael, still too much in the habit of seeing first his own achievements, erroneously took for a surprised hope. He offered his confession of faith.

"But the truth is, Daniel, that I've been tested, and I'm deep, deep blue. Shit blue. I've seen this spiritual technology change people and I've seen the difference it makes, and . . . and I'm closer than I've ever been to trying to take religion seriously. To take Jesus seriously." He might have admitted that referring to Jesus specifically was more difficult than he had expected, but he had said what he thought Daniel would want to hear. He had spoken, he thought, his brother's language. "So I've really considered doing the adjustment, maybe changing myself a bit. Maybe I could enter into your religious world after all these years, maybe meet that Savior of yours, and maybe be a bit more worthy of Marta."

There was a minute of strained silence, a silence that became more and more strained as it lingered. An external time-keeper would have barely noticed seconds pass, and for Daniel, his reaction seemed immediate. For him the response came like a flood, a flood of fear he later confessed as self-defense. Later he would regret the words he said next, feel that somehow anger or jealousy had driven him rather than love. Later he would cry for having failed to wait for wisdom and having missed the chance to offer his own brother a chance at life.

"Argh!" Daniel's groan was spontaneous. "You just don't get it, do you?" He groaned but couldn't have said why. "You can't come to that Savior of mine because your soul is blue any more than you can come to Him because you want to be loved by Marta. Don't you see?"

Michael didn't. He was taken aback, having expected Daniel to react positively, even happily, maybe at least offering again the old dying Savior story. Michael knew it well enough, didn't expect it would be anything new, and had genuinely felt himself open to the possibility of a new faith. It had been admittedly tentative, and he could have accepted a somewhat skeptical response from his brother, maybe a mistrust mingled with some excitement. But to be met with anger or ridicule felt to Michael like betrayal. "I was opening up like I never had before," he might have said, "and this is your reaction?" But Daniel was running ahead of him.

"Crap, Michael!" he was yelling. "You were always the smart brother, the one who could really think. You have always made that clear to everybody we knew. Yet sometimes I think you're dumb as dirt. Crap, Michael! Wanting to find Jesus so you can be loved by Marta is like, is like . . ." The pause was not tense, but for Michael, almost humourous. For Daniel it was something else, a scramble, but not of desperation. "It's like ordering tofu because you want to learn to speak Chinese."

Michael almost laughed. It was a wonderfully disarming line. But the feeling of betrayal was still there, fueling his defenses, bringing back the role of questioner. "Is that supposed to make sense?" he asked, with a tone of intentional disdain.

"No, I suppose it doesn't to you, Michael," Daniel responded quickly. His response felt too quick, and the words that followed, like those before, came back to him later with a sense of guilt. Had he somehow slipped away from a better calling? Wasn't he here to defend Marta? Wasn't he here to speak to Michael's soul? Wasn't he here to bring his brother to Christ? Yet, in spite of what the Holy Spirit should have spoken, Daniel let himself fall through the door of anger that had opened before him. "Of course it doesn't make sense," he steamed out. "Of course! Because you are the smart one. You're the thinker, and there has only ever been a kind of looking down on me and Helen and anybody who doesn't see your cynical side of life. Fine. I don't make sense. But you'd think the brilliant brother could see that coming to Christ in order to have sex with Marta is just, it's just . . . stupid."

Michael was ready. "Rather judgmental of you to imagine that it's only about sex, big brother," he said, deliberately hard. He wanted the charge of being judgmental to be a challenge.

"Fine," Daniel said. "Suppose it's love. Suppose you really want to love Marta. Fine. It's still stupid. If you look for God in order to find Marta, then she is God, and God isn't." Daniel suddenly felt his anger subside, as if his task were done. Then he was embarrassed, ashamed even, as if he knew then that he had gone entirely wrong. He looked at his big hands on the table top and wondered if he could cry. Yet it turned out there was one more idea, one more sentence he had to say. He saw Michael with something like anger in his eyes, and even so they were Michael's eyes.

"And the same is true of your Richard Gesar," Daniel said, and had nothing more. And for him, it was worse than not enough.

For Michael, it was too much, even though, on one level, he did understand what his brother meant, understood it perhaps even better than Daniel himself. For Michael was indeed the smarter brother, and the pieces of trained honesty he had cultivated, even if only from pride, served him well enough to see idolatry even when the Christian before him could not. But at the same time, even his recent struggles had not really softened him enough to help him avoid reacting with defensive assertion, assertion that by training came in the form of questions. Consequently, even having seen the previous point about judgmentalism fail, he could not help but press it. "So I'm to understand that no love or religious zeal is the right kind unless it's your kind?" he asked rhetorically. "There is no spirituality good enough unless it's the kind you have?"

To Michael's surprise, Daniel smiled or half-smiled, the kind of smile that might have been a sneer on Michael's lips, but on Daniel's it was more distant, deeper, sadder. Daniel's eyes grew softer yet reflected the kitchen lights like stars on a calm sea. For Daniel, that calm was indeed deep, almost a resignation, that kind of sad acceptance that some mistake for faith, even as he himself tended to make the opposite error.

"My kind?" Daniel felt disdain, though not toward his brother. "My kind?" he repeated. He looked away and sighed, and in that moment felt the need to tell someone, even Michael, the truth. For they, he and Helen, had been away, you see, away to sign up at last for in vitro fertilization procedures. There had been additional tests—not just the blood and semen and egg cell tests. It was everywhere now, wasn't it, this auroscopy thing? And it's a free public service now, isn't it? So both he and Helen were tested, you see, and they both came back blue. *Blue.* They were like old Pastor Miller, you see—a fact Daniel realized later he had no right to reveal—and it was like finding out you're dying, or already dead. And it's different for you, you see, because you who don't care anyway. But for me and Helen, well, it's like being infertile all over again. It's like . . .

Daniel didn't really know if he cried, nor was he even sure how much he had said out loud. Later he could only think that it made little sense to unload all this to Michael. But there at the kitchen table, it was too late. Michael was strangely moved, quieted, as he felt and resisted an impulse to reach across the table and touch his brother's hand. But he had no words of consolation. "Helen, too?" was all he could say.

Daniel coughed a laugh. "Helen, too," he said, shaking his head as if it were funny. "Me I can figure, but Helen?" He wanted to be silent. "And there will be no baby," he added.

"Wait. What?"

"It's the way the world is, Michael," Daniel was saying. "The physical tests are partly just to make sure everybody's got healthy cells. But there are other tests, too, normal ones I mean, for seeing if people can be good parents and stuff. And now there's some question whether we could give a child a good home if we ourselves are not at peace."

Michael had no words of wisdom or hope, and he knew it. Even so, "I'm glad you have Helen," he said, and even to him it sounded like a *non sequitur.*

* * *

An hour later, the kitchen was quiet, though Daniel still sat where he had been across from his brother. Helen was there, and she did reach across to hold his hands. He had tried to relate some of the conversation to her, but he had not managed it well. It felt entirely wrong to him, all the more wrong for having prayed for the Holy Spirit to guide him, to lead him with love and wisdom, and yet he had spoken with anger and sorrow and a failure to keep

Marta and Michael the focus of his concern. Nothing about it was right, and his soul was blue.

Yet in that hollowness Helen had prayed, and it brought Daniel back to life, at least a little. For he could not help but see the Spirit in her, as here was love, a love that came to him in the kitchen and reached out to touch his hands. It stepped up to him, looked into and beyond him, and in that prayer every word seemed just right. Yet if that were so, he reasoned intuitively, then she could not be blue, whatever the tests said. There had to be some other reality at work, something he was not getting right. And in that moment Daniel resolved, whether or not he could be confident of the guidance of God, to visit Pastor Ed one more time. Maybe there was one more conversation to have.

Michael, for his part, had reached a similar conclusion. He had been tempted to think that Daniel was indeed lost, confused, missing the very spirituality he had claimed for all these years. That would explain a lot. Yet Michael couldn't quite believe the story, the larger story that included a fatherly love of Marta, a devoted love of Helen, a singular and troubled love for Michael himself, all somehow broken by a failure to be spiritual. In Michael's often-tempted self-righteousness, he could not help but feel a strange sympathy for Daniel and Helen in having their desire for a child suddenly thwarted. Something was wrong, Michael felt, and knew in the branching logic of his thoughts that it implied there could be something wrong with his own blue soul. "I'm glad you have Helen," he had said and didn't know why, yet he had meant it. But he did not have Helen, or Marta either. There had to be still some conversation to have, and if it were going to be anything like reaching across a table in love, there was only one person he could think of, strange as it might seem. Michael resolved again to have one more talk with Professor Wacker.

26

QUESTIONS

Michael felt a little the sting of the lasers when he materialized in the phone booth at one of the transportation hubs at the University of Madison. For four days, he had tried contacting Professor Wacker, including going through the department office and a couple of his teaching colleagues, all to no avail. Finally, he had decided just to phone over and see what he could find out. As he stepped from the booth, a familiar voice greeted him.

"Well, hello, Michael Pryor," Marta said, smiling. Michael returned the smile immediately, strangely without the feelings of trepidation that had haunted him for twenty-four hours. It was about this time yesterday that Marta had finally returned his call, only after he had noted to her recorder that he was having trouble contacting Wacker. He had mentioned he was considering going to the university—noting as an aside that he didn't seem to have much work to do these days—and to his surprise Marta had called back. They had spoken at length about Michael's efforts to find the professor, only briefly about wanting to see one another. But as it turned out, Marta had said that she, too, didn't have much work, that the office at Abbott had hired another helper in her office and she was being encouraged—"mysteriously," she had said—to take a day or two off. Thus she could volunteer to go with Michael to Madison, arranging to meet at the transportation center.

So they met. Marta seemed to hesitate a short distance away, and for an instant he wondered if she was going to be standoffish. But she hugged him warmly, having waited, like people do, for the traveler's head to clear. Michael accepted her hug happily. It was good.

"So is old Wacker still in the same office?" Marta asked easily.

"All the same books in all the same piles, I suspect," he said, smiling, forgetting the catch in his lip, and he stood still as Marta strode toward the security station at the hallway to the right. He followed, felt a simple easiness in watching her walk up to the station and press her forehead toward the retinal scanner as she passed through. Michael used the fingerprint ID, and with the two signed in as visitors, Marta waited for him for him to catch up.

Michael caught her hand. "I'm—I'm glad you came to meet me," he said. Despite their presence in the hallway, with students passing as they came through the security station, he felt he might move right then into an apology. He had rehearsed it, but he had not been able to tell for sure if any form of apology would sound like he was being condescending. He had trained himself to insist that a woman—certainly every woman he had slept with—was a responsible adult and was making her own decisions. They had all agreed. What then was the need of any apology? And yet there was something bothering Michael about his last meeting with Marta, something lingering from Daniel's challenge.

"Fool," Marta said, pleasantly interrupting his discomfort. "I didn't come to meet you. I came to find Dr. Paul Wacker. You just happened to be going my way." She squeezed his hand.

Michael felt lighter, but after a few feet stopped her with a tug. She raised her eyebrows in question.

"I would like to talk to you about the other night," he said, looking into Marta's eyes. They were dark and pretty, and they looked back, and he felt softened. "I'd like to apologize, but I don't quite know how." He smiled crookedly.

Marta's own smile bent toward a thoughtful frown. She had rehearsed this conversation, too, probably better than Michael had. She thought he should apologize and guessed he would not know how. But she also knew that apologies were a bare starting point. They were important, and she had rehearsed her own but she had also established an argument, a discussion, a system of definitions and evaluations that came to her like a conversation with Michael, but which had really been a conversation with herself. She had let the conversations run in her mind, pushing them to make sense of what she felt and what she feared, to make sense of desire and principle, delight and will. Little of that conversation had been new to her—it had used references to virtue theory and yet clearly critical of the simplistic optimism of Aristotle or Confucius. She had reconstructed for herself a biblical Jesus who had turned a list of laws into concerns of love and then defined love as a kind of death. She had known all along she would not be able to carry on that conversation with the real Michael Pryor. She laughed a little.

"I'd like to talk about it, too," she agreed. "I have apologies of my own, though they might be different from yours." She began to walk the hall again, holding still quite consciously onto his hand.

"I didn't really mean to ignore you these last few days," she said, towing Michael, maybe allowing herself a little fear at staying closer to his side. "I sometimes have to think things through."

Michael couldn't help feeling a faint hope, more than a desire for sex, and yet not entirely separate. "Things about you and me?" he asked with as much innocence as he could muster.

"No," Marta responded with a slow drawling emphasis. "See? That's still your problem. Your world is still just too small."

Instinctively Michael felt an argument harden in his throat. He tried to swallow it. "What does that mean?" he asked, suspicious that they would be back to religious judgment.

Marta stopped in the hallway and looked at Michael with a kind of sternness that seemed like honesty. "It means, Michael Pryor, that I like you. I like you a lot." The stern look left her eyes, then became a shyness that caused her to look down, gather her thoughts. She started again. "But it also means that what you call 'you and I' is too limited." Michael wondered if she was going to talk to him about God. She didn't. "You and I," she said, stressing his phrase again, "are in a museum, standing in front of a tremendous painting. A masterpiece. And we can look at it and love it, holding hands and sharing our delight in the glory of the work. We can talk about it while we have a cup of coffee, knowing the painting is still hanging there, even when we're not looking at it, knowing it is still glorious, worth looking at again, over and over. 'Cause it's not just 'you and I,' Michael Pryor," she said with mock formality. "There has to be a third reality that is not *you* or *I*, something greater than you or I, or else there can be no *you and I*."

This was not how she had rehearsed the argument, but real conversations with real people never go as planned and she was OK with that. Still, she found herself at the end of an argument, slightly worried that she had forced more disagreement onto her audience, however cogent might be her point. Yet as the hint of embarrassment again touched her, she saw that Michael was smiling. "I haven't the slightest idea what you're talking about, Marta Sanchez," he said, "and I love it."

"Come on, Michael Pryor," she said. "We can talk about this another time, and I promise to use smaller words."

They spoke little on the remainder of the labyrinthine walk to Professor Wacker's office where they found only a locked door. Michael and Marta agreed this was a predictable dead end, and they then also quickly agreed to visit the departmental office for Philosophy. Michael vaguely remembered the way, and Marta believed she remembered it accurately enough. Soon they found an office, a front desk, and a receptionist who welcomed them warmly. She had been absent at Michael's first visit, so she greeted them as strangers with a friendly hello, followed by a mysterious sadness that neither Michael nor Marta noticed at first. The woman was squat and a bit wrinkled, grey-haired but spry. She wore a small crucifix. The plaque on her desk only said, "Vicki." Michael let Marta ask if they could see someone, perhaps the department chair; she mentioned they were interested in finding out about Professor Wacker.

Vicki nodded. "I thought you might be the nephew," she said, nodding at Michael. "We didn't think you were coming so soon."

"Er, no," Michael responded. He told her he was "an acquaintance," that Marta was a "former student," and that they had come to see the professor. He wondered if he should have pretended to be the nephew.

"Oh, dear," the woman responded, a shock of sadness in her voice that Michael recognized. "Then you don't know. But how could you? We only found out today, you see."

"What?" Marta inserted her question. "Did something happen to Dr. Wacker?"

"Here," Vicki said, coming out from behind her desk. "Let me get Dr. Rodgriguez. He should probably tell you the news. It's a little sad, of course, but peace will come. Peace will come." Murmuring, she disappeared through an inner door. There was an uncomfortable wait, and then a man strode alone through the door. Tall, thin, and dark, with a well-trimmed beard and deep dark eyes, he moved with long strides toward Michael and Marta, his black ponytail swishing. He introduced himself as Diego Rodrieguez, "head of the department this year." Marta and Michael introduced themselves. Vicki waited in the doorway.

"Marta Sanchez. Yes," Rodriguez said, "you were one of Wacker's graduate students. Some time before I got here. Isn't that right?"

"Yes," Marta responded, "some years ago. Listen; has something happened to Dr. Wacker?"

Rodriguez seemed not to hear her but turned to Michael. "Michael Pryor, right? Didn't you come to visit Paul recently?"

"Back in the spring," Michael responded coldly. "I'm surprised you remember. We didn't meet then, did we?" Something was bothering Michael about the man's inquisitive greetings, instinctively stepping back from the chat and looking for explanations where they might not be obvious. Marta was concerned; Michael was suspicious. "What has my previous visit got to do with anything?" he asked.

"Oh, nothing. Nothing at all," the man replied courteously. "But you know how it is: everything is recorded. You must have come through security some minutes ago today, so a computer somewhere knows you're here." He smiled like it was a humorous point. "Didn't come straight to this office, then?"

"No," Marta responded quickly, her concern growing, making her less cautious. "We went to Wacker's office, but it was locked up. Has something happened?"

"Ah, yes," Rodriguez frowned. "We've sealed up his office waiting for this nephew of his who is supposed to visit later this week. You can't have strangers looking through the man's things."

"What happened to Dr. Wacker?" Michael spat suddenly. "Are you going to tell us, or do we have to ask the computer that knows everything?"

The man smiled at Michael with a calm that seemed almost threatening. "I understand you are concerned, Mr. Pryor," he said softly. "So were we." He took a deep breath, looked sad. "Truth is, there has indeed been an accident. A traffic accident, and Paul has disappeared in a broken phone line somewhere. Seems like these accidents happen a lot these days." He paused. "I'm sorry you've lost your friend."

Even in her shock, Marta was a quick thinker. "But—"

Michael stopped her. He was certainly more mistrustful. "So Wacker disappeared in a phone accident?" he asked.

The man nodded. "That's what we've been told." Changing the nod to a soft shaking of the head, he added, "Tragic, I know."

"Do you?" Michael let the evident falsehood of the statement hang in the air. "But did you know Wacker didn't travel by phone? Didn't he in fact insist on driving a physical car?"

"Did he?" Rodriguez responded, apparently genuinely surprised. "I guess I didn't in fact know that. Hmm. To tell the truth, I didn't know him well." He paused, frowned thin-lipped again. "Of course," he continued, "when we were told it was a 'traffic accident' we assumed it was a bad phone line. Hmm. Still, tragic either way," he said.

"I think you might be missing Mr. Pryor's point, sir," Marta said. "If Dr. Wacker died, not in a phone accident, but in a car crash, there must be a body."

"Yes, I suppose that's so," Rodgriguez said, raising a finger to his lips thoughtfully. Then pointing that finger outward, he said, "I fail to see your point, Miss Sanchez. Do you think we have somehow been ethically negligent? We understood the meaning of terms the way the terms are commonly meant, and we are as capable of being concerned for our colleague as you are for your 'acquaintance.'" He indicated quotation marks around the word. "So if neither of you is Paul Wacker's nephew, I'm not sure what more exactly you expect from us."

"We expect nothing of you," Marta said with a hint of scorn. Michael felt strangely proud of her.

At that moment Vicki appeared at the professor's elbow, small and smiling sadly.

"Try not to be blue," she said kindly. "It must be hard on you, his friends." She sighed. "But peace will come. Peace will come."

* * *

Death and disappearance were in any event matters for the police; Marta and Michael considered it the most reasonable next move to go there. They weren't sure which police station to contact, since the accident would be a local matter and neither knew exactly where "local" was. Michael had recently driven the route to Professor Wacker's house, so he had to guess that the local police would be somewhere between there and campus. They guessed it would be a precinct in South Madison. Michael wanted to call them; Marta wanted to go there personally. Michael acquiesced. There was something in Marta he hadn't seen before, an anxiety that was more than concern for Wacker. Clearly they were too late, and both of them were practical enough to realize that no amount of lamentation or expression of longing for the company of the deceased would be helpful. They agreed he had been an odd, abrupt, and annoying man.

"And sharp," Michael had been willing to say.

"And good," Marta had added.

The station in South Madison had a phone booth, and it wasn't difficult to phone in to the otherwise vacant lobby. Nobody was waiting; hardly anyone came personally to a precinct office like this one, quaintly settled in a relatively quiet neighborhood of a wealthy suburban area. Even in the busier areas where drugs and crime and murders still occurred, the recent ideals of auroscopy were making headway, creating a few peaceful people among the angry and disenfranchised. Those who remained angry, those who refused to accept the peace and inner quiet of the red soul were increasingly understood as "ill" and "victims of oppression," until they, too, were more and more easily found, with aura scanners commonly built into every device that priced groceries or accepted payment for utilities. More and more, those "victims" could be considered "blue" and desperate, and both conditions, thanks to Gesar's wondrous technology, could now be cured without changing in the least the conditions of city and culture that drove them to their illness.

So especially in a place like South Madison, quiet and calm were thick in the air, and if there was any blue desperation in the place, Michael and Marta had brought it with them. As there was only the one booth, Michael let Marta go on ahead. By the time he arrived, still stinging a little from the lasers, he saw no one in the short hallway and wondered for a terrified moment if there had been another accident. With an uncommon and unexamined fear, he quickly moved ahead and around the bend of the hallway, where he saw Marta ahead of him, already moving up to the window of the station. Michael felt a sudden and unexpected flow of relief. He hurried. By the time he reached the window, Marta was confronting the large dark-skinned woman who sat there idly. Michael couldn't help but pity the receptionist for the difficulty she was about to face with Marta coming to her loaded for bear. That focused aggression, her evident zeal, Michael suddenly found intriguing, an attraction that replaced his earlier worry. He was intrigued by the intensity in her actions that was more than intelligent inquiry. Marta had seen something he had not, and she was chasing it, running ahead. It seemed she had a map he didn't. At the window of the police station, he found himself watching Marta, who reflected something odd and noble. She was being driven by an idea he couldn't imagine, and yet he didn't for a second suspect she had become paranoid or foolish. Uncharacteristically, he found himself silent, standing behind Marta, looking on as one following an honored leader. Aware of his own feelings, he trusted her; he had not yet the wisdom to call it love.

"Wacker," she was saying. "W, A, C, K, E, R. He's dead, for crying out loud, and there had to be some record here." In her push, Marta was not quite aware of her own zeal. But she had indeed seen something Michael had not. It was a hint, a vague awareness, a voice that came from prophecy and mystery, yet did not contradict philosophy. Indeed, like two arches built from different sites yet joining in the middle, she had seen in the philosophy department office a completed project that included the happiness of Vicki and the death of Paul Wacker. It told her that the former was obvious and that she had to make sense of the latter, and the two were connected. If Marta found what she expected, then indeed the arches were joined. And the result was terrifying.

"Yes, yes," the receptionist was saying after she had spoken into her computer. "We do show the death of Paul Wacker. A traffic accident. I'm sorry."

"No, not a traffic accident," Marta said in a tone that might have surprised her had she been able to view herself from the outside. "An automobile accident, somewhere on the highway between his house and the city. There must be a record of the accident, and there must be a body."

"Well, yes, I see," the woman said in reply, sitting back in her chair. She pointed to the screen. "Yes," she repeated. "You know, I should get one of the officers." The woman rose and disappeared through the door behind her. As at the university, Marta waited with Michael, barely aware of him, he distinctly aware of her and of her unawareness of him. He admired it.

They waited a long time, and Michael was on the verge of asking what could take so long when through the door came an officer. He was in standard blue uniform, his frame thin and tall, his hair and features dark. Behind him came another officer, this one shorter, lighter in skin, but with a more prominent nose and smaller eyes. From their name tags, Michael learned they were Officers Patel and Syed, two of South Madison's finest. With no flurry of motion or sign of special concern, the first officer placed his hand on the ID panel by the door that led from the receptionist's area to the lobby, and both officers came through. Almost casually, they invited Marta and Michael to a side room with tall, glass walls, where a table and chairs were the only furniture. "Sit. Sit," said Officer Patel to Michael and Marta. Neither sat.

"We're trying to find out what happened to a friend of ours," Marta started abruptly, and Michael let her go. She explained their questions at the university and expressed their dissatisfaction with the "misinformation" they received. For Marta, the briefest summary was enough, her mind focused, utterly without self-consciousness. Michael watched her natural intensity and forcefulness with admiration and a kind of mystified enjoyment that almost distracted him from his own participation in the inquiry.

"So we naturally decided you would have the right information," she concluded.

"You are a friend, not a relative, of this Paul Wacker, yes, Ms. Sanchez?" Officer Patel asked with seeming innocence.

"Did we give our names?" Michael inserted, trying to keep the offensive position.

"Well, you both phoned in," the policeman responded easily, "so, well, of course the system registered you both. It's a common precaution."

"Well," Michael began his own statement with a carefully veiled imitation of the officer, "Ms. Sanchez and I have had both business and friendly dealings with Professor Wacker. In fact, for some time we have worked together in some investigative journalism. With the professor's disappearance, I must say the investigation takes on a new dimension. So perhaps you can help us out."

Officer Patel nodded. "Well, his disappearance, you say?" he said. "No, no. Nothing so mysterious, Mr. Pryor, but all the more unfortunate."

"And yes, by Allah," the other officer suddenly spoke up from the doorway of the small room, "We know something of your investigative work, Mr. Pryor. You did some of the early interviews with Richard Gesar. Nothing recently however, it seems, but . . ." He let the sentence trail away, and Michael felt the table turned. What did they already know?

Marta, at once more naturally focused and less studied in manipulation, pushed aside the redirection of the conversation. "We were led to believe at first that Professor Wacker was lost to a phone accident, a 'traffic accident,' they said at his work. But in fact, that isn't true, is it? If it was in fact an automobile accident, a driving accident, then there has to be some clear record of the wreck, a body, wreckage of the car, a report, signs along the road. Can you tell us where and when the accident happened? I assume this is public information and not restricted to next-of-kin."

"Of course you're right, Ms. Sanchez," Patel said softly. "We do have the information you want. We have already drawn a little of it from the database for you."

"You knew what we were going to ask before we asked?" Michael posed.

"We are quite efficient here, Mr. Pryor," Officer Syed broke in. "We do our own investigations almost as quickly as you do yours, perhaps. Now it may not be all the information you desire . . ." He seemed inclined not to finish his sentences.

"Well, we know, Ms. Sanchez," Patel began again, "that your friend did die in an automobile traffic accident on the highway about ten miles from his home. We surmise that he simply fell asleep while driving and, quite unfortunately, veered off the road and directly into the concrete pillars of an overpass. That's like a bridge that carries one road over the other without the two actually intersecting." He said condescendingly, as if talking to a child.

"Our investigations suggest that he seems not to have died at once, but that he suffered significant brain injury. His own documents, which of course we had to access at the first opportunity, indicated that he did not want to, well, linger. So he was, let us say, peacefully and softly given the opportunity to enter his rest."

Marta at once knew what that meant, and she felt a sudden urge of argument. Yet finally, as if a new voice had emerged inside her, she paused and felt caution in her words, as if absorbing suddenly some of the curiosity and suspicion as first appeared in Michael's voice. "Wacker would never have wanted a quick euthanizing," she wanted to declare, but she didn't.

Michael didn't know the professor as well, and so pursued automatically the more obvious tack. "May we then see the body?"

"In fact, Mr. Pryor," it was Syed again, "it is common for hospitals that help the ill and injured onto their final rest to submit the bodies quickly to cremation. I'm sure you know this to be a fact, Mr. Pryor." Michael again felt a strange coldness. Indeed, after his father had been euthanized . . .

"Perhaps then we can see the wreckage of the car." Marta had taken charge. "Or at least you might tell us more exactly where the accident occurred, so we can see the place for ourselves. Maybe we can leave a memorial or something." Marta wasn't quite sure why she had added the closing deception.

There was suddenly an almost haunted silence from the two officers. The pause was only seconds long, but it was a thick silence, as if new calculations were taking place. The two officers glanced at each other, then Patel addressed Marta. "Ms. Sanchez," he started, "perhaps you feel unhappy with our interview, but there is nothing to be blue about. As we've explained, there is no body to view, and the wreckage of the car, well, that does in fact belong at this point to someone else, to some next-of-kin, for it does represent some minor material property. But if you believe, well, that you are not being properly served in this inquiry, you may certainly lodge a more formal request for information. We can log you in as having protested our policies."

"Perhaps, Mr. Pryor," Officer Syed came in, "you would like to pursue this investigation of yours more formally, declare that you suspect foul play?"

Michael heard a threat, and at once his heart rose to the challenge. "I begin to suspect something foul," were the words that came to him, but he was interrupted.

"No, no we have no official complaints." Marta was already moving toward the door, for she had felt again the change inside her, a sudden sense that she and Michael needed to leave. It was not fear, she would insist later, nor some despair at the inefficiency of bureaucracy. It was more like a desire to breathe different air. She had suddenly thought of Helen.

"Perhaps we have been a bit terse," she said, trying to smile. "You must understand that we are in shock at losing our friend."

"Well," Patel returned, "we certainly understand, don't we, Mahad? We have all lost someone. But you know we needn't be blue. We can pray together if you like. I pray to Lord Shiva, and Mahad here, of course, to Allah. But surely you, Ms. Sanchez, may pray to your Christ if you would like us all to share some peace."

Marta and her Christ? Michael ground his teeth against some questions forming in his mind. How did they know?

But Marta was already leaving. Officer Syed was moving aside as she called back, "No, thank you." She had to get out, yet something also told her to assuage the concerns of the officers. "We all do need to find some peace, and so perhaps Mr. Pryor and I should take a few days to recover from the news. But, please, if you could relay to us the details of the accident, we would appreciate it. Not that we could drive out to see the place, I suppose, but it would be a comfort to know the details." She felt her words like a mild dishonesty.

Almost too quickly for Michael, they were moving toward the phone booth. Marta seemed suddenly driven, and he felt her pulling him along. He had begun to feel the attraction to Marta as a kind of trust, as if it were a first step in a walk of faith. He followed her, not knowing where they were going. Around the corner and along the corridor to the phone booth they went, and he watched her press her eye to the scanner that opened the booth. Without a word, she entered, and instinctively turned around. "I need to go home," she said to Michael, "and you should, too." Michael watched her press the numbers inside the booth; the door closed, and the apparatus hummed. Michael waited for the reset light and raised his hand to the identity scanner. He paused, suddenly wondering what putting his hand there truly meant. Yet in the next second, he realized he had no other way out. He pressed the glass; it scanned his hand so he could go home.

27

LAST RITES

Michael was at work on Wednesday morning, although by noon it was clear it was pointless. At his desk, looking at a blank screen, he realized that he should have known nothing would come of his efforts. Melanie had not assigned him a real story for two weeks, and what she had suggested had only been nice stories of conversions and peace. Yesterday the president and vice-president had issued a joint statement about inner peace and their desire to work for peace with all people, something presidents and vice-presidents had been saying for a hundred years. But this time it was about acceptance of one's self and how that leads to the acceptance of others. This time it had been in preparation for a visit from the premier of North Korea. It seems we could tolerate even madmen as long as we don't call them such. There was a rumor that even Kim Lon-wa had undergone the adjustment and now considered himself a devout Buddhist.

Melanie had not even asked Michael to cover that trite story. "If there is no problem to report, you are likely to invent one," she said. So Michael had nothing to do, even with yesterday's story.

Michael had spent the day before trying almost desperately to follow up on Paul Wacker's disappearance. He liked calling it a "disappearance" because calling it "death" was too soft. After all, people die every day, many of them by choice, and in discussing death there was more about "easing our loved ones to a final rest" than there was about highway crashes and irreparable brain injury. The truth was that Wacker had indeed simply disappeared. Michael had checked with the police to request the digital video from the highway patrol drone that had found the wreckage, but it would take days to procure. He had asked about where the euthanizing of the "essentially already dead" Wacker had taken place, about where the body had been taken for cremation, and even about where the ashes might be now. To all of these questions he had simply been told this was information for the family and surely he did not want to intrude upon their personal time. Even exactly who "the family" might be was a bit of information Michael never quite uncovered.

The final frustration came when Michael tried to rent a car, determined to find the crash site himself. The same car company that had earlier rented to him told him there were no automobiles available. They would have one next week, but there just wasn't much demand for rental cars these days, so they didn't have one handy. "Where's the one I rented last month?" Michael had asked; the young woman on the other end said it had been taken out. "So there is demand," Michael snarled. With splutters and apologies, the woman repeated that nothing was available and asked if he wanted to make a reservation for a car next week. Michael declined.

Tuesday night, Michael had tried to call Marta. She had answered after several tries and told him she was in a library. "Library?" Michael asked with only somewhat feigned incredulity. "You mean like with books?" Marta had smiled at him through the screen. "I know," she said. "Weird, ain't it? Next thing you know we'll go back to using flush toilets."

In spite of her good humor, Michael could see that she was distracted. Yes, she had said, she was in a library with real books.

"Can't find what you need on the computer?" he asked.

"Of course," she said, "but when you research on the computer, anybody can track what you're reading. When you get a book in a library, read it, and put it back, you can finally, maybe for the last time, be alone." Michael hadn't quite known what she meant, but felt strangely like it might have been a subtle way of telling him to leave her alone. But Marta was not the subtle type. He had almost asked her to explain, but she stopped him.

"You know, Michael Pryor," she had said softly, "I don't know when I'll be able to talk to you again. If we do get to talk again, I'm not sure it'll be me." She laughed, sadly, but if it was a joke, it was one only she understood. "But in any case, I want you to know that we're OK, you and me. We're OK." She smiled weakly, almost apologetically. Then she made another joke about how talking in a library was the only crime still punishable by death, and she hung up. Later she and Michael would almost laugh to realize, of course, that she was wrong.

And so Wednesday morning, Michael went in to work. He phoned himself in but could not seem to log into his desktop computer. He had intended to ask Melanie to help him look into Wacker's disappearance. But even in the first moments of their conversation, he realized it was not going to work. She was too nice.

"I just don't see what you're trying to accomplish, Michael," she said. "Shit! You're just so damned macabre." She said it like she was patting a child on the head. "Sure, automobile accidents are rare, but people don't need to be reminded of how bloody they were."

"I guess that's one of the great things about phone accidents," Michael responded. "When people just disappear into mists of molecules, nobody has to clean up."

After a pause, Melanie changed the direction of conversation. "Guess what, Michael? Liz and I are going to have a baby." Michael had wondered what he was supposed to say. He was expected to be happy, happy for other people being happy. Isn't that the way it was supposed to be? But he wasn't. He didn't care. Or worse: for a second he felt stung for Daniel's and Helen's sake.

By the time Michael got back to his desk, he felt defeated. All this holiness and laughter. If all was indeed peace and holiness, he would certainly not have much of a job. If there is a heaven, he mused, there would be no job for the cynical reporter searching for lies, nor for evangelists or angry prophets of doom. In heaven there must not be any work for doctors and lawyers either. Of course in this world, this real world, whatever its other perfections, there had to be doctors to euthanize the unhealable and lawyers to write up the legal justifications. But there was no job for Jeremiah.

So Michael began to wonder if perhaps he was just wrong. He hadn't felt any joy at Melanie's news, and shouldn't a good person, a person who truly cares about others, want them to find happiness? The message of the "Don't Be Blue" campaign felt true, even to Michael. What had Marta meant when she said the next time they spoke it might not be she herself speaking? Was she, even she, intending to go through with the adjustment? What if, in the end, all this life of looking for liars and hypocrites were finally to end when the last liar, the last hypocrite, turned out to be Michael himself?

Michael stared at his computer screen and pressed his thumb to the scanner for the tenth time. Nothing. His very identity made no mark, changed nothing. He had nothing to say, and there was no one listening anyway. The world, it seemed, had shut him out, made it impossible to be himself. If he was wrong, then he had been wrong his whole life, and wrong in a much worse way than just having no angry job to do. In a world of peace and love, there was no place for anger, and that meant more than being out of a job. It meant having to rethink everything he believed. Was he simply guilty of misanthropy? Or was there truth to the sense that lies and deception are part of the human condition—not all of it, certainly, but indelibly a part? Indeed, deception was part of himself, he knew, although the thought came to him more easily that it would have even six months ago. Wasn't he good at self-deception, finding ways to justify what he did one way or another? It had been clear to Michael throughout his career that intelligent people could always justify what they wanted to do, including himself, Michael Pryor. That realization came almost naturally. It was something, no doubt, he had learned from his experience with Marta. Hadn't he always been able to find good-enough reasons to have sex, to abuse trust, to let someone die? Yes, it was true, and because Michael had always claimed to want truth, he had to face it. Whatever the cost, he thought, he would find the truth, even if the truth was that he, too, was a deceiver.

But what if the truth was no longer hard to find? What if part of his self-deception lay finally in his self-protecting mistrust of Gesar? What if it was, after all, simply true that every soul had a color and every color could be adjusted? That would mean his own doubt and despair and misanthropy could be healed. That meant he himself, even Michael Pryor, could be happy. Until then, he was just being a fool.

Strange, he thought, to have to make yourself willing to be happy. He pressed his thumb again to the computer screen and got no response. No doubt the computer even here at his own desk could—thanks to Gesar's technology—not only read a thumbprint, but could register his identity and personal history, as could every other hand scanner and retina reader that ran every phone booth and every grocery transaction, every record of complaint or computer-based inquiry. Consequently, every device, every transaction, every communication and transportation could tell him, could remind him, that he was blue. "Don't be blue," the voices said again and again, from machines and people and from the voice in his own conscience. What is the point of all this resistance that has no hope? What if it could all be fixed and if he, at last, could be happy? Michael wanted to be happy—and that made him angry.

Michael pounded his desktop. The frustration and impossibility of learning anything about Wacker's death had broken him nearly to the point of being willing to accept the adjustment. He would take the *tulku*'s pill, he said to himself, and awaken a new man. He could be spiritual, maybe find God, maybe find Marta, maybe get his job back, maybe find peace. In that momentary temptation, Michael was nearly lost.

But then Michael remembered something Wacker had said. And hadn't Marta said the same thing? And maybe even Daniel, though Michael couldn't quite remember what his brother had said. Wasn't it something about wanting God, or wanting whatever we want, whether it is God or not? Wasn't it something about the standard of happiness and whether we can desire more than we desire? Somewhere in that confusion, in that same moment of temptation to be happy, the urgings of his own honest habits and the call of truths greater than himself met in his soul. It was Michael alone, and yet it was not. It was Michael's own fervent insistence on truth, and yet it felt as if he were being lifted by another. It was his own importunate prayer, though he had never thought to pray. It was his own cry for a distant God, and yet it was an unexpected blessing. It said, "If there be a mystery, let me not run from it." It said, "If there be lies, let me unmask them." But it—or he—also said, "And if there be truth and peace, then let me find those as well. Let me find peace only if it is truth. I will bow," the thought said, "but only to the God who is God," Michael seemed almost to be speaking out loud, "even if it is Jesus." And perhaps in that moment, Michael was saved.

Michael breathed. There was after all another interview to make, and if he played it right, he could do it. He would have to talk to Melanie, and he might have to be deceptive. He would not deceive himself, but if he had to deceive Melanie to be honest, he would do it. He decided to try.

"Shit, Michael," was Melanie's immediate response, "I don't know what I can do for you. I mean, hell, you've talked to the Gesar more than I have. What's the point of talking to him again? He's a hard guy to get ahold of nowadays, and I don't have as many strings to pull as you think I do." She smiled with a kind of softness, and it seemed she meant it. "I don't think I can do much for you," she said, "and I have to be good to myself, too, these days" she said, at once proud and shy. "I have Liz to think of, and the baby." Michael had never liked Melanie's partners much, but apparently Melanie, too, was happier these days, and all was lovely at home. Michael didn't care who Melanie chose to have sex with, but he reminded himself that he had liked the angry Melanie better. Smoking had suited her.

As Michael felt his smiling lip curl into a snarl, he turned, looked away, hoping to look a little sad, at least from behind. "Yeah, sure," he said, "I don't suppose anyone can get through to the people in Albuquerque easily now. Certainly not a lost guy like me. But I thought if I could have one more assignment, it could be, you know, a kind of conversion story."

Michael heard Melanie turn in her chair. He didn't look back but wondered if he had piqued her interest. He had little practice in looking humble, didn't much like the idea of trying it here. So he kept his back to Melanie.

"Conversion?" she asked. "Whose?"

Michael risked turning around, but he kept his eyes lowered. "Well, mine," he said toward the floor, again almost afraid to see if Melanie would respond.

"You want to see Dr. Gesar to do the adjustment?" Michael wasn't sure if there was skepticism or hope in her voice. "I know I feel a lot better about myself since I did it," she offered. "Liz, too. I know you've been blue a long time . . ."

Everybody knew it, apparently. Every transaction, every transport, every effort to log into his own work station read him, checked his soul, told him what he could and couldn't do. Of course it was all for his own good—or so everyone said, over and over. Why would anyone choose to be unhappy? How could that not be a poor choice, a self-injury, a form of clinical depression?

"Yes," he said aloud, "I'm blue and always have been." He wanted it to sound like a confession, but it rang hollow in his own ears. "Daniel, too," he wanted to add, mimicking her announcement about Liz, but he held back. After all, that fact is what made him doubt the whole matter so vehemently.

"Well, maybe it would be a good thing," Melanie said almost hesitantly, and Michael felt exposed. "Maybe even a good story." Michael looked up; she was almost smiling at him again. Her eyes seemed to darken. "But I thought you were interested in pursuing the story of what happened to this friend of yours."

Michael felt his ire grow. Was she testing him? He turned away again. "Yes," he confessed, "I was surprised and scared about that. Maybe that's what has made me rethink my life. You know. Life is pretty short." It sounded plausible.

"I know what you mean, Michael," Melanie said to his back. There was another bit of silence, and Michael then heard Melanie's footfalls. She came up behind him, laid a hand on his shoulder. He turned. Her rough, barely blonde hair framed her head that was tilted slightly to one side as she looked up at him. Still her eyes seemed dark, distant, suspicious, but apparently she had believed him. "We can talk it over," she said with an odd, haunting care in her voice, "when you get back from New Mexico."

* * *

Daniel was in Ed Miller's office, but it was no longer Ed Miller's. He had been shown into the empty office by Lisa, who gave no clue with her smiles and friendly wishes of hope and joy for Daniel and Helen that anything had changed since Daniel last saw Ed in this office. But things had indeed changed. The messiness of the desk, dusty mismatched books on the shelves—all the clues that conveyed the warm confusion of Ed Miller—were gone. All was neat, and the books were newer; a whole section of video discs carried titles about the lives of the apostles and other saints, as well as the spiritual teachings of great figures from the Buddha to Gandhi. Saint Francis was next to Rumi. Daniel realized this was now the office of Pastor Jackson Hubble. "Um," he turned to protest and even leave, but Lisa was gone, and Daniel felt awkward. He felt even more awkward when Morris Hobbes walked in, slapped him on the shoulder, and shook his hand warmly, praising the Lord as he did so.

"What's the deal, Morris?" Daniel managed to break up the friendly greetings. "Looks like Hubble has taken over Ed's office."

Morris nodded and frowned at the same time, "Yes, I'm sorry to say Ed is no longer with us." Morris gave a moment's effort to trying to look sad. "But Pastor Hubble is here," he said happily. "I'm sure he'd be glad to see you. Me, too, in fact."

Daniel didn't doubt that. Morris was pretty much happy about anything. "Rejoice in the Lord always," he liked to say. He said it too often, Daniel thought then felt slightly guilty about his jealousy.

"I knew Ed was going to leave soon," Daniel tried to continue. "I know there was some unhappiness in his work there at the end, but—"

"Yes, yes," Morris interrupted. "He was rather unhappy there at the end, but I'm sure he's happier now."

Daniel winced inwardly. "Lord, I hope not," he thought to himself, afraid that even Pastor Ed had gotten the adjustment after all. For Daniel had come today hoping to talk to someone "blue," hoping to discuss a new idea, a strange and hopeful thought about hopelessness. It had come to him while reading Matthew's Gospel and hearing an echo of something he had said to his brother a week ago. He was convinced only someone "blue" would understand, but he wanted someone with training in the scriptures. Daniel didn't quite trust himself with these ideas, but he trusted Pastor Hubble even less.

"I think I'll just go," he suddenly said. "I mean, I don't want to bother Pastor Hubble while he's moving in and all. I could just visit Pastor Ed at home. I imagine he'd like a visit."

With trained compassion, Morris Hobbes smiled sadly again and cocked his head slightly to the left, as if amused by the innocent question of a confused child. "Gosh, I'm sorry, Daniel," Morris said softly, "but when I said Ed is no longer with us, I meant, well, that he's truly gone. He's with the Lord now."

"What?" Daniel was suddenly alert. All feelings of minor annoyance disappeared. "How?" he asked. "What happened?"

"Nothing happened," Morris said. "He rather suddenly checked himself in for depression and voiced his desire for a peaceful passing—"

"He was euthanized?" Daniel cried. With a rushing mix of anger and uncertainty, Daniel was flooded with memories of his own father. Ed Miller had somehow "voiced his desire," and it was done? It couldn't be. Daniel understood that everyone had a right to "die with dignity," but the standard phrase didn't seem to describe Ed any more than it seemed it had applied to Daniel's own father. Somehow depression itself shouldn't have been enough inspiration—or desperation. Daniel himself should have been there to comfort those men—his father, Pastor Ed—and somehow urge them differently, somehow change their minds. But wasn't it their freedom, their autonomy, to choose to die? Isn't it an act of compassion? Daniel knew the arguments, even almost believed them, product as he was of his age, yet he was haunted by some greater understanding. All the variant, conflicting understandings met as a quandary of guilt for Daniel, guilt for feeling an audacious insistence that he would try to change someone's mind and guilt for having failed to do so.

"I'm sorry, Daniel," Morris said. He put a hand on Daniel's shoulder, and that touch awakened him.

"You're not sorry, Morris," Daniel said with calm anger. "You're never sorry. That's why I can't stand you."

Morris was taken aback. He stepped away from Daniel, toward the open office door, almost with fear in his blue eyes. Daniel saw the fear and wanted it to be there. He felt himself swell and grow with a kind of power he might later have regretted had he not found the voice strong and liberating. The anger was accusing, but it was also calm, like honesty. For the first time Daniel saw dishonesty outside himself, and it freed him.

"You're never sorry, Morris, because you have never understood love."

Morris recovered, seemed to step forward a little. He adopted a smile that seemed to Daniel like he was raising a mask to his face. "But I love you, Daniel," he said. "I know you're upset."

"No, Morris," Daniel responded easily, "you don't love me. You may love loving people, but you don't love people. Only those who have been forgiven much can love much."

Daniel saw Morris's eyes go brighter. "By this the world knows that we are Jesus' disciples," he said, "that we love one another."

"And love is to give up one's life for a friend."

"But He came to give us life," Morris countered, "and life in abundance."

"Jesus wept."

Morris paused, thought. "But then he raised Lazarus."

"My God, my God, why have you forsaken me?" Daniel quoted.

"But it was for the joy set before him that he endured the cross," Morris insisted.

Daniel saw it all clearly, as if for the first time, and he coughed a slight laugh, nodded, looked down. "Tell me, Morris," he said, "did he actually endure the cross? Did Jesus come in the flesh?"

Morris stared at Daniel with a hard gaze, with a kind of bubbling behind his eyes that might have been thought, or calculation, or anger. "Maybe you should talk to Pastor Jack," he said. "I can see you're upset. And I know you've been depressed."

"Sure," Daniel responded, barely noticing the threat in the word, "you go get Hubble. After all, he's the one who killed Ed—as surely as if he'd stuck the needle in his arm, him and people like you."

Morris was at the door. "It's just the blue," he said, as he slipped out and closed the door behind him. It's just the blue. So Morris knew he was blue. Daniel wondered how.

There was a fumbling at the door, the sliding of a key in the office door, a click of the lock.

The sound of that lock was no surprise to Daniel. Suddenly it all made sense. What if, for all the value of compassion and happiness and the right of death with dignity, for all the peace of the soul and goodness of the abundant life, for the need to preach the love of Jesus and to lock the door on those who are depressed, for all the reds and blues and adjustments that could bring peace to the world—what if it was all just *wrong*? What if it's all a glorious statue of gold and silver and bronze, and yet the feet are made of clay? What if, after all, it was all just a lie?

Daniel smiled. It's OK, he said to himself, I'm ready. He considered the locked door and decided he wouldn't even try to open it. "I'm ready," he repeated and prayed a prayer of thanks. Then he thought of Helen. What if there are other locked doors? What if she—or others—weren't quite ready? What if they needed his prayer of thanks? Then Daniel knew that being ready was not enough and he needed to see Helen, to save her. No, he only needed to tell her what he had seen and to hold her in his arms. It's OK, he would say, "We're ready."

But the door was locked. For a brief moment, he thought he might not see Helen again. Then, in delight, he turned to Ed's window with the broken latch. He laughed aloud. "Of course," he said to himself. "God is good." And in a minute, he had slipped out into the late November air and was on his way home.

28

THE HERETIC

Michael wasn't quite sure what he was angry about, but everything that led him to Building 973 of the Sandia Laboratories this one last time seemed to fuel that anger. He had not been able to log into his desk computer until Melanie called IT and somehow got his login fixed. He had done his research, read as much as he could about what Richard Gesar was currently "up to," but had not managed to find Gesar anywhere. There was no news as to his whereabouts. Then Melanie had called Michael and told him the *tulku* was in Albuquerque after all and Michael could meet him there. "How'd you get this information?" he had asked. "I'm the editor, ain't I?" she had replied.

The frustrations continued. Michael had needed to purchase personal items before his visit to Albuquerque, but the catalog wouldn't accept his ID. "Don't be blue," it said to him, and Michael had whispered curses under his breath. Tim had come by, quite by accident he insisted, and bought the items for Michael. Finally, Michael had been sent on his way by Melanie. "Let me get that for you," she had said, placing her palm on the phone's reader. "See ya later," were her parting words. Michael had watched her watching him as the booth door closed, feeling that maybe she didn't trust him. Worried about sounding too angry or too humble, he had simply remained silent.

The laboratories were quiet, perhaps because of the Thanksgiving holiday or simply because there was nothing more to do. He had wondered if he would see Petra Eriksen, and indeed she was there to meet him. Before the trip, he had considered how he would resist Petra, making himself seem at once humble and distant. He had mentally rehearsed the scene in which she offered sex and he would pretend shame and sorrow and the need for a change before he could possibly "deserve" her attention. But Petra met him with hardly a flutter of interest, her professional demeanor making her so cold she was almost unattractive. Almost.

"It's good to see you again, Mr. Pryor," she said to him. "And good to see you hopeful at last."

Michael tried to smile. "Don't be blue," he replied with a slight nod, hoping it was enough.

"We have everything ready," Petra went on, turning from the reception area back through the double doors that led, not to the conference rooms where it all had started for Michael, but toward the labs where Michael had met Gesar, toured the facilities, and been introduced to the life-changing— now world-changing—technology. Michael understood the adjustment procedure well enough to know it no longer required special laboratories or complex procedures. Not anymore. The auroscopic process had been inter-woven with the miniaturization of the rematerialization process; the whole event was barely an outpatient procedure. It could be undertaken on your lunch hour. With a shock, Michael realized he might have made a mistake coming to Sandia too early in the afternoon. He needed time, had to know more, yet he did not want to appear suspicious.

"Petra." Michael touched her elbow to stop her in the hall, "I have to do this right. I have to change my life for the better with enough information that I can write it up when I'm done. Do you see? This isn't just about me; it's about what I need to say."

Petra smiled kindly, but not warmly. "But it is about you, Mr. Pryor," she said. "It's about health and well-being for yourself first of all. It is the free gift of grace and peace for you." She turned. "Come," she said, "and you'll see."

"But I can't," Michael protested, "not until I can talk to Dr. Gesar one more time." He was worried about coming across as angry. "I want to write this story for others as well as myself. Isn't Dr. Gesar's whole point that we learn peace and compassion with others after we find it for ourselves? I need to be thinking about everyone who reads my story as well as my part in the story itself." On that point, Michael felt he was being totally honest; he had always thought that this was the point of writing. Perhaps more than he had ever realized, he had cared somewhere in his work about someone, or at least about something, greater than himself.

"What is it you want, Mr. Pryor?" Petra Eriksen asked coldly. "Another exclusive interview with the doctor? That's impossible. He isn't here."

"But I was told he is here," Michael shot back, "and I want him to ex-plain . . ." Michael paused. "I would like him to explain for us all how he sees the changed soul. I would like to follow his care and concern, as well as his scientific insights, from blue to red, from burdened to bounteous, from ignorant to awakened, from sinner to saved." He looked pleadingly at Petra, and it was a real plea. "I can get his words and his encouragements at each step along the way, Petra. You know I can." He paused again. "And I think you want me to."

Dr. Eriksen looked at Michael sideways. "Richard is not here, Mr. Pryor," she said matter-of-factly, "at least not officially. Sometimes he has to get away from the crowds and noise. He comes back to these labs to rest sometimes, just to be in his rooms, practicing calmness and insight."

"So Gesar is here," Michael asserted.

"Yes," she replied, "and I think I can arrange for you to talk with him. Perhaps he would like to walk with you through the adjustment. I'll go see. Meanwhile, we do have a room ready for you. Richard had suggested we prepare one."

Michael was not surprised. She led him right instead of left, north down the long hallway away from the rooms of the staff, away from Gesar's room, away from the room he and Petra had briefly shared. They were both silent, and Michael was thankful. At the end of the building they turned up the hallway to the first visitor room. Petra opened the door and Michael passed through quickly, feeling strangely nervous. She followed him in, but merely walked to the bathroom door and pushed it open. "You know the place, I think," she said calmly.

Michael might have been unsure of himself, perhaps from years of confusing love and desire, and he watched with a hint of anger as Petra moved back to the door. "Petra," he called her name and wasn't sure even to that moment if he meant to ask her to stay. As close as he was to a new honesty about his own morality, and as driven as he was by a new duty, he couldn't help wanting to invite her to stay with him. And yet, as if with an unexpected wisdom, he stopped. "Thanks," he said.

But trials must come, even if only to show that they are indeed trials. So Petra smiled gently, her head turned slightly toward him as her body pointed toward the door. She was beautiful. "Do you want me to stay?" she asked as if to insist that this had to be Michael's choice.

And perhaps for the first time in many years, Michael was aware of temptation. Something in the question made him aware both of his own moral weakness and of the necessity of conscious choice. Petra was beautiful, an offered object of delight. Yet, at the same time, her beauty, the curve and form of her body silhouetted in the doorway, became a kind of darkness. In his slowly awakening eyes, her attractiveness was like the man who sells drugs to the addict, the peddler of alcohol in the depressed neighborhood. She was beautiful, a trap, an exploiter of weakness, an evil, but an evil he wanted, an evil he could choose. Or he could resist, perhaps choose something more than what he wanted.

"No," he said, and was surprised by the strength in his voice.

Petra smiled. "I didn't think so," she said. "I don't think you need me anymore."

"What does that mean?" Michael almost asked. Her words came to him as a sort of boasting, somehow about something she had achieved. No, he had not fallen to the temptation of her sexual beauty, but Petra Ericksen had nonetheless claimed some kind of victory, and Michael couldn't let the claim go without a challenge.

"Have you ever heard of Paul Wacker?" he asked impulsively.

Petra stopped just short of the door. She cocked her head a bit. Michael wondered if he had asked too much. Then she answered, "Yes, I know of him. I understand he was a friend of yours. I'm sorry you lost him."

"Then you know he's dead."

"Yes," she responded easily. "I imagine that's partly why you're here."

Did she imagine he wanted answers about Wacker's death and had vague fantasies that somehow Gesar would have them? Or did she imagine he was depressed at the loss of a friend? "Actually," Michael confessed with calm honesty, "I didn't know him well. What can you tell me about how he died?" Michael felt the question like it was meant, as if he were looking for truth.

Petra almost laughed. "How should I know?" she responded. "It's not as though we are gods watching all the workings of mankind."

"You knew he was dead."

"Of course," Petra responded, "and I assumed you were distraught over his death. We look again at the people who come to visit us, Mr. Pryor, even one as familiar as yourself. We saw that you had made inquiries—you and Ms. Sanchez."

Michael stopped, struck by the mention of Marta. Half of him heard the reference like a curious piece of evidence, part of the whole picture forming in his mind. It would have been part of his conspiracy theory if he had let it be. But at the same time, he realized there were ramifications to his being here beyond what might happen to him. To the credit of his growing sense of value beyond himself, he feared the effects of what he did here on those he knew and loved—yes, loved—back home. He could slip back into being the bold reporter, he could carry through with his plan, but the effects would not be his alone to endure.

"Yes," Michael tried to sound quieter, humbled. "Ms. Sanchez knew him better than I, of course. We were troubled by his sudden death."

"Of course," Petra Eriksen smiled her careful smile. "It was unexpected, but then I also understand he was a troubled man, lonely, something of a drinker. Perhaps he has at last found some peace, eh?"

"I wouldn't know," Michael replied with impatience he could not hide. Peace indeed? Does that somehow solve the mystery of death?

"But you shall know soon enough, Mr. Pryor," Petra said and stepped through the doorway. But then she stopped and turned, driven one last time, it seemed to Michael, to gloat. Or to confess. "There is peace for all of us who can find it," she said easily, "so let us not lose hope. We have entered the age of the science of the soul, Mr. Pryor. There is no longer any reason to be blue. It is both unhappy and irrational. There is peace for all who can find it. For you, for Ms. Sanchez, for your brother." She stopped with a confident smile. "Are you sure you don't want me to stay?"

Michael could only shake his head. As the door closed behind Dr. Eriksen, Michael's face hardened, his eyes became steely. His mind raced. For a moment there, near the end when the reporter in him was weakening because he was also a human being, the call to peace was another temptation. Peace and sex. What could be better than self-indulgence without moral qualms? But at the end of her speech, Petra's words struck Michael with a kind of threatening power. Petra Ericksen was beautiful and sexual; she was intelligent and clever. And she was satisfied somehow, like so many others full of personal peace and compassion for humanity. Yet, Michael chewed the thought: Petra had too much power. She had known about Wacker; Michael could understand that. She had known about Marta; that, too, was reasonable. But then she had mentioned Daniel.

How had Daniel gotten into the conversation? What did this have to do with him? Michael felt rage at the unknown danger, like an evil hand that reached out not to threaten him but to threaten his brother. How could it have happened? And yet how could it not have happened? In every movement, every transport, every transaction for food or utilities, there was the ubiquitous awareness of who was blue and who wasn't. This universal work of hope and peace, built on a universal sense of compassion, felt like a threat, especially when it seemed pointed at Daniel.

In a strange realization, Michael suddenly imagined Petra Ericksen trying to seduce his brother, and he was outraged. "Keep your paws off him!" he found himself thinking, though her paws were something he had enjoyed, something he was not sure he himself could resist if they were offered again. But what if it were Daniel? What if the tempters were coming after Daniel? What if he, too, could be ruined by his own desire? How evil are those who encourage us to fulfill our own desires!

Michael realized that this was a strange but genuine morality. In his anger he wanted for his brother something like goodness, and he realized with an unexpected warmth that perhaps it was something like the honesty he wanted for himself. He realized he loved his brother.

* * *

It could not have worked out better. Had Michael been a praying man, he might have seen the hand of Providence at work. As it was, he felt lucky, and that feeling emboldened him. Petra had sent a note via a messenger, saying he could see Gesar in the morning. He was told that the minimal staff was instructed to offer him whatever conveniences he needed, and that gave Michael a chance.

Michael decided to wait until five minutes after midnight. He had already taken a "walking tour" of the hallways, remembering his way to the labs. The few employees who saw him out walking said nothing. Michael had already planned simply to say he was feeling nostalgic, wanting to remember what he had seen and felt on his previous visits. He had his recording pad with him so he could claim to be taking notes on the building's physical layout, to get his descriptions right when he would later write up his story. But no one questioned him. Lab 4, where he had watched the early experiments on aura adjustment, was open but dark. Lights came on automatically as he entered, startling him. But his real interest lay across the hall in the archives, the office that should hold records of all Gesar's work. He had in mind a particular bit of data he needed to find. He wanted to find subject 001.

At 12:11, Michael was in the long north-south hallway again. He had been careful to pass the open labs without activating motion-sensitive lights, even while trying not to look stealthy. Past the labs on his right, past the double-doors to the reception area and the small common area on his left, he walked quietly. At last, with Lab 4 ahead on his right, he came to the door on his left that said, "Archives." He tried the latch, found it open, and passed through.

Light came on, and Michael at once felt exposed. But the door was solid, not transparent, and he hoped that no leakage of light in the hallway would betray him. It was too late anyway. The office he had entered seemed like a general library, with two desks with computers surrounded by shelves where books and clipboards lay about in a disorganized way. Whatever the books on the shelves and the notes on the clipboards might be, they didn't seem worth considering. He expected some kind of filing system, so he pressed on to another door in the far wall.

Sure enough, lights came on in the second room to illuminate another desk with a computer alongside multiple filing cabinets, each with a label indicating its contents. One indicated data accumulated on specific "light functions" and "wave analyses." Another said, "Test subject results." Michael pulled at that drawer. It opened silently.

The standard file drawer had dozens of tiny slots, each containing a small data drive. Michael searched numerically for the 401-450 drive and drew it out silently. Then he slid to the computer console and tapped the screen. What if it was digitally locked? Michael had to hope that security in the archives was considered unnecessary. But as the screen came to light, the login page required him to press his hand or forehead to the screen. Michael suddenly felt defeated; almost certainly he could not log in to a foreign service. Hell, he couldn't even log onto his own computer anymore. But there was nothing to do but try. Hand to the screen, the machine read his fingerprints and accepted him.

Michael stifled his surprise, realizing at once that, even without security lockouts, the system would register who was looking at the files. He didn't have much time. At once, he plugged in the data drive, and file numbers came up. Scanning through the list, he found the data he expected to see at number 431—information on the subject he had seen, the "lonely merchandise distributor" named Michael. The name was not included in the file, but Michael thought there had to be information that would link to another file, one with biographical information and more details of the subject's life. Gesar had, after all, known the man's name and occupation.

The first page that came up seemed to be a summary statement with two graphs, perhaps a before and after evaluation of the subject's spiritual state. The first graph indicated a spectrum reading around 450 nanometers wavelength, and the second indicated a color around the mid 600s; no doubt the change from blue to red, as Michael had learned. That was unimportant. The next pages contained numerical scores apparently based on a list of medical indicators. They seemed to simply indicate something about the subject's physical health prior to the first experiments. Another series of pages showed a graph of data that seemed associated with brain function, in particular as responses to specified stimuli. None of this helped Michael. It was only further into the file that he found what he wanted, a page that had in the top right corner an alphanumeric code that might be a link to another file. It said H7759-431-HM. If the 431 was the link to this file and the final letter meant *Michael*, then the *H* could be the initial of the subject's last name and the first five characters would be the subject's personal file.

Michael went back to the drawer, replaced the file cube in the 400-450 slot and searched as fast as he could in the all-too-revealing light for file markings to match the five-character code he had found. Nothing. He searched another drawer, then another, and then, there they were. There were only a few file cubes under *A*, a few more more under *B*. He took first the *H* file drive and moved back to the computer. Within a minute, he had the information he wanted: Michael Hendricks, it read, subject 431. The biographical information included his job as some kind of menial worker in a warehouse that shipped computer-ordered merchandise. Michael didn't check to see if there was evidence of him being lonely.

So that was the code. Michael wasn't actually interested in this other Michael, but only in the linking codes. At once he went back to the first drawer and withdrew the first data file, 001-050. In moments he had found the first subject, and then, bypassing the early pages, he found the code he needed: G2215-001-GR. Even without looking further, he knew that he had discovered what he had expected to find.

Even so, he wanted to look at file G2215, and began to eject the file block. He paused and looked at the first page of the 001 file. There were no before and after graphs. There were rather several pages of the same graph, or so it seemed to Michael. As he checked the graphs, he saw that each page contained several tests, each test done on a different date, and yet the color indicators were exactly the same in every test, right there in the red range between 660 and 670 nanometers. It was perfectly red from the beginning with no variation. The subject had always been perfect.

Michael knew what he had to know, and yet couldn't quite resist the chance to look at file G2215. Quickly, he ejected the file he was using, slipped it into the appropriate slot in the drawer, shoved the drawer closed and moved to the other file. He looked for the *Gs*.

The archives room door swung open, and Dr. Richard Gesar stood silhouetted in the light. "Find what you were looking for?" Gesar asked easily.

Michael's first instant of fear made his heart race. Yet almost magically, it disappeared as he hardened himself against the intrusion. Hadn't he, after all, found the truth at last? Hadn't he found a danger, a lie. "I think I did find it," he said with intentional boldness, "and I intend to tell everyone I can."

Gesar nodded. "What is it you think you have found, Mr. Pryor, that will be such a revelation to the world?"

If Michael hadn't been angry, he might have been more afraid. If indeed there were the kind of dangers he had only begun to imagine, that fear might have struck him with more force, maybe even silenced him. But he was practiced at looking lies in the face, and he could not quite foresee the danger of the world's kindness. For him, it was enough to strike with an accusation and see if it drew blood. Without revelation, of course, he would not really be able to tell if he truly had drawn blood or whose blood it might be. Without revelation, he would not even be able to recognize it as blood, or imagine how the subtlety of lies was greater than he could comprehend. Naively, he thought telling the truth was enough.

"Subject number one," he said. "It's you. You are the source and standard; you are the model and ideal. Everything you do and teach, it's just about you."

To his surprise, Gesar merely smiled. "So?" he said.

Michael paused. What he had said should have been enough. "Well," he continued, "you act as if you're helping the world be happy and at peace, when in fact you are trying to create the world in your own image. There is no God to be found in your spiritual health, unless that god is you."

Again, that should have been enough of an accusation, Michael thought, so it surprised him when Gesar answered with a shrug. "And why should that seem to you such an evil thing, Mr. Pryor?" he asked easily. "Why should it bother you that I have found the place of peace and wholeness and that I offer it to the world?" He smiled gently. "Unless you resent that you yourself are not god."

Michael hesitated. He knew enough of his trade to avoid being drawn into answering his own defensive questions. Even so, as the seconds ticked by, he wondered if that might be the only problem, if that is what, after all, made him blue. "I have failed to be god," he felt in his honest soul, a realization that could be a man's salvation. But the ensuing thought was to wonder why God should then in fact be someone like Gesar. Surely, he might have thought quickly, there is a third alternative, and for an instant the image of Professor Wacker crossed his mind.

Ironically, Gesar rescued him. "Come, Mr. Pryor," he went on, "let's be reasonable. Of course I am the standard of the healthy soul. Why should it be otherwise? I have trained diligently. I have studied those methods and insights that release the soul from ignorance. If I am thereby the measure of the spirit, can that really be so evil? You mark me as some antichrist bent on corrupting the world. Am I not rather here to save it? Have I not shown this salvation in what I've accomplished?"

Michael felt the pull of that rationale, but his saving obstinacy spoke up. "I do not need to deny the peace you bring to point out the arrogance of you pretending to be the world's savior."

Gesar laughed softly. "So obstinate, even to the last," he said. He shook his head. "I wish I could help you see the hope that is here," he went on, "and realize that I mean to be no one's god. I mean only to show others how they can find whatever god they desire. Surely you have seen, Mr. Pryor, that I have no need to become your god, for I am god unto myself. And all I wish is to share this freedom, to show you how you can find god in yourself." Gesar paused, smiled down at Michael with compassion. "I only seek to set you free," he said.

For a moment to Michael it seemed true. To be free, to be himself, without the demands of some arbitrary religion or moral code. To be at peace, like Melanie in her newfound calmness that made no demands to change, or like Desra, who could change her principles and feel no guilt. To escape the demands of any god by becoming godlike! Michael did want peace. He could let Gesar be the model and the bringer of peace.

Gesar himself broke Michael's trance. "So if I have found true peace in myself, why should it not be the standard of peace? If I have found the means to give that peace to others, why should I not provide it? Arrogant, Mr. Pryor? Was the Buddha arrogant when he proclaimed himself the Tathagata, the Enlightened One, the teacher of the Dharma that has liberated countless souls for thousands of years? Was the Prophet Muhammad arrogant when he declared that Allah had chosen him to speak the Recitations that would give truth to billions? Was Jesus arrogant when he named himself the Light of the World or the Bread of Life, when his death became the symbol of life that taught the world to speak of God as love?

"So what do you want, Mr. Pryor? What do you really want? Not what has someone suggested you must have, some god you must follow, preached to you from the sky or from some vain Olympus. I ask you what god will you find, there, in your own heart. What do you want, if it is not exactly what I have offered you: to be Michael Pryor with peace, to be Michael Pryor with a feeling of transcendence, to be Michael Pryor in harmony with the world?"

Honestly, Michael didn't know. Even still, he didn't know. Facing the silhouette of the *tulku*, with the light of the outer office glowing around him like a halo, there in the hypnotic light of Gesar's self-confidence and the promise of his accomplishments, Michael didn't know. Six months ago he could have blurted out the answer: "I want truth," and that might have saved him, even though at the time he didn't know the difference between his angry search for truth and the actual desire to find it. In the last half year, he had fallen from that strong tower, felt it wobble beneath him, as he realized he could not find peace in a search that actually had no intention of finding and yielding to its object. Now, even though truth had at last become something greater than his own inquiring, he hadn't yet flung himself into its grasp. So he was still vulnerable.

"I just," he paused, "I just don't know."

"Of course you don't know," Gesar said softly, "but yield to peace and you will." The *tulku* at last walked to Michal and placed a hand on his shoulder. Gesar seemed to wrap Michael in an arm and hold him, embrace him, nestle him. He reached his free hand out before them both as if displaying a vision. "There it is," he said softly, "the golden city. Kalki has come, riding his white horse, bringing the world to the end of the Age of Darkness. Maitreya

Buddha at last awakened starts again the golden age of the Dharma. Why not the Mahdi? Why not the new Christ? Come Mr. Pryor, come. So I am the measure of the Holy Spirit? Fine. Then believe in me and find life."

It was as if Michael melted. He felt himself let go and, yes, to desire peace. Why did there have to be rebellion? Why struggle? Why cannot we just rest with whatever gift comes to us? Let it be. Let it be as you will, Tulku Das.

In a moment, they were walking toward the hallway together, still together, Michael bent as if under the weight of the greater arm. They might have gone directly across to the laboratory, might have gone directly to that place of peace where, some months ago, a different Michael found peace. Except Gesar kept talking.

"You see, then," Gesar said, "even you can come to peace. And when you have found peace, you will write again your articles and tell the world what you have found. From your example, the lingering few, those who for reasons unimagined—their depression, mental insufficiencies, their intransigent bigotries—they, too, will come to peace, and all will be well.

"Come, Michael Pryor, come to peace. In you others will find hope. Perhaps even your brother and his wife. Perhaps Marta Sanchez. Unhappily, it is too late for Professor Wacker, but why not help save those you love ?"

And it was those he loved who saved Michael Pryor. Gesar had made the same mistake Petra Eriksen had made: the confusion of loves. But how could they know? For those who love Gesar and for whom Gesar is god, all love is self-love. But for those who love another, who love the Other, those words, meant to be words of hope, finally woke Michael to his own reasons for rebellion. "No," he said in his mind, "not them. Not my brother!" He stopped in the middle of the hallway. Gesar stared at him, smiling but curious. Michael bristled. "No," he said, "you keep your damned hands off my brother."

"Excuse me?"

Michael erupted. "What do you know about my brother? Why is he even part of this conversation? What is really going on with you that you try to reach into his life? Leave him alone! He's no one special! My god! He's just a laser technician! You leave Daniel alone, or I swear I will hit you as hard as I can with every power I still possess."

Gesar frowned. Michael fumed, letting silence carry the smell of his burn into the air, letting it permeate the environment. Finally Gesar spoke. "Perhaps I've misjudged you after all, Mr. Pryor," he said. "Perhaps after all you are destined to be one of the heretics, one of the fallen. I would not have foreseen it, even as you resisted, time after time, the call to peace." He paused. "But, Mr. Pryor, so be it. Is your brother no one special? So you shall be, too. You might have been one to help us find peace in the world; instead you seem determined to be alone, broken, unhealthy, crippled by your own demands. It is a mental illness, Mr. Pryor, or so we shall insist."

Michaels anger softened. He didn't know what was happening.

"We shall carry on without you, Mr. Pryor," Gesar was saying, but not to him directly. As if speaking into the air, he continued. "It might have happened with your help, with very little confrontation. Over time and with your words behind us, we might have brought peace without troubling the few. But we shall simply move on, perhaps more quickly than we'd planned, and we shall bring peace to this world, peace to the unhappy many, without your help."

Richard Gesar, the *tulku* of Sandia, stepped back from Michael Pryor and looked at him kindly. "Michael," he said prophetically, "I leave you to your unhappy God. Someone will help you find your way home." And the savior of the world walked away, leaving Michael alone in the hallway.

29

THE THEOLOGIAN

For Marta, the problem was both much simpler and much more difficult than it was for Michael. She understood the basic role of philosophical presuppositions—which are not quite matters of faith nor matters of proof. She had long ago spent time questioning fundamental ideas and following them out to their implications, tracing the implications of their opposing assumptions. So Marta started by knowing more than Michael, though she did not doubt any less. Hers would be a real struggle, but a different struggle.

In the same way, her struggle would be both more difficult and easier than it would be for her friend Daniel, though she was sure she would end up with a similar conclusion. She trusted Daniel even as she trusted her own epistemology, but she had never quite been able to read the Bible the way he did. She envied her Protestant friends, that whole *sola scriptura* thing, even while she challenged it. For her, the holy text was part of the struggle, something that fit into, enhanced, relied upon, and then informed the theological questions. The scriptures were not for her a solid foundation, but one of the first stones. Along with all the other stones, no matter how heavy or how foundational, the Bible had sometimes to be lifted down and studied then put carefully back in place, assuring once again that it could carry the weight it had to bear.

That labor was Marta's job, and she understood it was not everyone's job. She settled down to the task once again in her quiet apartment, a bottle of red wine on the table beside her, open and breathing. She had tried to have a bottle sent in, but the scanner seemed to be out of order, not recognizing her fingerprint or even retina identifications. But she had found an old bottle of red in her cupboard, one she was going to use for cooking. It tasted better than she had expected, indeed perhaps better than the bottle she was going to order, like the later wine at Cana. So she happily turned to her thoughts—ready, because that was her job.

Marta was a smart woman; that truth was not a statement of arrogance or pride. It was like the basic recognition that reason was a valuable tool. It was not as though reason alone was a key to salvation. She knew there were good people who were not very good reasoners and there were many great reasoners who were not good people. But good thinking was possible, and it was a good thing. It was part of what convinced her that she was made in some divine image. And if there were divine images, there must be the divine. Therefore, she insisted, those who would scoff at reason had to be wrong. She had once made a philosophy professor angry by laughing aloud at Nietzsche, as the great German skeptic declared the folly of evolved reason and its inherent errors. "So what's he using," she had blurted out, "digestion?" She had thought humor was allowed. It wasn't.

So Marta intended to use reason and use it well. She did not easily accept grand conspiracies nor look for evil where it was not. She was too smart for that. But Paul Wacker was dead, and nobody knew why or how or where. There had always been unknowns, mysteries to the minds of the greatest knowers, yet in this case there should be no mystery. The people they had sought out had seemed to know everything else, everything except this one thing. They knew names and acquaintances, knew the colors of their auras, knew even whom their new visitors had talked to most recently. This discrepancy had alerted her to the problem. "Fact: I am not a fool," she told herself, "but there is something wrong. Something is being hidden, and that, too, appears to be a fact."

So, why did Wacker die? He was a fool, driving foolishly. Maybe. But while that could explain the accident, it didn't explain the cover-up. Something was wrong. Why would Wacker die?

It would have been easy to think Wacker had been killed, but Marta resisted that thought. In these days, people were done with conspiracies, done with wild explanations of secretive methods for disposing of those we find annoying. How annoying was Paul Wacker to this old world of peace and harmony? He was a curmudgeon, certainly—Marta smiled at the memory of Professor Wacker—but not a troublemaker. Even if he had been a troublemaker, nobody kills such troublemakers. Those who seem socially unfit, we help. We counsel. We heal. We help them adjust. Adjustment. And if they cannot be healed, we encourage them to pass away peacefully. To die. Marta put a period there and left a footnote in her thoughts, even as the idea gave her the connection she needed.

Adjustment. Whom do we adjust? Blue people. Why? Because they are unhappy. And to be unhappy is to be unhealthy. If red is the indicator of spiritual wholeness, then blue is the indicator of spiritual disease, dis-ease, uneasiness. So why are some people blue? She felt the strength of honesty. "Why are we blue--people like me and like Michael?" She stopped, poured some wine, held her place in the line of reasoning. "Hardly a surprise," she said to herself, thinking of her own lonely contemplations, the angry rebellion of Michael, even the bristling rational impatience of Dr. Wacker. All blues. With a humph, Marta remembered why she had never liked the idea of karma, the idea that somehow all people who suffer in this world deserve it from some effect of a previous life. Did all the people that died in the last California earthquake just happen to be living in the same place with the same karmic background? What? Did all the people who died in the last African pandemic just happen to have the same karma and just happen to live in the same area of the world? Are we really saying that all of us, somehow, every blue soul is blue because of the same kind of lingering illness? What is that illness other than blueness itself?

No, she insisted, we blues are not unhealthy, we're just not happy. Why? Do we hate happiness? Are we chronically depressed? That would be a useful avenue to consider, she realized, and already had an inkling of where it would lead. She shuddered.

Starting again, Marta thought, blues are not evil or depressed. They are—and here, Marta called upon her own internal sense as her first witness—waiting. "We are . . . waiting." Even Michael Pryor was waiting, she decided, although she laughed a little because he himself didn't yet realize it. Michael was waiting. So was Daniel. But waiting for what?

Waiting for God. Waiting for God to do what? To act. Waiting for God to do precisely what the adjustment is supposed to do. We wait for God to fill us, to make us whole, to complete us and make us as we are intended to be. We wait. And what if God chooses not to complete us, to make us whole? Then we wait.

"No," Marta thought, "this is nonsense. We do not wait to take medicine because we hope God might cure us. We have long recognized there is no science in Christian Science, even as there is very little Christianity. We do not wait to find security in the love of others as we wait for God to comfort us. We do not let the mentally troubled struggle with their brain chemical imbalances while we wait for God to heal them. No. We heal them. And if we cannot heal them, we ease them into a peaceful death." There it was again, and Marta stopped.

"This is different," she said aloud. "No, this is different, because we are not trying to be happy. Hell, I can be happy. Anyone can be happy. That's a mediocre accomplishment. We're trying to be something else. We're trying to be spiritually whole, we're trying to be in the presence of God, and for that we must wait on God, as it is His place only. One must be invited into the presence of the King."

Marta felt the truth. "There it is. We do not want happiness or even wholeness. We want the presence of God. But God does not grant it. Maybe I can't know why. Let us leave the ancient Problem of Evil to itself for now. Let us instead recall that of all the things the King must control, it is the King's own presence. If He deigns not to grant us admission, then it is to show us His presence is, after all, *His* presence, and not a presence of our own making."

This was finally familiar ground, and Marta followed its pathways easily. "God does not grant the presence of God precisely because He is God. He is God in himself, and not the God of our desires or even of our needs. This is not the God of adjustment, but *God*. He is not the God who fills us and makes us whole, but He is God. He is not the God who completes us or gives us spiritual awakening, but He is God. So it must be, for any god that is the God of my adjustment is not the God who is God." Marta smiled and spoke aloud, "Thus no god I want is the God that I want." It was a lovely and reasonable paradox. She might have thanked God in that moment of worship. Perhaps she did but didn't know it.

Marta sipped wine, felt it warm in her mouth, dry on the back of her tongue. She repeated her conclusion. "No god I want is the God I want," she said again, satisfied. "Yahweh, He who Is. Not 'he who is my friend' or 'he who is my peace.' Not 'he who is my helper, my healer, my delight,' nor any 'my.' Of course God may be these things, but He is not these things. He is Himself only, the One who is.

"How could it be? Look, how the Israelites, having just come from being saved by the mighty power of Yahweh Sabaoth, stood at the foot of the flaming mountain and could not keep faith for forty days. Look how in the silence of Yahweh, there in the shadow of the holy mountain, they demanded the divine presence. And if God would not come, they would make him appear, make him a calf, cover him with gold. In the same way, we hunger for his presence. Of course. But then in hungering, look how we turn to make a god that will satisfy us. So we become idolaters, worshippers of a golden calf because it is a god we can carry with us and see when we want to. 'O God who is my only peace' we say, and we mean it. 'Give us peace,' we cry, and we mean it. When he does not, we say, 'Then I shall make a god that gives me peace.' And so we are adjusted.

"Thus any adjustment-god is not God, and therefore adjustment is idolatry. If so, then those who will not be denied a god of peace will find him where they must, in whatever god or meditative technique, whatever 'adjustment' is at hand. But what if they find it in Christ? It is no better, for the Christ that is found in order to find the Christ I want, is not the Christ who is. He is an idol-Christ, an anti-Christ. In contrast, those who wait for God, those who refuse to worship an idol Christ, must deny their 'Christ' and therefore must be blue.

"But why would the God of love, the God who is the giver of peace, not give peace to those who call upon whim?" There it was again, Marta realized at once, the Problem of Evil, again appearing in one of its many permutations. Marta knew this question in a hundred forms that non-theists barely recognized as dangerous to their ways of thinking. But so few would risk being unhappy with the answers they found that few found the answer. Marta replied to her own question: "Because, by not speaking, by not entering into our world to make us happy, God who is God says he is not the god of our desires. He says, 'Look, I am not the god of your hopes or of your fears, and that is why you may fear Me and hope in Me.'" To Marta, it made perfect sense, almost too much sense, and she tingled with fear and hope.

"What shall we say then?" she went on in her internal dialogue. "Shall we refuse the desire to be at peace with ourselves, with others and with God? By no means!" She smiled, hearing the language of her mind mimic St. Paul. "The desire for peace is right and good, God-given and full of meaning. But we cannot demand it; we cannot take it by force. It comes from the hand of he-who-is or it does not come at all. To force its coming is to guild the idol of ourselves. And therefore," Marta paused before the elenchus, "we must refuse to worship the god of adjustments. God is not the god of the red aura."

"So," she said to herself, "we are rebels after all. We rebel against the false god, even when that god is seen as spiritual health and wholeness. What folly must it seem to deny peace, to deny contemplative wholeness!? Who in their right mind would insist on being unhappy or unhealthy?" It was not a rhetorical question, and Marta knew the answer: no one. No one "in their right mind" would make such a choice, and therefore rebellion against the false god would only be perceived as mental illness. There the mantra of compassion led in a wonderfully logical, if strangely anfractuous line: if one is unhealthy, then we, in our compassion, seek to cure them; if we cannot cure, we ease their suffering, and if we cannot ease their suffering, then we help them to a peaceful death. Marta calmly spoke aloud: "And Paul Wacker is dead."

So the Israelites made a calf of gold. Of course they did. Peter declared his belief in the Messiah and then insisted Jesus could only be the kind of Messiah Peter wanted. Of course he did. And our world, tired of the failure of naturalism and the spiritual void, finds a god that models and makes for us the spirituality we desire. Of course we do. Of the three, only Peter came to see the folly of his idolatry, and he died for it, crucified, they say, upside down. Marta spoke aloud again: "Upside down indeed!"

Did it come back to Peter, then? The first pope, depending on how one reads history. What kind of Messiah do you want? What kind will you demand? One who defeats the enemies of Israel and drives the Roman legions from holy ground? One who fights a bloody Armageddon ahead of an army of vengeful angels? One who can adjust the aura of the soul and give one peace? Or one who simply says, "I Am?"

For Marta these were not rhetorical questions. They were existential ones, and Marta knew what the answer had to be. She smiled again, content with the clarity of her conclusions. She was even happy—or something like happy—with the practical implication. What should one do if other Messiahs come? One should flee to the mountains. Marta sipped her wine to the bottom. Putting down her glass, she wondered if she had time to drink the last fourth of the bottle. No. She decided she would not even try to phone herself out. She could walk. There was a little snow in the air, not really early for the end of November. Advent: wasn't it next week? She had a good coat, and it was only a few miles.

30

THE INEVITABLE

"Don't worry about coming in, Michael," Melanie had said when Michael videoed in. "I've been in touch with Gesar's people. No one is going to press charges."

"Press charges?" Michael had been incredulous. He had been trying to explain that the information he had from Sandia was tumultuous. There was something sinister in all this change during the last year, he had told her. She had only cursed him mildly, laughed, and told him he was full of shit. But he had a story, he had insisted. People needed to understand that Gesar considered himself some kind of savior, that he was making himself the model of all human happiness. "He thinks he's Christ, for God's sake," he had almost screamed. Melanie had only asked, "So?"

Michael's curses were more vehement, and he ultimately accused Melanie of being one of the *tulku*'s converts. "But I haven't converted to anything," she had replied without defensiveness. "I'm unchanged by the adjustment, except that I'm happier than I've ever been. No one has to be anything except what they already are."

"Or is it, Melanie, that everyone needs to be like Gesar? 'Don't be blue,'" he mocked.

Melanie had to have seen his point, yet she did not respond. Rather, her response returned almost automatically. "Why do you insist on being depressed?" she asked. "It's not healthy, you know." Michael had ignored her. Only later did he realize her question contained a threat.

That was five days ago, when he had first realized he couldn't phone out from home. Thus the video call and Melanie's comment that he didn't need to come in anyway. "Take some time off," she had finally said. "Get your phone fixed."

The phone company computer had told him there was nothing wrong with his machinery. All the diagnostics, reported the pleasant, mechanical voice, indicated no interruption of service. That was three days ago, and then he had tried to call Daniel.

It was not the first time since Albuquerque that Michael thought to call his brother. Indeed, it had been almost his first instinct upon awakening the next day to tell Daniel about Gesar and his Christ complex. He thought somehow Daniel would understand, and Michael couldn't forget it had been Gesar's mention of Daniel that brought him to his senses that night. This whole story involved Daniel, but still Michael could not understand how, as he was still not quite conscious of his own belief in a reality greater than himself. Michael could not yet imagine being called to purposes beyond his own understanding. As a consequence, he doubted his own desire to talk to Daniel, couldn't exactly explain why or how it was important. Somehow it had to do with Daniel's Christ, and Michael couldn't yet explain that either. It was mystery. Below the conscious surface of Michael's own analysis, he wanted Daniel to explain it to him.

Even so it wasn't until Michael needed Daniel as a phone repairman that he felt he could call Daniel as a Christian, or even as a brother. But when he tried to call his brother, even the video phone wouldn't work. Michael felt stranded. Then he found he could no longer order food either. Hand on the scanner, forehead to the retina reader—and nothing. The automated diagnostics continued to report that everything was working normally, yet instead of gaining access to his accounts at the markets, he only received the recurrent message: "Don't be blue!"

Finally, after five days, there came the phone calls. Three of them. First, strangely, Desra called. "Hey, Michael," she said easily. "How are you?"

"Pissed as hell, actually," he said just as easily. "How are you?"

Desra laughed softly. She looked away from the phone and seemed to wipe a tear from her eye.

"I'm serious, Michael," she said. "How are you?"

"I told you," he responded honestly. "Nothing's working here. Can't phone out, can't call, can't get food. Called the phone company, and they told me absolutely nothing."

"Well, of course, you old goat." Desra's easy laugh caught Michael by surprise. She was soft and attractive. Some back-lighting came through her blond hair as she turned her head, seemed to look off sadly. "Haven't you seen the news?" she asked.

"Er, no," Michael responded, strangely embarrassed. Surely he should have looked at the news programs. "Actually, I didn't think that would be working either, once the phone company proved to be no help," he said, as if excusing himself.

"Well," Desra started, "you should check it out. It's a good thing, Michael. People care about you, you know. I care about you." There was a pause. "Don't be blue."

"What the hell, Desra?" Michael exploded. "Why do we have to keep using that stupid phrase? It's become the most overused advertisement in history."

Desra looked at him warmly. "It's not an advertisement, Michael," she said. "It's an encouragement."

"What does that mean?"

"Well, it isn't like it's a billboard," she explained. "It isn't there for everybody. *My* phone doesn't say that."

Suddenly, Michael was awake, shocked by his own failure to see. "Of course," he said to himself. "It isn't an advertisement directed to everyone; it's an accusation directed at me."

"Damn it, Desra," he said back. "Have I got to have a red aura to make my phone work? What has blue got to do with anything? Why would anyone care one way or the other?"

"I care," Desra said softly. "Of course I care. If I don't care, who would? I only want you to be happy." An awkward silence followed.

"Why'd you call, Desra?" Michael finally asked straightforwardly.

"I told you," she said, "I just want to help. There's no reason to be blue. No one has to be unhappy any longer, not even you." Michael felt the intended softness in her smile. Yet he no longer felt the enticement of her, not because her love was too far distant in his past nor because she was unattractive. Had he paused to analyze himself, he might have guessed that a mild anger could interrupt desire. He might have discovered he had started to learn to desire something more than the fulfillment of desire.

"Maybe I don't want to be happy," Michael responded. To his surprise, he saw Desra nod.

"That's probably true, Michael," she said. "And that's too bad. Everybody says there are always those who would rather have a disease than yield to the cure."

"And who is the everybody who says so?" Michael asked directly.

"You know, the experts and all that," she answered. "You know it's true. It's always been true. Some we can cure of their disease and some we cannot."

"What disease are you talking about?"

"Dis-ease, Michael. Just dis-ease." Desra looked away, then back to her camera. "Only someone very ill would prefer the illness to a simple cure."

Michael quit. It was enough. Desra was there, warm and inviting, beautiful as ever, somehow warmer than ever, and yet her words were all wrong. They were true words, or almost true, and yet they weren't Desra's. The words were no more Desra's than her Japanese vocabulary.

"You know, Desra," he said, looking hard at her, "if you really want to help me, order some food and have it sent to me. Nothing's working here."

"I'll see what I can do," Desra said. "But there's still time," she finally added, though it seemed a non sequitur. "There are people you might still listen to." She smiled warmly. "People maybe you love more than you love me."

Michael hardly heard her goodbyes. Her closing words made him think only of Daniel and Marta. What if they, too, were like Desra? What if they, too, were happy now? For a few moments, Michael's fantasy ran into a conversation in which Daniel urged Michael to be happy. It would not be the first time. Daniel had in the past invited him to embrace God, to find the Savior, to be, in some sense, happy. Yet in the current haunted fantasy conversation, Daniel's voice sounded as foreign as Desra's, horribly different. Hadn't Daniel confessed that he, too, was blue? No, please! Not a happy Daniel!

The temptation shifted to a fantasy conversation with Marta. "It's true, Michael," she said in his mind's ear. "There is at last rest for the weary mind. There is peace after all for those who will take it. There are the traditions of the Church, the chant of the prayers, the release of forgiveness. And as we find peace, we naturally desire peace for others. Come to peace, Michael . . ."

Michael could. He could. He could come to Marta's peace, to Daniel's peace, to Desra's peace, to the *tulku*'s peace. He could give up anger and sorrow. Or he could be alone. As he shut out those loving invitations to peace, while left necessarily in the vacuum of the Spirit's call, he heard nothing but silence. "I'm sorry," he said into the silence where no one seemed to be listening, and he suddenly felt alone. Utterly alone.

The call from Melanie came twenty minutes later, but in those twenty minutes Michael remained alone. That brief time delivered the existential reality of death, made Michael recognize loneliness as something like the consciousness of falling asleep. No one was there. Michael knew the vacuum not as peacefulness nor as fear, both being emotions that require consciousness. It was simply emptiness without purpose. So what was the peace of nirvana supposed to be? What is the peace of heaven? What is this peace of mind everyone promises and yet still requires oneself to be oneself? How can one be dead and yet alive? How can one be more without being less? What if there were no Daniel, no Marta? What if there were only Desra and Gesar? What if there were nothing to live for except to keep living, with nothing better than an "adjustment" to make you happy with meaninglessness?

What does the adjustment do except make me incapable of wanting better? Was Desra better, or only satisfied with Desra? "No," Michael thought, "give me Daniel's unsatisfying Jesus rather than Desra's satisfied Desra." Yet what if there were no Daniel? What if he, too, had only a satisfying Jesus? And then Michael felt a call, not knowing it as such, to that which is greater than that which is satisfying. Michael wanted a God he didn't want.

So he was prepared when Melanie called.

"Are you ready to come in?" she asked easily, as if he had been on vacation.

"Sure," Michael said, "but I can't seem to phone out. Can't even call out, though apparently you can call in."

"'Course I can," she responded off-handedly.

"Can you get food, too?" Michael asked.

"'Course I can," Melanie repeated. "Guess you're still blue, eh?"

"'Course I am," Michael mocked in response. "Jesus! Isn't it my business?"

"We're all everyone's business, Michael," Melanie said. "You'd know that if you weren't so damned recalcitrant. Acceptance of yourself leads to compassion for others."

Michael let that last sentence resonate, wondering if he should consider the logic of the claim. Or was it supposed to be an observation of fact? What had compassion to do with being blue or going to work? Michael chose to pursue the answer to that question, though the other question might have been more important.

"So I can come in to work so you can have compassion on me?" he asked with acid in his voice. "Gee, thanks, Melanie."

"Don't be such an ass," she responded, laughing. "I want you to come to work because I want your work to continue. You're damn good at what you do, or at least what you used to do. But times have changed. Maybe the despairing and cynical reporter is no longer needed. That's not to say you are not needed. It's just to say, hell, stop being so damn blue."

Michael felt himself form a resolve. "Melanie, I don't want what you have. I've seen through the romance you seem to have accepted. You can become like Gesar if you want, but I know better. He's dangerous, Melanie, and I could show you if you could still think for yourself. Meanwhile, I can't accept your peaceful and compassionate invitation. I won't accept it."

To Michael, his point seemed clear and thoughtful, a statement of strength and understanding, but clearly Melanie heard it quite otherwise. On the screen, she thinned her lips in a frown and sighed. "We thought you might say that," she responded. "But listen to yourself. Be reasonable, if you still can, and just listen to yourself. Half of what you say is sheer paranoia; the other half is depression." She looked at him intently. "You're sick,

Michael," she announced as if it were obvious. "But there are cures. Almost anyone, they say, can be cured with the adjustment and given again the kind of self-esteem and hopefulness and, yes, compassion it provides. That makes the world a better place."

For a second, Michael almost believed it. In the next second, however, he wanted to argue about how one should define the so-called "better" quality of the world. Then he caught the further implications of Melanie's point. "You're sick, Michael," she had said. Those we can cure, we save; those we cannot cure, we ease; and those we can neither cure nor ease . . .

Melanie sighed and shrugged. "Watch the news, Michael," she said. "Everything you need to know is there, and you can still change your mind." She nodded. "We're here to help," she said, "but if you can't accept help, well, I did the compassionate thing calling you in." Then she was gone without a good-bye.

Michael was in shock—not from Melanie's abrupt disconnection but from his own realization. But, of course, it was inevitable. With some fear, he called out to the television wall and it lit up. The giant array of small screens appeared with the common barrage of entertainments, the comedies and dramas and explosive action shows on a dozen screens, payment options for new movies and the usual pornography options. There were no special interruptions of programming, no "breaking news" announcements. Whatever the news, it was not interrupting entertainment.

Yet the news Michael wanted, the news he expected, would be life-altering. "News," he said aloud. At once the flashing shift and shimmer of the dozen changing screens became the normal five or six that had always been his choices. On two screens there were general scenes of people milling about, not exactly celebrating as if it were a party at New Year's, but happy, somehow both calm and pleased, like an anniversary of a long-married couple or the board meeting of a successful company. One verbal scroll at the bottom of a screen described a gathering of legislators from a state government, then it shifted to a different state, a different legislature, but the scene seemed no different. The other milling scene was a bar, where patrons toasted and patted one another's backs, not nearly as wild as bar celebrations for a winning sports team, but more like patrons watching a pleasant summer weather report. From those scenes, Michael's eye quickly fixed on the images of talking heads, several apparently like the hosts of public programming, sitting at tables and announcing their programs above a scroll with a phone number for "pledges." For Michael, the more important screens had written scrolls identifying some speakers as medical doctors, one as a sociologist, another a psychology professor at UC Boulder. From those screens, Michael chose a Muhammad Awuka, some kind of press representative for the "Christ Hospital" across town. Michael called up the screen and the audio.

"Of course," the man was saying, "one of the effects of greater mental health is greater physical health, so we expect the incidents of minor illnesses, literally from stress-related heart problems down to the common cold, to fall dramatically. We have already seen a drop in those problems since aura adjustments became common five months ago. Naturally, the genuine physical problems with heart and kidney damage, *et cetera*, we handle as we always have, healing where we can, replacing organs when they fail, easing into death those we cannot save."

Michael had heard most of it before, but this time he shuddered. He switched screens to the psychologist. "David Brookfield," as the screen announced him, was more focused and more effusive. "The potential for human healing," Brookfield was asserting, "is profound, and for society, far-reaching. Studies done by Osterman, Temlar, and, of course, Richard Gesar, and those studies we have done ourselves, continue to show great gains in mental health, peace of mind, self-acceptance, and all the benefits of those greater states of mind. Thanks to the innate neuroplasticity of the brain, the chemical pathways that determine quiet and self-confident behaviors have been consistently reprogrammed in every case, literally without exception. This development is for psychology what mandatory polio vaccination was for physical health, or what mandatory in-vitro genetic tests were for obstetrics, and no one questions the value of these developments. We will all be healthier for —"

Michael recognized the parallels, but it was the word *mandatory* that caught his ear. He called back the larger screens and sought another kind of expert, finding a scroll that read, "Stella (Starlight) Vallis, JD, LLM." He called up the audio.

"... admittedly brief," she was saying. "There were some in legislature who argued for a longer time allowance, but for the most part, it was understood that there is little threat of overburdening the various clinics. No doubt the majority of us have already found peace with ourselves and have found peace with these decisions. The only real difficulty in the legislative decision was more logistical than legal."

"Get on with it," Michael murmured at the screen. "Give me the legal arguments." Instantly the live video stopped, the system searched whatever parts of Vallis's speech were already recorded and skipped to that portion.

" . . . nor requiring difficult legal justification," she apparently had said twelve minutes earlier. "The precedents are clear and the social benefits unambiguous. It is of course primarily for the benefit of those patients themselves who still need to find mental comfort and spiritual peace. In the end, these are acts of compassion, as we all recognize, and there are no violations of religious rights when there are no requirements of any specific religious belief or practice. We are concerned for spiritual health, not religion, *per se.* Prominent teachers and leaders of many religious groups have enthusiastically endorsed this program."

With a quick shift of camera angle, the visual picked up the interviewer raising a question. Michael might have recognized some face; he didn't care. The reporter asked, "What about the interruptions of services for those who are blue?" he asked. Michael nodded at the kind of question he would have asked.

"These procedures are merely systemic limitations on the economic activity of those still blue," the lawyer said.

"Merely?" Michael called to the wall.

"And of course they have been properly conjoined with individualized efforts to reach the unfortunate few who may continue to remain lonely and depressed, urging friends and relatives to call them to health."

"That explains Melanie and Desra," Michael humphed.

"All this is naturally in addition to the constant communications through open media to give the unhealthy direct access to any clinic or religious institution they choose." She smiled. "The limitations have shown themselves to be very effective. We are reaching thousands of the lost."

Then Michael suddenly understood the "pledging" stations. He abandoned Ms. Vallis and called up the first station he saw. Pledging indeed! "Don't be blue," was the theme, and across the bottom of the screen rolled transport numbers for phoning in to various places with names of clinics and charitable organizations and religious establishments. Michael tried another and then another pledging station and found the same message repeated in various permutations. Several had a countdown clock on the stage with the speakers, a clock that showed thirty-one hours and some minutes.

Michael chose another station at random, one where a man and a woman sat on their video stage, the phone information and the countdown clock moving across the bottom. It was practically the same picture as the last, and carrying the exact same message. The man pressed his lips together into a thin, but not unhappy frown. "There is simply a better way to be," he said, looking at the woman, who nodded with sincere agreement. "And there's a better world in the making." How great shall it be, he went on, when all are at peace. He expressed his own amazement and wonder at the possibility of a world without worry, without concerns, without the nagging existential questions that lead to depression and anxiety. What if finally the meaning of life were clear to everyone in his or her own way? What if all could be so satisfied within themselves that there would be, naturally, no more conflict between individuals, no more conflict between people groups, no more conflict between nations?

"But you know, Jim," the other speaker took up the easy, but clearly scripted pledge, "there are still some out there lost and alone in their depression, somehow unable or unwilling to come to peace and to find wholeness." Then followed sorrowful looks and sad frowns, as those who are sad and lost were described in their loneliness, uncertainty, and fear. Even as health waits within reach, even as cures and the end of suffering wait for anyone willing to come in, still how sad and unfortunate it was that some remain blue. "Shouldn't we care? Shouldn't we help? Shouldn't we feed the hungry? Shouldn't we reach out and give happiness to those in need?"

Michael found himself torn. It was compassion, wasn't it? Hadn't they in fact accurately described the emotions of fear and loneliness he had himself experienced all day? Why then did something inside him cry, "No!"

"You're right, LeeAn," Jim responded. Then he turned to the camera. "And it's still to you in need that we call. The number is here, right at the bottom of your screen. You can come in any time to whatever church or mosque or temple or humanitarian clinic you choose. Follow the numbers or just call out to your video, and we'll unlock your phone, so you can unlock your own peace of mind."

"But what if I don't want your damned peace of mind?" Michael yelled at the wall.

And the wall responded. At first, it seemed simply to go blank. It took a moment for Michael to realize that the search mode was still active. Though it seemed the search took a long time, it was only seconds. At last the video-searching program found an interview that seemed to hold the response to his question. It was an interview, said the on-screen data, from three days ago, and the clip began with the face of an interviewer who, to Michael's surprise, seemed to ask his own question almost explicitly. "How then do we help those who cannot seem to want peace of mind?" The interviewee was none other than Dr. Richard Gesar himself.

"This illness, this dis-ease," he said calmly, with compassion, "is like the hundreds before it that we have cured. But in all cases, there are some we cannot help, often for reasons we still do not understand." Gesar smiled softly, kindly. "Our response is as it always has been: Those we can cure, we save; those we cannot cure, we comfort; and those we cannot comfort we ease into a peaceful death."

The camera angle switched back to the reporter who smiled as compassionately as Gesar. "For people have the right to die with dignity, just as they have the right to live without suffering," he said.

"Of course," Gesar said with honest and forthright love. "Of course."

Of course. Michael was not surprised. In fact, he felt strangely foolish, like he should have seen the inevitable outcome of love. It all made sense. He saw suddenly, as if by a flash in darkness, a whole picture that included his own loneliness and his own complicity in his father's euthanasia. It was a picture of compassion and human rights, of technology and sensuality, of individual health and of social harmony. It included his relationships with Desra and with Petra Eriksen, and even with Marta. It was his world. And suddenly to him it was evil, an evil of his own making.

Michael felt calm resignation. There was an inevitability to these events. He saw for the first time his own possible "death with dignity." To rest at last, to just give up on this confused and messy reality, to let it carry on with its own version of peace, while he slipped into a different peace, a dreamless sleep. He could just let it go, he realized, like his father had.

But with that thought the evil returned. Yes, he could find peace, or whatever that kind of peace might mean, but there was still that big picture, and still his own role in it. Yes, there could be an end, but there had to be something else, some other peace to come before the end. Michael, almost at the door of heaven, still didn't know what it was, though he knew it was not the peace offered on the television wall. It was a different kind of peace. It wasn't death; that was too easy, too much a part of the evil picture he had helped to draw. Yet it would be like death. It would be like laying down a burden, a release from the ugliness—not the ugliness he was suffering, but the ugliness he himself had created. Michael couldn't call it confession or repentance, but he heard it call him.

Michael thought of Daniel and somehow guessed his brother could explain it. He guessed that his brother knew something about peace that Michael did not know. The maturing flow of love and respect for Daniel mixed unexpectedly in him and made him wish once more to see his face. And that was when Michael prayed. "Let me," was all he said.

Then the third call came in. At once, it seemed, the video-phone buzzed. Michael thought it indeed had to be Daniel. But it couldn't be, since he wouldn't have phone access unless . . . Michael paused. What if it was a call from Daniel and Daniel was as red as everyone else? Michael's heart sank. It would be a cruel miracle if he could indeed talk to his brother only to find that he, too, would urge him, "Don't be blue."

"Who is it?" Michael asked the wall.

"No identification," it said.

That was strange—strange enough that Michael felt courage flow into him. "Yes, phone," he called. The wall went blank. No image appeared, and only a soft crackling interrupted the silence. Michael acted on faith. "Daniel?" he asked.

"Michael. Michael, is that you?" It was indeed Daniel's voice.

"It's me, Daniel," Michael answered, almost surprised by the desperation in his voice. "I can't see you."

"No video," said Daniel's voice. "I hacked in. I've probably only got a few seconds, so listen. Michael, brother, if you're still OK, I mean if you're . . ." There was another pause, Daniel's characteristic uncertainty and hesitation.

"I'm still blue, Daniel," Michael confessed, and it was as if there were a sigh of relief on the other end of the audio line.

"Michael," Daniel spoke with a renewed strength, "if you're still OK, you need to get to us as soon as you can. I'm not sure if you can do this, but you might—" Daniel's voice stopped.

"Daniel?" Michael called to the wall. There was no sound, not even the soft crackle. The wall blinked, and the news returned. LeeAn and Jim were back on display, expressing their concern for the suffering. "There's no need to be blue," Jim said with honest compassion. Michael believed him.

Michael suddenly realized what the countdown clock meant. He questioned the wall anyway. "What does the countdown indicate?"

"According to recent legislative action, those depressed and unhealthy individuals with blue auras are being urged to admit themselves for voluntary adjustment. This service is totally free and for the benefit of all. After midnight tomorrow, local time, all remaining blue individuals will be evaluated on a case by case basis."

That, too, made sense. It was compassion for the individual and peace for society. Michael understood his world at last. "Why should I be a burden on others?" his own father had asked rhetorically, and Michael knew there was no reply. There still was no reply. It was unhealthy to be blue; it was harmful to others. To offer peace to those willing to take it was an act of love, as was the offer of a painless passage into the silence of death. It was compassion to offer everyone the dignity of choice, whether it was a religion or a charity or a secular hospital that represented their own beliefs. Or it could be the choice to abandon them all and take, as we all must, a final rest. Michael could choose what peace he wanted, but apparently he could not choose against peace.

But he could try to find his brother. And he had less than thirty hours.

31

FLIGHT

"It makes no sense to resist being happy. It's like they say: It's a kind of mental illness. It's like people who cut their own flesh." Michael was half aware of the complexity of the arguments he was running through. He was alone, with no one to help him think or help him choose. "But there are also all those mentally ill people who cut their flesh for religious reasons, who fast or practice asceticism, all to obtain their own peace of mind, whatever that is. That's the point, isn't it? There is no limit to how one seeks peace of mind, even self-mutilation; the only sickness is to refuse to find peace of mind.

"What could you possibly argue against hope? I mean, sure—if someone were to offer you a deadly drug that promised to make you happy on the way to a painful death, no sane person would listen. But temporary sadness for a greater joy later is entirely reasonable, and an easy, painless effort to find happiness is best of all. So why would any reasonable person refuse a harmless, peaceful means to a full and final joy? Only if they were ill and could not seek happiness.

"And even those who are ill we try to help. Don't we offer mood-improving medication to the depressed? Don't we offer euthanasia to those whose suffering cannot be alleviated? Peace is the goal, both the inner peace of the individual and that social peace Gesar says arises between individuals. That's what they keep saying, isn't it? And the latter is the natural result of the former.

"There is, therefore, only good in the work of the great *tulku*, Richard Padmaram Gesar."

Michael could follow his own argument that far, and he had no reply. There could be claims of violation of individual rights if indeed any specific means of peace were being forced on anyone. But look at Melanie. Atheist lesbian from first to last, but she found peace and didn't have to embrace some bizarre religious claim.

"Think of it like practicing yoga or meditation. Right?" Michael was trying again. "We've had these practices taught to children in secular schools for a generation, and does anyone complain? Are they being indoctrinated or violated? No. They are being taught to relax or to relieve stress. Do your yoga and pray to the Buddha. Do your yoga and pray to Jesus. Do your yoga and pray to a duck. Do your yoga and pray to nothing. Whatever! It's like learning to breathe. Breathing techniques help anyone, and so does the great *tulku*.

"Perhaps calling him 'the great *tulku*' isn't fair," Michael thought. "If I were considering sitting down with a glass of wine in order to relax, there would be no hesitation. If I take an aspirin to relieve a headache, do I mock 'the great medicine man'? So what if I just say I want Gesar's adjustment in order to find peace of mind. How is that any different? Why call it *his* adjustment at all? I'll just say, 'I want peace,' and I don't care whose it is. Why would anyone not accept the gift of peace? Why wouldn't I?"

Michael knew where he wanted this argument to end: he wanted it to end with seeing Daniel. But he had to consider that it might as well end with him going to a clinic. If both were not possible, then it was not a fair argument. Consequently, he chose to entertain doubt about Daniel: What if even the call from Daniel was another invitation to be changed from blue to red? A call had come from Desra and failed. Then one from Melanie. Why not also a more veiled, more mysterious one from Daniel? Perhaps he, too, was one of them. Michael laughed aloud. "One of them."

"All that conspiracy thinking does is change one option into the other. I mean, OK, suppose Daniel is 'one of them.' So what?" With a flurry of thought, Michael realized that placing even Daniel on the side of the adjustment still left him having to decide what he ought to do and what he ought to be. He was still blue; red was still an option. If Daniel was red, that only made Michael all the more alone.

"Fine," he said to himself. "Fine. Suppose Daniel is red. Hasn't he always had his Jesus and his God beside him offering him peace? Hasn't he always told me—maybe not in so many words, but still, over and over—that I need his Jesus?" Yet despite all those years of claiming Jesus, Daniel was blue. Daniel could therefore represent for Michael the second option, a real option to being happy. But what was it? "Just to wait and be unhappy for no good reason?" Michael rethought, and with Daniel in mind, restated: "Just to wait and be unhappy for reasons I don't understand?" To Michael, that seemed a plausible option. It sounded more honest to his awakened respect for his brother.

"And yet there is a third option, isn't there?" Michael was being drawn inexorably on, perhaps not so alone as he imagined. "Perhaps the third real alternative is suicide." He shuddered. After all, wasn't such a thought only one more sign of the overwhelming illness, the 'dis-ease?' Aren't those who contemplate suicide proving themselves to be in need of the very medicine being offered? The irony struck Michael. "In fact," he said almost out loud, "if events play out as they might, suicide is one of the options, not in the form of a bullet in the brain, but in the form of acquiescing to euthanasia. Isn't that the same option as being blue? 'Those we can help we heal, but those we cannot we ease into peaceful sleep.'" Michael coughed derisively at the quotation and felt briefly the sting of guilt for his use of it. "To refuse to be happy is to choose suicide or at least the ease of sleep, which," Michael had to admit sardonically, "certainly seems better than the bullet option."

He laughed at his own logic. "So it's peace in the end, one way or another," he said to himself. Why did it still seem like a threat?

He started over. "Peace is good. Some people find it easily, I guess, and some find it only with great labor. Maybe some never find it. For those who struggle, there is the adjustment, a process that brings peace and makes no intrusion on the health or freedom of the individual. Fine. Only a few, surely, would refuse such a gift. Peace is, in the end, a state of the brain that Doctor Richard Gesar knows and studies and understands, maybe better than any of us. It is through him and his gift to the world that this brain state, this peace of mind, can be enhanced and, for the struggling, healed. If indeed there are some of us," Michael smiled at himself again, "who cannot be healed, there is another kind of peace, the final peace we have always offered to the suffering. The kind of peace my own father chose."

Michael felt again a haunting, intrusive sense of guilt. It was strange to him, stranger still for the context of his argument. Isn't guilt the very opposite of peace of mind?

Michael was frustrated. Trained as a questioner more than as one who must answer questions, he didn't quite have the skill of Marta Sanchez. Nor did he have the faith—whatever that was—of Daniel. Still, through all the argument, something pulled him toward his brother.

"How can this argument, all this damned pondering, run honestly if I already know the ending?" He shook his head, and yet the very point offered in honesty helped him refocus. "OK, I already know I have to go see Daniel, because, well, that's how the story ends. I can try to doubt even his call, but that's not realistic, nor does it really change the issue. The only real alternative is to call the clinic. Maybe that's the point. I keep asking why anyone would deny the value of happiness, and I keep reaching the conclusion that, in fact, no reasonable person would.

"But maybe Daniel would say no, because, for him, it has to be Jesus. OK, fine. Let it be Jesus. What then can be the problem? Maybe Daniel would say, no, it has to be *only* Jesus. OK, fine. Just like for the Reverend Dr. Roberts, let it be only Jesus. Why not? And let us then breathe peace and think peace and rest in each other's friendship. Let Daniel truly be my brother; let Marta truly be my love. Let us finally rest. We return to our jobs, return to our lives. Maybe we have children, maybe even Daniel and Helen will have children. And life goes on until it no longer can. And then we die in peace as we lived in peace, trusting only in Jesus. How can there be any possible counterargument?

"So instead of a clinic, I go to a church." Michael knew the options. Why not? Still the rhetorical question haunted him, reminded him of Daniel, and that church or clinic or mosque or temple were all the same option. They were not-Daniel.

"Why? Is it finally that I just don't want to lose? Is it that I just don't want Gesar to win? How can such a juvenile desire be considered in this context? So Gesar measures peace of mind by the standard of his own experience of himself. If others, too, find that peace in themselves, what is the problem? Let it be peace, then, after all."

Then Michael ceased from his arguments because it seemed he had no more. But he was far from satisfied, for he still heard the voice that called him to Daniel. Simply being angry at, or jealous of, Gesar was no reason to flee to Daniel. And Michael was tired of being angry.

"There is no difference between Gesar's adjustment and taking aspirin. Or, better, it is no less a divine miracle to be given a red aura through adjustment than to be given peace through a vision of Jesus Christ. Why should Gesar not be the Christ? Why not a new hand of God? If the lost child prays and then suddenly sees a light in the distance, does he refuse to follow it because, after all, God did not Himself descend to lead the child out of the woods by the hand? If a man is wounded and he finds a doctor, does he deny the work of divinity because an angel did not appear and heal him with a flaming touch? Let the light in the distance be the work of God; let the doctor be the healing miracle. Let Gesar's adjustment be the peace of God. That's the great freedom of the matter, that I can perhaps find peace in Daniel's God or perhaps in another. Let it be the god of my choosing." In so thinking, Michael had found the argument for peace as well as the argument against it.

"But that's the problem, isn't it? What did Daniel say so long ago about the God of my choosing not being God. This isn't aspirin. This isn't being lost in the woods. This isn't even being miraculously healed. This is about finding God, and the difference is that any God I can find the way I want to find him, or any God I can say is the god of my choosing is not God. I can want peace of mind, and maybe it's OK, even a good thing, to want peace of mind. If I want that peace by finding God, that's a good thing, too. But am I the one who makes it happen? If I am the creator of the peace of God, then it is not the peace of God."

Daniel came back to his mind. "What if I assume that the phone call was not a ruse? What is going on with Daniel? What is wrong with him that he does not accept this happiness? What is wrong with him that Daniel does not have it already? Maybe it's a family trait." Michael suddenly found that slightly amusing and thought of his father.

"No!" Michael wouldn't accept some claim that there was a genetic cause to their morbidity. His own father's death had not been a failure to want happiness. It had been deep sorrow, and his euthanasia had been, Michael knew now, the work of a society that let death be too easy a solution. It was Michael's own society; it was his own ideal. Michael himself was to blame—he barely knew how to say such a thing—and blame could not be lessened because it was unpleasant. The thought was liberating.

"Because if it is true and it is also unpleasant, then isn't it better to be sad than happy? Isn't there something better than being happy? Isn't there—maybe—something better than peace with the God I choose? Maybe it's to be unhappy with a God I don't choose." That brought him back to Daniel.

"Daniel thinks his God is the true God and yet does not find peace of mind. He does not have to pause, like I do, to worry if he is being deceived by an idol. He's sure he isn't. So why does he not find peace? Could it be that Daniel is saying the very same thing? I cannot worship the god that gives peace, lest I worship only my own peace. So what does Daniel want more than he wants the peace of God? Is it that any God true enough to give peace must also be true enough to deny it?" Michael understood. "Of course! There is something Daniel wants more than God's peace," Michael realized, and he realized that Daniel was right. For a second, Michael felt the peace of God.

* * *

Michael had slept a decent if not long sleep. With the first light of day he ate the last of his bread and found a little wine left in the rack. He retained that odd feeling of acceptance, a sense that he knew what to do, even if, after eating his paltry breakfast, it took an hour or so to prepare. By eight o'clock, he had managed to draw enough courage, or perhaps find enough humility, to act. He took a deep breath and let it go, closed his eyes and thought of his father's death. He thought of Desra and Petra and Marta and the mistakes he had made all his life, it seemed, in his treatment of women. He thought of his brother and decided to see him at last, see him even with a red aura, someone he could trust to lead him to a church or a clinic where he could find peace. Feelings of dejection mixed with vague hope pressed upon Michael, and he turned on the news channels again to find out the proper way to phone in for adjustment. This was the only way.

The news still had the crawl running, and Michael, finally looking ready to surrender, looking as tired as he felt, video-called the number and told the attendant he was ready. "I think I need . . . I need to be healed," he said softly. "I finally realized that I need help."

The young woman who answered leaned her head to one side and smiled. "We're here to help you, Mr. Pryor," she said with honest concern. "We see that you have a booth in your apartment. We've reactivated it. The number to an open clinic is already dialed in, but if you have another choice in mind, a church or a temple of some kind, we can change the number to whatever you want."

"No, the clinic is fine," Michael said almost sadly.

"It's your choice," the woman said. "So just put your hand to the panel."

Michael barely heard the instructions; he nodded and finally hung up. Sitting on his couch one last time, he put his hand on his chin, felt the scratch of the growing beard, and tried to think. One last chance.

Another shake of his head, a sorrowful glance around his home, and he stepped to the phone booth. He put his hand to the panel that read his identity, the door slid open, and he stepped inside. Silently the door slid closed and Michael noticed the number from the new program was already entered into the panel. He took a deep breath, preparing with more than just habit to avoid breathing in the gas that could calm him and allow him to avoid the first sting of the lasers. Opening his eyes wide, ready, expectant, he activated the booth, felt pain and disappeared.

For Michael, no time passed. Whatever those few seconds had meant to those waiting to receive him at the clinic, he at once simply found himself in another booth, his eyes wide and his heart beating hard. With a hiss, the door began to open, and he bent his head into his hands and leaned forward. He stumbled, murmured unintelligibly as he had seen thousands of people do before as they emerged groggy from the transport. Immediately a small young man—what luck, he was a little fellow—came forward to steady him, as Michael stumbled back against the closing door of the phone booth. The young man slipped his arm under Michael's to hold him up.

With a sudden jerk, Michael grabbed the intern around the throat with his arm, dragging him back into the phone booth with him. Outside the booth, other helpers stood, ready to help other arrivals but not at all ready to deal with an act of violence. They were frozen, and in the second of their inaction, Michael slammed the young man's hand against the panel of the phone booth and shoved him forcibly outside. The door slid closed, and Michael tapped in quickly the number of the booth in Daniel's building. They would know where he went, but it didn't matter. The gas hissed, and Michael, breathing hard from his excitement, had to cover his own nose and mouth with his hand. The sting again, the flash, and his last phone call.

32

RAPTURE

Michael felt almost sheepish standing at Daniel's door. His heart had calmed down, and a peculiar shyness had taken its place. What was he doing? What did he think this would accomplish? The door opened, and it was Daniel.

"I broke the law," Michael said immediately.

Daniel smiled. "So did I."

Michael stepped into the apartment. In the middle of the living room stood Helen, her eyes weary, but her smile at Michael's presence somehow genuine. Beyond her were others, people Michael didn't know. One was a woman from Helen's work, two others a couple from their church. One was Reuben Meyers, whose wife, Alexis, Michael found out later, was already "at peace" and had left him when he repeatedly refused to find his own happiness. She had told him it was hard being around him, hard to see him "like this."

And Marta was there, appearing from the kitchen, wiping her hand on a towel. When she saw him, she smiled wryly, her eyes bright. With efficient matter-of-factness, she stuffed the end of the towel into the belt that held her blue skirt at the waist and walked across the room. Michael waited, as if he knew he had to be welcomed before he could speak. Her eyes spoke softly; he hoped his did the same. Both Helen and Daniel moved aside for her, and she stopped in front of Michael. He felt himself smiling without reserve. She hugged him strongly, and he hugged back, felt himself relax into her. When she stepped back, she was crying. "I prayed you'd come," she said. She coughed a little laugh. "Want a sandwich?"

"I'm starving." Michael smiled down at her. She took his hand and led him to the kitchen. The others let them pass. "My brother," Michael heard Daniel say, as if announcing him to the strangers. And *brother* sounded right.

Marta had "seen it coming," she said. She had bought some food before her retina and handprint identification stopped working "so at least I got to contribute some of the food." She had sliced meat and bread; with quick ease she began slapping together a sandwich. "When I got here," she reported, as if it were merely the news of the day, "Allen, the neighbor guy with the grey hair, and Leticia, Helen's friend, were already here. You know," she spoke more softly as if releasing a secret, "for a while I felt sad, kind of disappointed with myself for having failed to bring anyone with me. But Daniel and Helen always were better people than I am. Kind of figures the last refuge would be here." She handed the sandwich to Michael.

"But why, Marta, are you—"

She put her hand on his mouth. "Just eat your sandwich," she said. She felt an odd joy in watching him eat. It was love, she knew, and yet it wasn't. She might have loved him in a different way, and maybe she could still, but there was also a strange delight in watching him eat. There was a simple normality in it, a beauty that was part of him being Michael, being hungry, being here. She was puzzled too, but she let the puzzlement go and saw beauty in the love and hunger of a man she couldn't help but feel attracted to. She let all of it be. She had no illusions about her future, about their future, but that made things easier: she could let them be. It was all in God's hands. She smiled at him.

"What?" he asked, smiling back. He wiped mayonnaise from his lip with the back of his hand.

"I love you, Michael Pryor," she said, and it was true.

Michael stopped chewing. He wanted to speak of love, and he strangely hoped it might even be true. His hesitation was not, as it had been at other times, in other relationships, some fear of commitment, as if some words carry intrinsic promises. He rather didn't know at this point what love could mean. For though he understood the finality of these hours less well than Marta, he felt it as much. Perhaps more, for the call of God was heavy on him.

Marta put her hand on his lips again and saved him from any effort to speak. "Don't talk with your mouth full," she said and laughed. Then she turned and stood beside him, leaning against the countertop as he was doing. "I saw where things were going," she said, "and I came over here. I've been here two days. Managed to buy some food first. Just had to hope the water wouldn't stop running." She nodded toward the kitchen sink, then back toward the rest of the house. "They have to keep the toilets working," she said, then smiled up at him, adding, "though if you really wanted to flush someone out, one sure way would be to keep them from flushing."

Michael smiled at her simple humor, amazed at her odd calm, puzzled and perplexed by who "they" might be. He shoved the last of his sandwich into his mouth.

Marta, however, did not miss the questions in his eyes, and she felt the need to answer. She felt the sadness of the truth, even though the softness of love was unchanged. "The world will change tomorrow, Michael Pryor," she said, looking away as if talking to no one. "Maybe it will be finally peace and goodness. Maybe. Maybe it will finally be the Kingdom of God on earth. It's what we all want; it's what we have to want. Yet for some of us, for those of us huddled here in your brother's home, it is a final doom. A strange and lovely final doom." She looked at him with a nodding frown.

It was a fact. Michael had no doubt. He saw the doom and even the loveliness. That was the problem, wasn't it? That it was a goodness of terror. "I know something of what you're talking about," he said, "but I don't understand it. I see it coming, but I don't know what it is."

Marta nodded. "Yep," she said, "it's pretty strange, although I both love and fear that the strangest thing about it right now is you being here. But, tell you what. If you really want to know what's going on and you're finished with your dinner, we should talk to your brother. He seems to understand it best. He's a good man, your brother."

"I know," Michael said honestly, and he felt a sting. It was not a familiar sting; it was a kind of pain. Michael, perhaps for the first time exploring the calm honesty of guilt, recognized the pain as wholesome and right. "I'm sorry I didn't see it sooner," he confessed.

Marta grabbed his arm, offering consolation or pardon. "You should be sorry," she said matter-of-factly. "You wasted a lot of time."

Michael was mildly surprised at her words, and then he wasn't. Even as the sting of guilt could be painful and good, so were her words somehow both condemning and loving. Before he could sort through the paradox of justice and love that lies at the very root of the world, Marta's hand looped through his arm. "Come on," she said, "let's see what Daniel has to say."

Daniel was speaking as they entered the living room, responding to a question, it seemed, from the neighbor. No one had appointed Daniel the spokesman; no one had made him a leader. But it seemed right, even to Daniel, that he was speaking, not because he felt full of some gift, empowered by the Holy Spirit. It was only that, when the others had questions, he felt himself reply, because he understood what it was like to have questions. When they expressed doubt, he knew what it meant to doubt. Uncertainties, loneliness, and pain were in him already, echoes of other loneliness and pain that made him want to respond with compassion. It was natural.

"That, in the end, is the point," he was saying. "We were so often looking in the wrong place. Visions and revelations and mysteries of numbers and times and half-times and all that." He smiled because somehow that language seemed funny. But he felt a bit guilty for seeming to be flippant. Yet the guilt, too, went quickly, marching off to its proper place.

"If someone knows when the thief is coming to break in, he stays awake and catches him. So if a thief is going to be a good thief, he has to come when nobody's looking, or he has to come in a way that no one suspects.

"If it were possible, even the ones who know better would be deceived. Even those who were warned. Even those who were looking for it. And maybe when Jesus says, 'If it were possible,' he doesn't mean that we somehow catch it. It doesn't mean we somehow see it coming. Maybe he just means we get out alive, barely.

"So if the thief comes, and if even those looking for him, even the good people of the earth, can be deceived, then it has to be something good that deceives us. You know what I mean? The only kind of deception that will work is the kind we want." Daniel rubbed his chin. "If we had seen it coming, it wouldn't have been it."

"But what is *it*?" Michael was almost surprised to hear his own voice, automatically asking a question, perhaps for the first time in his adult life not out of a desire to challenge, but out of his own muddle. For he knew somehow there was a work going on in the world, a movement of such importance even his own sense of conspiracy couldn't grasp it. It still lingered in his mind that the world out there, all of them—Melanie, Desra, the *tulku*—were right, and all his resistance and fear was misguided. He might still just be wrong, even though there was a change in the world, a stealth, a thief in the night.

"It?" Daniel repeated the question. "It? It's this." Daniel spread his arms out and swept them around the room. "This place and these people, and the fact that tomorrow none of us will be here." There was no melodrama in his voice.

"I know what they're saying, Daniel," Michael said. "I hear it, too. And I can see why it has to go where it's going. It has to be peace, and I see why peace means conformity or death. But, but . . ." Michael's problem was not that he didn't have the categories for seeing his choices. He saw those choices clearly enough to feel the gravity of the demand that had brought him into this room, made him part of Daniel's "this." The sweeping of his brother's hands had included him.

"But how can they get away with it?" Daniel helped his brother. "Of course they can, and they will. Because it is kindness. It's compassion. It's peace and love. It is not intrusion or killing; it is healing and helping. We ourselves—us—we made the world this way. We ourselves have made our love this way." Daniel sighed with the burden of realization. "We ourselves have made our Christ this way." Although Michael could not understand all that Daniel meant, he felt his sorrow bloom as his brother spoke of how "we" had made the world. Daniel, perhaps not greatly more aware of what he meant, felt the sorrow of having made his Christ into one of the gods of love.

"And so tomorrow," Daniel continued, because he had to, "we will all find peace. It is the end of us, Michael, my dear, dear brother. The end of us. For we will all be changed, changed in the twinkling of an eye." He smiled to himself again as he quoted his scripture; then he took a long breath. "Changed one way or another."

"But changed which way?" Michael drove his question. "Which way?"

Daniel smiled, and Michael felt it almost calm him. "I think you already know which way," Daniel said. "That's why you're here and not out there." Daniel laughed a little, sadly. "What you don't know is for sure."

"What?" Michael was lost, yet it seemed clear that Daniel wasn't. He was somehow encouraged as Daniel laughed out loud.

"I'm sorry, Michael," he said. "I just don't say stuff right, you know. I mean, we do know. All of us here know. We just don't know for sure. We are—all of us here—unsure. We don't quite know what world we want. We have helped bring the very Kingdom of God, and in the end, the kingdom turned on us and destroyed us. We don't know. We can't know. That is the point." He took another deep breath. "Even so, when the Son of Man comes, will he find faith?" He smiled again at his scripture quoting, almost certain no one understood clearly what it meant.

"But we have faith, Daniel." The plaintive voice was that of Reuben Meyers. "We have had this faith so long, and yet here we are. And I'm tired."

Daniel looked at his friend and loved him. He couldn't help it. There was no decision involved. Michael looked at Daniel and saw the love.

"But faith, Reuben, isn't about believing good things," he said easily, because he knew it was true. "The world around us has faith, now, Reuben. That is another of our gifts to this Kingdom of God we have helped to make. But faith isn't just optimism or even hope. It is to bear up and to go on. It is to act in our uncertainty. It is not to find peace, Reuben. No. Think about Gethsemane.

"No, you guys. Sorrow and uncertainty, like sin itself, have to be—I don't know—lifted up, carried, done something with. Sin has to be lived through, or else we mock it. Sin, if it isn't carried, is simply made into nonsense. The evil of the world is not merely healed. Or rather, the evil of the world is healed. It must be healed, and we must love and long for and celebrate its healing. But it is not just healed, like 'ta-da!' No. It has to be carried."

To Michael, this was incomprehensible. To Marta, this was the part of Daniel's speech that made sense. She nodded. "In the classic Problem of Evil," she inserted, "some answers to the problem of suffering fail because they answer the problem too well." She smiled at the intentional paradox, then turned to Michael and winked. "This was one of Wacker's arguments."

"OK?" Michael returned, unsure what to expect. But Marta began a simple explanation that only started to make sense as it unfolded. "Some philosophies respond to the sorrow of human life by saying that it's wholly a matter of perception, and that ultimately the suffering is itself an illusion. Our own failure to see with a 'pure mind' or to escape our perception of selfhood makes us think there is a problem with reality, when—so they say—there is no problem and therefore no real suffering." Marta paused, trained almost by second nature to let the argument sit before replying. "But such arguments, Professor Wacker used to say, cannot account for the error of perception in the first place. Worse, they make mockery of the tears and sorrows. The logical inconsistency is that they must take those tears seriously in order to raise the question, but the answer denies the tears. The moral problem is that they make foolish any real notion of compassion, at least in the literal, etymological sense."

Michael wondered if anyone in the room understood what she meant, but then he realized it didn't matter to Marta. Explanation was its own purpose, seeing and telling the truth because it's true. He admired her integrity. There was no extraneous purpose to thinking and talking, no art of persuasion. It was worth speaking because it was honest speech. With the same admiration, Michael listened again to his brother.

"I'm not sure I understand half of what you say, Marta, but if you see the connection with what I'm saying, it must mean that, to understand the sorrow and suffering, even the sin of the world, someone has to feel it. It would be justice, I suppose, if only those who caused sorrow or suffering felt the pain they caused, but the world doesn't work like that. And yet the pain must be borne. Someone must bear it, and I'm afraid it's us. We who remain have come to the end of a world where sorrow has been overcome, where peace has been achieved, and yet not by taking it seriously. The good has come too cheaply, and that leaves us, this odd bunch of us, to become the world's evil." He took another deep breath. "We will make up what is lacking in the sufferings of Christ."

Michael again wasn't sure what Daniel meant, but he thought he had understood something in the Wacker-Sanchez argument. There was something right about even his own uncommon and unpleasant feelings of guilt, and there was something in him that made him not simply desire to have those feelings removed. He wanted no assurances. He wanted no excuses. He might have wanted to bear those feelings himself, might have fallen into the trap of pursuing some ascetic purchase of his own innocence. But there was no time for such ideas, and the imminent end of things was a mercy.

Michael could not follow Daniel's words all the way to the end, for although he was on the threshold of life, he did not yet know the story he thought he knew. "But this is where I falter," he inserted into Daniel's exposition, easily because it was honest. "You guys, all of you, but you especially, Daniel." He shook his head. "I don't get it. You talk of your faith and your Christ and yet here you are, as lost and bewildered as I am."

Marta laughed. "Lost and bewildered, yes," she said, "but not as lost and bewildered as you are." She put her arm back through his.

"You guys, you Christians, drove this 'Kingdom of God' thing. Shouldn't you be the first to love it, to embrace it? Shouldn't you of all people be reddest among the red? How can you have your Jesus and still be blue?"

"I don't know, Michael," Daniel said, shaking his head. "Again, maybe that's the point. Where are all our proofs? Where are the beasts and the dragons, the plagues and trumpets, the bloody moon, the false prophets and ten-horned monsters? Where is antichrist and the numerical mark of the beast?" He shrugged. "I don't know," he said, "but I can tell you something about divine grace and divine power.

"Divine grace can give peace, but divine peace cannot be created by human beings, not even by Dr. Richard Gesar. Divine love can be given freely, but it cannot be taken by demand. What God gives we can delight in thoroughly, but if we create the delight and just insist that it's from God, we are idolaters. Blessing—don't you see?—blessing has to be received, not created, and the relation between the sinner and divine holiness is, well, a relationship, not a business deal. God gives, and that means God must be able to refuse to give."

"OK," Michael replied with hesitation in his voice. "I get that." And partly he did, although partly he longed to see a larger picture. He did already feel the stir of the call in Daniel's words, felt the possibility of surrender to that which was not his own invention, and he knew it was right. Yet the argument remained, not just his own argument, but that of the world around him. He had to press it in order to be honest.

"But people take analgesics for a headache," he said, "and they accept counseling for their psychological turmoil. We have the technology to fight pain or anxiety, and only a fool or a fanatic would deny himself health, as if pain had intrinsic value." For a second Michael was scared, afraid that Daniel would not have a reply. Michael knew he himself had already tried these arguments, arguments not quite his own. Yet he felt like he had invited the vampire over the threshold.

Daniel was nodding. "All that is true," he said, "but with this one difference. The peace of God is the one thing we cannot snatch. It is precisely it being from God that means we can't create it. We can't make it with technology and meditation. Being able to make it is precisely what proves it is not God's peace, but our own. That's why, in the end, the peace of God must be something beyond all understanding. It must be something not like any kind of peace the world gives."

Daniel paused. Michael realized the others in the room recognized the words and saw something in them that still eluded him. He felt alone, although he was here with his brother and Helen, with Marta and the others, still strangely on the outside. Something was missing, and he didn't quite know what it was. "But how can you be sure?" he asked aloud, but perhaps not to anyone there.

"Haven't you been listening, little brother?" Daniel said as if it were amusing. "You can't be sure. If assurance is what you want, get the adjustment. Then you'll be sure." He paused, his smile faded, his eyes dark, because he realized that he had an offer to make. It was necessary, though he felt it tear at him. "You still have that option, Michael."

But Daniel needn't have worried, for that was no longer truly an option for Michael Pryor. No, the adjustment was not possible, for Michael saw, as he had expected to see, that his brother was right. Sorrow must be borne. Guilt must be borne. Even sin must be borne. But how could that be now, in this last hour of the world? What? Shall I undo what I have done? What? Shall I deem it unimportant? What? Shall I declare it merely the path of my life, somehow justified because I am not yet dead? Shall I cut my arms? Shall I whip my own flesh? There is no bearing of the sorrow of life, certainly not one that would deny its meaning or deny life's glory and beauty. "I'm sorry," he could say, but it wasn't enough. He knew it; and to his own surprise, he found he had said so, had said all this, aloud.

And of all the people there, of all the voices possible, one spoke softly and easily. "He doesn't know," Helen's voice said. "Daniel, he doesn't know."

As if suddenly created out of nothing, Helen came forward. She seemed to appear as if she had stepped out of a large crowd, but of course she hadn't. Helen, out of all of them, had seen beyond explanation and circumstance into the heart of a lonely child. Without deciding to, she stepped up to Michael and grabbed his hand. "He doesn't know," she said to herself in silence and loved her brother-in-law like the child she had never had, the child she would never have.

Michael looked at Helen. Her eyes were green; he had never noticed before. He saw as she smiled that one of her front teeth was slightly crooked; he had never noticed before. She spoke his name and told him a story. It was a story Michael had heard many times, and yet he had never heard it before. It was simple, and Michael thought it could actually be true. The story somehow made sense of all he knew, of all he had heard, and of all he had felt, even the unsureness itself. The story fell upon him, and the world was changed.

In the hour or two that followed, there were strange tears and strange laughter. Michael hugged Helen, then his brother. He might have cried, but he wasn't sure. Ironic jokes about the last-minute convert were funny and sad. In the middle of these exchanges, Michael discovered an unexpected fondness for Reuben and the others present, as if suddenly they, too, had become family. And for them Michael became comfort, as if a proof that God still calls and God still loves. For this family of strangers and loved ones, he was a closing and final, sad and lovely reminder of grace. After a while, Michael held onto Marta, and she to him, and he saw and felt love in her dark eyes. He in return fell in love with her, imperfectly and impurely, and yet with neither guilt nor dishonesty.

All too soon it was midnight, and there were sounds outside the door.

THE END